GUARDIAN

THE LIMINAL CHRONICLES

AMY WINTERS-VOSS

SHY RED FOX PUBLISHING

First edition.

EBook ISBN: 978-1-7366720-2-0

Paperback ISBN: 978-1-7366720-3-7

Hardcover ISBN: 978-1-7366720-5-1

Editing by Sarah Buhrman and Sarah Templeton

Sensitivity read by Rihoko Colwill

Cover art by Odette.A.Bach

Library of Congress Control Number: 2023906671

Shy Red Fox Publishing

Sioux Falls, South Dakota

CONTENTS

— ◆ —

AUTHOR NOTES

I'VE USED ASPECTS AND events in Japanese myth, culture and history as the basis to write this tale, but the universe in the book series is a Japan-based fantasy world. Please note that any people, places, and beliefs in the Liminal Chronicles are used fictitiously, and I have done my best to treat them with respect.

In this series, I wrote out of an excuse to dig deeper after my trip to Japan in the fall of 2017 and to deal with the growing desire to return. Though I am not Japanese, I love Japan and only wish to do my best to portray the 'Japan' in Guardian as truthfully and close to the real one as I am able. While Japan is not a perfect country (there isn't such a thing!), it has an incredible and unique culture. I feel even in researching and asking my Japanese friends—that I can only touch the surface of each topic's depths.

I hope that this humble tribute to a land, society, and mythology I adore brings enjoyment and expanded interest in the country to all who read it. Many aspects this book shares are lessons I've learned after meeting amazing, patient, and kind people from Japan.

Also, I hope this tale will inspire my readers to take a stand and support others. Everyone, from every faith, can do this. Be the difference.

— ◆ —

CULTURAL NOTES

Just a few quick notes for you.

Names

In Japan (and many Asian countries), the family name is presented first. This ties in with the idea that the group is more important than the individual. People referred to each other by their family names until a certain level of familiarity is reached. Then they'll use personal names.

Respect is king. A suffix is almost always used to show respect and levels of familiarity. Lack of a suffix is either rude or the speakers are on such a familiar basis that both sides agree the lack of a suffix is acceptable.

Name Suffixes

-bou - a less common suffix. In this book, it refers to an ascetic mountain hermit, though there are other uses.

-chan - an endearing and cute name suffix often used for children, young women, or by a significant other

-kun - friendly suffix for young people, especially boys and young men

-san - equivalent to Mr., Mrs., Ms., or Miss

-sama -polite, formal suffix to show great respect

-sensei - teacher, master, and professionals such as doctors and lawyers

Words

I have done my best to describe and give hints for words that aren't native to English. Sometimes a loan word from Japanese that made its way into English doesn't mean quite the same thing to a Japanese person as it does to a Westerner.

You'll find this with words like 'futon' which is a stuffed mattress that is put on the floor to sleep on in Japan, but in America is a folding frame and mattress that can be used as a couch or bed. Same for the idea of the bath, American baths and Japanese ones differ greatly. In Japan, one washes and rinses off outside the tub, before getting in to soak. I just wanted to give you a heads up.

The vowel sounds are similar to Spanish, where 'a' is 'ah'-as in father, 'e' is 'eh' as in elk, 'i' is 'ee' as in 'eel', 'o' is 'oh' as in boat, and 'u' is 'oo' as in 'moon'. So the name Date is 'Dah teh'. It doesn't sound like 'date' the fruit.

Locations

Only the large cities such as Kyoto and Tokyo are actual locations in this book. All others are fictional, modeled after the area.

Further Help

I try to help you remember who everyone is, and what words mean along the way. That said, the Cast of Characters and Glossary are in the back of the book to help you with names and unfamiliar words.

— ◈ —

ACKNOWLEDGEMENTS

TO MY READERS - for your continued excitement for this story and for your patience.

To my husband, Mike - for your never ending support of my crazy endeavors.

To my friends - for your support, belief in me, and encouragement.

To Kyoko, my Sis - for always telling me to do my best and cheering me on.

To my beta readers—Angela and Laura, my editors—Sarah and Sarah, and my sensitivity reader—Rihoko - for your insight and honesty. Your remarks really helped shape Guardian.

Without all of you, this novel would not exist. Thank you very much.

どうもありがとうございます。

1

Mt. Kurama

Today, I take my first official step toward becoming a Guardian. I'll request training with one of the senior League members ranking above my aunt, Nakamura Hisako.

Who would have thought a former yakuza like me would have the chance to be a part of the secretive League of Guardians? I don't care what it takes. This is my best chance to make something of myself and have a future outside of the mob. I'm not going to waste it.

My aunt, my girlfriend—Ohno Suzu, young Suzuki Sojirou—who goes by Jiro now, and I all moved to Kyoto so we could learn more of what it meant to have natural magic inside us. We live with my aunt's kitsune family. The kitsune are the mythical, shape-shifting foxes. To think that one of these beings would take me under their wing, let alone claim to be related, still blows me away.

Cantering along the forested hiking trail up Mt. Kurama, on the outskirts of Kyoto, Aunt Hisako and I keep out of sight as the sun descends in the sky. We ensure no one's watching, bow before quickly ducking under a hidden torii gate just outside the tiny town named after the mountain, and lope into the realm of the sacred. *Why didn't we take the path to the temple?*

My fur fluffs and the pads of my paws tingle upon contact with the path where the kami, the gods, have been. Since I gained kitsune magic, passing through these gates is intense, like suddenly smelling coffee again after having a severe cold. Is it something magic users get accustomed to?

Learning to shift shapes into a fox is my favorite of the new abilities I gained after receiving natural magic. It's a childhood dream come true. The learning curve on the language of gestures for fox-kind has been steep, but worth any temporary embarrassment.

Magical signs, in an ancient scrawl, glow on the markers and torii gate. Aunt Hisako veers from the trail and scrabbles straight up the steep hillside. Following, I sift through the myths I memorized as a kid, stories of who might live on this mountain.

None of it provides a clue to who we're visiting, though the nagging niggle in my mind says I ought to figure it out. No matter how often I ask, my aunt refuses to tell me.

She's panting hard, and stumbles a few times, but she won't slow down. My throat tightens. *Is she pushing herself too hard?* She hasn't recovered from Date Sari breaking her hoshi no tama, the ball that holds her magic and spirit.

Do I dare disturb the tranquil silence of this sacred forest to ensure she's ok? Pressing more speed into my lope and digging my claws into the hillside allows me to catch up. The barest whisper comes from my muzzle. "Aunt, do we need to rest?"

Her head jerks up and her black lips press together. Heaving in air, she flops to the forest floor. "A moment's rest... won't make us... late."

To help her save face, I force my breathing to be a little harder. Truth be told, my muscles burn from the climb.

But one of her nine tails snaps my side. "Stop pretending, already."

My head ducks. Aunt Hisako knows me too well. Our bantering relationship is a stark contrast to when I first met her and she ran over my toes with a shopping cart. Back then, she thought I would return to the criminal life. After I saved her and kept her secret about being a shape shifting fox spirit disguised as the prim dowager of Nonogawa, things changed.

Birds sweetly tweet in the cedars and cypress farther down the mountain, though none directly above as if to warn others of our presence as foxes. Aunt Hisako points out that we're close to Lake Biwa, though several ridges bar the view.

When she's caught her breath, I ask, "Should I carry you?"

Harrumphing, she sticks her nose in the air. "You will not drag me in like a wounded animal to the house of my master."

Stubborn, prideful old fox! I'm just trying to help. "Aunt..."

"He's expecting us. Let's not keep him waiting." Her lope isn't as fast this time as she takes off.

Finally, we halt in front of a shimmering bubble that reflects the surrounding forest. Aunt Hisako flicks her head from one side to the other and sniffs as she trots around what must be some sort of force field.

Unless I look at it from the right angle, it's invisible, blending in so perfectly one could bump right into it. *Why does this teacher spend so much magic to hide from the world?*

A twitch starts between my shoulders, telling me to get the heck out of here. The urge grows stronger every second, but it's not my gut telling me something's wrong. It's artificial. If the magic was a sweetener, it would have a distinctive aftertaste.

"What are you looking for?" I ask, keeping close to her side. "This place gives me the creeps."

She chuckles, then coughs. "The ward drives off humans. Sorry, I forgot to warn you. You're the first human I've brought to meet this yokai."

The population of powerful spirit beings, called yokai, has been dwindling the last few centuries. To meet a high-ranking one will be an incredible privilege.

When my aunt approaches a scraggly pine tree with a bare branch stripped of bark, she says, "Put your paw on this tree."

We touch the wood and the strange shimmer retracts to reveal a walled in compound with a towering, gold filigreed gate and stout wooden doors. *Whoa. Is that real?* I reach out.

"Wait, Tatsuya! You'll set off the alarms." Her paw glows upon contact with the door, and it creaks open ever so slowly. Aunt Hisako mutters, "He could at least have one of his servants oil the hinges."

"Aren't you gonna tell me who we're meeting today?" It comes out as more of a whine than I intended.

"Soujou-bou. You're familiar with the myths about him?" How she speaks his name is almost akin to being on a first name basis.

"The King of the Tengu?" And famous hermit priest. My voice raises before lowering to a more respectful volume. "You can't be serious." He'd be positively ancient! We're talking in terms of millennia. *He still teaches?*

She pshaws as she trots inside. "After everything you've seen, you doubt my word?"

Quickly, I bob a bow. "Sorry. You've just been so..." Then my words cut off as I take in what lays beyond the gate.

This estate is so immaculate it could be a home for the Emperor himself. Stone paths, lined with trees that bow inward, lead to another enclosure with a tower. Enough buildings surround it to house an army. The secluded one is probably a teahouse. Such perfectly groomed grounds would draw everyone in Kyoto if it were a park open to the public. And tengu bird-men, ranging from raptors to ravens, scurry about the grounds as if every task is an important mission.

King of the Tengu, indeed!

"It's not like I can talk about him in front of anyone else. This is League business. Anyway, if we hadn't followed the exact path, we'd have walked right past this castle. Part of how he stays hidden even in this modern age with the temple, shrines, tram, hiking paths, and tourists sharing his mountain. It's a liminal space of sorts."

So Soujou-bou is part of the League of Guardians, the secretive group that protects Japan. Turning my head this way and that, I take in more of the vast estate. Dark wood buildings with their tiled roofs and golden cloud-peak ornaments contrast with the dusky winter sky.

Then a yellow-eyed crow squawks a greeting to us. He's dressed in a pair of gray hakama and a dark blue kimono with white tie-dye patterns and sports an ancient style of starched silk hat.

My aunt beelines straight to him, bowing, then exclaiming, "Kairi-san! It's been a while!"

Despite her warm greeting, he's curt. "It has. But Soujou-sama is waiting. He will not be pleased." Stiffly, Kairi leads us through the inner gate, grudgingly allowing us to wipe our paws at the entry. The winding maze of rooms has me lost and the polished wood floors announce every step with a loud creak. They're nightingale floors, like I'd read about in Nijo Castle.

Our guide tucks his wings back and kneels to open the sliding panel before bowing and announcing us. "Great Tengu, they have arrived."

A short man with gray wings at his back and a humorously long nose rises spryly from a meditative pose. He greets us with a scathing tone, but respectful actions. "Nakamura-san, you never were early, were you? And this is my prospective student?" His red ascetic monk's robe and flowing white beard wave freely in the breeze trickling in from an open door. The view beyond hints at a picturesque rock garden raked into a swirling pattern.

My aunt's ears twitch, but the jab about the rudeness of not being early bounces off her. "Soujou-sama, this is my nephew, Umeji Tatsuya." She still breathes heavily but gives a deeper bow than I've seen her do before.

Next, the tengu king's eyes narrow and his wings ruffle. "Let us see you in your original shape, boy. Your magic doesn't quite match the kitsune form you present."

He waves his feathered fan, popping me back into human shape. At least I had the sense to dress formally, in a navy suit and a tie that Su-chan picked out for me. Though, I still feel out of place. Besides my aunt and I, everyone else wears a kimono and hakama. It's different from the streets of Kyoto, where you see the traditional clothing only occasionally.

Then Soujou-bou raises a bushy eyebrow. "Nakamura-san, why do you associate with a magic thief?"

"That is his story to tell, Soujou-sama. Know that I believe him," she responds in a flat, neutral tone that raises my hackles. She's never this submissive.

As I give a deep, reverent bow, he remarks, "Boy, Nakamura-san's recommendation does not excuse the evil in which you've partaken. Why did you stoop so low and steal kitsune magic?"

My insides twist at having to contradict the tengu king right off the bat. Taking a deep breath, I keep it simple. "We did not steal it, sir."

But he snaps, cutting through the air with his feather fan. "No one gives such a gift! It destroys the owner. If I do not find your explanation satisfactory, you'll not leave my palace alive."

The declaration sends a shiver down my spine and my words spill out. "The fox I was fighting was Date Sari. She'd repeatedly attacked me and Aunt Hisako because of an old grudge and used her magic for evil—mixing it with that of an oni to add to her power.

"When she attacked my girlfriend, I tried to stop Date without killing her by dispelling her abilities. We didn't know it would split and settle into each of us. The kami judged Date for her actions and Inari Okami was merciful. He didn't require us to return her magic or hoshi no tama, which would have killed us.

"My aunt gave me a chance to start again after leaving the yakuza, and I wish to honor her and follow in her footsteps."

"Yakuza, you say?" His eyes flick to my aunt.

I whisper, "I have much to atone for, sir." Pressing my palms together in front of me, I bow as low as I can and remain in the position as I ask, "Please, teach me so I can serve as a Guardian."

"Humans aren't suitable candidates. The fifty-year appointment uses up too much of your brief lives. I fear your criminal past prohibits you from forming the support network needed for working in a remote area like Nonogawa. Guardians don't work alone, you know."

Fifty years is a long time. But what Aunt Hisako taught me about the Guardians calls to me more than anything I've ever wanted before. And I can rely on Su-chan, Satou, Matsuo, and probably Mie.

"This would be for the rest of my life." *Fitting for my atonement.* "And, yes, at first, I had a hard time in such a small town, because the rumor mill picked up news of my mobster tattoos before I could prove I won't go back.

"Some in Nonogawa may never accept me. That's part of the price I pay for my past. But there are a handful of friends I trust. I'll have to work hard to prove to the residents that I'm worth the risk."

He says, "What about compensation? I assume that because the law says you can't have a bank account for five years after leaving the mob, you have no savings set aside."

"Yes, sir. I'd need a livable wage, at least what the PSIA paid me for contract work. The day might come when I want to raise a family. If I understand it right, I can't really have a second job."

Aunt Hisako's eyebrow raises. Whether it's from Soujou-bou's question or my answer, I can't tell.

"Why do you aspire to the position?" His voice holds a disapproving coldness.

"I'd like to make the world a better place by maintaining peace in the area I'd serve. I can't undo my past, but I can protect those around me."

"Nakamura-san, is he violent?"

She knows the truth of what I was, that I'd taken lives. To be yakuza requires you to smother your conscience. But she's also aware there was nowhere else for me to go.

Clearing her throat, she says, "I, too, was concerned because of his past. No yakuza escapes being a bully or hurting others in their line of work. But he's handled difficult situations since leaving the mob by trying for peace before fighting. And he's had multiple opportunities to take revenge, but he chose not to kill. So I believe he's no more eager to spill blood than I am."

Soujou-bou's hands run over his chin and snowy beard as he appraises me. "Then I will consider this request while I speak with Nakamura-san about a string of weapons robberies. Fetch wood for our fire tonight. My servants can show you where to harvest the wood and how to dry it quickly for use."

"Yes, sir." I bow and kneel as Kairi did to open the shoji panel and exit in the proper traditional style, then I ask the nearest tengu for instructions. As with the other bird-men we've encountered, his reply is as brusque as a slap across the face. Though I get the gist of the drying spell.

A selection of work shoes sits available for the servants as they go from building to building. Slipping into a pair, I dash off in the direction shown.

'Fetch', he said. There's no pile of wood here or even an axe, and the light is fading. No time to hunt for the proper tool and no one's here to ask.

Figures. Such a mundane task. But I'll have to use my sword with a touch of magic.

So I set my suit jacket on a stump, then mumble an apology to the sword and to the tree I'm about to take down as I draw the katana from its sheath. Frigid cold runs down the handle, seeping into my hands and burning like holding ice, as the sword's ghostly blade glows and crackles. Why didn't I pick up a pair of gloves to shield my skin when I use the katana?

Gathering my ki and speaking a phrase of kotodama, the magic of the word, makes the task easy. A quick spell warms my hands, too. In less than twenty minutes, I have the wood piled neatly for the Great Tengu and use a bit more magic to dry it so it's ready to burn.

Planting a few pine cones ensures the tree will be replaced. Then I carry a stack piled high into the house. Was the sword especially cold because it didn't approve of being used for the task? *Too late now.*

When I return, Soujou-bou and my aunt are in deep discussion about ancient weapons being stolen from several museums. He directs me with a dismissive wave. "Clean my shoes and make us curry rice."

Stew for a king? A humble meal, but he is an ascetic monk. "Yes, sir."

Then he returns to his conversation as if I'm not there. "Nakamura-san, are you saying the sword is part of the collection that would allow someone to take over Japan?"

My feet root to the spot in the hallway. *Why can't I stay for that discussion?* Maybe I can linger outside for just a moment.

She responds, "Yes. We thought time had erased these legendary weapons, called the Ring of the Rising Sun. A secret society spread them out over Japan, to avoid anyone using them to steal the royal regalia. One of my contacts says that at least a few may be in the hands of Tokyo's criminal element. Plus, rumors have it that Ibaraki Douji, the old oni king's second in command, may be building an army."

The royal regalia—the three items needed for the ceremony to crown a new emperor—is at risk? My eyes bulge and I hold in a gasp. Something big's going down in my old stomping grounds. *Can I become a Guardian in time to help?*

Soujou-bou's words turn quiet. "Too much power in one place. So, why would Ibaraki be popping up now of all times? Oh, we've also lost contact with our agent in Sumichou." His words turn choked. "Another operative likely... dead."

Where's Sumichou? Dead? I gulp.

A throat clears as my aunt's stern voice calls out, "Tatsuya, Soujou-sama gave you a task."

Damn her incredible hearing! I have no excuse. So I shuffle off in borrowed house slippers, muttering silent curses at myself the whole way.

Soujou-bou's shoes are filthy from the mud after the recent rain. I cringe at having to touch where someone's sweaty feet have been, and I don't want to get my suit dirty. Rolling up my sleeves, I ponder how to do this. Another use for magic.

Then a tengu servant pops in, ordering me to hurry as I wash and don an apron in the suspiciously empty kitchen. Did Soujou-bou give someone the night off so he could test me?

Pride can't get in the way. Just like when I was in the mob, I'm being assigned the most menial tasks to test my humility and ability to follow orders. *I did this once; I can do it again.* Pasting on a neutral face, I nod, then with ruthless efficiency chop the ingredients laid out on the counter.

There's nothing to light the cooking fire with, so I have to resort to ki use yet again. I'd rather not have to keep using up my magic energy for things like this. Though, there's no choice if I want to have the food ready in a reasonable time and avoid interrupting Soujou-bou's talk with my aunt or having to ask the curt servants.

When I bring in piping hot bowls of curry stew, I take the same care I used to serve my old yakuza boss as I set chopsticks down on rests on the low table. The spicy aroma makes my stomach rumble. I'll grab a bowl in the kitchen and eat out of the way.

Aunt Hisako avoids looking at the Tengu King. He paces around with unnatural halting, bird-like movements, and says, "No complaints, proper manners, curious, and more humble than I expected for a strong-willed, yakuza pretty-boy."

"Humility is my only choice if I wish to repent for what I've done, sir." Giving a quick bow, I deflect his compliment, blunt as it was. Though, I'm not sure what to make of it.

I'm about to ask to be dismissed when he blurts, "Honjou Masamune, how is it you found this former gangster worthy?"

My head jerks back. *Honjou Masamune?* The famous sword that Tokugawa Ieyasu, the shogun who helped unite Japan, owned? The very blade made by Gorou Nyuudou Masamune—one of the most famous smiths that ever lived? It disappeared after WWII. And wouldn't Masamune have forged a tachi? The sword I have is too short to be one of those.

Wait, some tachi were remade into katana to fit the times. I gulp. My old mentor, Hiro, never said that the katana he gave me was legendary!

Suddenly, the blade tucked into my belt vibrates as it hums. Its song thrums through me with the same positive energy as a cat's purr. I knew all things have a soul, but it's done nothing like this before!

"I see. So you accept him." Then the Great Tengu says to me, "She's always so formal. I don't know why she speaks like an old woman."

It talked?

My aunt shakes her head. Later, I'll pester her until she explains. Way too many questions unanswered right now.

"Umeji-kun, I will train you to perfect your swordsmanship, just as I trained Minamoto no Yoshitsune nigh a millennium before. Then perhaps you can do credit to that treasure you carry. And we will bring your case before the Council of Guardians. What say you?"

He taught one of the greatest samurai in history. Closing my gaping mouth, I gather my wits and give a deep bow. "It would be an honor, sir."

Aunt Hisako wouldn't steer me wrong. But her careful composure and tight mouth makes the back of my neck prickle. *What isn't she saying?*

"Bring your supper," Soujou-bou directs.

On cue, I zip to the kitchen for my bowl. As I balance it and dodge a servant in the hall, Aunt Hisako's voice rings true, "Soujou-sama, you fall for the handsome ones in your care, whether they be men or women, just as you did for your first student. But you told me to speak the truth to you, above all. So hear me when I say Tatsuya won't take it well. Centuries ago, people accepted this kind of behavior. But in these modern times, they would see it as an abuse of power over a student."

His voice turns dismissive. "When I was young, a master had total control over his pupils."

"With all due respect, Master, for a tengu, you're not that hard-nosed, and you know it."

His "hmm" is half growl.

What the? He's a Buddhist priest. Queasy, I whip out my phone to do a one-handed search on the internet for what legend I missed about the tengu king. A Noh play pops up. Scanning it provides the context. *Yep, he was interested in his student.* Though, it doesn't say if anything happened.

That's why my aunt acted weird.

"We in the League keep talking about the need to modernize, yet fail to do so. Attitudes are where we have to start. We need fresh blood for that. This is only one reason I want to bring Tatsuya in as a Guardian. My nephew is bright and will speak plainly. He's young enough to help us utilize technology, too. The criminal world is leaving us in the dust because of the internet."

"Worse, our numbers dwindle by the year. No one else on the Council would take Umeji-kun as a student. Why couldn't they see the potential?" Soujou-bou adds.

Aunt Hisako actually stood up for me. And Soujou-bou is my best ticket to becoming a Guardian. *Shit.* Food sounds terrible. Eating is out of the question after what I heard. I zip back into the kitchen to dump out my stew and rinse the bowl, then slide the door to the room open.

Aunt Hisako's ears perk up. "Tatsuya?"

Upon being spotted, my muscles tense as I debate on whether to say anything about what I heard. Speaking my mind goes against everything I've been taught.

"Your expression is so dour. Out with it. I value the truth." Soujou-bou plops his chin in his palm as if tired and motions for me to speak—an unheard of trait in leadership.

But my throat constricts, so I spit out something bordering on safe. "Your voice carries, sir." *I'd have had to been deaf to not hear.*

"Does it? My old ears are not what they used to be. Then tell me this, boy. Is a romantic relationship between a teacher and student inappropriate?"

Awkward!

Aunt Hisako's eyes fix on the floor. I'm on my own.

Here goes nothing. So, I bow to soften my answer. "Y-yes, sir." The words tumble from my mouth as if racing to get out. "The student will have a hard time saying no because of their respect for the master."

He leans in. "Even if the student came to care for the teacher?"

My instincts scream, 'Trap!' and I clamp my arms to my sides to avoid stuffing them in my pockets. This is too formal an occasion for that.

Training in the yakuza was brutal to force agreement with my superiors. If the clan head said the crow was white, we all said, 'Yes, it was'.

But just going along with what the group wanted was a big part of why my life in the yakuza was a mess. And I'm still paying for it. *What am I if I can't speak the truth? Trust him or leave.* "The student should wait to express such things until their time as a student is over. It could harm the teacher's reputation otherwise."

"I agree. Therefore, you will remain here for training. My servant will show you to your room."

Holy shit. He just said I was right? So different from what I'm used to. Hopefully, it won't be too bold if I ask a question. "Sir?"

"Yes, Umeji-kun?"

"Will I be allowed to visit friends and family?" When his eyebrow raises, I add, "I'm bound to another because of my kitsune magic, sir."

He glances at Aunt Hisako. Primly, she states, "It's true. Before I could warn him about aspects of his new nature, he took a lover and found himself mated to her for life. We haven't determined if the bond is reciprocated."

A sparkle enters his eyes. Barking a laugh, he slaps my aunt on the back. "Like teacher, like student. Impulsiveness runs in your family, Nakamura-san."

When he turns his back, her lips purse and her eyes roll.

He says, "This lady of yours must be a rare beauty for a man to be smitten enough he'd make reckless choices and pass up one of the most sought after kitsune in Japan. I'm surprised Nakamura-san wasn't the one who seduced you."

Blinking, I avoid my aunt. She's not the only blunt one here. *Che!*

Soujou-bou isn't the first to suggest a romantic relationship between Aunt Hisako and me. We're not blood kin. I'm related to her through her first husband's side of the family. Despite her old lady human disguise, she's in her prime for her species.

I've seen her in her younger human form, too—the ideal of our culture's beauty. But that's just not how we've accepted each other. I see her as a mother figure.

When she speaks, Aunt Hisako's voice carries an edge. "Soujou-sama, he resembles my first husband. So it's an impossible match. Our clan witnessed what happened when Date seduced my husband's twin. While my nephew is generations from that union, and I'm glad he's here, the result was my brother-in-law secluding himself in a monastery, never to speak with us again."

Hot on the heels of her declaration, I blurt, "Sir, besides, my aunt encouraged Su-chan and I to date, and I strive to be worthy of her."

Putting a finger to his lips, he says, "You accepted a match made for you?" His intense stare burns, despite me trying to keep my eyes on my feet.

"Aunt Hisako suggested, but never pushed too hard. And Su-chan's amazing—a talented mage before natural magic augmented her abilities. Su-chan saw value in even the likes of me, sir."

"Then you must let me meet this woman of quality and character. Now, clear the table."

If he can accept me just as I am, as a student, maybe this won't be so bad?

While I clean the dishes at the old-fashioned pump outside, I take in the forest's glow from the lights of the tiny town of Kurama below and the metropolis of Kyoto beyond the ridges. The force field surrounding the estate barely hinders the view.

Then the hint of a shining fox shape streaks across the sky toward Soujou-bou's domain. My muscles tense and I hurry with my task. Last time I saw that phenomenon, a messenger kitsune from the god, Inari, delivered news that I was going to be tested before I could become a Guardian. *News for me?*

After putting the dishes away, I see my aunt bowing to a beautiful white fox sitting in the position of honor by the tokonoma display alcove.

"Hisako-san, Inari-sama has heard of your plight. He awaits your presence to offer counsel. You have difficult choices ahead."

Sensei's hackles raise for a moment, then settle. I've never seen her do that outside of a fight. Kneeling at her side, I offer the comfort of proximity.

Turning to me, the messenger says, "Ah, Umeji-san. I have news for you as well."

I probably couldn't tell most foxes apart, but he's the only messenger one I've seen. Giving my respects, I try to suppress any eagerness. "G-good evening."

"Now that you are among the ones I watch over, you may call me Yoshirou." After the obligatory pleasantries, he says, "The message is that your trials will increase. Dark days are at hand for kitsune-kind. The tasks ahead, should you choose to accept them, will set the course for our people."

Pain creeps up the back of my neck and into my head. That's not what I wanted to hear, but I close my eyes in respectful acceptance. Curiosity gets the better of me and I raise my hand as if about to ask a question, but let it drop because it might be rude.

"Yes?" the messenger prompts.

"Uhm. Yoshirou-sama, were you the one to visit me at the shrine near my cousin's house?"

The kitsune's eyes sparkle at the recognition. "I was, indeed. The Nakamura clan is a family I serve. Few kitsune remain, but I am fortunate to be assigned to a clan of our kind. Others serve Inari by watching over various species."

I probably should shut up. But something wells up inside after the freedom Soujou-bou granted. It's hard not to squirm as I debate asking.

He says, "Umeji-kun, speak. I will answer if I am able."

"What happens if I don't accept or complete the tasks? Will someone else accomplish them?"

"The future is always uncertain. One can follow portents, but never with an exactness that an intelligent mind desires. Truly, there are only actions and consequences. Each choice makes swirls in the mists of the future, sending those droplets to various places. Some become part of raging rivers, some evaporate to rejoin the mists again. This is the nature of things." He dips his head. "Now excuse me, I have business with your aunt."

He approaches her with his tail low but curved up, then tilts his head toward the outside in invitation. With dignity, they trot outside.

"Umeji-kun, close the doors for the night," Soujou-bou says.

My brows furrow, but I do as told. When I see them chasing and pouncing as they head deeper into the forest, I wipe my hand over my face and slide the doors closed. Soujou-bou gives a deep belly laugh at my reaction toward their date, but kindly changes the subject. "So, Umeji-kun, tell me how you came to possess this sword of legend, Honjou Masamune."

2

REFUGEES

A GRUFF VOICE BOOMS like a blow to my ear, "Umeji-kun, get up already! We have weary guests who need nourishment!"

Springing from my futon on the floor to a defensive crouch, I scrabble for my sword and stiff muscles protest moving in the chilled air. *Where the hell am I?* This plaster walled room filled with antiques isn't mine.

Then Soujou-bou peeks through the door before disappearing again. Taking a deep breath, I let the shakiness dissipate. I'm at my new master's house for training, and he put me through hell yesterday, despite my being in good shape already.

He bellows down the hall, "The Date clan arrived after the messenger told them you and Nakamura-san were here. Hurry, now!"

So, I holler as I snag the tray that holds the formal clothing Soujou-bou expects me to wear. "Be right there! Did my aunt return last night?"

"Yes. She's still sleeping. Don't wake her with your yelling!" His shouting echoes into my room.

"You decent, Tatsuya?" The quiet voice of the one I'm not supposed to wake comes through the paper of the shoji door.

"Decent enough."

In her kitsune form, Aunt Hisako yawns as she uses her snout to open the door, then pads into my room. "Soujou-sama, as good a king, leader, and teacher that he is, couldn't be quiet to save his life."

Don't laugh. The Great Tengu might hear better than he lets on. My fingers fumble as they quickly wrap my obi belt around my waist and create the specific knot with the thick fabric.

Switching to her human form, my aunt tsks. "Tatsuya, that's a terrible knot for your obi. It'll come out in no time. I know you're in a hurry, but the Date clan is worth making yourself presentable for and you need to get used to wearing a kimono daily. Your master is a stickler for some aspects of tradition."

So, I close my eyes. My aunt and I have had nothing but trouble from Date Sari. "How do we know the Dates aren't bringing more problems?"

"We don't." She tugs at the knot in front of me and turns the sash so it goes to my back. "I hunted a pair of rabbits and dressed them last night, knowing you've never had to deal with that. Soujou-sama will help you, if you ask. He's an excellent teacher. Though, he'll chide you for being a city boy."

Her teasing warms me inside and gives me hope that this meeting won't be a disaster. She waves her hand toward the door. "Off with you, now."

"Ki boost first," I volley and share energy. To conserve her limited ki, she returns to fox form.

A few moments later, Soujou-bou has me grill the meat. I've never had rabbit before. Each of the pieces is so tiny, but the charred aroma makes my mouth water.

"Stop turning it so often. It can sit there for a few minutes while you prepare the rice." As he creates the side dishes, he grumbles and his feathers rustle, "Umeji-kun, for being Nakamura-san's apprentice, you're rather worthless."

Ouch. "I've lived in Tokyo most of my life, sir. Never tried rabbit meat or any other wild game. But I'm a quick study," I respond.

"Indeed…"

That tone. *Something's up.* Movement catches my eye thanks to a quick word of kotodama magic. He slips in chestnuts as he moves to block the view. I wouldn't have put them in with the variety of vegetables, though there's no way I'll say so or he'll think I'm judging his cooking skills. So I mumble, "Chestnuts." *Remember that.*

He harrumphs. "Pay attention to what I told you to do."

"Yes, sir. Uhm, may I ask why you help with the cooking instead of having your servants do it?"

"Being able to provide for yourself and those under you is a skill everyone should have. No tengu nor student should be above even the most menial of tasks."

Aunt Hisako said Soujou-bou prefers tradition. But this is the second aspect where he breaks from the old ways. Usually, leaders expect to be served.

Bringing out breakfast gives me a first glance at the guests. The morning sun peeking through the shoji panels on the window highlights bandaged wounds and the foxes' tired eyes speak of dangers faced. Old smoke and singed fur scents hang in the air, diminishing the tang of the fresh pickles on the tray I carry. They're both leaning on the wall as if exhausted.

Hackles raise on one of the kitsune pair, as I kneel and set dishes of grilled rabbit, natto, rice, miso soup, and pickled vegetables in front of them on the table.

"What thievery was allowed at the Date clan's expense?" a red male growls as he advances on me.

Backtracking before he decides I'm a threat, I put my hands up. "Please forgive what appears to be stolen magic. It wasn't intentional. I'll be happy to explain after you've had your fill. Please, enjoy."

"Polite words don't cover for the travesty you've committed. That's my sister's magic you have. I'd know it anywhere."

"Quiet!" the silver female snaps at the younger fox.

"But Sari's dead because-"

"Now, Hoji!" When his head dips, she continues, "The human is correct. Inari-sama required my attendance for your sister's judgment."

I'll be damned if I apologize for Date Sari's death. I'm not the one that caused that witch to die. But I can at least respect their grief.

"Please," I say, gesturing to the bowls. "I'll leave the room so you can enjoy the food while it's still warm."

"Did you prepare it?" Hoji asks.

"I assisted."

After shoving the bowl away, Hoji curls up by the table as his stomach growls. His mother barks and nips his rump, then digs into her meal.

Out of no where, Soujou-bou's thundering voice from behind makes me jump. He extends his wings as if he's a raptor about to pounce on prey. "Date Hoji, you would dare to refuse my hospitality or that of my student?"

We all shrink in the Tengu King's imposing presence.

Hoji's head and ears droop as he kneels. "N-no, Soujou-sama. Forgive my rudeness. It won't happen again." He retrieves the bowl and wolfs the rabbit meat down.

"You may not know when your next meal will come." Sitting with the fox family, Soujou-bou says, "Umeji-kun, you need not sit apart from us when you eat. Bring in bowls for everyone. Then let us find out why Date Miwa and her son dared use a teleportation spell on my mountain."

Not long after I sit, I end up refilling their bowls. *How long has it been since they've eaten?*

"Thank you for the meal and your hospitality, Soujou-sama," Miwa says as her son nods in appreciation.

"It was delicious," Hoji adds, then glances at my aunt. Perhaps he wishes to make up for his snobbery?

"As to our intrusion and going against your wishes, my good Sou-jou-sama," Miwa continues, "Please forgive our actions done only in the flight for our lives. My husband and daughters are dead at the hand of the oni, Ibaraki Douji, who claims my eldest enthralled her." Her paw covers her face, and she takes a deep breath.

Soujou-bou runs his hand over his chin and beard. "A single kitsune en-thralled Ibaraki, you say?"

"Likely," she sobs.

How did Date Sari manage it?

Hoji nuzzles his mother's shoulder and picks up where she left off. "My eldest sister died defending us, despite her reduced animal state. She still rec-ognized and protected our family, becoming the oni's target of choice. When Ibaraki shouted 'Death to all kitsune', we fled. As they gained on us, I shoved my mother through a hastily made portal before closing it behind me."

"Could they trace you?" Soujou-bou asks as he purses his lips.

What's it take to track a portal?

"We entered on the edge of your lands, hoping it would be indistinguish-able from other forested mountains."

Then my aunt pipes up, "Is Ibaraki intent on your family only?"

"What are you insinuating?" Hoji narrows his eyes.

Straightening her posture at the challenge, she adds, "The Date clan isn't the only one to suffer losses. The messenger, Yoshirou, brought news of other clans being attacked."

Under his breath, Hoji mutters, "What has Sari started?"

"I'm hoping it's not the extinction of our race, Date-san," Aunt Hisako says with a dead calm that gives me the shivers.

After swallowing the last bite of my meal, I ask, "Aunt, do you think I should train away from the clan if the kitsune are in danger?"

"You're Nakamura-san's relative?" Hoji's voice cracks.

It takes effort to keep the grin off my face. "Technically, I'm more closely related to you. Your sister was my seven-times great grandmother. Aunt Hisako's brother-in-law was the father of the child your sister bore. Small world, huh?"

"So my daughter's line continues?" Wiping the tears from her eyes, the mother perks up.

"Yes, ma'am." I give a bow because of her positive response. "My name is Umeji Tatsuya. I'm honored to meet you, great grandmother. Please, be kind to me."

Returning the pleasantries, she pads closer. "Grandson, I am Date Miwa, and I am pleased to find you at last. I knew my daughter had a girl, but she hid the child, and we could not find her. We heard snippets but had troubles tracing her line. You're a connection to the grandchild I never knew."

"Don't expect me to be an uncle to the brat that caused my sister's ruination." Hoji turns his nose up.

But Grandma Miwa snaps, "Hoji! Your sister chose the path that led to the death of herself, your sister, and your father!"

Hoji's grieving. So his anger is to be expected.

Aunt Hisako scoots beside Grandma Miwa, letting the proximity to one who's been her enemy speak. "Tatsuya is common kin, linking our families now."

"Will it be possible for us to put aside centuries old enmity for the sake of our species?" Grandma Miwa asks.

"Perhaps we can work toward that end." My aunt at least has the decency to leave the avenue open. How hard will it be for her to set aside her feelings about the Date clan after they declared they were on different sides of the Meiji Restoration over two hundred years ago?

Hoji's staring at my aunt again. *What's up with him?*

As I clear the table and do the dishes, my new grandmother directs Hoji to help me with the work. *So much for a moment of peace.* Too bad Su-chan had to stay at the Nakamura clan den to research her half of the magic she received from Date Sari. It would have been much more fun. *Damn, I miss her.*

3

ENEMY AT THE GATES

MY MUSCLES PROTEST WITH every swing as I chop wood for the cooking fire. This time, I have an axe—unlike yesterday when the tengu servants played a trick. *Bastards.* They even tattled, saying I used my sword to fell a tree a few days ago. *Should've used only magic for the task.*

As punishment, I had to read translations of the Heart and Diamond Sutras aloud three times, scrub every floor of the twenty plus building estate with a rag—pushing it with my hands while running it across the floor, and then promise that I'd never use my sword for such a low task again. My back and neck hurt so much I could have sworn I was eighty-years-old. Aunt Hisako wasn't this harsh when I used her sewing scissors for paper!

Soujou-sensei freed me from most chores to focus on my training. At this rate, I'll build awesome core muscles from chopping wood several times a day and the constant exercises and sword drills he makes me do! Fast draw and cut techniques, stretches for limberness, a host of torturous push-up and lunge versions, and the list goes on.

Maybe Su-chan will notice a difference when I see her again. *Wish she was here.*

The top of Mount Kurama overlooks the forested valley cradling the Anba River. I could stare at the breathtaking view forever. But movement in the sky makes me shield my eyes from the sun and squint until the object comes into focus.

A falcon tengu dives from the clouds toward the estate at a blinding speed, chittering a shrill warning as he homes in on Soujou-bou's garden path. His massive wings spring out from a tucked position, extending with a whoosh, louder than a parachute opening.

Fallen leaves swirl as they're tossed off the path. Then, tucking his wings back in, he lands at a run, not missing a beat. He bounds, with kimono sleeves flapping in his wake, into the master's sitting room. The shoji doors are wide open to view the courtyard garden.

To fly like that. How many others have witnessed the tengu grace, not just their trickster side? Tearing my eyes away with a shake of my head and one last swing, I bury the axe in the woodblock and follow to see what the commotion's about.

Inside, the tengu kneels as he reports to his master in a grating, scratchy voice. "My Lord, Ibaraki Douji leads an oni horde. They've reached the base of the mountain. She was screaming 'Death to the kitsune.' We estimate the horde to be four hundred strong."

Shit. She followed the Date pair. I'll help defend my master's estate. Will even Soujou-bou, the old priest, have to fight?

"Light the flares! Sound the alarm!" Soujou-bou shouts.

The messenger strikes a gong that sends a thrum reverberating through the vicinity and spurring all around to action. So I move out of the way to keep from being trampled. With deafening pops, portals form in every direction.

Taking his swords from their perch, Soujou-bou shouts, "Kumagai, prepare my armor! Zumi, gather the troops!"

In a softer tone, he says to me, "This is the reason I don't allow portals to be created just anywhere on my land. It allows my troops from across the country to arrive in an instant. Each province's portal has an assigned location, so there's no worry about overlap and losing soldiers to the void. Newcomers don't know the open areas."

Meanwhile, the sky fills with a cacophony of beating black and brown wings, caws, shrieks, and whistles from tengu that barrel down en masse. Did the intruders think taking Soujou-bou's lands would be easy? *Guess again!*

Energy thrums through my veins as I force myself to be still and wait for orders.

Aunt Hisako skitters from the house to my side. "I heard the summons. What's happening?"

"Invasion. You ok for ki?" My hand hovers over her fur, ready to share my life force.

But she holds up a paw. "Keep it. You'll need what you have."

"Kitsune-kind, go, now!" Soujou-bou barks at us.

Pressing my hands together before me in my bow, I volunteer. "Master, let me help defend your home."

"Protect your aunt in her weakened state, at all costs. Ibaraki will focus on both clans of your family when she realizes how many kitsune are here. My people will buy you time," Soujou-bou says, then directs his captains to hold the gate.

"Understood, sir!"

Grandma Miwa arrives. Her head whips around to Aunt Hisako. "What do you mean, weakened state? I saw you low on ki, but..."

Aunt Hisako won't meet her gaze as we retreat inside, with Soujou-bou and his retainers hot on our heels. She gives the unvarnished truth. "Sari stole my hoshi no tama and broke it, leaving me magically crippled."

Gasping, Grandma Miwa hangs her head as a tengu servant rushes in with Soujou-bou's armor. In a glowing blur, the bird-man servant helps his master into the many pieces. Black and brown feathered soldiers open the house's sliding doors and line up the troops outside.

While Soujou-bou puts his helmet on and casts a spell to tie the laces, he barks, "Umeji-kun, I suspend the restriction on you. Create a portal out of sight and get your family to safety. Keep your destination secret."

"We don't need your protection, yakuza." Hoji sticks his nose in the air, then turns to the others. "Mother, let us leave."

Instead, Grandma Miwa slaps the top of his head with a forepaw. "Baka."

From outside, the chaos of thunder, the clashing of swords, and continual pops from new portals forming makes my muscles twitch.

"Kami-sama, protect us. They're using an anti-magic battering ram." Aunt Hisako's voice turns tight and my mouth goes dry as a desert, just like it did those years ago in the surprise attack on the Hiragi clan yakuza headquarters.

Soujou-bou and his servants stride through the hall toward the outside. His barked "Now, boy!" enhances the purposeful presence he emanates.

We double time it to an interior room. "Create cover for us." Thinking better of commanding my elders, I add, "Please," as I gather my ki.

With their agreement, I whisper a word of kotodama and scribe a glowing blue circle in the air that sizzles with sparks. My aunt's family den lies just beyond the hole and a shimmer around us grows as the fox pair provides the illusion of an empty room.

My aunt and great grandmother jump through. But when we hear my master's war-cry, Hoji dashes off. Swearing, I close the portal despite the Nakamura clan's protests and at a dead run, I draw my sword.

"Umeji, get the foxes out of here!" Soujou-bou's voice booms from above as his massive wings beat and fling dirt and leaves.

"On it, Master!" Bailing off the veranda in a ki enhanced leap, I belt out a kiai to sail over Hoji and slash the oni running at him in half.

"I had him, yakuza!" Hoji howls and points to the host of ash piles around him as his sword hovers, shimmering in the air above his fox form. "To avenge my family!" He switches to a human guise and dashes toward the fray.

The stench permeating from the wave of red, green, and blue oni invaders rushing the gates fills the air with a sickly green haze that almost causes me to lose my breakfast. So, I improvise a spell to eliminate the nausea still roiling my stomach.

Hoji's face, sharply planed and framed in glasses, is a grim mask. His jeans, Doc Martins, and blue wool pea coat will keep him warm while I shiver in just a button-up shirt.

Next, an oni archer takes aim at the idiot kitsune, so I incant a shield around us both.

"Back off or you become the enemy, too!" Hoji growls.

The archer's movement blurs. Our defense falls when a second arrow hits the spell wall. Screaming as the arrow pierces his shoulder blade through to the other side, Hoji collapses.

I manage a stronger shield and drop to his side. Tengu warriors carrying axes and pikes flock to form a shield wall between us and the oni.

A deafening, scratchy voice calls out. "Don't bother denying that the Date clan is sheltering here. Surrender the kitsune, and we will cease our fight!"

"Ibaraki, get your filthy oni off my land!" Soujou-bou's voice rings clear above the din.

"One hundred pieces of gold for every kitsune head laid at my feet!" the leader volleys. Bass voiced cheers erupt and echo around us like a tsunami rushing in and crashing over everything in the way.

Can we get Hoji outta here?

He spits, "See what your inexperience in battle caused!"

So, I mutter, "The point is getting you to safety and healing. Your kind's in danger, not mine."

"They killed my father and sisters!" The stubborn idiot struggles to get up, but a rain of arrows glances off the barrier as he winces and tries to get up for another charge. "I didn't ask for your help, whelp."

Arrogant ass! Placing my sword under his chin, I say a word of kotodama to extinguish his human disguise so he'll be lighter to carry.

Defiantly, he shoves aside the blade and scoops up his sword in his jaws. In response, I incant a field around him to keep the embedded arrow from hitting anything as I grab the scruff of his neck. His curses ring out as he tries to break free.

As if things couldn't get worse, a shrill female's shout makes me turn my head. "The Date family will pay! There's one over there!" A green skinned, stringy-haired figure in a vibrant kimono raises a metal hand to point at Hoji and me, alerting the entire army as it pours through the gates. *Fuckin' peachy.*

We make it inside the main house. My legs tremble, but I steady myself to scribe an arc in the air. Picturing the alley close to a city park that I used to visit, I create a portal, then stumble into the bustling cityscape before closing the gate behind us.

Panting and wincing with each breath, he growls through gritted teeth. "Couldn't create a portal all the way to your clan's den this time?"

You little shit. "Didn't want them to follow us. We're in Tokyo, a hell of a lot farther! Shut the fuck up so I can concentrate on getting us back."

But my hand goes numb as I grab a fistful of his fur. *What the?* Energy is being sucked out fast. "I hope to the kami I have enough ki to do this again!"

Deflated, he coughs up blood, spattering the ground in a waste of life giving paint. "You didn't do things the honorable way." Every rise of his chest causes the muscles around the arrow to tighten, stretching the skin around the puncture.

Resting a moment allows my breathing to slow. "My master said to get you out of there."

"Let me die here."

"Not on my watch. There are so few of your kind. Your job is to find a mate and have lots of babies to re-establish the numbers of kitsune. Soujou-sama wouldn't have said to get you out of there otherwise." Despite the bravado, my legs threaten to give out. "Ki's draining too fast."

He shoves his phone toward me with his canine nose, as he says, "Use the energy from this to create a portal."

"What?"

"Fine, give me energy to do it. Just hold it up for facial recognition."

When I comply, he hits a speed dial setting, creating a yellow portal. But it twitches and freezes like a program glitch. I drag us through to a tatami mat room with a sunken hearth, a den I know well.

Hoji shudders as blood oozes from his mouth. Easing him to his good side, I back off as the Nakamura clan crowds in with Grandma Miwa.

"That portal didn't seem stable," I croak.

"It wasn't. We didn't have a choice," Hoji whispers between coughs. "I never thought I'd step foot in this den. Our clans were enemies from before I was born."

Next, Great Uncle Nobu uses a spell to create a glowing knife and slices away the blood-soaked fur to investigate the wound as Hoji's breaths turn shallow. Behind me, a squeak precedes quick barefoot slaps on the floor. Suzuki Soujirou—Jiro as he's called now—asks, "The fox isn't d-dead, is he?"

"His ki pulse is erratic. All the ki I pour into him dissipates." Great Uncle Nobu's voice waivers. Suddenly, he shouts, "Stay with us, Date Hoji. Look at me!"

Poor Jiro collapses and crab-crawl skitters backward. "D-d-date?!"

Hoji's eyes fly open and flick to Great Uncle Nobu's, but don't stay there.

When I squeeze Jiro's shoulder, I whisper, "Not the one who hurt you." *Anything else I can do?*

Nakamura Asako, Aunt Hisako's mother, fetches paper, brush and ink with lightning speed. Her writing sloshes ink onto the tatami mat floor. The black stain and that of Hoji's blood will never come out.

She asks, "Tatsuya-kun, how long has he had the arrow in him?"

"Less than 10 minutes?"

Then she drapes an ofuda charm on Hoji's neck, as close as she can get to the wound. "This should help stabilize him."

But the paper only sizzles out of existence.

Grandma Miwa howls, "Not you, too, Hoji!"

"Miwa-san, tell us what's happening," Great Uncle Nobu says.

"It's..." She heaves in a breath, "...like a bomb. The kind that killed both Sari and my husband. I don't know if there's enough time to dismantle it."

Su-chan kneels beside us, laying her hands on Hoji's shoulder. "I'll buy him time." She snaps, "What are you all waiting for? My ki pool will last maybe five minutes!"

Then the gentle scent of Su-chan's cherry blossom perfume hits, reminding me of how she kept me sane during the craziness in Nonogawa. Why did my first time seeing her in days have to be one I can't just scoop her up in my arms? *Damn you, Hoji.*

Grandma Miwa says, "Don't give him too much. Let it dribble in. You'll last longer and the bomb won't reach capacity as quickly. It's about 80 percent full." Her hands shake as she grips the arrow and mutters words too fast to understand.

Meanwhile, Hoji struggles to breathe, and each jolt sends a fresh wave of agony through him. Grandma Miwa rasps, "Almost there."

"His ki pulse is erratic! We've got to remove it now!" Great Uncle Nobu hisses.

So, Grandma Miwa utters a word to slice off the end of the arrow and slumps. "It's disarmed."

Did it steal her ki, too?

Great Uncle Nobu sheds his button-up shirt, wads it up and stuffs it into Hoji's mouth. *This is gonna be bad.* I can't tear myself away from the grizzly scene, but I pull Jiro into my side and cover his eyes.

"Asako. Miwa-san. You hold Hoji still while I pull it through because we can't remove it via magic. The directional burrs mean it has to come through the front," Great Uncle Nobu says, and everyone's hands press and clamp down on Hoji to hold him on his side. "Ohno-chan, keep feeding him ki, even if his pulse stops. Do you understand?"

Su-chan gives a definitive nod.

"Ready?" my uncle asks.

Uncle Nobu shoves Hoji with one hand while he yanks with the other. The arrow jerks through halfway, with its burrs dragging through already angry flesh before it stops in what must be Hoji's lung. Hoji cries out and bites through several layers of the shirt.

Nobu soothes, "Sorry. Once more and we'll have it."

The second yank makes the young fox jerk and Great Aunt Asako puts an ofuda over both sides and affixes it with first aid tape. Hoji shivers, whimpering.

Next, Great Aunt Asako steps into her matriarch role like a battle field general ordering troops. "Energy isn't draining from him anymore, but he isn't out of danger yet. Jiro, fetch a futon and blankets for Hoji. Hisako, warm stones in the hearth."

Aunt Hisako scrambles to fetch rocks from the garden.

Without pause, Great Aunt Asako continues the string of commands. "Tatsuya, please fetch the kappa healer at the base of the mountain. Suzu, help my other daughters prep the bedrooms for our guests and be sure to prime the pump." Her directions continue to everyone in the house.

The kappa isn't at the pond. Waiting in the cold for an hour puts me in a sour mood, but he says he'll be by after gathering supplies. Thankfully, my great aunt has warm food ready to feed us all.

Afterward, I check on Hoji and lift the corner of the talisman covering his wound. His eyes open, so I ask. "Can I get you anything? Water? Pain meds?"

"If I close my eyes, will someone else be there instead?" he asks. Trying it doesn't work. "Food. Pain meds. Strong ones if they'll let me have them." He takes a shaking breath. "I was an ass."

Sure was. But his family's murderers were at the gate. *I'd have been in a rage, too.* So, I shrug it off.

Grandma Miwa pads over. "Son, how do you feel?"

"Like shit."

She chuckles as she pats his shoulder. "That's to be expected. Count yourself lucky to have survived a ki well destructor. Hisako-san says all yokai courts banned them."

"Can I get a bath?"

"After we get some food in you, a cool bath would be good."

"A hot one?"

"Not yet. That open wound has to finish healing. We focused on your ki well and lung first. Nobu-san didn't feel we could do more without shocking your system. Hopefully, the kappa will arrive soon for a professional opinion. After the wound closes, a hot bath should do wonders to help you recover mobility in that arm."

Great Uncle Nobu peeks in. Since Hoji is awake, Nobu changes the bandages and helps Hoji to the sunken hearth. Because of the chill in the room, I drop a blanket from the futon over the fox's shoulders. Warm rays pour through the skylight above and Hoji's head tilts back to take it in as he whispers, "I shouldn't have lived to see the sun again."

Zipping off to the kitchen, I return with a bowl of miso soup, a cup of tea, and a funky black paste that makes me wonder what dead thing got dragged through it. I say, "Eat this. If you finish it, your mother says you can have something heavier. The salve is the strongest pain killer they'll let you have until the kappa arrives. Lay down and let me apply it."

"Can it wait until after I eat? That stuff..." Hoji's nose wrinkles.

"Uh, sure."

Grandma Miwa chuckles as she pads in. "You're feeling better."

A few sips of the hot tea perk Hoji up. The miso soup is simple, just a fish and soybean paste broth with diced tofu, seaweed strips, and scallions. But as soon as his tongue touches the salty umami, he wolfs it down as if he'd not eaten for a week.

"Ready for more?" Grandma Miwa asks.

"Please."

"Tatsuya-kun, if you would be so kind. I'll administer the pain killer while you fetch the rest of lunch for Hoji."

Along the way, questions assault me. How many times will Date Sari's sins haunt us? What if the League can't stop Ibaraki before she wipes out the kitsune? What if...

'The what ifs do you no good' Aunt Hisako likes to say. *Deal with the problem at hand.*

A tray of various foods known for their health benefits sits on the counter as Aunt Hisako dries her hands after washing the dishes and asks, "What's on your mind, Tatsuya?"

"The ki bombs are how Ibaraki is taking out entire kitsune families, right? So, how do we stop them?"

For a moment, her mouth twists to the side. "Magic itself may not be sufficient. One of those arrows can suck spells dry, allowing for another to penetrate a defense."

"How hard do you think they are to manufacture?"

"I'll have to consult the archives to be sure. They'd be costly to make—as in, more ki than the average yokai has. But the real question is, how are they made?"

A few hours later, the blare of multiple, high-pitched, tea kettle whistles makes us all jump. Great Aunt Asako murmurs a vision spell and, in a hollow voice, says, "Intruders at the edge of the property. Hisako, gather everyone. Tell them to bring only what they can grab in five seconds."

Su-chan scampers off to fetch Chou, her semi-sapient pet slime, and her bag of potions. I snag my sword and the book of myths from my dad and throw on my shoes and coat.

Before everyone gathers, another whistle blasts our ears. Great Aunt Asako shudders. "They've found the den."

They traced us?

Great Uncle Nobu and Great Aunt Asako shove ki into today's healing spell to patch Hoji up as best they can, then they scramble for their weapons. I tuck my sword and Hoji's into my belt.

Hoji says sadly, "Too bad I can't grab the research notes."

Just then, Grandma Miwa scurries in. "I have them."

When everyone is in the room, Aunt Hisako's brows furrow in concentration. "Everyone but Tatsuya, create a portal to a place as far as you can. We have to redirect the intruders."

Great Uncle Nobu, in human form, tucks Hoji under one arm and grasps a polearm in another.

"Suzu-chan, please lend me ki. Your pool is the greatest of us all." Aunt Hisako says as she holds out her palm. So Su-chan claps her hand into the outstretched one. "Thank you." My aunt slaps a portal talisman in the air, and she scribes a long series of circles around it. A flick at the talisman makes the portal duplicate, expanding out like a magician's card trick.

Woah.

"Miwa-san, please be the battery for Tatsuya and his on-the-fly training."

My great grandmother nods and sends a rush of sunshine warmth into me.

"The enemy's been tracking our every move and tracing our portals. That's a tremendous skill not even I can manage. To counter, we'll wipe out the trackers," Aunt Hisako says.

When she finishes the spell, she collapses. A corridor made up of over twenty portals opens to a river, then an alley, and finally a cabin. "Suzu-chan, carry me. I don't have the energy. Mother, Father, please provide cover for us. Jiro-kun, as soon as all of us are through the fifth portal, you will close them behind us. But only that one and those after it. Tatsuya and I will monitor the others so we can catch as many of the intruders in the in-between as we can. Do you understand?"

Jiro's mother, Chiyo, grimaces at the thought of her middle school-aged son having to help in the group's escape. While I agree with her, I know he can do this.

So Jiro nods. "Fifth portal."

"Enemy at the front door," Great Aunt Asako says with a quaver in her voice when there's another whistle.

Deftly, Su-chan scoops up Aunt Hisako and adjusts the strap of her potions duffle. Chou clings to the bag but holds out grabby hands toward me.

Before I can respond to the pet slime, Aunt Hisako says, "Tatsuya, I'll create a mental link with you so you can see how the spells work. You and I will be last through." She heaves in a breath. "Everyone, go with my parents into the portals they enter. Now!"

So Great Aunt Asako and Great Uncle Nobu race through the portal line toward a shrine. Everyone follows, hot on their heels. Behind us, crashes and wood splintering precede the shouting, thuds, and slaps of heavy bare feet on the floors of the genkan entry.

My heart sinks at the violation of the Nakamura clan den. *It felt like home.*

"Shield, Mother!" Aunt Hisako barks.

"T-two, three, f-four…" Jiro waits for Su-chan and me to pass before closing the fifth portal.

It doesn't stop after that; our group moves as one.

"Father, open a new portal corridor!" Aunt Hisako shouts as the eighth closes. "Tatsuya, can you feel the dozen piling through the first portals? Let the next one go fuzzy around the edges, then release it just as they step through. If we're lucky, we'll catch them in the void between. And I doubt the regular oni troops can manage the magic."

"We've doomed them." I shudder but obey and head for the tenth portal. Then my footsteps falter and Grandma Miwa shifts to human form so she can put an arm around my waist.

"Better them than us," Aunt Hisako growls.

Pressure grows around us so heavy in my head it's hard to think.

"Protect your ears!" Aunt Hisako shouts and whispers a spell as she leads us through another set of openings.

Just then, a sonic boom tears through the closed portal behind us. The blast whooshes past and we close three more gates on the pursuers.

"Father! Another portal corridor. Now! I'll choose our final destination!"

I can still hear her? How? I didn't have the ki to enact the spell to shield my ears.

When Jiro tugs at my arm, blood runs down the sides of his face and nose. *Aw shit, he protected me.*

"Tatsuya, can you sense the power building behind us again?" Aunt Hisako asks.

"It's weaker this time."

"You're going to disperse it before they can use it. You don't have a seal for full access to League powers, but your connection as a student should be enough. Mother, give us your strongest shield. The rest of you run like hell to the last gate!"

"Come on!" Jiro tugs at his mom's hand. She has a tear-stained face and furrowed brows—does it mean she's had to flee like this before?

So Grandma Miwa and I settle into fighting stances, though I'm a little unsteady. She slaps my leg with another ki infusion. With Aunt Hisako tucked under one arm, Su-chan joins us.

Through the mental link, Aunt Hisako says, 'Imagine the power on the other side of the previous portals as a ball that keeps growing smaller. Focus on this and imagine it exploding like a supernova.'

I draw ki from my well and press my hands together, picturing everything on the other side of the portal compressing into the center of that glowing ball of power, and I hold the image of an atomic blast.

Heat fills my ki well, scorching my insides. But I keep pushing down on that power. The magic scrabbles for a handhold, screaming to be released.

When I sway, Grandma Miwa puts an arm around my waist again and more bonfire-like ki flows in. Aunt Hisako and I press harder until the magic squeezes into a centimeter-sized cube.

"Now!" Aunt Hisako screams.

The release knocks the four of us back several meters. Blinding light sears my retinas. The shock wave ripples past the barrier, flinging us toward the last portal. But Grandma Miwa's shield keeps me from being buffeted around.

Another flutter of doors appears, and a mirror-like shift bends everything in a wavy mirage. Tugging us through the door, Aunt Hisako allows the illusion to engulf everything behind us with a flash as we tumble through the last portal.

Aunt Hisako rasps, "Summer home, Father. I'll erase any trace of our portal there."

When Aunt Hisako, Grandma Miwa, Su-chan and I step through to solid ground at last, we collapse in the snow, spent. The refreshing cold seeps through my coat and pants.

I gasp in the country air. That was some crazy magic back there. *I'll be learning that? Fuckin' cool.*

Shoving herself to her four feet, Aunt Hisako wobbles and whispers something I don't understand. She whips her tails, and the air glows where the portal had been. "Shield your eyes!" she shouts.

White-hot flames engulf the area, and I put my hand over my face before the air crackles and the scent of ozone permeates the area.

"How did you do that?" Hoji's eyes are wide as he lays in the snow beside me. "It shouldn't be possible."

Su-chan picks up Aunt Hisako, who collapsed. Meanwhile, Great Uncle Nobu and Great Aunt Asako scurry to place wards around the property.

I ask, "Aunt, could that blast have killed whoever was dogging us?"

"Possible, but not likely. They were more powerful than most yokai I've encountered. It would have killed a lesser oni. Any who survived won't be happy with us."

Gently, Su-chan squeezes my hand. "That was insane."

"Bat-shit crazy. I can't believe we survived." My hand wipes over my face.

All of a sudden, Aunt Hisako laughs. "I haven't had to use that kind of spell in decades. Japan's been relatively peaceful. Speaking of...Miwa-san. Suzu-chan. Thank you for lending ki to Tatsuya and me. We couldn't have pulled that off without your help. I'm watching you closely, Su-chan. Your talent is incredible."

My girlfriend just shuffles her feet.

After a moment, my aunt sighs. "I don't want to waste energy for a seal. So, know that what you just saw is not to be spoken of. Ever."

Hoji's eyes go wide. "That means you're a G..."

In a flash, her tail flies up to his mouth. "I meant no speaking of what you think that means. At all! How else do you think I got my nine-tails when I'm only a few centuries old?"

Unable to pick his mouth up off the floor, Hoji gapes before shaking his head to clear it. "That means you have the experience of one who lived over a thousand years!"

Grandma Miwa whispers, "And the wisdom to match."

Next, I offer my great grandmother and Su-chan a hand up before carrying the still awed Hoji inside. *Have we done everything we can to keep everyone, especially the kitsune, safe?*

4

HEALER

"Tatsu!" Su-chan's voice chimes in the air when my eyes flutter open. Scuffling says others heard my girlfriend's exclamation and a host of foxes all peek into the room.

Her palm presses to my cheek as she explains, "In the commotion over Hoji's near death experience, we'd not thought to check everyone else out. Then you didn't wake up when I tried to roust you and I freaked out. We were all so worried!"

As I reach for her hand, every muscle in my body protests like it's been wrung out. She squeezes back and I feel sunshine-warm ki flow in, as if the well inside me had been scorched in the desert sun.

"Hoji's the one to worry about." Though, my voice comes out scratchy. *Why do I feel like shit?*

"Call the healer now that Tatsuya is awake," Great Aunt Asako pads in, then gives orders to someone outside.

To me she says, "Someone designed the arrow that hit Hoji-san to pull ki from and corrupt everything it touched, including a user's magic. It affected all of us who helped him. But you were the worst case. Why?" The question hangs in the air.

"Umeji-san?" Jiro's brow furrows deep, but I nod for him to enter. He kneels beside my futon.

"What's up, Jiro-kun?"

"I'm so glad you're awake!" Then he deflates. "Mom wants to go back to Nono-gawa."

What the hell do I say? "Does she think it will be safer?"

He nods. "But I don't wanna go."

I can't blame him. He's being tutored by mythical kitsune who can teach him more about life than the school in the tiny town could. Through the Nakamuras, he's learning magic and traditional arts beyond the usual subjects. And he's thriving so much more than he did back in Nonogawa.

Great Uncle Nobu even thinks he can have Jiro ready to pass the mandatory Middle School exam at least a year early. The boy's blowing through lessons so fast. *Way smarter than me.*

"Can't blame you." *Will it be safer if they return? He's got fox magic too, which makes him a target.* Maybe I can chat with the Nakamuras about the issue? When I become a Guardian, I can be there to help watch over him. Though, I can't if they leave now.

So, I change the subject. "You seem to hear me fine. Are you ok? Yesterday, it looked like your ear drums got damaged."

"Yes. It tickled when they fixed my ears." He brightens until Grandma Miwa enters, then he goes still. "I can fetch the healer."

"Let me accompany you, in case there's trouble." Grandma Miwa creates a glowing portal to the pond with a flick of her tail.

But Jiro backs away.

Closing her eyes, Grandma Miwa turns her head. After a moment, she insists. "Let me atone for the evil my daughter did to you. You are safe with me."

I add, "She's my great, great grandmother and was kind to me at Soujou-bou's."

That decides it for the boy.

Everyone gathers around the hearth in the main room before breakfast. This area is smaller than in the old den, but cozier because the fire's warmth fills the entire space.

Su-chan giggles as she sets out a cushion for me. "You walk like an old man." When my eyes roll, she adds, "It will get better. The rest of us recovered. I'll be back. The Nakamuras said we should have a bucket of water ready."

Within moments, Jiro and Grandma Miwa return with a blue, scaly skinned creature that resembles a long-legged turtle–a kappa, who bows shyly. His shell is solid, and water sloshes in the dome of his skull.

My aunt's mother brings a cup of water, offering it to the kappa, "Here, Sekiguchi-sensei."

So the turtle-like creature pours it into the dented dome of his head. The brightness of his ki well rival's Su-chan's, that means he's powerful.

Then Jiro asks, "Sekiguchi-san, why do you put the water there?"

He puts a finger to his beak for a moment, as if weighing whether he wants to answer and a few drops slosh onto the tatami. His turtle-like beak makes his accent thick. "I trust you, young one, so I'll answer. It's my source of magic and my weakness. But know, if I ever hear of you using that knowledge against one of my kind, you'll wish you hadn't."

"U-understood." Jiro bobs as he stammers. "Thank you for trusting me."

"Let me check the patients," Sekiguchi says.

Kneeling to investigate Hoji, he rousts the fox and pulls back his eyelids. Then he re-bandages the wound on Hoji's shoulder and splays his webbed fingers on various points of the fox's body. More water spills from Sekiguchi's head, and a stale scent fills the room. The kappa tries to close the wound in Hoji's ki well, but it reopens. Only after a fifth try does it stay shut.

"For the kitsune lad, I'll return tomorrow to heal the rest of his wounds. It should go faster after that. You all did well, considering the dire situation." The kappa's hands glow as they hover over Hoji's hoshi no tama, the ball that holds his magic. "The smidgen of ki inside him is stable. You may allow him more. He's also dehydrated and weak. Ensure he drinks and gets salts to stabilize him. A long soak in a bath would do him good, too. Warm is fine."

Then Su-chan returns, sets her bucket by the door, and plops beside me. Instantly, Sekiguchi pales, scrambling backward into the stone wall. He hisses.

Aunt Hisako's head swivels from him to Su-chan and I. "Sekiguchi-sensei, what is wrong?"

"Magic thief!" He points his scaly finger at Su-chan. "How can you allow that witch into this den?"

I shift to be in between Su-chan and the kappa. *Why not accuse me too?* Granted, Su-chan received an unknown form of magic when I got my kitsune version.

Great Uncle Nobu says, "You had no issue with my nephew's accidental acquisition of kitsune magic. Why do you take issue with the girl's, which happened the same night from the same kitsune?"

"S-same kitsune? How can that be?" Warily, he crawls over animal-like on all fours to inspect Su-chan, craning around me faster than I can block, and his eyes narrow.

Leaning away from the intrusion, Su-chan says, "It's true, Sekiguchi-san. I'm sorry the magic I have startled you. We don't know what kind I ended up with, though. Do you? I'd like to know."

Sekiguchi sits back on his haunches, covering his face for several moments. A sob escapes his mouth as the water empties from the bowl in his head. "Finally. A clue."

Great Uncle Nobu, in human form, places a hand on the kappa's shoulder. "Suzu-chan, please fetch our friend some water from the bucket."

So she zips off, returning to hand a glass to the kappa.

"Sorry." Sekiguchi wipes at his eyes. "I-I just didn't expect to see that particular magic." Gathering himself, and giving a reassuring smile, he says, "I'll be ok."

"Can you tell us what you mean?" Great Uncle Nobu prods.

The kappa shudders and waves off the question.

Taking the glass from Su-chan and refilling the water in the bowl of his head, the kappa speaks to me, "Young man, your family told me this was not your first time risking yourself. You aren't seeking the end because of your past, are you?"

My head shakes.

"Good. I've seen a few cases of that in my time." As he hands the glass back to Su-chan, his gaze flickers between her and the floor. We all hold our breaths.

Eventually, he turns his attention to her. "Young lady, what is your name?"

"Ohno Suzu, sir. Nice to meet you."

"Ah. Miwa-san said you were a help in saving her son and that you have knowledge of the art of healing." To the rest of those gathered in the room, he asks, "Can anyone else speak to this young woman's character?"

Everyone's hands shoot up, including mine, and our eyes are bright. The kappa nods to himself, muttering, "That settles it." Addressing Su-chan again, he asks, "I have been looking for an apprentice. You would do. What say you?"

She smiles, meekly. "I'd like that Sekiguchi-sensei. It would give me a purpose here. Everyone's been so welcoming, but I feel a little out of place since I have no kitsune kin and don't have that specific magic. I need something to keep busy."

She feels left out? "Su-chan." I grasp her hand and squeeze.

"Excellent. It will also give us time to help unravel the mystery of your magic. Tell me more as we get to know each other." At her wide eyes and eager nod, he adds, "I'll leave the kitsune and young man in your care until this evening." Sekiguchi gives a slight incline to keep most of the water where it belongs, and Great Uncle Nobu sees him to the door.

Unlike the main Nakamura den, the little summer home doesn't have as much space for everyone. So we doubled up. Su-chan and I get ready for the day in our room.

"So there's a clue now for your magic."

She turns glum. *Change the subject.* Besides, she's safe to share my inner feelings with. I grumble as I throw on a sweater. "I'm an adult, the kappa didn't need to call me 'young man'."

"Sekiguchi-sensei did that to all of us. I'd bet he's lived a very long time." Leaning over before she returns to the central hearth, Su-chan says in my ear, "If you behave, I'll hop into the bath with you."

Several of the foxes look away as we enter the main living area. *Did they hear us?* Poor Su-chan goes beet red.

A few moments later, Hoji gives a wracking cough.

"Take it easy, Hoji-san," Aunt Hisako urges. "You've been out for two days. That arrow almost claimed your life after your efforts to protect our species."

Che. My hands shove into my pockets, pressing hard against the seams. That's not how I'd describe what happened at all! Hoji ran off and it was my duty to stop the frickin' idiot.

Speak of the devil. He winces as he crawls over to kneel by me. "Soujou-bou came to see how we were doing. While you were out, I told him what happened."

Biting my tongue, I nod.

Hoji scrunches his eyes shut and takes a shaky breath before continuing. "He refused to take me as a student because I caused our predicament. I didn't obey his commands. He said I should learn from you."

My mouth opens and closes a few times. *Really?* Jiro gives an almost imperceptible nod from around the corner.

Placing his good paw on the tatami mat and lowering his head just shy of touching the floor, he shudders with the effort. "Umeji-san, please teach me."

But the guy is a loose cannon.

Aunt Hisako interjects, "Date-san, couldn't this wait until you've both recovered?"

His head whips up, causing him to wince. "Of course. No need to respond now."

"It would drive me crazy to wait for an answer." So, I gather my thoughts. "Date-san, Jiro and I don't trust you because of what your sister put us through. It'll take a while before we'll have faith in you. Regarding your request, the lessons I learned in the yakuza were brutal."

He grimaces.

"I don't think I can teach such a thing, because I refuse to treat you how they treated me."

"That means I won't be able to train under Soujou-sama." Wilting, he nods before returning to his futon. "Thank you for answering."

Then Grandma Miwa places a bowl of steaming donburi in front of her son and Hoji rallies. My stomach growls from the scent of the meat and rice. She says, "Now that news came of the murder of a powerful Date clan ally—a tanuki by the name of Seta-san—we're opting to stay hidden here in the Nakamura clan's summerhouse in the spirit realm. The whole kitsune community is spooked."

"Is Soujou-sama ok? What about his tengu soldiers?" *Spirit realm?* When humans visit a yokai kingdom, the legends say they return to a different time. Months, years, or centuries have gone by in the human realm. I didn't think about that when I signed up for Guardian training. That's gonna be a mess for those of us with connections back in Nonogawa. *Satou, Matsuo, Mie—how old will they be when we return? How am I gonna break this to my girlfriend?*

Su-chan answers, "Yes. He retreated to the spirit realm, too, after fending off the first oni wave. He's recovering from his own injuries and many of his people died in the battle from those ki-bomb arrows."

"Soujou-bou is worried about the tengu numbers, too. He said now many shrines and towns are unguarded," Jiro adds.

"That includes Nonogawa and the shrine Aunt Hisako and I watch over in the at-risk category. I don't want our families back home caught in the wake of Ibaraki's terror campaign." My stomach clenches and I get up to fetch my sword. *Gotta help.*

"Ta-kun, take it easy. I notified my family before we came here. Your aunt and my parents have connections." Su-chan gently presses me back down to the futon as she moves a stray lock of hair from my face, letting her touch linger.

Ta-kun. My heart skips a beat. She gave me a nickname on her own. Does that mean we're especially close?

"Soujou-sama gave you strict orders to heal before he'll come to train you and test Jiro." Turning to the boy, she asks, "I don't suppose you could make sure the fire is going for the bath like Nobu-sensei showed you. All of us taking turns means not everyone can get in at night."

When the water is warm, Su-chan and I slip into the tub, and she leans against my chest. We soak up the light cedar scent and skin to skin contact.

"I need time with you, even if we're both exhausted. Just to be next to you." Then her whisper turns barely loud enough for me to hear. "Remember when we first took a bath together?"

"Yeah. Best night of my life." Wrapping my arms around her, I kiss the top of her head. "Wish I had the energy to show you how much I appreciated that night."

"You're looking for a repeat?"

Chuckling, I grin at the mischief in her voice. "Maybe."

"Perhaps after you're healed, we can sneak away for some time to ourselves. This house is so..."

"Busy?"

"And they hear everything! At least we have a few moments together."

When we dry off, Su-chan says, "Sekiguchi-sensei thinks Hoji will make a quick recovery now that his ki well isn't leaking like a sieve."

"Wanna hear something wild? I helped Hoji phone his mom via a spell to home in on the location for a portal."

"How in the world did the Date clan merge technology with magic? They don't appear to be using oni as batteries like Sari did," she says. "And do you think Jiro will ever be able to trust Miwa-san and Hoji-san?"

"Maybe Grandma Miwa. Hoji? I'm not sure what to make of him."

Sunlight streams through the skylights in the den. Trudging toward the kitchen for a bit to eat, I overhear Aunt Hisako's voice.

"Yoshirou brought news of yet another slaying. This time, it was a single fox, not someone I knew. Did you know Uehara Chidori?"

Grandma Miwa nods to me as I shuffle in. She says, "I knew her. She was so sweet. What was she doing out alone?"

"No idea. If we go anywhere now, we have to go in groups and time will pass at a different rate for us." My aunt's lips purse. "How does Ibaraki get away with these attacks?"

"Shouldn't the police and the PSIA be on her trail? Why isn't there more of a government presence to protect our people?" I add. When I'm a guardian, I'll be able to help stop this insanity.

The two foxes give fleeting smiles.

When did I start identifying as kitsune? I'm technically not one. But I'm not just human anymore because of the fox magic inside me.

"Well, I'll check in and report the incident to Satou-san," I say as I reach for my cell.

"Let me get you some breakfast first." My great grandmother, Miwa, rises from her seat.

"I can do it."

"I insist. It's the least I can do for a grandson I've not been able to dote on for decades." She sets out a tray for me with a tempting assortment that makes my stomach growl before checking on Hoji.

After she's out of the room, Aunt Hisako whispers. "You made quite an impression on her when she saw you leaping to help her son. I wasn't sure if the whole Date clan would be like Sari or not. But they seem to be decent folk."

What made Sari turn so selfish?

Oh, I need to ask for Su-chan's sake. "Aunt, about the time rate being different in the spirit realm. How big of an issue is this going to be?" Then my throat tightens. "What if..." *Su-chan's parents are dead before we return?*

Her voice turns soft. "Always the tender heart. It varies from location to location. Here time goes faster than for the outside. So you and Su-chan won't be missing out on years with family and friends."

Are we gonna be old when we see Su-chan's family? "How much faster?"

"I think it's about one week there to one year here. Not centuries difference, like in the tale of Urashima Taro. So use that to your advantage."

Doable.

After breakfast, I dial Satou—my parole officer, former employer, and PSIA contact. My foot taps as I wait and count the rings. *Maybe he's busy at work.*

"Hello?"

I ask, "Boss, have they updated you on the news about the kitsune?"

"What happened?"

Post retelling and several muffled swear words later on his side, I ask, "So I read up about Ibaraki Douji. In the legends, she was the only one left from her oni outlaw band. How could she have gathered such an army?"

"You tell me. I know Date Sari conjured oni and turned even more men into them."

"Does the PSIA Paranormal Division know how they're targeting fox families? They shouldn't have been able to trace Date Hoji and his mother to Soujou-bou's estate. Aunt Hisako's best guess was a rare portal tracking spell. But the clan hid the den well."

"Damn." He lets the pause build.

"Is there anything that we can do to protect the yokai that are being targeted, particularly kitsune-kind?"

"I'll see if there are any strings I can pull. But this is more the L-" His words cut off, and he growls, "Stupid seal keeps me from talking about that organization!" He huffs before continuing. "Our aunt's territory. Since she has connections, maybe she can contact her leader."

"I'll ask." Satou doesn't know Soujou-bou is the head of the League.

"How is our aunt doing? Do I need to come to Kyoto?"

"Inari Okami-sama sent a messenger. Aunt Hisako has to make a trip to hear from the kami himself. For now, we are safe. Did you find those talismans I left?"

"Yeah. And I'm using them, even though I hate hanging stuff on the walls. Keep Aunt Hisako safe, you hear, Umeji?"

Before dinner, Sekiguchi stops by to check on Hoji and me. Now that Su-chan will be his student, he sends her to fetch an ingredient from the Nakamura family garden. Then he murmurs as he runs splayed glowing hands over the base of my ribcage. "I'm still trying to figure out how that arrow affected you so badly, because it didn't hit you."

"Several of them hit my shield, sir. Did it go through my magic to my ki well?"

"That is likely the culprit." His hands wring. "Umeji-kun, has Ohno-san discovered what magic dwells within her, yet?"

"No, sir."

"I see."

I don't. My eyes narrow. "Sekiguchi-sensei, what does that mean?"

"You should be able to return to your training within a few days. Just don't overdo it."

"Sir, please don't dodge. If you know something, Su-chan should be told."

Clicking his beak, he shakes his head.

"Why not, sir?"

He shudders. "I haven't seen that magic in over a century. I took her on as a student for her healing talent and the chance to monitor her. If I am ever ready to share, I'll say so."

"Is she in danger?"

"I fear she could be the risk." He shrugs and gathers his healing supplies. "I shouldn't need to check on you again. Though I will monitor Hoji-san."

Jumping from my cushion to intercept him, I try to control my voice. "What do you mean, she could be the risk?" He ducks to go around me. But I slap an arm across the doorway. "No offense. But if there's a problem for Su-chan, I need to know. Especially with all that is going on."

"If I see signs, I will let you know. Right now, it's inert."

"What is? How will we know if this whatever-it-is becomes active?"

A guttural growl escapes his throat. "There was a yokai I knew once. It's his spirit's energy she has. Since you two didn't steal it, we just have to wait. That is what you need to know. Do not tell her yet, for I need to research. The case of obtaining magic from another spirit is rare. That it happened to three of you in such a short time? This can't be a coincidence. I also need to find her a proper teacher. But she can learn much of the healing arts from me in the meantime."

Then my hand drops, and he ducks out. *He knew the spirit?* If his reaction says anything, it was more than a simple acquaintance.

5

Nakamura's Visit

Thick fog nestles into the valley as if getting ready for a good nap, and the chill of the morning sticks to my exposed skin. Pulling my stocking cap from my pocket, I throw it on and unroll the brim to cover my ears.

Today, Aunt Hisako asked Jiro and me to accompany her to Fushimi Inari Taisha. The popular shrine on the southeast side of Kyoto is the site for her consultation with Inari Okami, the god of rice, smithing, harvest, business success, and a host of other things. The foxes worship Inari because they often become his messengers, an enviable position in kitsune society.

Aunt Hisako opts to go early because it's all the way across town and she wants to avoid the worst of the crowds. So we hop on a bus before sunup. Poor Jiro yawns, but he stays glued to the window since he's not ventured into Kyoto proper before.

The areas with rows of traditional houses catch his attention. "Will we see a geisha?"

Aunt Hisako says, "They are called geiko here. Likely not. They sing, dance, perform music, and play drinking games with their customers into the wee hours of the morning, so they wake up late. I had a friend who was one. She led a demanding but rewarding life."

Several bus switches later, we reach our stop. Bowing and passing under the first giant torii gate gives me the shivers. The bright incandescence of the gate and path leading up the mountain isn't noticeable to most people, but those of us with natural magic sense it.

I'd only seen a minor effect of it at the shrine back home. At this mountain, one place Inari resides, the innate magic seems to want to show off for us.

I whisper, "Jiro, is this your first time visiting a shrine after you gained your powers?"

The boy nods, beaming from ear to ear and my aunt chuckles despite the seriousness of our visit. "Seeing the power emanating from the area is always impressive. Shall we offer a prayer before beginning the hike?"

In a few moments, we reach the large red and white main gate with its stone kitsune statues in their vivid red bibs, seated on their pedestals and looking down on us as if judging the souls entering.

Jiro approaches each one, taking a snapshot with his phone. Holding up his screen for me to see, his eyebrows raise. "I can't get a good picture. I wanted one of the wink the spirit gave me."

I shrug.

"That it graced you with such a gesture is a good omen." So my aunt glances over my shoulder to see the picture before guiding us to the prayer area.

Innumerable strings of paper cranes hang under the wish plaques depicting white foxes and various scenes from the shrine grounds.

When I glance back, Jiro investigates the plaques, then he trots to catch up. "I wanted to see what people write on them. I mean, what if I buy one and the wish I make sticks out too much? They're on display!"

Ruffling his hair, I offer, "I'll put mine in front of yours if that will help."

His steps turn to a skip. "Okay!"

After offering our prayers, Aunt Hisako faces the mountain, and sets her shoulders back. "I can do this."

We find the trail to the top. Why did Aunt Hisako not have me create a portal to the spot she needs? It would save her energy, because I've heard the hike has a ton of stairs. Despite the early hour, there's still a mob of tourists.

Then Jiro halts in front of one of the red poles. "Why does it say a business name and date?"

Patiently, Aunt Hisako reads the left side of the gate beside him. "The name is the business that donated it. For example, this one says Kansai Television. On the other side is when it was dedicated. Can you read it?"

"Third month of the 24th year of the Heisei Era." He grins at being able to read the formal date.

"What year was that in Western style?"

His mouth scrunches to the side.

"Gah, Aunt, don't make us do math so early. I didn't get coffee this morning." Grumping, I scratch my head as my brain cells refuse to cooperate.

"2012," Jiro declares.

She nods and then her head bobbles in an 'I told you so'. "See? Not hard."

Soon the gates are stacked so tightly they touch each other. We can barely see through the posts. Are we in another realm or something? Sure, there are birds singing, but the glow from the spiritual energy is intense.

The mist thickens as we climb flight after flight, creating the myopic illusion that there's only us on the path, and muffling everything but our footsteps. Fox statues grace most every landing.

"Is it true there are thousands of torii along the way?" I ask.

"Tens of thousands—including the little ones. They keep adding them, too. When I first came here, there were a lot fewer torii," Aunt Hisako adds.

In the 1700s?

"How many stairs are we gonna have to go up?" Jiro can't quite hide the whine in his voice.

Determined, my aunt tightens her jaw. "As many as it takes to reach the top."

She's slowing already. Is that a sign that her ki is waning too fast? At least the steps aren't uneven. Each stop along the way has vending machines and a place to buy souvenirs. We rest at stop number three, and I pick up warm drinks for our group.

How do they get the vending machines up here? Are there roads? I didn't see any in the fog. Do they carry them in like the couriers with packs lugging items up the hill?

Handing a bottle to Aunt Hisako, I sneak in a ki boost. She'll need it. Her eyes narrow, but she says nothing.

"We won't get lost in the fog, will we?" The boy shuffles his feet.

"I've made this trip many times, and we just stick to the wide path. I can do it with my eyes closed. At stop six, there's a magnificent view. Now, if only the fog would clear." She cradles the warm drink in her hands and begins the ascension again.

Beyond the large torii are tons of miniature ones leaning against the rock walls of the path and more kitsune statues. Different people must maintain the stone carvings of the foxes because they have inconsistent styles of bibs in varying degrees of wear.

Small paths veer off, but we stay the course and we rest after every other set of stairs. As we look down the hill through the trail of gates, we can see the winding course of red below us ending in the mists as if that's where reality ends. *So otherworldly.*

Reaching stop six, Aunt Hisako opts to enter the little open-air restaurant for breakfast. The fog prevents us from seeing the view, but my aunt, sitting on a cushion, leans against the low wall. Her gaze locks on the hidden city beyond.

"Aunt..." I lean in to ensure her full attention. "Are you doing ok? Should we stop somewhere to make a portal?"

"I will do this on my own strength. Inari Okami would not have asked me to come if I didn't have the ability."

After the longer break and a boost of ki, she seems to perk up for several flights. But I offer an arm to support her after she halts again.

"How many more stops until the top?" Jiro asks.

"We just passed eight. Fourteen is the summit."

"Oh." Then he points. "Should I scout ahead for an empty bench?"

"Please," I answer and receive a scowl from Aunt Hisako. In return, I let grit fill my voice. "We'll get there without you passing out from lack of ki."

They say it takes three hours to complete the trip to the top and back down. But we're already past an hour, not counting the stop for a bite to eat.

Never the less, she plods away. I won't say anything, but my thighs and calves burn from the slow steps. I'll pay for this tomorrow in training.

After the two-hour mark, we reach the top.

"Are we the first ones to arrive?" I ask.

"Few people make it this far," my aunt pants as her arm, wrapped around mine for support, shakes. A real trooper, Jiro stabilizes her on the other side.

Aunt Hisako huffs and puffs. "It used to be so much easier... There was a time I could run the entire way... I'll rest so I can pray and not fall over. So set me on the bench over there and take Jiro-kun to get his top of the mountain souvenir. If they still have the noren with a prayer on it, I'd like this year's one."

When she digs in her coat pocket for her coin purse as we park her on the bench against the store, I shake my head. "You rest. I'll get one for each of us and help you up the last stairs."

"I'll do it myself, Tatsuya."

Okay. I know better than to argue. "We'll be here if you need us."

The tiny shop sells the noren curtain topped in blue with a meandering line of torii and a white fox. Jiro hugs his souvenir tight. Suddenly, he zips to the door, shouting, "Naka-"

Outside, she's climbing that last set of stairs with painstaking slowness to the little shrine adorned with a bright red noren and grass tassels. *Stubborn kitsune.*

Tugging my sleeve, he whispers, "We should help her."

"Not this time. She is determined to do it. Respect her choice."

His lip sucks in, but he nods. With every jerk of her body, my legs twitch, urging me to run and catch her. *I will honor her effort.*

Crumpling, she reaches the top. Jiro is skipping every other step before my legs engage and we arrive at her side as Jiro asks, "Nakamura-san, are you ok?"

"I'm fine..." She gasps between sentences. "Just exhausted... Let me kneel here to pray. Tatsuya, please put up a barrier of silence."

Stubborn old fox. When the glow of the privacy shield pops into place then fades, Jiro and I head back into the shop to grab another drink for our trio.

His legs swing as they hang from the bench, not quite touching the ground. "Will she be ok?"

"Yeah. Do you want me to show you how to share ki when we retrieve her?"

A grin forms and his head bobs. "Can I be the one to help her today?"

"Sure."

Twenty minutes drag by. *What's taking so long?* So, I send Jiro to hunt for the next stop to see if there are souvenirs he'd like to buy. Time continues to crawl. Usually prayers are short—a few seconds to a minute.

Looking at my watch again shows Aunt Hisako has been kneeling up there on the hard stone for longer than I could stand. Difficult for anyone, but I can't imagine doing that in the body of an octogenarian.

A few moments later, Jiro bounds up from the next shop waving his find, a tenugui towel printed with a host of white foxes in formal kimono on it. The cartoon stylization with the enormous eyes and dark whiskers warms my heart.

Then he stills, and his gape causes me to check on my aunt. Her head touches the ground as she kneels before a man with shocking red, bushy hair and stripes on his face. He's decked out in a light green outer robe and white hakama. A glow surrounds his form. His mouth moves, but I hear no words.

Inari Okami. The god himself! Jiro and I give a deep bow. *To be in his presence.*

When Aunt Hisako's hands cover her head and she convulses, Jiro jumps to his feet, but the mysterious being holds up a hand. So I grab the boy's wrist to keep him from approaching.

My aunt dares to raise herself to gaze at Inari-sama. But he shakes his head, and hers falls. When she presses her forehead to the step again, is it acceptance?

Inari-sama winks out of sight. Racing to my aunt's side, we help her to her feet. Her mouth opens and closes, though no sound reaches my ears and tears trail down her face.

Jiro pokes me, saying, "Silencing spell."

Idiot. I undo the magic. "Sorry, Aunt."

But she shakes her head. "At least one of you remembered." Her accent reverts to the Okayama prefecture one with its odd verb ending.

"Let us carry you."

Stubbornly, she starts off. Then her third step falters and her voice cuts out. "Anyone watching?"

"Nope." Jiro calls as he runs through the mists to check the flight of stairs on each side.

With a flash, a dark nine-tailed fox replaces the old lady before us. She sighs. Her voice barely registers in my ears. "This is humiliating. But will you carry me, Tatsuya?"

"No prob." Hefting her over my head and onto my shoulders, I whisper a quick word of kotodama to make her invisible and another to keep her in place. Now there won't be stares as we descend the mountain.

Still a trooper, Jiro doesn't ask to visit the remaining shops as we return to stop six. The restaurant is crowded now. But we visit the ice cream stand for a lunch that we won't tell Jiro's mom about.

Aunt Hisako eats hers when we are safely out of view. Her fur tickles my ears and keeps my neck so warm that I'm sweating and Jiro fetches ice water. Relieved, I gulp it down. "The crowds have swelled."

Whispering in my ear, my aunt says, "Go to the lookout. The fog lifted, so you should be able to see across Kyoto."

The valley cradling the city within the mountains beyond sprawls before us. The view below shouldn't surprise me. But after the mist encompassing us for the last several hours, the buildings jam-packed into the valley stretch toward the sky and seem out of place.

"We can't see Mt. Atago from here, can we?" I ask under my breath.

Jiro's head swivels. "Where is it?"

"No. It would be to the northwest." Then Aunt Hisako's weight shifts on my shoulders. *She's looking for it, too?*

At Jiro's quizzical expression, I point to the right at about sixty degrees from straight ahead.

"But there's the old imperial palace in the north central area, if you look past the s-curve in the raised section of Highway 89."

"Can we visit there and Nijo Castle?" The boy's eyes light up, but he quickly adds, "Someday. My legs are too tired right now."

"We should." After a few odd looks from the old-lady voice emanating out of nowhere, she whispers again. "You two haven't had a chance to see the sites yet, have you?"

At the den, Hoji, with an apron tied around his waist, meets us at the entryway. "Welcome back! Where were you guys off to today?" His head jerks. "Oh my, she's so low on ki!"

As we kick off our shoes, I carry in the sleeping fox. Even Hoji giving her an energy boost doesn't cause her to stir.

"Yeah. She insisted on making it all the way up Mt. Inari in human form."

Immediately, he scowls and his voice raises. "You let her do what? And you didn't take me with you to help?"

Why's Hoji so protective? My finger goes to my lips and my head shakes as I mouth, "Later."

His brow furrows, but he nods. Pointing to himself, he mimes lifting.

Fantastic. I'm ready to collapse, but I need to wash off. Her fur on my neck was roasting me. When I nod, we transfer her, taking great pains to not disturb her slumber.

Later, after I clean up, we meet in the kitchen. Great Aunt Asako directs Jiro and me to chop vegetables for tonight's stir fry. Moving his cutting board laden with enough pork to feed twelve, Hoji makes room for us. Though Jiro shuffles a step closer to me and away from the Date clan member.

"Why in the hell did you let her hike up that shrine mountain?" Hoji's sharp words slash at the peace in the room.

Whatever. Though, my shrug only increases his glower. "A messenger told her to visit, and who am I to stop an elder from making that journey?"

"You could have tried. Don't you know how rare my people are?" he growls as his teeth grind.

"Yeah, I'll let you try that with her and see how well that goes over. She's more stubborn than an Akita Inu! Hiro had one of those dogs and even he couldn't get it to listen."

Scowling, he says, "So you didn't care that it would exhaust her?"

"Jiro and I ensured she had enough ki. What is it with you today? Why do you care?"

Instead of answering, he harrumphs and cuts the meat into thin slices with such force that it digs into the wood slab. His hand flies back from the cutting board, blood running down his finger.

Click. He's been staring. So, he's got it bad for her. *Nice one, Romeo.* "Let me see your hand, dummy."

"I'll do it myself."

Jiro only snickers.

"What?" Hoji growls before his hand glows and the bleeding stops.

Why do I still expect kitsune-kind to say the words like I had to before I gained fox magic?

Then the boy zips his lips, but a laugh escapes me before I can stifle it.

Clearing his throat, Hoji says, "Did she tell you what Inari-sama required her for?"

Ok, we'll allow him the grace of a subject change. "I just know it had to do with her being magically crippled. We didn't hear what either of them said at the shrine. But we could tell she didn't like what she heard. When she wakes, I'm tempted to ask. But I also am concerned about prying too much."

Then his shoulders slump. "I should have been there. My sister is the reason her tama is broken."

"You want to help her?" Jiro asks.

"Of course. I only learned how much of a monster she was to Hisako-san and to you this week. I'm sorry." Hoji bows deep and longer than necessary.

So Jiro gives a quick nod and goes back to work.

After dinner, Aunt Hisako's sisters, Tsubame and Yoko, arrive for a visit. She curls up by the sunken brazier with them to catch up. When I approach, the fox sisters make an excuse that they have something to work on.

"Aunt." My throat tightens. *Do I want to intrude this much?*

"You're going to ask about my meeting earlier today, aren't you?"

"Uh, yeah."

"I don't wish to talk about it."

"But-"

"The price to heal me is too high. So that's the end of it."

She's a Guardian, dammit! She'll need the power to do her job. So maybe I can ask again later when she doesn't feel so raw from the experience.

In the morning, Hoji and Jiro both pounce on me as I chop the wood for the breakfast fire. *Woah, Jiro isn't afraid of the Date clan anymore?*

"What did she say?" Jiro blurts.

"You two are up early." Crack. *Ugh.* My swing didn't hit the center.

"Don't play around. Tell us." Hoji's hands go to his hips.

But I shrug and chop again. "All she would say is that the price to heal her was too high."

"Shit," Hoji mutters.

"Agreed." There's enough in the stack for today's use of the fuel-efficient rocket stove, so I scoop up the wood in one arm. The others follow.

"And what are you going to do about it?" Spit flies as Hoji sputters.

Hoji, you little... I pause, placing the wood by the central hearth. 10. 9. 8. Don't be a smart ass. 7. 6. 5. You'll just end up in a fight with him again. 4. 3. 2. 1. "Any ideas, genius?"

That shuts him up, so my wood stacking in the main room resumes.

"I broke Hisako-san's tama. Healing her will hurt someone? That's what she means, right?" The boy's expression crumples and his head hangs.

"Jiro-kun, we've been over this before. It wasn't you."

In the evening, Hoji approaches me in private. "Hisako-san wouldn't tell me, either. I offered to pay the price since it was my sister that crippled her magic. She just shook her head and walked off."

She's even more stubborn than you. "Give her time. It must have been shocking and she'll need to process it. Though, thank you for offering."

His lips purse, but he nods.

Later, I can't find Aunt Hisako in the den. She and Yoshirou must be off frolicking in the forest again. She's been gone a lot and I'm not sure it's safe for just the two of them to be out and about. *Worry wart.*

After that, Su-chan and I join Great Aunt Asako for tea.

"We haven't had a messenger in the family for some generations now," Asako mentions, as if a part of the future of her people isn't hinged on this match. Aunt Hisako, her daughter, hasn't had a kitsune mate to date, much to her mother's dismay. "Until Yoshirou-sama, she's always been interested in humans, and they've been good to her. But they have such short lifespans. No offense, mind you."

"None taken." It's funny how she often speaks to me as if she forgets I'm not of the same species.

"It's just hard when so many generations of grandchildren pass before I have. Still, I'm curious, Grand Nephew, how your situation will turn out."

"Asako-san, do you think that Tatsuya and I will have longer lives?" Su-chan asks.

"Possibly. Your circumstances are unique enough we don't know." Casting a spell on the set, she serves tea.

6

BLOOD ON THE TATAMI

"TATSUYA, SOUJOU-SAMA SUGGESTED MOVING your training to this summerhouse, so that you're available to protect the clans," Aunt Hisako says.

"Interesting times." Despite the urgency of the situation, the tightness in my shoulders relaxes a little. It's better to stay with Su-chan and my family.

"Even so, to get that old mountain priest to leave his home is a miracle." Then her tone quiets. "Your training continues tomorrow. But I have a meeting with him now. I'd like you to come."

"What's up?"

"Just join me for the meeting. It's about your training."

A little notice. That too much to ask? Though, she knows me too well. I'd have wound myself up so tight, I'd be shaking when we finally left.

Then Aunt Hisako holds up an unusual ofuda.

Soujou-sensei said no teleporting. When I lean in to get a better look, all I see is a splash of red as she slaps it into the air.

"Stop gawking. I have permission, and it goes to a location that won't interfere if there's an emergency."

So, we step through the portal into the audience room of Soujou-bou's estate, an area untouched by Ibaraki's oni horde during the attack.

Paintings of animals hiding in a forest of pine trees cover the gold on every wall and ornate wood inlays of hexagons and crest patterns cover the high ceiling. The walls only go so high to allow for circulation.

Before us, Soujou-bou sits on an elevated dais surrounded by a dozen yokai. Instantly, my stomach tightens from being in the presence of so many powerful beings. There's a koma inu, a guardian dog; a baku, an elephant-like dream eater;

something like a phoenix—perhaps Suzaku, the Guardian of the South; and a yuki onna, a snow maiden, among others.

Their ki signatures radiate way more power than my aunt and their hard gazes fix on me. *Oh shit.*

"Welcome, Nakamura-san, Umeji-kun. Have a seat." Soujou-bou indicates two cushions before the dais.

As I bow and kneel on one, glancing at my aunt reveals nothing, which makes prickles form on the back of my neck. Her gaze locks on the floor and her voice hushes. "Tatsuya, this is the Ruling Council of the League of Guardians and one of the newest members, the baku Mishima-san. He will be taking a recruit under his wing."

The head honchos for a legendary group that's not supposed to exist. I gulp and avert my eyes.

Soujou-bou flicks his fan. "Let's get down to business. We're here to discuss the fact that Umeji-kun is not yet a Guardian, but he has possession of one of the most powerful swords in Japan, Honjou Masamune. I deem him ready to learn our secrets and he has shared his story and that of how he obtained the artifact with me. You all know the details. Any questions for him?"

The yuki onna, decked out in a snow white kimono that makes her skin look blue, raises her chin. "What makes you think you are worthy of carrying a sword that should be a national treasure as a personal weapon? We heard you used Honjou Masamune in a way that was far below her."

Grilling time. When am I not gonna have to prove myself? "My aniki, who was an undercover officer with the PSIA, gave it to me. He told me the sword couldn't fall into Date Sari's hands. And I learned my lesson, ma'am. A sword, especially Honjou Masamune, needs to be treated with respect." I was also setup for that problem, but I won't whine.

Next, the yokai, that I swear is none other than Raijin the Kami of Thunder, asks, "How did your mentor come by it?"

"I don't know, s-sir." And there are the taiko drumsticks. *Yep, it's him. What the hell am I doing here?* My hands tremble, so I ball them up to keep control. When the gods seemed more distant, it was way easier to avoid fear.

"We know that Inari Okami supports you training for the position of Guardian. But what makes you feel you are worthy of the post?"

Looking for excuses to get rid of me. Taking a breath, I try to slow my racing pulse. "I wish to atone for my past. Serving those around me will show my intent."

Jumping in, a reptile that resembles a T-Rex with a line of spiked plates running down its back adds, "That is the only reason you wish to serve?"

Godzilla? What did Dad call this guy? Honengyou. Pressing my hands to the floor in front of me and lowering my head to almost touch them, my voice quavers. "Uh, no G-" *NOT Godzilla!* "N-no, Honengyou-sama. My aunt offered to train me 'for a different destiny'–if I was willing–to earn 'a proper place in society again'. I didn't know what that was, but I knew I wanted to take the offer from the first real friend I made after being released from prison."

"What makes you think you have it in you to take up the prestigious position of Guardian? When things get tough, you'll just go back to being yakuza and tarnish our ranks." The baku's tone turns nasal. His elephant like trunk raises, and he looks down on me in more ways than one. "I don't see why he needs to continue the training nor carry that weapon. Pick a yokai at random, and they would be a better replacement. One of us should carry Honjou Masamune then it would be safer from Ibaraki."

My breathing speeds up. I still haven't dared to raise my head. *They want to take my sword?* Sure, becoming a Guardian wasn't guaranteed. But they don't see anything worthwhile in me.

Idiot. My aunt picked me because she thought I had potential. And if she couldn't find anyone else, that would mean it's hard to find a replacement. Maybe they don't know what I've been through already to help their cause and my aunt's people.

Clenching my fists so hard my knuckles crack, I say, "It's not about the prestige. I'll do what I can to protect my town and kitsune-kind. My prayer every single day is to be worthy of the training of my teachers and live up to the expectations of those who claim me as a friend or family."

"And you think you're worthy?" The baku scoffs. "We don't need to waste our time with this."

His reaction is all too familiar. The same judgment I used to get in Nonogawa. But I won't hide from the scorn this time.

As I'm about to answer, the koma inu cuts in. "I feel I must challenge this nomination, Soujou-sama. Normally, I keep my peace. But this student's past permanently stains him. How can a human even think of becoming a Guardian? Let alone a mobster joining our ranks? This cannot be borne. Besides, his species is so short-lived the fifty-year term takes most of their lifespan."

"I second the challenge," the snow maid says.

"Enough!" A rush of wind roars through the room as Soujou-bou booms. "Umeji-kun is my student. I find him worthy!" Then his voice lowers to a growl. "We chose to modernize, to ensure the human world doesn't leave us behind, and we created the council so that a single yokai wouldn't be the breaking point of the League. But make no mistake, I am still head of this council."

No one else speaks for several heart beats.

Not unified. Most organizations ratify the leader's opinion.

Then my aunt's voice rings in the hall. "Before this meeting, I consulted the archives. The council has never challenged a candidate unless the candidate broke our code after starting training."

Thank you. Aunt, your unwavering belief in me means more than I can ever tell you.

"Never has a criminal entered our ranks. He'll sully our reputation," the Godzilla-like yokai rumbles in a voice deep enough to shake the floorboards.

Despite the growing need to run from the disapproval of powerful yokai here, my hands ball into fists at my side again. *I'm the problem.*

"I don't want to be a cause of division." Cleansing the emotion from my expression, I continue. "Yokai need to be united to stop a common threat. Ibaraki Douji isn't just murdering kitsune. She and her minions are killing anyone who sides with them."

Again, silence from the Council. So I heave in a breath and forge ahead. "If I'm right, my presence here means it's difficult to fill your ranks with normal yokai. Yet you think you don't need all magic users right now. Were you aware I was here when Ibaraki attacked? I pray I'm wrong. But I predict she'll return.

"So, know that no matter what, I'll still be doing what I can to protect those around me. Thank you for even considering me."

When I stand, my aunt gapes. Suddenly, Soujou-bou pounds the floor with his fist. "Umeji-kun! Do not leave this room unless you wish to resign from being my student."

I freeze and my head droops. "I-I wish to learn more from you, sir."

"Then hold out your hand to receive my personal seal. Stay still. It will sting." He motions me forward and when I comply, he turns my hand palm up and waves his feather fan over it. A red glow hovers there as stylized line-art of a fan with a long-nosed tengu face settles onto my skin.

Damn, it hurts. I hiss as the brand scorches, leaving that awful burned flesh stench. Clenching my muscles prevents further twitching as the glow sinks into my hand.

Investigating the mark reveals the lines are tiny characters of a passage from the Diamond Sutra.

"You spoke well," Soujou-bou says. "And you are correct. Ibaraki will return. And the lack of candidates is a problem that plagues the League. Fewer and fewer yokai are born. But we will table this subject for another time. To activate the seal, just whisper my name and think of the symbol. You'll be able to access my power until I cut off the flow."

I blink. That's the second time he acknowledged my opinion. Soujou-bou isn't your ordinary leader.

Wait. His ki well holds more energy than I can imagine. *I get to tap into that?*

Then the yuki onna blinks, whispering, "That's a Guardian privilege."

"Incorrect. It is mine to give. I had reserved it for Guardians before this," Soujou-bou says crisply.

"May I say one more thing on the topic?" Aunt Hisako asks.

"Go ahead." Soujou-bou snaps his fan closed.

"You gave me permission to train him in magic and, after that, to recruit his girlfriend, Ohno Suzu. As a pair working together, humans are better suited for the responsibility. If it weren't for Tatsuya and Su-chan, Date Sari would still be on the loose."

Su-chan, too? Since when?

"Do not forget, Date is the reason we are still dealing with Ibaraki Douji's horde." Aunt Hisako's shoulders straighten and her chin lifts before her voice turns to quiet steel. "I will resign if the Council rejects Tatsuya."

A collective gasp passes through the hall. Soujou-bou's brow furrows. "That is unprecedented, Nakamura-san."

"So are the times we are living in, with all due respect." She leans on her paw as if about to get up. "With your permission, Soujou-sama, Council."

The tengu king nods.

So, she tilts her head toward the door. "Shall we, Tatsuya?"

Our steps echo before the looming chamber door booms shut behind us. She slaps another ofuda with that stripe of red into the air.

Aunt Hisako left them speechless. *Over me.* "Aunt?"

Stepping into the den and closing the portal behind us, she explains, "My resignation was imminent, anyway. I won't be healed." But she paws at the tatami. "The council hasn't had a serious nationwide threat in centuries beyond pandemics. They can't keep expecting to handle things as we always have. It's what the Shogunate did in the 1800s. Look where that got them."

So they're outdated, and Su-chan and I would have been the start to reviving the League. *What'd she just say?* "Aunt, why won't you be healed?"

"I told you the price was too steep." Shifting to human form and knocking on my forehead, she shows a glimmer of the perkiness she had when I first met her. "Did you forget?"

"No." My hand swipes hers away. "You've dodged every attempt to find out just what that price is. It's time to tell us. Lean on your family."

Slowly, she blows out a breath.

That's when Great Aunt Asako pads up. But her head and tail hang low, and her steps are slow. "Hisako-chan..." Her strained voice chokes off.

Aunt Hisako returns to fox form, sniffing the air. "I smell blood."

"Come. There isn't much time," Great Aunt Asako whimpers to her daughter. Aunt Hisako scrambles down the hall and we book it after her.

Next, the coppery tang assaults my nose. *Another victim.* As I skitter around the corner, a wail comes from the room. *Aunt Hisako's voice.* I find a prone white fox smeared in so much red and brown the pools threaten to spread out the door. *Oh fuck, it's Yoshirou!*

Sekiguchi slumps in the corner, the divot in his head devoid of water. I'm bumped out of the way as Su-chan rushes in with a bowl that she pours into the kappa's head. Only then do Sekiguchi's eyes open, and he shuffles back to the messenger.

"Another, Ohno-chan," Sekiguchi croaks.

She zips past on her mission, not even acknowledging me. Glowing with blinding intensity, the kappa's hands move over the messenger's form as he half murmurs words. Wounds close, only to open again.

Stunned, I stumble to my aunt's side as she clings to Yoshirou's paw. Before I can stop my mouth, words tumble out. "Was he hit with one of those ki bombs?"

Sekiguchi's head hangs. "A variant. They used a ki leech poison on the weapons and it spread too fast for me to stop it."

"Can I add to the ki to help override it?"

"You may try. The poison's effect doesn't spread to other magic users like the arrow that hit Hoji-san did." Sekiguchi's gaze stays locked on the fox as my hand slaps over his blue scaly one.

So I give everything until the last flame presents itself, and release as the room spins.

Yoshirou rasps, "Hisako-chan."

"Shhh. Save your energy."

"I love you." Then his body wracks with a cough that spews crimson specks. "You know this, don't you?"

She nuzzles into his fur as she sobs. "I do. And I love you."

Sekiguchi's well is dry again, but Su-chan rushes in with a large bucket using a ladle to fill it again and again. *He's using all his energy, too.*

"Dammit," Sekiguchi sputters. "I-I can't stop the bleeding."

Yoshirou rasps slurred words, "I'm sorry I can't be the one."

Quietly, Great Aunt Asako ushers us all out. "Let them have their moment."

A small puff of sunlight enters me, enough to get my carcass off the floor and Su-chan helps me up. In the hall, she falls into my embrace as her tears wet my shirt. Her ki well has never been this dim. She must have used all her reservoir, too.

"Nothing we did helped. Nothing!" Her fist pounds my chest.

"Aunt Hisako got to say goodbye," I whisper into her ear.

Don't let my aunt have heard that. *Please, Kami-sama.* It's hard enough for her to experience it. Slowly, Su-chan's hands unclench, and sobs rack her body.

Everyone in the Nakamura household huddles in the hall, waiting. Jiro meets my glance as he holds his mother's hand. His face shows a pain no kid should know. So, I pull a hand away from Su-chan to place it on his head.

Hoji rushes in, almost unable to see over his stack of blankets and towels, and nods in acknowledgment. But, glimpsing Aunt Hisako in distress over her lover, he backs out double time.

"So they're a couple." Disappointment flashes before the emotion melts from his face. *Didn't he know?*

"They were engaged as of last night and looking forward to sharing the news with everyone today," Great Aunt Asako whispers as she wipes the tears from her cheek with her forepaw.

Why did this have to happen now?

Most of the household gathers in the stone-floored main room around the sunken hearth. The skylight shows the stars of the night sky. Lamps give a soft warm glow. Great Aunt Asako has the fire going low and serves tea. As we sip, the drink thaws us.

Afterward, she shares, "Yoshirou-san was on a mission for Inari to the Watabe clan when Ibaraki's minions struck. As best he could tell, he was the only one to make it out. Watabe Hoshi shoved him through a portal. A tengu on patrol spotted his white coat and flew him here. They not only killed that clan, Yoshirou-san said they stole a powerful weapon."

"How many kitsune?" The cold numbness creeps back into my chest, like after the attack at the Hiragi Clan headquarters. *When's this senseless violence gonna end?*

"Yoshirou-kun didn't say. But Nobu sent word via the tengu to Soujou-bou to see if he will send a scouting party, as we speak."

When Great Uncle Nobu pads in with Aunt Hisako, she collapses to a cushion and clutches the key that Yoshirou carried as a sign of his office. Vacantly, she stares at the floor. Her mother pushes a cup of tea in front of her. No movement.

"Hisako-chan, drink."

Only Aunt Hisako's mouth moves. Her voice is a tiny squeak. "I'm pregnant."

Fuck.

Everyone, including the Date duo, gathers around. Her father puts a hand on her shoulder. "Lean on us. We'll help you raise the kits."

Biting her lip, she nods as tears fill her eyes and her face falls to her paws.

Great Aunt Asako coaxes some tea into her, then Aunt Hisako whispers, "I'd like to lie down."

Her mom offers to tuck her in and keep her company until dinner. I help where I can. No one dares to speak.

After we go to bed, a cawing ruckus startles me awake. Grabbing the sword, Honjou Masamune, which rests by my pillow, I scramble out of bed.

"Tatsu, what's happening?" Su-chan bolts up, pulling on a robe over her pajamas.

I shove a portal ofuda into her hand, so she can get help if need be. "I'll find out."

Slamming the shoji door open, I bound out to find that the noise was a pair of tengu messengers. Aunt Hisako cradles two howling, mud-encrusted kits with singed whiskers.

"These little ones were the only survivors. They must have hidden and wandered out looking for family or food. Bodies of the parents and an older kitsune were in the smoking remainders of the den."

Unfortunately, the tengu's report makes the kits cry even louder.

"They seem unharmed, but only time will tell how their minds fared." The speaker's companion tilts his head side to side in a distant, bird-style curiosity.

"You're safe now, little ones," Aunt Hisako croons, running a paw down the nose of the one snuggling into her chest.

"Your clan will find a home for them, yes?" one of the bird-men squawks, poking his head and beak forward, but not leaning otherwise. *So unnatural.*

"Yes," my aunt says as she nuzzles the fox pups.

"So be it." In their raspy language, the pair chants and a puff of blue flashes over her. They use one of those ofuda with the red characters to create a portal to Soujou-bou's.

Unable to help themselves, Su-chan and Jiro peek over her shoulder. But the male kit growls.

My girlfriend tuts, "Poor tykes. They must have been through a nightmare. Let me hold one."

Aunt Hisako's strained posture softens and her puffy eyes close. "Thank you."

Next, Hoji, in human form, plops down cross-legged with them as if it's the most natural thing, pulling out a set of five otedama bean bags. Eyes and ears perk up, and little tails wag as he performs juggling tricks. Even Jiro claps as Hoji executes a difficult catch behind his back.

When one of the kits' tummy rumbles, Hoji is the one to speak. "I think we have some leftovers from dinner. How does gyuudon sound?"

Everyone, but Su-chan and I, heads toward the kitchen. As I kneel beside her, she looks me up and down, lifting an eyebrow. "If it weren't a shitty day…"

Oh. All I have on are my boxers. *At least I had those!*

After the kits have food in their tummies, yawning commences while they stagger back into the main room.

"No sleep yet. Into the tub, you two," Aunt Hisako commands. They whine with quivering jaws that would break most anyone's heart. The sight just brings a sad smile to my aunt's face. "Human or kitsune, it's universal."

"Would you like me to do it so you can rest?" Hoji asks.

"Oh." My aunt pauses mid-step. "Thank you, but I think this will be therapeutic. Though I could use help. They're going to be a handful."

Their conversation carries down the hall. "Sure."

"Have you ever dealt with children?"

"It's as good a time to learn as any."

"You'll end up wetter than they will. These two rascals…"

When Su-chan and I crawl into our futon a few hours later, my chest and throat tighten and I pull her close. "I don't know what I'd do without you. How is Aunt Hisako holding up?"

Her arms encircle my neck in return. "Did anyone offer to stay with her tonight?"

I should have thought of that. "I'll check on her."

It nets me a kiss on the cheek. Su-chan says, "That's what I adore about you. Your heart is always in the right place."

At least this time, I throw on a pair of pajama pants.

Hearing the pad of my steps on the stone, Hoji freezes, holding a futon and pillow. Aunt Hisako and the kits are piling up on a few futons in the main room. At my nod, his face and shoulders relax.

So, Su-chan and I drag our bedding out to join them. I'd heard sometimes kitsune sleep in a pile, but never understood why. Tonight, it's solidarity. We will not leave my aunt alone.

Breakfast is catch as catch can. Not surprising, considering the events of last night. I had to tiptoe away from the pile of sleeping foxes and humans. My heart tugs again at all the support for my aunt, who was the first one to believe in me after I got out of the slammer. So much has changed since then.

Grandma Miwa is the only other one up. When she pads in, not even her claws click on the stone floor. "How are you, Grandson?"

I shrug as I dig in the fridge for a bite to eat. "Could be worse. You?"

"The same. Did anyone pass on the news from the messenger?"

That stops me in my tracks.

"Oh, sorry. In the chaos, I suspect no one remembered. Well..." She takes a deep breath. "His message was 'Questioning you is part of the test. There is a difference between humility and giving up'."

I blink. "He was talking about the meeting yesterday?"

"I don't know. Those were his words for you, verbatim. Neither you nor Hisako-san said where you went yesterday, which vexed us all."

"Sorry. We should have said we were heading out on business." My hands shove into my pajama pants pockets and I can't keep the whine out of my voice. "Everything is a test."

Instantly, my great grandmother's mouth turns up. "If one is destined for greatness, I would say that is accurate." At my sigh, she adds, "They entrusted you with secrets that even I am not privy to and you carry a blade that no one has seen since Japan's surrender in WWII."

"How does everyone know what that sword is? Does it have a label only I can't see?"

She huffs such a quiet chuckle I almost don't hear it. "I saw it well before Hisako-san was born. I would know that aura anywhere."

Woah. That's humbling. "Gotcha, Grandmother." After warming some leftover rice, I crack an egg over it. "Want me to prep some for you, too?"

"That would be lovely. Thank you."

Quietly, we eat while enjoying each other's presence until there's a knock at the den's front door. Whispering the word for a shield of silence for me and the visitor, I book it to answer before the visitor makes any more noise. *Let my aunt sleep, please. And don't be more bad news!* The door opens to the kappa healer.

"Can I help you?" My hands rub my bare arms and I shiver as a frigid blast rushes in. Don't want the cold air to wake the crew. So, I usher him inside the summerhouse and into the spell's effect.

Upon seeing the pile of sleepers past the entryway, he whispers. "I wanted to check on your family. How is Hisako-san?"

"Last night was rough." To keep him from worrying too much, I share about the kits that arrived. "I think it will be good to have the little ones around."

"Agreed. She'll need to handle a passel of them." At my incredulous look, he backtracks. "I hope she shared the news of her pregnancy."

"She did, but how did you know?"

He shakes a webbed finger at me and tuts. "Did you forget my specialty? I saw their light inside her. In other news, Soujou-sama also asked me if I could testify about your character."

Uh-oh. I swallow. The issue of my being a Guardian is still ongoing. *Is that a good thing?*

"I have not been around you as much as Soujou-bou and the Nakamura clan have. But I shared what little I knew. Anyway, the reason I am here is to escort my student to the river. Since she insists on making the trip daily, I don't wish for her to go alone."

"What?" My heart stops. Su-chan's doing something foolish on her own and she didn't ask me to go along?

"You have been away much. Your duties and training take you elsewhere. But your destinies intertwine. Exactly how is yet to unfold."

So I blow out a breath. *He's not a threat.* Stop letting the need to protect your mate get in the way. But my insides knot up again. "Why is she going to the river?"

Then his beak closes so tight it clicks and he shakes his head.

He knows something. "Does it have to do with the part of her magic you won't tell me about?"

Instead of answering, his eyes narrow.

"Fine. I'll take her there."

"You think you can?" he quips.

Huh? My head whips to the dog pile of my family. "She's gone!"

7

SECRETS

Sekiguchi's beak clenches. "You won't like where she is or what I suspect is happening."

Su-chan's in trouble! My heart pounds so hard it threatens to leap out of my chest. Slamming where the glowing magic box surrounding us intersects the wall, I snarl, "Take me there already!"

Grandma Miwa and Hoji pad up to my silencing spell and draw an arc in the wall of my shield of quiet. They enter, only for her to chide, "Grandson, your silencing barrier didn't include the wall. Don't wake the house. Tell us what is wrong."

An apology would be in order, but I blurt, "Su-chan's gone," and point to the kappa, not caring one wit how rude the gesture could be considered. "And he knows where she is."

"Get clothes on, then we'll go," Grandma Miwa commands.

But the delay only revs up the squirrels in my brain. Where is Su-chan? Why would she sneak out? Is taking the time to put on warm clothes going to make us too late to help her?

When I return, the kappa holds out his hand and requests, "Ofuda, please."

Can't he make a portal? Calm down, idiot. You can't help if you can't think straight. So, I whip a paper out of the stash I keep in my pocket.

He slaps the talisman into the air, and we emerge into dawn's golden light, illuminating a moss-covered stair path enclosed on both sides by cedars. A bubbling stream greets those who hike near it. Sekiguchi points up the path, then presses a finger to his beak.

Why not go straight to Su-chan?

Wind whips through the surrounding trees. The foxes sniff the air and their ears prick. Hoji's head sweeps side to side, testing different directions, and he points his snout up the path.

As we ascend, the wind and the water grow louder. The path widens before a stone torii and shrine. Behind that is a waterfall. Su-chan, with her eyes closed and arms spread wide, turns in circles under it. Something shimmers on her skin. There's no steam from a hot spring. *How can she stand the cold?*

Then my heart stops. A translucent, shimmering, blue-green dragon writhes around her as if inspecting, reaching down toward her uplifted face and she stills.

Its clawed hand hovers over her ki well just under her ribs. "My magic-"

"Leave her alone!" I scream, whipping Honjou Masamune from my cargo pants pocket to free the ghostly blade and, in a ki-infused leap, bound toward my girlfriend.

Her head jerks toward me, and her eyes fly open. The dragon, or whatever it was, rises out of reach as Su-chan shrieks, scampering out of the water. Picking up, the wind howls with such force I'm driven to my knees to keep from being blown away.

Then Su-chan crashes into me. Soaking wet, her arms wrap around my chest in an uncharacteristic public hug. "Tatsu! Why am I here?" Her body wracks with shivers. The cold water seeping into my clothing makes goosebumps on my chest and neck and her skin is ice.

The others surround us, scanning the area.

Running a hand over her drenched hair, I say, "You're safe now. We were hoping you could answer that question."

Sekiguchi asks, "Did you see the dragon spirit hovering above you?"

Chattering, she shakes her head. "W-what? The l-last thing I knew, I was sleeping b-beside Tatsuya, and then I woke up here."

"Let's get you somewhere warm," Grandma Miwa says.

"Will the dragon spirit follow us through a portal?" Hoji points to the sky as the wind swirls in the grove.

"Should w-we ask what it wanted w-with me?" Su-chan shivers so hard it's difficult to understand her. "B-because I sure as hell don't want to be cont-trolled by something again!"

"It's the magic inside you. You'd been wondering what it was. Now you know." Sekiguchi's voice turns quiet.

"But-"

"He was my friend many years ago. Though this is not his river."

Need answers now! "How can she have the magic of a fuckin' dragon?" My harsh voice contrasts with the reverence in Sekiguchi's.

Without warning, his palm lashes out faster than I can dodge as his voice turns steely calm. "You will speak about him with respect!"

Ow. My hand automatically goes to the impact area. "Sorry."

"My friend died over one hundred years ago. The presence of Shion's spirit here today proves my hunch: Su-chan has his magic. That kind of thing doesn't happen without deeds so dark no one will speak of it. I know it wasn't this innocent girl. So what did you do, yakuza?"

"Me? No way!" *Oh, shit.* "That has to be how Date Sari kept Ibaraki under control—with the power of a dragon."

"Daughter..." My great grandmother's voice trembles. "The spirit chose this waterfall close to where his power remained, while he waited to connect with Su-chan. He must have died near here. The magic of the word at work in the wild."

Then another click. *Waterfall's character is dragon plus water.*

Grandma Miwa continues, "This is a sign that powerful forces are at work."

Behind me, Hoji opens a portal. "Dragon Spirit, please allow us to get this woman to warmth. She has no fur coat to keep her warm. Then please tell us what happened to you."

Debris swirls around the fox and a raspy whisper seems to come from every direction before it fades out. "Find the vixen's records. Let the world know what happened and let me not be forgotten. Then I will retrieve my magic."

Like hell he will!

Hoji swallows as he asks, "He means my sister, doesn't he?"

"Sari, what did you do?" Grandma Miwa closes her eyes, then grits her teeth. "It's up to us to help this unfortunate kami's spirit find peace."

"Where might those records be? We want to help you!" Hoji shouts to the sky.

No answer.

"Su-chan, let's get you warmed up." So, I tug her gently.

Hoji's portal glimmers in the air before us, and Grandma Miwa dashes through. "I'll warm some stones by the fire."

Sekiguchi says, "Shion may remember me. I will stay and try to calm his spirit."

Gratefully, I nod my thanks.

The crew that had been asleep when we left rushes us with questions.

Padding up, Aunt Hisako sniffs my girlfriend and her eyebrows knit. "Su-chan. You found out something, didn't you?"

She nods, still shaking violently. So my arm slips around Su-chan's frame to guide her toward our room. I help her into dry clothes and she snuggles into our futon as Grandma Miwa and I place warm stones a few at a time in with her.

Next, Great Aunt Asako enters the bedroom and shoos me out, much to my consternation. *Why?* It's not like Su-chan's naked, or that I didn't just see her that way. Come on! I want to crawl in with her.

In the main room, Hoji and Sekiguchi are relaying the story to the Nakamura clan the best they can.

Aunt Hisako returns and takes a seat beside me. "How is Su-chan?"

"I don't think she's had time to process. How did I not know she was sleepwalking or..." *Being kidnapped?*

"That may continue if we don't appease Shion's spirit."

Hell no. "Not on my watch." My fists clench. "When others controlled her, she didn't handle it well."

"Do you know anything about this? You're a Guardian, are you not?" Hoji adds.

Instead of responding directly to that, she says, "This may be the answer to an old mystery from the Nonogawa Valley. A river dragon named Shion disappeared about a century ago. He was Nonogawa's Guardian, before me."

Grandma Miwa hisses. "Sari, the more I learn of your deeds, the more I wonder where we went wrong."

"If you're the town's Guardian and you're magically crippled, you must be healed! There is no other choice," Hoji demands as he gets into Aunt Hisako's face.

"Back off Hoji. She knows what needs to be done." So I push him to the side. *Maybe he'll buy a clue.*

"Clearly not." Staring down my aunt, he adds, "Because you said the price was too high. I think it's time you told us."

"I said back off, Hoji!"

Aunt Hisako deflates. "Tatsuya, Hoji-san is right. Very well. I had hoped you would complete your training before I had to deal with this."

"B-but. Him? A Guardian? Is the League desperate or something?" Hoji squirms, continuing his griping under his breath and his mother snaps at his ear, but he dodges.

"Again, he's right." My head bows. "I don't know if they will accept me. But I will do everything in my power to protect Nonogawa and kitsune-kind, either way."

Everyone turns to Aunt Hisako.

Clearing her throat, she dives in. "To seal the crack in my hoshi no tama, another must give up the same amount of power that was lost. The donor will lose the power permanently."

Hoji whistles. "No wonder you're reluctant."

"Yoshirou knew this and had planned to retire from Inari's service so he could do it. I didn't want him to and would have done my best to stop him. No one's abilities should be stunted just so I can be back to full magical capacity."

Padding over to Aunt Hisako, Hoji bows. "It's important that the League have all its Guardians, especially right now. I volunteer."

"We don't know how much magic ability is actually required. How can you flippantly volunteer?"

Then his ears flatten and his words rumble in his throat. "My sister is the reason for all this suffering."

"But you're so young. You have your whole life ahead of you and you just got healed."

"You're only a few centuries older. I could say the same of you."

Awkward. "I'm going to check on Su-chan. She'll want to know what we figured out."

So Hoji says, "Let's continue this conversation somewhere private."

To squash his prodding, Aunt Hisako stomps her paw hard on the tatami. "I said no! That's the end of it!" She trots off toward the kits' happy yips.

It makes the fur on Hoji's back bristle.

Cedar and pine scents linger in the air from the hearth fire. I gather a few more stones near it in a blanket for Su-chan and Hoji tags along. After a moment, he says, "Your training from Soujou-bou has to do with the Guardianship, too. That's why he won't let me be his student."

"I don't think that's it. I hate to break it to you, Hoji, but you're too impetuous. While you have the soul of a samurai, you don't have the discipline."

"You just haven't seen that side. The situation we find ourselves in has been insane. You've done some stupid things, too."

I admit, "Point taken. So how do we show Soujou-bou your best side?"

"You'd help me?"

"Why not?"

Then his paw scuffs the tatami. "Every time we learn some new atrocity my sister did, her shadow darkens any future my mother and I have."

"I'd not be able to stand it here if you were anything like Sari."

"Che. I idolized her, though we never got to spend much time together. Now I know why."

Instead of dwelling on the bad, I try to turn things around. "Everything I saw said 'she needs to be in control'. How about you show the world the good your family can do?"

"Ok. What if I train you in the magic that my clan is developing? I'm on sabbatical right now because of the issues we're dealing with. But the down time is driving me crazy."

Suddenly, I stumble on a rough spot on the floor. "Not the oni based tech magic?"

"No! I was talking about using electricity. It was for my PhD thesis." He mutters, "Tell me she didn't use oni like that…"

Jiro, wide-eyed, pokes his head out of his room. "New magic?"

"You think Nobu-sensei will let you take on another subject?" Hoji raises an eyebrow. "And you'd learn from the likes of me?"

The boy bites his lip as if deciding. "You aren't like her. I can ask Nobu-sensei."

At that, Hoji's ears perk up. "Maybe our clan won't always be the black sheep of kitsune-kind. How can I simplify it enough for humans?"

"Hold on." My arms cross and my steps halt. "How is what you offer different from Sari's magic? I may not be well educated, but a brief explanation goes a long way."

So Hoji gives a little bow. "Sorry. What I've been developing is powered by electricity. Not whatever abomination Sari must have practiced. Since electricity has the character for ki in it, I figured there might be a way to make it work."

"Oh?" I ask.

"Many others have tried, but not succeeded because they tried to use it like they use natural magic. Ki users usually break through with a particular style, but this is so different from the natural version we have, it won't be easy to learn. Are you willing to try?"

"Count me in. Though, I'll have to put most of my time to my other lessons." I offer a fist bump, which takes him a few seconds to return with his paw. Has he not kept up with human culture?

"Fair enough."

"Me, too!" Jiro says enthusiastically and Hoji offers the same gesture.

Then my hand pauses on the inset handle for the sliding shoji door to the room I share with Su-chan.

"Jiro-kun, let us see if there's a snack in the kitchen," the fox says.

Thanks, Hoji. You're ok.

As I shut the door behind me, Su-chan sits up. She's wearing a sashiko coat and the white-stitched wave patterns on the dark jacket radiate a faint blue glow.

Great Aunt Asako nods before leaving us alone.

Should I crawl in too? "How are you feeling?"

"Physically? Better. Emotionally? I don't know. Your grandmother had to make sure I was only being controlled. That's why she sent you out."

The damn dragon made her fear of being puppeteered come true. My stomach turns. *If he laid a hand on her...* "Su-chan..."

But her hands wave vehemently in front of her. "It wasn't like that!" Taking a shaky breath, she continues, "How could he take over my mind every day? I think it started a week ago." She rubs her arm as she looks at the tatami. "I'd wake so cold next to you. Yet you never stirred when I'd snuggle for warmth. You're such a light sleeper. Did the dragon make you sleep more deeply?"

"Shion has a lot to answer for," I growl as I set the stones under the blanket and grab her shoulders, forcing her to look into my eyes. "What can I do to keep this from happening to you ever again?"

"Miwa-san said we may stop it if I keep covering the vulnerable areas of my body, like my neck, with this embroidered coat. The designs are lovely and they're like protection talismans." She turns away and her fists clench. "But I intend to go back to the waterfall while I'm awake—to deal with this once and for all."

How can she be so composed, considering the circumstances? Slipping into the futon next to her, I pull the cover up over us.

Idiot. She's not calm at all. Su-chan's still shaking, despite the heat. She's holding it all in.

So my arms wrap tightly around her. Her head tucks into my shoulder as I say, "We'll get this figured out. You don't have to face it alone." *She always puts on such a brave face. Can't let that fool me anymore.*

Her hands clutch my shirt, and she rasps, "Why couldn't this Shion just talk to me?"

The Nakamura and Date clans reluctantly agree with Su-chan's plan to confront the spirit. The last thing we need right now is another member of our group being threatened.

Afterward, Great Uncle Nobu takes me aside. "A messenger from Inari came for Yoshirou's body. I'm also allowing Jiro to learn from Hoji. And Hisako will join in. She insisted the lessons would take her mind off her loss for a little while."

After lunch, Hoji gives Jiro and me our first lesson, and several others join in, including Su-chan, Aunt Hisako, and Great Uncle Nobu.

Hoji, in his human form and sporting jeans, a button up, and tie, has us all fetch a cellphone and open it to reveal the battery. At Aunt Hisako's furrowed brow, I'm about to scoot over to help. But Hoji zips to her side and flicks his fingers to do it.

"Do you think I can learn?" Suzuki Chiyo asks. So, Jiro pats the ground for his mom to sit.

Hoji nods, pushing his glasses back up on his nose. "Everyone can perform magic. It just fell out of favor around the Meiji Restoration when the West called it a superstition.

"Just because they couldn't see it, they refused to believe. No magic user was fool enough to share it with those boisterous foreigners."

Aunt Hisako nods. "I remember. It was the best way we had at the time to protect yokai, like us."

"Now keep in mind, the effort to break through varies from person to person. For some, it can take years or decades. There's no way to tell how much effort it will take to access the ki well inside you if you weren't born with it open. This is a new field. I don't know how easy it will be for a person to break through."

"If I don't try, I won't know, will I? Bye-bye warranty." Chiyo sets her shoulders and pops open her phone.

Hoji continues, "When I first figured out how to do this, it was hard. I couldn't pull the energy from the phone. But having contact with the power source helped. So place your fingers on the battery. You need to feel the flow and see the energy field. Unfortunately, I don't have my research equipment here. So I'll simulate it for you." Holding up his iPhone, his free hand pulls something from the device. Then the air about ten centimeters from the phone glows yellow, writhing and pulsating.

"This inside part of the toroid..." Hoji pauses at my questioning look, "...the donut shape is the most powerful area of electromagnetic radiation... uhm, the energy field. The closer you are to a source, the more of the emitted energy you can interact with. The effect drops off quickly the farther you're away from it."

An energy field from our phones? Like around power lines? Is that healthy?

"Your exercise today is to see the field. If you manage that, then focus on the most powerful area. If you're used to accessing natural ki, this will feel uncomfortable."

Behind us, the click of claws on the floor draws everyone's attention. "Hisako-san, what are you doing?" The female kit, Yuri, asks.

"Trying to learn something." She pats the kits' heads. "You two can stay if you're quiet."

"Can we learn, too?" Their ears perk up.

My aunt gives a questioning look to Hoji, who nods before setting his own phone in front of them as he offers a quiet explanation.

Then Taka, the male kit, presses a forepaw to the battery. "Ooooh. Wavy things." His sister's head tilts, and she shoves his paw out of the way to try it.

Everyone's heads swivel toward the kits and Aunt Hisako's lips purse. I have to stifle my laugh. *Outdone right off the bat.*

What if...? So I cast a spell for clarity of sight. The phone only seems to pop out at me from the stone floor.

Hoji doesn't move, but his tone turns stern. "Natural magic won't do you any good, Umeji-kun. Didn't you hear me?"

"Yes, Sensei." My head ducks at being caught.

Stretching, Great Uncle Nobu says, "Well, time for my student to continue his studies." When he gets no response, he pads over and puts a paw on Jiro's head. "Were you concentrating that hard?"

The boy jumps. "Uh. Sorry Nobu-Sensei. I figured something out."

"Oh?" It makes Great Uncle Nobu lean in.

"The energy flows like a stream and, if you follow the lines, you can change them." Light streaks appear around the phone in that distinctive donut shape and Jiro follows the flow with his finger, then draws one section out as if it's bread dough.

"Fascinating!" Great Uncle Nobu exclaims and the rest of us scoot over to see better.

"So, the younger ones catch on quickly." Hoji scratches his chin, admitting, "I won't tell you all how long it took me to manipulate the field."

"As with everything," Chiyo sighs, but pats her son's head.

Hoji gives the rest of us homework to keep trying for a breakthrough. Afterward, Jiro asks him more about electricity based magic. Their conversation turns to programming and Jiro's so excited he can't sit still.

8

THE SIN

As I read a book of newly published myths and folklore at the table, Hoji sorts through a stack of documents. Pointing to various crumbling, charred papers in their protective sleeves, he asks, "Are you familiar with magical encryption? I can't seem to make heads nor tails of this."

"I dabbled in web traffic sniffing for the yakuza but haven't seen the magic side. What kind of decryption key would that rely on?" When I lean in, I could swear the blurred script squirms under scrutiny. The musty, acrid scent makes my nose wrinkle and there's a suspicious-looking brown stain on one of them, making me queasy.

"Could be anything. Most likely proximity. But to what?"

"Do you know who wrote it? That might provide a clue."

"I'm hoping it was my sister, so we can solve the mystery Shion wanted us to look into. Maybe I can have it fingerprinted. Father must have had reason to keep it in a separate safe deposit box." When my eyebrow lifts, he explains, "After Mother presented my father's death certificate for access to the family's box, the bankers gave her a key to another."

Suspicious. So I get up to pace and shake off the twitchiness building inside. "Sometimes secrets should remain buried. My gut says this is one of those times. Yes, I want to know how to help Su-chan. But do you really want to know, especially if it's bad?"

He harrumphs. To get a better look, I drag a page over. Green sparks ignite under my fingers, making me spring back. *What the?*

"Do it again!" Hoji's eyes go wide, and he shoves the paper in my direction.

77

Upon contact, the glow reappears, and the writing coalesces to legibility. Hairs raise on the back of my neck as if a ghost passed through me. "Hoji-san, something's off. You don't want to see this."

His paw stomps the floor. "For good or bad, my family should know."

Stubborn fox. I read aloud what I can from around the burn holes and charring.

1861 May 1

...convinced him, after a year of servitude, to give me his ability. Now to wait.

1861 September 30

Learned from a kumiho to mask magic identification, in exchange for one male kitsune in human form ... couldn't save him and kill the kumiho witch before she devoured ...

Never make a deal with anyone who wants to hunt a fox.

1861 November 4

Female oni agreed to the terms... my assistance in helping her become ruler of the oni horde and sacrificing the life of my teacher for the merging of her magic to mine.

1862 April 3

Tomorrow, I shall have more power at... fingertips than any other kitsune in history. After masking my... the oni and I created the occult circle. Now to ensure Master will be there.

1862 April 4

We mimicked the forest echoes to lure him. The fool always rushed in to help ... blood and fire of the symbols rendered him defenseless. His strength gave out as the circle drained his ki. When he was too weak to move, I sliced...

Can't get the blood off my hands. No amount of washing works.

Oni isn't happy that I got the dragon's magic on top of binding her power to take the ki drain for me. Not my problem. She wasn't smart enough to negotiate well. Took most of the ki from myself and the dragon spirit to quell her attempts to turn me.

Will I always fight her for control?

1862 April 6
Moved the bind to the collar ...successfully entwined ki use and technology.

Holy shit. It mentions "the dragon". *That's Shion, isn't it? And she murdered him.* My stomach lurches.

"This is indeed my sister's journal." Then Hoji's head hangs. "You must have unlocked it, because you have her magic. Dad was the one that insisted we work to combine magic and tech. That means he knew..." With bulging cheeks, Hoji dashes toward the toilet.

Damn you, Sari. Cold fills my insides and my hands shake. So I scoop up the papers, unwilling to read anymore of the dark tale, and I jog down the hill trail to the burn pit. A flick of my fingers starts the blaze, despite the snow covering the ashes.

Even if the fire is hot enough to incinerate the pages, we'll need a priest to cleanse Hoji, myself, Grandma Miwa, and the building.

"Stop! Tatsuya don't destroy those!" Aunt Hisako shouts as she races in fox form from the summerhouse.

My head swivels toward her as I hold the papers above the flame. "It's Date Sari's journals telling of the sickening evil she did. No one should have to read this ever again!"

"No!" she blurts, "Hoji-san told me what you two uncovered. That year! It was when the first protector of Nonogawa, Shion—the dragon, went missing, and many legends popped up to explain his absence. It's what Shion wanted you to uncover! Plus, the priests and the League of Guardians need to know the truth from those papers. Then they'll dispose of them. Wait while I grab an approved portal ofuda."

Warily, I do as I'm told. Though, I insist, "I'm coming." Not that I want to see the members of the League again after how they treated me. Well, except Soujou-bou. But Aunt Hisako shouldn't go anywhere alone, especially in her depleted state.

"Stay. League business. I'll be back soon."

When her portal closes, I trudge up the hill to let both clans and Satou know that Date Sari did indeed kill Shion and Ibaraki was involved.

Aunt Hisako returns about an hour later. "It was dragon blood on the pages."

We did what Shion wanted. *Now, I gotta become a Guardian to stop this insanity.*

9

CONFRONTATION

LATER, GRANDMA MIWA ASKS Hoji and me to join her at the low table as she preps gyoza dumplings for lunch. "I will expunge my daughter, Sari, from our family register as soon as I can get to the records office."

My head hangs. *That means...*

"Grandson, I will not cut you off. When I mentioned this to Hisako-san, she shared how your mother has refused to accept you because of your past. If you like, I will adopt you officially into the Date house."

I'd be her son... and Hoji's brother?

Hoji's ears twitch, but he says nothing.

A generous offer, but don't run from the problem. So, I stare at my folded hands on the table. "Thank you for your kindness, Grandma. My mom hasn't seen me since I turned yakuza at fourteen. I'd like a chance to show her who I am since I left." *When I've become a Guardian, even if I can't really talk about it.*

"Of course. I thought her answer was definitive and a spurn to all of us. But if you think she might change her mind, I won't push." She pats my hand. "It's good you wish to keep her in your life. On a different topic, I keep getting calls asking where Sari is. They want her to speak at several women's empowerment conferences and I've told them they have the wrong number because I couldn't face telling them the truth. At least she was involved in some good things."

After dinner, a typhoon moves in, hitting Kyoto hard. Lightning flashes. Thunder peals above. And the rain pounding the skylight roars down at us as a messenger, soaked to the bone, arrives with news about Yoshirou's private funeral arrangements.

His family invites my aunt and her parents to attend two days from now. Then the messenger turns down the offer of tea and a warm spot by the sunken hearth. She'll only have to head back into the howling wind and chilling rain.

Great Uncle Nobu turns on the radio, which says our area has a landslide warning, so we need to be aware of our evacuation routes.

Meanwhile, I text the news about Yoshirou to Satou. Kneeling by Aunt Hisako, I whisper, "Su-chan and I'll keep you company tonight. Satou-san says call tomorrow. He's worried sick about you."

"Thank you, but I wish to be alone. I'll be ready to go with you and Su-chan tomorrow." Her voice cracks.

She even turns down her sister's offer, instead asking Tsubame to take the twins for the night. My throat tightens as she retires early and shuts the door to face her grief.

Then Hoji shuffles in with his arm raised, about to ask a question, but sees her heading to her room and his head hangs.

Aunt Hisako's mourning is affecting the entire house.

Sliding her hand into mine, Su-chan gives the comfort of her presence. *Dunno what I'd do without you.*

That night, we take turns watching the kits. Hoji, Tsubame, and Jiro teach them to use magic to perform the toughest otedama juggling tricks. Finally, the kits' eyes droop.

Hoji scoops Taka up by the scruff of the neck, and Tsubame does the same for Yuri. With little protest, they get the kits tucked in. Though the young ones ask for Jiro to sleep beside them. Cheers erupt when Jiro's mom grants their wish. Soon the trio is engrossed in chat about Hoji's lessons and how Jiro is learning how Kyoto Jidai Arcane University thwarts hackers trying to access their network.

How old was I when I started learning about hacking? Probably about sixteen. *Maybe he's not so young for it.*

As he walks by, Hoji ruffles the trio's hair and fur. "You three sure are catching on fast to whatever we throw at you! Oh! And Jiro, that back door you found, IT just patched it."

Afterward, the voice of Aunt Hisako's sister, Tsubame, carries down the hall. "Hoji-san, do you have a moment to speak outside? We can portal to the storage shed to stay dry."

"Sure. What's on your mind?" he asks.

As Su-chan and I finish cleaning the kitchen, my eyebrows waggle and she stifles a giggle. She suspects it, too. *I won't pry.* There are so few secrets here in the tight quarters. Let them have theirs.

Tsubame returns a little less bright in spirit, and Hoji flees, bobbing his goodnight. Then Su-chan mouths the words that echo my suspicion, 'Love confession.'

Poor Tsubame. Didn't she notice Hoji only has eyes for Aunt Hisako?

Su-chan sets an alarm to wake up just before the time we estimate the dragon drew her to the waterfall. When it goes off, I growl and throw my arm over my eyes. But my hand hits her head.

"Tatsu, just because you're a grump in the morning, doesn't mean you need to blame me."

Caressing her cheek, I soften my words. "Sorry. I was grumbling at the alarm and tried to hide from the light. But I know being puppeteered is tough on you."

Outside, rain batters our window. *Don't wanna go.* "It's still raining hard. Should we wait until the storm is gone?"

"No!" She stiffens.

"But you were drenched yesterday and so cold. I'm worried about you getting sick."

"I need to find out what Shion wants." She slips clothes on and puts on the sashiko embroidered coat she slept in over the top, ensuring the talisman-like patterns are against her neck. She's not taking any risks of being controlled again.

But he wants his magic back. My insides wind tight. "I know. I just don't have a good feeling about this." *At least we won't go alone.*

Aunt Hisako—with a ki boost, Hoji, Su-chan, and I fight our umbrellas as soon as we step through the portal. Wind rushes around us as we push toward the stone torii.

Unfortunately, Su-chan is the only one with a raincoat. My cheap plastic umbrella I bought at the combini yesterday collapses under the wind's battering.

Why bother? If I try to put it back up, it's just going to happen again. Maybe Su-chan's obsessive packing isn't so bad?

As we bow and pass under the gate, the gusts drive us to hunker down. That's when a tingle begins on the back of my neck, so I stick close to Su-chan and pull my katana from my pocket. Her determination makes my heart swell.

"Shion-sama, I've come to you, so you don't have to drag me here again." Clenching her fists and leaning into the gusts, Su-chan shouts against the storm. "We did as you asked–uncovered what Date Sari did to you."

The gale contorts the trees and bamboo surrounding the waterfall. Every cannon-like crack causes me to flinch.

Like a war zone. In my peripheral vision, Hoji's hands fly up, and a glowing yellow shield encircles us just before a cedar crashes into it, causing us all to cover our heads.

A torrent gushes over the waterfall, bringing the stream's flow over the banks and our feet. If it gets much deeper, the water might sweep us away.

Nevertheless, Su-chan's brows knit together and she slips her hand into mine. Giving a squeeze, she casts a spell to help us defy the wind.

That's my girl.

Lightning strikes pummel the ledge of the hill with the water cascade. *Like Sari's storms?*

The ghostly form of the dragon, iridescent blue green, with his teeth bared and claws extended, undulates toward us. "You dare summon me? Do you think because you have my magic that I am helpless?"

Where's he get the energy if Su-chan has his magic?

My girlfriend drops to her knees with a splash and bows her head, letting her umbrella wheel away. Her voice cracks as she shouts over the roar. "I requested your presence, Shion-sama. Since I've been possessed by others, I could never force anyone to do anything!"

The ghost slithers effortlessly through our shield, to lift Su-chan's chin. His words echo around us in the gale. "It's not possible for an innocent to have my magic."

Steeling my nerve, I crouch beside her in the frigid water. "It is, Shion-sama. Please, hear us out."

"Witch! No matter what form you take, I know that magic, too!"

When one of the dragon's claws swishes through my chest toward my ki well, it sends a shudder down my spine and my words tumble out. "Date Sari attacked Su-chan and me. The only way I could attempt to stop her was to remove her magic."

"I see the ink you hide from the world. A yakuza's word means nothing. You only wanted the power!"

"My sister was the one who took your life and stole your magic. I'm here to report her death." Hoji, in human form, drops to his knees beside us.

So the dragon hovers over Hoji, breathing in his scent, and reels back. "Kin to the betrayer, and you turned Sekiguchi against me. Your word, too, is worthless!"

Aunt Hisako changes from her silver fox form to her elderly human one and puts a hand on Su-chan's shoulder. Then she holds out her other palm, activating her glowing Guardian seal. "Will you listen to a fellow member of the League?"

The ghost huffs, tendrils of smoke radiate from his mouth as he writhes in impossible serpentine knots. Finally, he nods.

"I can attest to the truth of their words. Date Sari also stole my tama and magically crippled me. Her crimes are innumerable." Then my aunt's words soften. "Great River Kami of Nonogawa, Shion, the Guardian of the valley. That is who you are, yes?"

Reptile eyes close as the dragon exhales steam. "I am not forgotten..." Then smoke returns, and his breathing turns ragged, "...even though the League failed to send help when I called!"

"There are no records of a call to the League. In Date Sari's notes, I found she lured you into a circle that kept you from sending messages. Again, not forgotten."

The dragon hisses and points to Su-chan and me. "Sari may be dead, but the Date clan and those with my magic must pay! Starting with them!"

On instinct, I lunge between the dragon and Su-chan.

"A Guardian would never demand the blood of innocents! In your rage, have you forgotten the oath you made?" Aunt Hisako whispers Soujou-bou's name. Her palm glows.

But Shion's scales bristle in waves all the way down his long form, and he darts forward into my aunt's face. "No one is truly innocent. And these two killed Date Sari for the magic they carry. Your support for them is hypocrisy."

"Inari Okami punished Sari for her crimes!" Hoji sputters.

Shion's head jerks back and his clawed hand presses to the shield Hoji raised to protect us from the storm. On contact, the yellow glow transfers to fill his entire body as the spell collapses. He utters, "Truth," and the spell's ripple runs over us all. "How did the kitsune witch die?"

A tingle forms at the back of my neck and my hand tightens on my sword. *Ki theft?*

Then Aunt Hisako gasps, "That's how you've powered your magic, siphoning ki from spells already cast."

Hoji's eyes narrow and he spits his words. "Ibaraki Douji killed Sari shortly after the kami punished her. We discovered the depths of my sister's evil and we expunged her from our family register."

Careful Hoji. Shion doesn't trust us yet.

Sweeping over to Su-chan and me, Shion waves a clawed hand over our ki wells and asks, "Is it true, Sari did not die at your hands?"

"No, Shion-sama. We regret the unintended theft. Removing her magic was the only way I could stop her without killing her. I have too much blood on my hands already. Though, I don't regret stopping my seven times great grandmother from her evil."

"That is why your magic resembles hers." He nods to himself. "So her family must be the ones to atone for her atrocities."

His words make me bristle. "Atone? How?"

"What of me, Shion-sama?" Su-chan asks, still with her head bowed.

"You are his mate, are you not? Family."

Su-chan's head swivels and she glares. "You haven't mentioned this mate thing."

Shit. My palm wipes over my face. "I was waiting for a good time to tell you." Belatedly, I add, "When we get back to the house, I'll explain."

"You asked how atonement would be paid. I require the return of my magic. Though, it will snuff the life from her fragile human body, which wasn't born with natural spellcasting. Something is killing off yokai much faster than we can repopulate and I must restore the balance."

My mouth goes dry. In one motion, I raise Honjou Masamune and lean in to shield Su-chan. "Spare her. Take my life instead."

Instant silence smothers the surrounding forest. No wind, no rain, no thunder. Just droplets falling from the trees and the waterfall beyond. *The eye of the storm?*

Next, the dragon poises like a snake about to strike. "You dare bring Honjou Masamune against me, boy?"

"Only if you hurt her!" I say with steel in my voice and my hand grips my sword tighter.

"Tatsu! Don't! I'm the one with Shion-sama's magic. And you need to be Nonogawa's Gua..." Her foot stomps as the seal Aunt Hisako put on us cuts off the word. "...protector. It's ok."

But I can't breathe as she presses her hands on each side of my face and rests her forehead against mine. "Not ok! We're supposed to fill the position together!" My breaths come ragged. I shout so hard my lungs burn. "There has to be another way!" *Come on, idiot! What is it?*

"Then you can be free. Kitsune mate for life. I bet you didn't intend for it to happen, did you?"

Honjou Masamune clatters to the ground and my head shakes as I clasp her to me. A cold deeper than I've ever known gushes in. *Don't want anyone else. Ever.*

"I didn't know how to tell you because I didn't want you to feel you were stuck with me!" I growl to Shion, "Take what you need from me!"

"Enough!" Aunt Hisako's booming command rings so hard that trees crack and fall around us, though her shallow breathing draws my attention. Hoji rushes over, pouring ki into her.

She pants, "Shion-sama, Ibaraki leads the oni. She and her horde were enough to breach the defenses at Soujou-bou's estate. The Oni Queen is intent on wiping out my race and our friends. She even claimed she wants to be the new Shogun!

"Japan cannot go back to that system. With yokai declining in numbers, we need everyone we can get to fight her. Tatsuya is correct. Soujou-bou also intends for Su-chan to be a Guardian, so she and Tatsuya make the first human pair to fill the role."

Slowly, the dragon's mouth purses as he paces tight circles around our group. "I must see this done." Hovering before Su-chan and I, the dragon looks into my girlfriend's eyes. "However, you are a rare, pure-of-heart soul. And it is fitting that both the holder of my magic and the spawn of my murderer bring justice. You, girl, will be my eyes and ears—the body I am denied. When the time comes, I will work through you."

Su-chan stiffens in my arms, so I state through clenched teeth. "You won't possess her! She's dealt with that too much."

He gets right in my space to stare me down. The smoke from his breath mixes with the rainwater dripping down my face. "You dare tell a god what to do?"

Defiant, I roll my shoulders back to be at my full height. "I'm volunteering to be your tool, instead."

"No, it must be the girl. She has the dragon magic and is more powerful than you will ever be. Even if she's an innocent, every human craves power. This will be her chance."

Sizzling behind us signals intense magic. A peek over my shoulder reveals Sekiguchi stepping through a portal.

Straightening but shaking hard, Su-chan pulls away from me. "My life is for healing others, studying to improve potions for that healing, and giving the energy I have to those who can use it best."

Shion waves her words off, but Su-chan persists. "A prophetess in Hokkaido foretold you in my life. She said I would become a terrible dragon, raging over a town and wreaking destruction in my path. I won't kill. It goes against what I believe. Plus, Tatsu has told me the price he's paid for taking lives." She digs her feet into the muddy ground. "So, I will resist that with all I have."

Why didn't Su-chan tell me?

Be here for her. Talk later. Scooping up my sword again, I state, "I stand beside her. Anyone who tries to possess her will answer to me."

Honjou Masamune's metallic hum reverberates around us.

"Foolish mortals. If the pair of you are to become Guardians, killing is necessary sometimes. I learned that the hard way. I should have killed Date Sari. If you will not give up the magic inside you, then you leave me no choice!"

Instantly, I raise a shield and my sword. The dragon lunges, sucking up the energy from my spell and freezing me in place. Then light blasts from the sashiko patterns on Su-chan's embroidered jacket, sending the dragon flipping away head over tail backwards.

"Shion!" A staccato voice rings in the waterfall's clearing as the kappa steps forward. "I won't allow you to possess my student! If you continue to pursue this path, then you aren't the river god I loved a century ago. I was hesitant to approach you since you puppeteered the girl. But this ends here.

"You're consumed with rage. It turned you into something I don't recognize anymore." Sekiguchi drops into a fighting stance and his hands glow a vibrant blue.

Loved?

"Stand down, Sekiguchi," Shion snarls.

Instead, the kappa barks, "Get the girl out of here!"

Without hesitation, I scribe a portal. "Come on, Su-chan."

"But-"

I grab her hand and tug. *Idiot. She needs the choice.* "Your teacher said to go."

Finally, she nods.

"I'll cover you." Hoji steps between us and the oncoming confrontation, giving my aunt a shove. "You too, Hisako-san."

My aunt glances back as the portal closes behind us and "Hoji" falls from her lips.

"You're all soaked to the bone and shivering! Let's get you warmed up!" Grandma Miwa offers.

"Hoji's back there with Sekiguchi, facing off with the dragon." I point to where the portal was. "I've gotta go back for him!"

But Great Grandmother Miwa's tails fluff. "You're too low on ki. I will help him." She hollers into the other room, "Asako-san! Your family needs you!"

As Great Aunt Asako skitters in and Grandma Miwa flicks a tail to make a portal, a glitchy door forms and sputters. Hoji drags a limp Sekiguchi through.

"Kitsune, this is not ov-" Shion's voice comes through before Hoji's fingers snap, and the portal shutting clips off the sentence.

"It is for now." Hoji gulps in another breath as he shouts, "Someone fetch water immediately! His well is empty."

"Thank goodness you're alright!" Grandma Miwa's paw goes to her chest.

Still dripping wet, Su-chan and I stiffly race to the kitchen's water pump. Great Aunt Asako beat us there and already has a bowl.

But Su-chan shakes her head. "He'll absorb a lot."

Each of us rushes back with a container. We pour it into the dome of the kappa's head and zip back for more.

"He spent what he had and all I could give him," Hoji rasps, letting his human guise extinguish.

Several bowls of water later, the kappa opens his eyes. "You should have left me there, but thank you."

Su-chan kneels before her teacher. Her hands glow as she waves them over his vitals. The light emission spikes over his ki well and her hands press to his chest.

"You're still dangerously low, Sensei. Accept some of my ki, please." At his nod, her hands glow bright blue and the light settles under the kappa's ribs.

"The Shion I knew was not like that. The betrayal must have broken him. For your sake, Ohno-chan, I will keep trying to reason with him. But we must give him time."

Words pour out of me from the need to protect my girlfriend. "Did he take back the demand to use Su-chan as a puppet?"

"No."

After that, we move the kappa to a quiet room and Su-chan keeps him company.

Hoji takes a seat across from Aunt Hisako and me. "Now what?"

"I will contact the League. This recent development does not bode well. The fools in the council think they've seen this all before. But the events are a culminating series of smaller squalls, threatening to converge into a perfect storm they might not be able to handle," my aunt says before she pads off.

"Thank you for watching out for us, especially my aunt." I give a deep bow to Hoji, but he waves it away. I'd bet good money he wants her to notice, but it's too soon.

That night, instead of sleeping beside me, Su-chan offers to watch the kits while my aunt is away on League business. Hoji and the Nakamura clan could have done that. Su-chan asks Sekiguchi during lessons if she can access books in his library and she's gone much of the day.

Is she avoiding me?

When I can catch a moment with her, I'm so touch starved that I scoop her up into my arms, squeezing to hold her there for a few moments, even when she squirms. "Damn, I miss you."

She turns rigid as a board and her voice goes flat. "Let me go, Tatsuya."

Not Tatsu?

Reluctantly, I release her. My hand reaches out to caress her cheek. But it drops when she steps back, and my chest tightens. "What's wrong?"

So I sort through everything that happened recently with threats to the kitsune, her being puppeteered, the death of Yoshirou, the stress of being cooped up with so many other people in a small house with no privacy. *What the hell did I do?*

Her words turn clipped. "It's not you."

Grabbing her shoulders, I get her to look at me for just a second. I don't want to make her uncomfortable. But she needs to know I care. *Maybe I haven't told her enough lately?* "Su-chan, I'm here for you."

Then her look turns haunted.

Click. "It's the possession and prophecy. Isn't it?"

She looks away.

Slowly my arms encompass her, to give her a chance to refuse. This time she doesn't fight me. "I'll help you through this. No matter what."

10

BOND

AUNT HISAKO STAYS BUSY. Unless she's with the kits, Taka and Yuri, she keeps to herself. Yoshirou's funeral was hard on her.

Two days afterward, we head to the kits' old home. Aunt Hisako makes the little ones stay behind until their parents' bodies are prepared for the funeral. Even then, it's a tough call if it's the right thing to bring them back to the place their family died. I don't know how Aunt Hisako manages to help, since this is where Yoshirou was wounded.

The neighbors, checking on the commotion, come with magic at the ready in case it's another attack. *Can't blame them.* But they gather around the kits with warm welcomes and offers of a home.

After that, the kits are downright clingy, fearing Aunt Hisako, too, might go away. They ask to stay with her, much to her relief. She needs them as much as they need her.

Then the neighbors fetch the Shinto priest from the shrine the family attended to help purify the area. Soujou-bou, being a Buddhist priest and Aunt Hisako's boss, volunteers to officiate the private ceremony for the kits' family. Everything, my clothes, my hair, the air all smell like singed fur and smoke for days from the funeral pyre. Kitsune aren't afforded official cremations, I guess. It's a rough week, but the little ones need the closure.

Afterward, Satou visits to check on our aunt and brings greetings from my friends, Matsuo and Mie. He loses it when he finds out Aunt Hisako refuses to be healed. While I agree with him, I'm less in a position to argue with her.

We give him several portal ofuda and show him how to use them. From Nono-gawa, he texts me, 'The efficiency of the portals is amazing. But I prefer the downtime on the Shinkansen. The bullet train ride is quiet, an in-between time that allows you to transition between one place and another. Portals abruptly throw you into a new location.'

Satou didn't get to meet Taka and Yuri. They were too shy, and Aunt Hisako didn't want to push them. The kits haven't been sleeping well since the funeral, often waking from nightmares of what they experienced in the attack.

Now, Su-chan sleeps with them to keep them company if Aunt Hisako is away on League business. I volunteer to help, but she shakes her head. The constant interruptions in her sleep and demands on her schedule leave bags under her eyes.

Shouting that others can watch the kits isn't gonna help, nor will hitting something. But I use each morning's workout to imagine slicing clean through the issues between us. And I punch a tree a few times when I'm out of sight of the den. My knuckles get pretty bruised.

Unfortunately, someone must have tattled because I get cussed out by Great Uncle Nobu for taking out my anger on a living thing. He offers to listen. But after the lecture, who would wanna talk?

The kits aren't making progress in their studies and are acting out at the adults here by throwing tantrums. Grandma Miwa says it's expected, especially after what the twins have been through. The best thing is to give them a stable, loving home.

It's been a few weeks since the last attack on a kitsune or a friend. So, we've moved back to the main Nakamura family den. The Date duo returns to their own home to clean up and hold a funeral. We help them through it, of course. Though everyone asks them to stay with the Nakamuras until the threat to kitsune-kind is dealt with. Reluctantly, they agree.

Despite having more room, both clans clamor to get away from the cramped conditions for even a bit. We go out in groups of at least two, with each of us carrying scads of portal and healing talismans, and we always let the others know where we're going.

Inari-sama sent a messenger the other day to teach all kitsune to mask our fox and dragon magic and pass it on to trusted friends and family. It's not a perfect solution since a true-seeing spell can penetrate it. But it allows us a little more anonymity from the yokai community, which has gotten nosy as hell of late in their concern for our clans and kitsune-kind.

On top of that, the sword drills and muscle building exercises Soujou-bou has me do several times a day are killer, but I'm not as winded when we spar. And I was in decent shape before I started training with him! For a tengu that looks like a senior citizen, he's damn spry.

It's been about two weeks since the kits' family's funeral. This morning, I snapped at Aunt Hisako. She didn't deserve it. And poor Su-chan keeps having to deal with my moodiness in the few moments I get to chat with her until I get a workout in.

After training, Great Aunt Asako drops several coins in my palm and asks Su-chan and me to buy a new fire protection charm for her kitchen.

Not like my aunt can't make her own. She probably needed me out of the den for a bit. *Can't blame her.*

Sekiguchi also asks Su-chan to pick up a few ingredients for his potions. He's been busy restocking after the craziness of the last month. She's soaking up everything he can teach her. Sekiguchi even gave her permission to add the recipes to her family's tome of magic healing, as long as he gets credit. *Like she wouldn't do that, anyway.*

I hate doing the masking spell each time before we go out. When it hides my fox magic, the spell constricts the space under my ribs where my ki well resides. I described it in a text to Matsuo, my friend in Nonogawa, saying it was smothering like wearing a mask when I'm sick on a muggy summer day.

So Su-chan and I head out. My hands stuff into my coat pockets and my feet scuff the ground as we walk. *Stupid being cooped up all the time and requiring an excuse to go outside. Stupid me for snapping at Aunt Hisako. Stupid that Su-chan has to be so tired and that we have to hide our magic.*

Freshly fallen snow covers the ground, stone steps, and roof of the bare wood torii. We bow before passing under it. The shoveled path through the dense trees feels like a shadowy tunnel threatening to close in on us, and I don't even see a trace of the kami like I usually do.

Su-chan gives the barest tilt to her head. "What's wrong?"

"Dunno. It's not like just one thing sets me off lately. It's everything. And... you're avoiding me."

Then she looks up at the sky. "Maybe this walk will help? We haven't had a moment to ourselves in quite a while... and we need to talk."

That sends a jolt through me. *Nothing good comes from that phrase.* The cold seeps through my jacket and pants to the deepest parts of my soul.

But her hands wave in front of her face. "N-not that way! I've just had a lot to think about."

It's not like her to be so distant. She wants to be with me right now. *Be present, idiot.*

So I hold out my hand in an offer. She accepts, giving a slight squeeze. For the first time in days, we make contact.

Her warmth resets something inside. The tight ball near my ki well unwinds just a little and the surrounding forest isn't threatening to trap us anymore. This time alone with her is a gift, even if I'd like more than a walk and holding hands.

After a few strides, our footfalls sync and we slow to climb each step together until we reach the top. The frigid water at the station to purify ourselves is refreshing as we pour it over our hands and rinse our mouths.

The flat, open area contains the shrine and a little stand. We head to pray first. Clapping and ringing the bell, Su-chan says, "Kami-sama, please heal my teacher's broken heart, protect our friends, and help us find a better way to appease Shion-sama."

I'll protect her.

Clapping my own hands, I plow ahead. *Su-chan won't let me help her. There's been so much death. And the League doesn't want to let me be a Guardian. I'd pinned my hopes on it. Why can't I have that position?*

Suddenly, a falling pinecone thunks the top of my head, much like Aunt Hisako did when she was teaching and I didn't pay attention. "Ow!" My hand automatically goes to that spot instead of staying in a praying position. *Why can't I stay focused?*

Click. My prayers had changed from being worthy to selfish whining. *When did that happen?*

Politely, Su-chan steps back to let me finish.

Kami-sama, help me be the man I need to be. Not just to be a Guardian. But to continue to be with Su-chan. I still don't have a good feeling about 'the talk' she alluded to, and I'm gonna have to tell her today how she ended up as my mate. Help me protect kitsune-kind, too.

When we head toward the deserted talisman and amulet stand, there's a single cashier garbed in winter gear with a white shrine coat over the top. His hands are as big as plates, and at least two, maybe three, of me could fit in his coat. He'd put many a sumo wrestler to shame with the power he packs.

Odd stripes of light and dark brown run through his hair and his beard is more like a bottle brush than whiskers. The back of my neck tingles and I stiffen. But he flashes a smile that offsets the gruffness in his heavy brows and gives a deep bass chuckle. "You're safe. I'm dedicated to this temple. Welcome."

Su-chan rushes over, tugging me along. The number of fire protection talisman options boggles the mind, causing my mouth to push to one side.

Then she nudges me. "I know that look. Did you see what kind she had already?"

My head shakes.

"Well, how much did she send you with?"

I whisper back, "Enough to buy the biggest paper ofuda. So I guess that's what we do. She lived through some of the most dangerous fires in Kyoto, you know."

Passing off the coins, I get a raised eyebrow from the clerk. But then I see the glow in the shape of a boar in his chest. It clicks.

Wild boars cover the top of the main building. The creatures are the servants of the tengu, Atagoya Tarou-bou, protector of this shrine. Either Tarou-bou grants this clerk the shape shifting power, or he's special.

He chatters about how deserted the shrine is in February because of the snow that only covers the mountain top and we bid him a good day. When we're out of hearing range, I stop to shove my hands into my pants pockets. *It's time.* "I owe you an explanation."

"You do."

As we descend the ridge in search of the mushrooms and wild bamboo shoots Sekiguchi had requested, I berate myself for a good ten minutes to gather the nerve. *Just get it over with.*

Su-chan keeps expectantly glancing at me and I gulp, scanning our surroundings to ensure we're alone. "Su-chan, about the first time we made love. Did you notice anything afterward?"

"That came out of nowhere." She blinks. "Should I have? Is this about what we need to talk about?"

So I nod, and my throat tightens. "Things were different for me. I hoped it was for you, too."

"You were my first. I don't know what I should have expected beyond what I could glean from romance novels, movies, and my brothers' unwanted advice."

"Makes sense." I heave in a shaky breath. "The thing is that when a kitsune is with someone the first time, it forms a mate bond. That was my first time after I gained the fox magic. So, in my eyes, you are my mate. And I'm glad about it. I would have chosen you, anyway. But, as best Aunt Hisako and I can figure, it isn't the same for you."

"So what does being your mate mean? Not like marriage, right?"

Kinda. "It means..." I pause as my feet shuffle. "It means I am yours as long as you'll have me." *And if she'd leave, it'd be pure hell.*

It's as if she'd smacked me when her voice goes hard. "Tell me that's not code for you being stuck with me. Because I'm not cool with such a thing. At all."

My insides clench and my head whips around to her. "What do you mean by that?"

A breeze picks up as if to stress the increasing emotional distance between us. Her hand rubs her other arm and her gaze drops. "Because... well, what happens when the prophecy about me destroying Nonogawa comes true?"

"You're the sweetest person I've met. Not gonna happen!"

"You don't understand!" she shouts as her fists ball up and her voice shakes. "My grandmother's prophecies always come true!"

As if emphasizing our fight, the words echo on the mountainside as I step back from her fury. "But-"

She croaks, "And the string between us isn't there anymore! I can't see it!"

I broke us. My eyes scrunch shut as those words turn into a kick in the gut.

Or she thinks she did...

"The red string of fate you talked about when we started dating?" There can't be any doubt about this, so I whisper a word of kotodama for true seeing.

When she nods, I share what the spell reveals, moving closer to her. "I see it! It's faint, but still there!"

She looks away and I lift her chin. "I'm not gonna abandon you just because of a prophecy!"

"Don't promise things like that!" Her expression degrades to something wild and desperate. She tears away from my hand. "I don't want you to be bound to a monster!"

She always felt sorry for the dangerous yokai—the monsters. Even taking some in as pets, like Chou—the ki sucking blob. *This's why.* "You're not a monster, Ohno Suzu. Never have been. Never will be. And I'm bound to you so you know I won't abandon you."

Next, she tries to shut me out. "Because you have to!"

"Stop it!" Grabbing her shoulders, I halt just short of shaking her. It won't help. My heart squeezes so hard it might implode. *Don't fuck this up.* "I. Need. You. You've stuck by my side, even when I didn't think I was worth the effort. Lean on me for once."

But her head whips from side to side and I catch her face, pressing my forehead to hers. "Let me help you through this! I can tell it scares you because you wanna run. Even if you break up with me, I'll be there for you! That's my purpose in all of this. Not being a Guardian. Not learning magic. None of it! Just you, Suzu!"

She crumples in on herself and sobs wrack her frame as she sucks in huge breaths every few seconds. Clutching her to my chest, I kiss the top of her head.

It's why our fates are intertwined. "My brave, brave girl. You don't have to fight this alone. Look at the string again."

Together, we watch it pulsing bright and strong. The doe-eyed gape turning to a smile on that sweet, tear-stained face makes my heart skip a beat.

"Don't leave me," she croaks as her head thunks against my collarbone.

"The hells will all freeze over first." I rock with her, refusing to let the contact break soon and the twisted-up ball inside unwinds a little more. We still have a big storm ahead. *But we'll face it side by side.*

When she's cried out, I lend her my handkerchief.

Su-chan says, as she wipes her eyes, "How about we finish our errands? The last thing on our list is the potion materials."

She could have asked me to count every sand grain on the beach ten times over. I'd do it just to have more time with her before we head back to the crowded den. Tugging me along, she finds the potion ingredients close together. Then a sparkle enters her eyes as she leads me down a secluded trail that barely counts as a path.

"This is the way I take to train with Sekiguchi-sensei when it's safe enough, but we're going to take the left fork instead. I want to show you something."

"I thought he lived near the summerhouse."

She shrugs, pointing to a mountain across from us. "Didn't you know the den and summerhouse were near each other?"

"Uh, no?" Evidently, I need to learn the Kyoto area better. Keeping my sense of direction in a forest is so different from in Tokyo.

The trail opens to a city block-sized meadow in the cypress and bamboo grove. Each tree standing in the circle bordering us has a set of tassels or paper streamers that mark them as having a kodama, a special type of yokai that indicates a healthy forest. And since the kanji for the word also means echo, they must have repeated our words during our fight.

I shudder. Those echoes will haunt me all my days. *Stop it. Things are ok now.*

Finally, Su-chan brings me to a cypress, tall but spindly. It must be quite young, and she pats the bark. "Can you sense something special about this tree?"

A glow inside it expands and contracts. "I can see the spirit's heartbeat."

"There's more than the ki magic. There's a being connected to it. Can't you see the difference?"

It's a kodama tree, right? *More than the magic pulse?* As I blow out my cheeks, I respond, "Uhm. Should I?"

"I was hoping you could. You have so much in common with everyone here, and I'm the odd one out. Just like when we left Hokkaido."

Failed that test. Is there a way to help her feel included? "Could you show me? And I could show you what it's like to be a fox?" If no one but the trees sees us shift, it should be safe.

Her face lights up. "I'd like that. You go first."

Cupping her cheek in my hand, I ask, "The feelings and senses might be a little overwhelming. You ready?"

At her nod, I murmur the word to transform us. She leaps into the air, giving a high-pitched yipping laugh before she sprints away.

Eagerly, I give chase. The sounds of her joyous barking and her paws beating a rhythm in the dry leaves guides me, even though she's out of sight. Glimpsing her effortlessly leaping over a fallen tree, I pour on the speed to course alongside.

Just as I'm about to catch her, she veers back the direction we came. Her scent calls to me like nothing I've experienced before, giving me a burst of energy that I put into quickening my pace. I use a touch of ki to flip through the air in front of her before she's off like a shot again. *Playing hard to get?*

When I don't follow immediately, she yips for me to join. The game continues until we reach a boulder by the base of the tree where we started playing. She nips and gekkers as we pounce and tumble together.

Sunshine warmth radiates through me just like a ki boost and blood pounds in my ears. *She's inviting you.* So my nose buries into the fur of her neck.

Wait a damned minute. We aren't foxes and there'll be consequences.

But it's been so long since we made love. *Damn it.*

Growling, I drop the spell on both of us so abruptly, we crash to the ground in a heap.

"Why'd you stop?"

It's an accusation, not a question. *She wanted you.* Make sure she's not gonna regret this.

"Su-chan..." I pull her close as the overwhelming scents fade and my clothes scratch my tingling skin. "'Cause I'm pretty sure you'd end up pregnant. That's not something we should rush into."

Then she curls up, covering her face. "I've been so jealous of the closeness you have with your fox family, while I'm stuck as a freak. I thought you wanted it, too."

Aww shit. Try to be a guy who thinks about the girl's side, and I still get it wrong.

Running a hand through her hair, I snuggle into her unyielding form. "I won't ever take you at the cost of ensuring you have a choice—especially when the result would be long-term consequences. It doesn't matter if I want you more than I've ever wanted anyone before. Understand?"

Slowly, her muscles thaw. "It's that important to you?"

Letting my head sink to her shoulder, I nod. "Yes."

"Right here, as we are. Nothing between us."

My lips lock onto hers as I cast a privacy silencing and camouflage spell to shield us from the rest of the world. *We need this.*

Then she whispers, "Warmth," and the cold flees as she tugs at my clothes. A carpet of moss forms and softens the ground underneath us.

Soaking in the feel of her skin, I give her all of myself—nothing held back. Together, we respond quicker than ever before. Her moans and hands pulling my hips to hers harder and faster undo me. Even after pleasing her, I just want to soak her all in, to never let this moment end.

Afterward, the sun descends toward the horizon as we lay there reveling in our reconnection.

"That was my first time without a condom," I mention as I nibble her ear.

"Really?"

"Yeah. Best sex ever."

She curls up and pulls my arm tighter around her. "Best so far for me, too. Not that I have much experience."

"You're a natural." Having her close stirs me again. Then her laughter catches me off guard and her touch washes away all other thoughts. I can't separate my choice from my desire as her mate. Not that I'd want to. "Do you know the power you have over me?" I ask.

Her answer? She bends me to her will a second time, and I couldn't be happier.

The sun kisses its mountain ridge lover when we emerge from the privacy spell.

"I promised I'd show you what I can see in that little tree."

Oh. All I remembered was us and amazing sex.

Laying her hand over mine, she whispers a word of kotodama. My mind swims for a moment with a vibrant blue phosphorescence, until I'm seeing myself blink in surprise and the light of dusk warmly tints my face.

Creepy.

Then Su-chan's gaze flicks to my chest, where I see the ever-so-faint fox shape. We hid our magic. She shouldn't be able to see that, should she? I can't see hers.

Next, her focus turns to the tree. But it's not just the bark. There's a tiny translucent creature grasping a thin branch. The pulsing light at its center twitches, and the leaves that make up its large ears wrap around itself as if I'd seen it naked.

"This is a kodama," Su-chan announces.

"Whoa. I just thought they were trees."

She giggles, then whispers reverently, "Now that I have the dragon magic, I see every single soul if I focus on it. Put your hand to the bark so the tree can know you."

What do I say? My "Hello. Nice to meet you," seems lame.

In response, the spirit unwraps giving a shy, polite bow.

"I met this sweet little tree when I got lost the first time I walked to Sekiguchi-sensei's without him, and now I try to visit each time, even if I have to portal here."

"That's why you've been burning through talismans?"

She giggles. "Yeah. That spell is so hard for me." Patting the tree again, she tugs my hand and bids the kodama farewell. "See you later, little one."

11

GRAVITY

THE NEXT MORNING, MY phone buzzes with a message from Satou while I scarf down a bowl of rice with a fresh raw egg for breakfast at the warmth of the central hearth. 'We need to talk about the desecrated graves.'

Before I left for Kyoto, he mentioned that someone was taking ashes from cemeteries and had tried to do so with the remains of Hiro, my big brother from the yakuza.

Aunt Hisako joins me, saying in between bites, "Tell my nephew we can meet at his house in an hour."

"Is this because you don't trust the Paranormal Division over Shion's disappearance?" I ask.

She spits, "Chief Arai." Then her face contorts into a deep scowl, the kind that was reserved for me when I first met her. *She'd run over his toes with a grocery cart, too. If the ghost had any…*

"He refused to help investigate because it was a cold case. The hypocrite got to investigate the mystery of his own death. Not everyone gets that. My predecessor, Aya-san, pestered Arai about a Guardian's death, and even got kicked out of his office. The tanuki could annoy the heck out of just about anyone. But Aya-san curbed his tongue and was respectful when he did League work."

This meeting is another thing that my girlfriend isn't a part of. Yet. "Should Su-chan come along?"

"Arai won't like her."

"What? Su-chan's the nicest person there is!" *The Chief gets another tick in the evil column.*

She chuckles, "Oh, Tatsuya. Look at you, so protective of her. He's on your blacklist now, isn't he?"

My eyes dart to the tatami and my hand runs through my hair.

"It's a good thing in a mate. Just know it makes you predictable," she says.

"Understood."

"In time, we'll bring her in on League things. She just doesn't have a Guardian sponsor yet. I can only back one candidate at a time. Besides, she might like the chance to catch up with her family."

Why wouldn't Chief Arai help Aya?

I'm about to hurry off to wash my dishes and ask Su-chan if she wants to tag along when Great Aunt Asako peeks around the corner. "Can you two help with dinner prep?"

But Aunt Hisako's head dips. "Sorry, Mother. Business in Nonogawa."

"Do you need help to prepare anything? A ki boost?"

My aunt Hisako's eyes brighten. "Thank you. I could use a ki boost before we go. Tatsuya and I-"

Just then, Taka bounds in with Yuri and Jiro on his heels. "Where are you going, Hisako-san?"

"To visit one of my nephews and a few others for work. I'll be back soon."

Yuri's tail wags and she blurts, "Can we come?"

"I wish you could. One man I'm meeting, I don't trust him. So my parents will watch over you until I am back."

Pitifully, the kits' ears droop.

"I'll see if I can bring you something."

That brings a swish back to their tails, and a relieved smile to Jiro's face.

So Great Aunt Asako gives her daughter a ki boost, takes my dishes, and shoos everyone else off to the kitchen to help make homemade udon noodles.

Jiro does a fist pump as he walks in and the kit twins leap in the air. "I've never gotten to make them," Jiro says. "They're my favorite noodles!"

Su-chan isn't anywhere in the house. She better be here after the dragon kidnapping fiasco. *Or I'll have choice words for Shion.*

Finally, I find her in the shed, where she and Sekiguchi have set up a potions production lab. She's elbow deep in some funky, rotten smelling goo that makes my eyes water. At least she has a magical barrier to protect her from it.

But Chou peeks over her shoulder. The black blob pet leans precariously over the simmering pot, stretching hard to reach it.

"No! Chou!" Su-chan shouts too late.

Sploosh, blerp! And Chou falls into the viscous liquid, causing waves of the disgusting stuff to cascade over the pot's edge.

Su-chan growls and fishes the blob out of the goop. "Need anything, Ta-kun?"

We're back to Ta-kun. Good. I have to bite the inside of my cheek to keep from laughing. No way am I gonna incur her wrath right now. "I'm going to Nonogawa for a few hours with Aunt Hisako. Wanna come?"

So Sekiguchi shoos her out. "Go. Things may turn troublesome again before this is all over. See them while you can. I'll clean up here."

She beams, rushing off to wash off the awful, stringy goop. Her smile warms me inside. *Her old cheerful self.*

While we wait for Su-chan, Aunt Hisako and I compare notes to ensure we don't have any info gaps. She scribbles in a ragtag flip notebook using a pen that's about to run out of ink.

She says, "Arai will dig into anything he doesn't deem fully explained. I don't want him asking any more than necessary. Kazuo, on the other hand, he should know everything. We've got half an hour before the meeting."

"I've kept him up to date, as best I could," I say as Su-chan slips on a jacket, texts her family, and joins us.

Next, Aunt Hisako switches to human form. Satou always seems more comfortable with her old lady guise, since it's what he grew up with. "I have a few things to firm up with him. Let's head over early."

In the end, I'm the one to set up a portal in a less recognizable location away from the den, just in case Arai is there, and the three of us stride through and bow.

Satou peeks at his watch. "You're early. It's not that you missed me. So what's going on?"

"Sorry for interrupting your down time," I say.

My aunt waves him off. "Be careful around Chief Arai. He was the one who denied the previous Guardian of Nonogawa access to the Paranormal Division's records. He shut down all mention of it."

"Aunt," Satou's lips purse as he asks, "Are you able to tell me why?"

"My predecessor suspected involvement, but he wasn't able to prove it. Rumors say he prevented Guardian involvement in Kyuunan, though I'm not aware of how. I was informed Arai-san was stationed there before he was promoted to Chief."

"Shit. He's highly respected in the department, even if he is a jerk." Satou hisses through his teeth. "Thank you for the heads up."

Then Su-chan pokes me. "Ta-kun, should I stay? Or should I call Mom and Dad for a ride?"

With a raised eyebrow, Satou asks, "Why would you need to stay? Enjoy your family. I'm sure they miss you."

Aunt Hisako says, "See your family today. We'll bring you in on things when you have a sponsor."

"Sponsor?" Satou queries as he steeples his fingers.

"She and Tatsuya will be the pair that replaces me." She shrugs and ensconces herself on a cushion.

How can Aunt Hisako be so sure about it? Everything I've seen has said otherwise.

In the meantime, I can help my girlfriend. "Su-chan, I'll make a portal for you. Then you don't have to wait for them." She allows me to pull her out of sight for a quick kiss.

"The portal was just an excuse?" Her eyes sparkle as she taps my nose.

So I tuck a stray wisp of hair behind her ear as I shake my head. "It's the safest mode of travel right now. Knowing your independence, you'd start hiking to meet them and leave yourself vulnerable. It's my privilege to watch out for the most amazing woman in the world."

It nets me another smooch that should be enough to carry me through the meeting.

Ten minutes later, Officer Takahashi carries a small box and Chief Arai's ghostly pale form trails behind him. So, I set out cushions for them at the low table as Aunt Hisako prepares tea.

Then Takahashi places the box in front of an empty cushion, and Arai settles there.

An urn makes Arai portable? *Interesting.*

The spirit's hands hovering up in front of him like discolored folded puppy paws and floating above his cushion give me the heebie-jeebies, worse than when I met him via tele-meeting.

After everyone enjoys the warm tea, Satou opens his briefcase to toss a few photos in front of Aunt Hisako and me. "Do you recognize the names on these gravestones?"

All of a sudden, my aunt's hand covers her mouth, and she whispers. "Yes. These were Yuki's students and some of the dead at the Battle of Toba Fushimi."

The remaining names I know only too well and a nod is all I manage. My hand runs over the kanji that spell Kentarou and my fist clenches, wrinkling the photo. My little brother from the Hiragi Clan.

Then swiping through the others reveals every one of my brethren that died in that fateful clan clash. Grave markers lay toppled and cracked. It takes extreme effort to control my breathing as my blood boils. *They should be at peace!*

"Umeji, if you would refrain from wrecking the evidence photos..." Officer Takahashi's voice is emotionless, but that warning style harkens back to my mob days.

"Yes, sir," I mumble as my shaking hands spread the pictures as flat as possible.

"Show them the surveillance footage." Arai waves for things to move along.

Complying, Satou sets his iPad on a stand. "Knowing that someone had attempted to do this to Otsuka Hiro, we set up cameras near key Hiragi clan graves." He runs through the video. "At 11:47 on the 13th, the reconnaissance team reported a paranormal incident."

A muscled arm dragging a club comes into view on the black and white video. It bashes the drawer open, destroying the entire grave, and dumps the contents of each pot into a separate bag.

Satou continues, "As you can see, the perpetrator either can't verify which ashes are of the yakuza or just doesn't care."

I want to scream. Though digging my fingernails into my palms centers my thoughts. "Why would they do something like this?"

"Let me verify." Aunt Hisako summons a book out of thin air, flipping through the pages. "The remains can help identify a soul that hasn't passed on."

After a moment of everyone's gaping at the wondrous magic, Arai says, "Correct. Ash and their name might be enough for a strong mage to bind them as servants."

That makes me cringe. "Like shikigami paper puppets?"

Aunt Hisako nods. "But they'll keep their original form."

Then Takahashi leans in to add, "Mobsters and gang members have been reported missing in Tokyo and Kyoto. I wouldn't have considered it significant, except the timing and the sheer number of reports."

"How many?" Satou sucks in a hissing breath.

"Hundreds. Though, as reports keep pouring in, it may end up much higher than that."

Bile rises in my throat as I offer, "Ibaraki may have learned how to turn them into oni like Date Sari did."

"Underground reports say there was an ugly woman yokai selling weapons after a series of thefts. She demanded some sort of sample, like DNA or something, for an incredible price on pistols and Uzis. Are those the missing riff raff?" Arai asks.

Next, Takahashi shoves another photo in front of Aunt Hisako and me. "That's not all. Kyoto police say Ibaraki left a declaration at Rajoumon, the old marker for the famous oni-haunted gate here in Kyoto."

'To the kitsune and any who shelter such vermin: As the Queen of the Oni, I declare war on you for betrayal and enslavement of my kind. Your end is nigh.

To the holder of the witch's magic: I know who and what you are. You deprived me of the reward I worked toward for centuries.

So I shall take from you, and all involved, what you took from me.'

The message makes me shudder and Aunt Hisako furrows her brows. "Tatsuya, she'll target you. And a seething horde of yakuza ghosts, Samurai spirits, and an army of angry oni all chained to an ambitious, revengeful leader is a recipe for disaster."

To keep her composure, she takes a few deep breaths before saying, "The League needs to know this if they don't already. Thank you for bringing this to my attention. Is there any other news?"

"The PSIA will continue our sentry duty, as always," Arai says.

But a glance at my aunt nets her stony expression. Goosebumps form on my skin. *Did the temperature in the room just drop?*

"Nakamura-san, you and Umeji-san went north to Kyuunan, correct?" Takahashi asks.

"Yes." Her word comes out in a flat neutral.

"Well, the police department says strange things have been happening, but something cut the connection before they could say what it was. I wish I could give you more details."

"Thank you for sharing Officer Takahashi." Aunt Hisako's gaze flicks to Arai, who stills. "Was the PSIA aware?"

Shifting, Arai clears his throat. "Yes, but that is another case. Details are not available for this meeting. Did you have anything to add?"

My aunt only shakes her head.

"Then I believe that confirming a link to the disappearances concludes this meeting. Rest assured, the PSIA is increasing our surveillance and will do all we can to protect kitsune-kind."

Better than they guarded Hiro? His words leave a sour taste in my mouth.

As the others leave, Satou pulls our aunt aside. "How are you doing? Have you arranged the cure yet? If it's a matter of money, I can pay for it. Believe me."

But her shoulders slump. "I will not be healed, Nephew. The cost is in magical ability, which has to be developed. Though thank you for your generous offer."

"Why not?" he parries.

"It would leave someone unable to defend themselves. Better me than anyone else."

He rubs his face. Sheer frustration embeds itself in his features. "Is there any-thing I can do to help?"

"Just assist the Ohno family and Aya-sensei as they watch over Nonogawa until a replacement Guardian arrives. Those who know Tatsuya and me may be targets."

Pacing, Satou says, "Aya-sensei called from the hospital today. He was elbow deep in surgeries. I can't say he's the best choice for watching over Nonogawa."

"He has a network to call on for backups. The troublesome tanuki has more friends here than he can count."

That stops Satou in his tracks and his head juts back. "Aya—the doctor—he's a tanuki?"

"And a drunkard. And he sent me a large cactus that had a 'Sit on This' sign." She clasps her hands, sheepishly. "I suspect it was because I sent him a but-tocks-shaped topiary last year. Though that's a story for another day."

After Satou shuts his gaping mouth, he asks, "Do I even want to know?"

I have to cover my mouth and turn away to choke back my laughter.

Instead, Satou barrels past the tempting tale. "You trust him?"

"Yes. Just because we have some bad blood over a stupid issue doesn't mean he's not a capable defender." She hands Satou a slip of paper with a scribbled address. "Change of topic. If things go bad in Kyoto, I'll be sending two kits to you for temporary placement with another kitsune family."

That's when footsteps and claws scrape the floor behind us, and we hear sniffles and whimpering. My aunt's eyes widen as she whips around. "Taka-kun? Yuri-chan?"

The pair of kits, with fluffed tails as big as daikon radishes, slink into the main room from behind the stairs. Their heads and tails lower.

Then a portal forms behind them. Great Uncle Nobu shouts, scooping them up by the scruff of the neck. "There you two rascals are! We've been searching all over! Why did you leave Jiro-kun?" Quickly, he bobs a greeting. "Sorry for the interruption. Last trace of them ended at the same wall Hisako-chan portaled through."

Taka wriggles and yips, "Hisako-san's gonna send us away!"

Yuri howls.

So Great uncle Nobu's voice softens as he tucks the twins under his arms, "We want you to stay and would only send you to Satou-san if there was no other choice."

Aunt Hisako says, "Come here, my mischief makers."

When Great Uncle Nobu puts them down, Aunt Hisako gestures to the one person the kits don't know. "Little ones, this is my nephew, Satou Kazuo. And these are Watabe Yuri-chan and Taka-kun. Soujou-bou's servants brought them to us after the tykes were orphaned."

Satou holds out a hand to let them sniff. "So you'll raise them?"

"Yes." Aunt Hisako says and kneels beside the kits.

Yuri just sniffs, then ducks behind my aunt, but Taka butts his head into my former boss's hand.

"Brave lad." Satou scratches him behind the ear. "I've never met a kit before."

"You know what we are? But you're a human!"

Conspiratorially, Satou nods and cups a hand to his mouth as if about to reveal a secret. "Want to know the funny part?"

The girl pokes out from behind my aunt and ears perk on both the kits.

"My job is to contact the kitsune, so we at the PSIA Paranormal division can help. Yet, I didn't know my aunt and her family were kitsune until a month ago. One of the slyest foxes will raise and love you. Listen well to her."

It causes the kits to giggle and their back feet thump the floor.

Then Aunt Hisako says, "One more thing, Kazuo. I cannot return to Nonogawa for the long term. I have property in Kyoto that I will move to when things settle down."

That's my cue to herd the young foxes elsewhere. Great Uncle Nobu helps. Shifting into fox form, I offer, "Should we head outside to play?"

As we go, my aunt's voice echoes on the stone floor and carries down the hall. "My human children are not interested in my old home, because they don't want to deal with the taxes. Will you hire a lawyer for me since I can't be in human form for very long these days?"

"Aunt, I don't need nor want your property," Satou chides.

"I'm aware. Though, I want to discuss a simple sale..." Then her voice trails off.

"Will do."

Not returning to Nonogawa? And gonna sell that beautiful old house? My heart sinks. Nothing will be the same when Su-chan and I return.

What if Su-chan doesn't wanna live in Nonogawa again? When we came to Kyoto, she said she couldn't continue in Nonogawa with her business. *Shit.* More uncomfortable conversations to have.

As if reading my mind, Nobu says, "It'll be alright, Tatsuya."

"Hey Umeji-san, you said you were going to play!" Yuri nips at my tail.

The next day, Aunt Hisako pulls out one of the special red-edged ofuda. "Come with me again. The council should get to know you better. I'm choosing the time as best I can to give the worst of the sticks in the mud heartburn."

Uh-oh. The back of my neck prickles, but I nod and follow her through to Soujou-bou's cavernous meeting room, and the tang of ancient cypress wood washes over me as we give our greetings. *Is it bigger on the inside than the outside?*

Emitting a ruffled snuffle, Mishima—the baku seated with the League's leader—glares.

"Never mind Mishima-kun. He needs to remember the priority open-door policy for all our members. So, Nakamura-san, Umeji-kun. What brings you two here today?" Soujou-bou says as he gestures to cushions.

On cue, we share the news from the meeting with Satou, Arai, and Takahashi.

The baku just sneers. "Humans are behind the curve, as always. I was suggesting a plan for our attack on Ibaraki's forces in Kyuunan. The Oni Queen learned many of the fox witch's tricks while she was a slave, long-distance portals and puppeteering of other beings included."

"Mishima-san, do you remember when I turned down the appointment to the envoys? It was, in part, because I don't view humans as lower than us." My aunt's words turn steely and silence looms like a specter.

Then Soujou-bou's harrumph cuts the stalemate. "Save your energy. We need to focus on the largest threat we have seen in centuries, and it affects an entire species of yokai. The rest of the council and the envoys should arrive any moment now."

Gazing at me, his mouth turns down, and silence hangs for a few heartbeats.

My palms sweat.

Soujou-bou says, "Umeji-kun. I formed the council and gave them powers so that all of Japan would have input in the League of Guardians and not rely on a single head. That way, if the leader falls the League does not. Today is one of the few times I have regrets about the decision."

Not good. My stomach twists. *So they're saying no to 'the yakuza.'*

Next, Soujou-bou's words soften. They don't sound like my boisterous teacher. "Until you came into possession of the sword, it had been lost since World War II. A member of the League commissioned it before the organization existed. Those who held it were always members.

"The council requests you return Honjou Masamune to us. The blade's physical whereabouts remain unknown. But unsheathing the magical encasement, summons the spirit of the blade from its resting place. Usually, museums house these historic weapons for safety reasons. We hope to track down the actual blade. Rumors say it's in a private collection."

A ton of bricks crashes down. *They wanna take Hiro's sword.* The one thing I have from him. *How am I gonna protect my family and kitsune-kind?*

"Soujou-sama..." My aunt's voice rings in the chamber, clearing the darkness hanging over us all. "What if he places himself under the command of the League? There's precedence for one of your students doing that."

"True." Soujou-bou lets out a long breath. "But-"

Instantly, Mishima pounces. "That sword is one of the most powerful katana in existence and there are guardians without the enchanted weapons they need!"

Soujou-bou parries, "Such as yourself, Mishima-kun?"

Shrinking, the baku quiets.

"I wish to spare you the public handover, Umeji-kun." Soujou-bou's eyes go to his hands, folded in his lap. "The rest of the Council will arrive any second. Please, return Honjou Masamune to us. Perhaps, if you become a Guardian, we can entrust the sword to you."

The sizzle of portals opening on the other side of the heavy door spurs me to action. With gritted teeth and purposeful steps toward my teacher, I pull Honjou Masamune from my cargo pocket. The sword bucks in my hands and vibrates so violently I almost drop it. But I place it in front of my teacher, letting the weapon rattle in its scabbard.

"Honjou Masamune, your protest is noted," Soujou-bou whispers before the council pours in.

The yuki onna from the last meeting approaches. "So, Yakuza, you surrendered it? There was a bet you wouldn't. I guess I owe Shunosuke-san a hundred thousand yen." Her mock disappointment causes my teeth to grind, but I wipe the emotion from my face.

When the baku stretches his trunk over to take it, I growl. "I surrender it ONLY to Soujou-sensei."

As if it understood me, the sword lifts on its own and slaps the extended snout. Mishima's eyes water as he rubs the spot on his trunk.

Soujou-bou leaves the sword to rattle like it's cussing everyone out. He says, "Umeji-kun, if you will remain my student, place yourself under the League's direction. It will allow you to fight at our side in times of need. But one of us must request your assistance."

"I mean no disrespect, Leader. But we did not approve his Guardian apprenticeship. Umeji's not even yokai. What did Inari-sama see in him?" The snow maiden bristles.

Soujou-bou shrugs. "He is both yokai and human. A most unusual case, I admit. The only thing I see tainting us at this point is prejudice."

So They're playing politics over me? *What a load of bullshit.*

And I am yokai.

After a moment, Soujou-bou crosses his arms, leaning back and narrowing his eyes as he continues, "I know you did not approve of him. This one has had to work harder to prove his loyalty and obedience than any of you. Do not forget. Inari Okami, in a rare intervention, gave his blessing for Umeji-kun to be trained. There is more to the young man than you can see."

Putting my shoulders back, I lower my eyes. Such praise is unheard of from a teacher. Soujou-bou's doing this on purpose. *To what end?*

But the baku and yuki onna purse their lips. They won't speak against Soujou-bou, in public at least.

First Arai, and now these two.

When my aunt and I return to the den, the numbness creeps in. *Never shoulda gotten my hopes up.*

She seethes, venting about the leadership's gutless octopi. That brings the kits in with lowered tails. "We're sorry, Hisako-san! Whatever we did, we won't do it again!"

Aunt Hisako blows out a breath. "It's not you, sweet ones. Did you get a snack?"

It makes their tails wag and warms me inside a little again.

"Alright, I'll cut some apples into bunny shapes for you," Aunt Hisako offers.

"Yay!" Little claws scramble for purchase on the stone floor as the pair races for the kitchen.

Shaking her head at their innocence, she chuckles. But my aunt's mood darkens again. "Tatsuya, you are being used. The council will not say it outright, but it couldn't be more obvious. As tempted as I am to resign, Soujou-sama is right—I need to stay on, at least for now."

After hours of training that started at sunrise, I'm washing up when there's a knock on the door to the bath. Steam rolls off me after the relaxing soak. *Maybe the West is on to something with washing in the mornings.* Though I miss the evening's relaxation. There's just not time for everyone in the two clans at night.

"Ta-kun?" My girlfriend's voice is hesitant.

"Come in. What do you need?"

When she closes the door, her brows furrow. Her gaze doesn't even linger over my naked form like it often does as I dry off. *What'd I do this time?*

"A baku brought this. He had a symbol like your aunt did when she showed her seal." She sets the envelope with my name on a dry counter spot.

"Did he say anything?"

"Just that it was for you, and you only."

"Then why do you look upset?"

Slowly, she blows out a breath and unclenches her fists.

He better not've been a jerk!

"He was rude. Didn't even bow, and his speech was so plain and curt," she says.

"Mishima, you little shit!" A sempai, one above you in seniority, should act honorably, not treat their underlings like garbage. Though, sometimes I saw guys doing worse to their little brothers in the yakuza. Ensuring my hands are dry, I snatch the paper off the counter and open it.

Your presence is required at the guest house at 11 AM.
The League Council

My hand crumples the paper. *Why isn't Soujou-bou's signature stamp on it? And what the hell do they want?* "I gotta get ready, Su-chan."

Cautiously, she takes the paper from my hand and smooths it out to read. "That's fifteen minutes from now. He can't be serious."

They set it up, so it's impossible to be early, let alone on time. "Oh, he is. Can you grab my coat and my..." *sword.* I don't have Honjou Masamune anymore.

They're stripping me down. *Breathe.* "My phone. Oh, and ask Aunt Hisako if I can borrow one of her special portal ofuda. I'm not allowed to teleport there. But one of those should get me in."

Her hand goes to my cheek. "I'll come with you."

Don't drag her into this trap. I shake my head but draw her up into a kiss that leaves us both a little breathless. "Thank you, anyway."

Rushing to get ready still takes me longer than I want. I'll have to show up with a five-o'clock shadow.

Aunt Hisako's jaw shoves forward as she hands over one of the ofuda with red characters. "I shouldn't do this. But they've set it up so you can't make it on time. Something stinks."

"Tell me about it." I say as I bow my thanks. "I won't make a habit of asking for them."

With haste, I step through the portal into Soujou-bou's empty hall in my sock feet and zip off to the guest house. I throw one shoe on and use magic to enhance a leap. Then I speed boost from the porch as I throw the other shoe on midair, only to wobble ungracefully upon impact. At least I don't fall on my face. The wet strands of my chin length hair soak my shirt. *Just great.* I look like an over eager lackey.

The yuki onna greets me with a pasted on neutral expression, though she watched me book it over to avoid being later than the polite five minutes early. *Not as late as she expected.*

Inside, the guest house isn't as ornate as Soujou-bou's audience chamber. Still amazing though, with the nature scenes painted on the sliding wall panels, and ornate carvings above those and in the ceiling.

Kneeling in front of a pair of the League's best, my stomach ties itself in knots. Their stares fall cold, causing warning prickles on my skin.

Of course Soujou-bou isn't here. So, I lift my gaze and roll back my shoulders. *Face the hazing like a man.*

The baku shuffles over, his lion like paws sliding across the tatami with effortless silence. He gets into my personal space. "What could you possibly offer the League? It may be hard to find recruits, but a yakuza? And one that isn't humble enough to lower his gaze in the presence of his seniors?"

"Why isn't Soujou-bou here?"

"You gonna cry to him because we don't want you?"

Don't sink to his level. "What do you want?"

Then the yuki onna calls Mishima back before she says, "We require proof of your desire to join and the dedication you'll have to the League. Our glorious leader, Soujou-bou, is too fond of you to have good judgment for this conversation."

My eyes narrow. That's all I'll let them see. Bile burns my throat, though I'm as calm as a sea of glass on the outside. Innocently, I ask for clarification, "Sempai?"

But Mishima crosses his arms and leans back. "We need to know you can handle tasks in a professional manner. So you'll do our dirty work. Show us how much you want to be a Guardian."

"Of course." This is gonna be ugly.

"Soujou-sama hasn't been forthcoming in his plans to deal with Ibaraki. We need you to report anything you hear."

Be a spy against my teacher? No way. I'd lose the slim chance I have to be Guardian and maybe my life. After meeting the gaze of each, I get up and head for the door.

"We haven't dismissed you, yakuza," Mishima snarls.

Disgusted, I give only a passing glance. "In the mob, I learned loyalty to the boss was the most important thing. You've just shown your true colors."

"So you're going to run to Soujou-bou like a pathetic tattletale?"

My head shakes. "A good leader will know the strengths and weaknesses of each member. He's seen my intentions; I'm sure he sees yours, too." I don't bother bowing to them as I reach for the door.

"What do you mean?" Mishima asks.

"He's King of the Tengu and Head of the League. He earned those titles." Sliding the shoji door open, I step into the hall and stiffen to attention.

In front of me stands Soujou-bou himself, with his feather fan outstretched. I bend in reverence, but every muscle inside shakes. *He overheard.*

"This test is concluded," his voice booms. "Umeji-kun, go tell the cooks you'll be staying for lunch and meditate until I arrive. I need a moment with these two."

I bow and leave the building.

Unless every bit of that meeting was a test, there's a traitor in the ranks. My Oyabun—the yakuza boss, along with almost all the members of the Hiragi clan, died because someone ignored signs like that. And the hairs standing on the back of my neck say something's wrong.

Protect Soujou-bou. *Don't be the weak link.* So I use a spell and sneak over to the side.

Mishima's whining carries outside, "Soujou-sama, I'm sorry. I didn't..."

"He has betrayed you, League Leader. I have proof," the snow maiden says.

That's when I book it to the kitchen as ordered. I shouldn't have doubted my teacher's ability. But I also didn't want him facing a two on one situation with powerful yokai.

The cook directs me to help serve the meal and have it ready for the master of the house in his quarters. Then I wait in the seat for the lowest of rank. Though, meditating is nigh impossible.

Of course, my stomach growls because I didn't get breakfast. The tempura and fish make my mouth water. Not even the amazing details of the room's decor distract me from the food. *Please hurry, Sensei!*

Finally, Soujou-bou's voice booms from outside. "Reo-san, did Umeji-kun come to you as I asked?"

"Yes, Soujou-sama."

Upon his entry, I bow. Soujou-bou takes his time removing his shoes, watching me all the while. "How much did you hear?"

Caught. My bottom lip sucks in, but I bow again. *No sense dodging.* "Until Mishima-san apologized and the snow maid said she had proof. Sorry, Sensei. I had to ensure they wouldn't betray you. My yakuza leader and clan all died because someone didn't report the signs."

"So you don't know what else happened?" He asks as he sits on a cushion.

I'm curious. "Not my business, Sensei."

One of his hands rubs a black spot on the palm, where his seal is. *He had to use his mark today.*

"Then let us eat." His hands clap together. "Itadakimasu."

Something went down, but I don't dare ask. So, I too say thanks for the meal and dig into my food.

"Umeji-kun, the League is preparing to act. I will also speak with Nakamura-san about her predicament. Am I correct it is possible for her to be healed?"

"Uhm." My chopsticks stop halfway to my mouth, and I set them down on the rest. Aunt Hisako won't like me tattling on her. But, if what Soujou-bou means is that they're going to war, he's got to know all the variables. "Yes, Sensei."

"You were hesitant to answer and did not give details. That means she won't like hearing what I have to say. She's stubborn as a mule. But it helps to know her reaction. Now, regarding your appointment as Guardian..."

Suddenly, I can't breathe. *Don't look up.* Don't show how much you need this break.

"Yes, there is resistance because of your background. But also, considering the position will take so much of your human life and you don't wish to shed blood again, I would like you to see what we deal with. Everything that happens of late is unprecedented. Thus having a trainee with us will just be one more of those things. Can I count on you?"

"Always, Sensei." *So, my rejection isn't a done deal?*

12

PRICE PAID

MOST EVERYONE HUDDLES AROUND the sunken hearth and the kotatsu heating table during the chilly afternoon. The rise in humidity makes the temperature seem colder than it is.

Returning from a meeting with Soujou-bou, Aunt Hisako storms through the living area. Everyone stares. The kits hide behind Hoji and Su-chan. When Aunt Hisako slams the door to her room, my chest tightens.

It's my fault.

Every crash causes us to flinch.

Hoji pokes me as he whispers. "Do you know what has her in such a huff?"

"Maybe." My head ducks and I motion for him to follow.

Outside in the frosty air, I toss up a privacy spell. His head tilts. But he waits for me to speak. My hands shove into my pockets as I force the words out.

"I got her in trouble yesterday when Soujou-bou asked if it was possible for her to be healed. He needs her to be at full capacity for her duties. So, I said, 'Yes'."

With tails drooping, he paces. His words come out rough, almost harsh. "I think there's more at play."

"How so?"

"I overheard her parents urging her to consider a kitsune husband again. They mentioned me as a possibility." He stops and kicks at the grass and the scent reminds me of gardens and soccer fields in Tokyo.

Then a chill breeze runs right through my shirt. *Should've grabbed a jacket.*

"Why can't they leave us alone?" he huffs.

"You're afraid they'll ruin your chance."

"She's so independent. But she's still mourning, too. Their timing was terrible."

He sits to stare out over Kyoto as the pause builds. But not uncomfortably so. "I'm growing fond of the twins. Never thought about what it would be like to be a dad before. You know the pressure on my kind to reproduce. I kept shoving it from my mind because I thought I had time."

Sure, Hoji's been helping with the kits a lot. "And you don't want to be kept out of their lives?"

"Shit, I don't know." This time, his paw's scuff sends a clod of dirt flying. "Maybe?"

That's when the door to the den opens. Aunt Hisako sprints out in her silver fox form up the hill and Great Uncle Nobu hollers after her, "Hisako!"

An eerie high-pitched shriek echoes in the hills. Hoji stiffens as his claws dig into the dirt.

So, I shove him. "Let's go! What are you waiting for?"

"You know why. She wants to be alone."

Baka. I shrug and transform into my red fox form. "Don't be an idiot. She's being forced to do something. We gotta go after her."

He growls with hackles raised. "It's my price to pay."

As I make for the path she followed, he scrambles after us. He may be twice as old as me, but I could swear he's still a pup some days—so easy to predict.

The twins scamper behind, shouting because they can't keep up. "Where are you all going? Are you coming back?"

Lately, they ask that of everyone. *Poor things.* We'll return soon. *I hope.*

When we catch up to her, Hoji creates a portal right in front of her to the top of Mt. Inari, where the highest building for the Fushimi Shrine is. Inari Okami is waiting, with a sour face and his arms crossed. He calls out, "Nakamura Hisako, stop this foolishness!"

Oh man, I don't wanna be in my aunt's shoes right now, in trouble with a god.

Immediately, Aunt Hisako skitters to a halt, mid-dodge of the portal. Backing up, she slinks through with her tails down. Hoji reverently bows and follows to the other side.

As I'm about to do the same, Inari-sama holds up a hand. "Not you Umeji-kun." With that, the portal snaps shut.

About an hour later, a portal opens from a path with a plethora of torii gates to reveal Hoji in human form carrying the curled-up silver kitsune form of my aunt.

He stumbles as he steps through. Dark circles under his eyes highlight the hollowness in his cheeks and weakly, he states, "She's healed."

He's gonna fall over. So I rush over to help.

Aunt Hisako's ears are flat, and her tail fluffed. The press of foxes surrounding them swamp the pair with questions.

"I didn't agree to you paying the price," she mutters.

He says through gritted teeth as he sways, "And you know why I did. Besides, Inari-sama called you on your reluctance. Were you going to keep arguing with him?"

That makes Aunt Hisako's lips purse.

So, Great Uncle Nobu relieves Hoji of his burden, while I help him to a seat. Nobu asks, "Where do you both want to rest? Here in the main room?"

Aunt Hisako motions toward her quarters. Her mother and sisters follow.

"Anywhere," Hoji pants.

When he grabs a cushion, Nobu asks, "So what did you have to pay, Hoji-san?"

At the same time, animated voices come from Aunt Hisako's room. But I can't make out the words.

"My son, it's significant, isn't it?" Grandma Miwa doesn't hide her concerned sniffing.

"That's between Hisako-san and myself," he mutters as he tucks his legs up to his chest to rest his head. "I'm exhausted. Think I'll lay down."

Yuri, who trots in from playing with her brother and Jiro, nuzzles Hoji's hand. Out of the corner of my eye, I see the ladies return. Aunt Hisako pokes her nose around the corner.

"Yes?" Pulling the fox kit up to his lap, he boops her nose.

The kit blurts in typical childish style, "Will you be our daddy, since we don't have one anymore?"

Then Hoji's mouth turns up. "I hope to be in your lives. Perhaps something like that."

"Are you gonna marry Hisako-san?"

At the question, every kitsune ear perks up.

"Che," Hoji says in dismissal.

Yuri's head droops as she asks, "Why not?"

He sighs, but he ruffles her ears. "We'll talk about it when you're a little older. Let me rest now."

Instead, Yuri zips back to her room. She and Taka drag a pillow and blanket, cover Hoji, and curl up next to him.

Hoji is the first to wake from the pile of nappers. So, I help him extricate himself from the kits.

"Thank you," he whispers as we head to the kitchen to see how we can help.

"Are you ok? What happened?"

Dismissively, he waves it off. "I'll be fine. My ki well is intact. And now Hisako-san's is, too."

"You sure? You looked wiped out." I grab his shoulder so he knows he can't change the topic.

"I'll be fine. Just won't have as much power."

"Thank you for helping Aunt Hisako."

His small, genuine smile gives the answer I seek. None of us could've stopped him from making the sacrifice.

While Hoji takes his turn cleaning up after dinner, Su-chan, Jiro and I watch the little ones. The adults discuss concern over the price paid.

Soon, Aunt Hisako skulks into the kitchen to help Hoji. We try not to overhear conversations in the den's tight quarters. But with eleven kitsune and humans, it's impossible.

My aunt's voice reverberates against the stone of the kitchen walls. "You still haven't changed back into fox form. Are you that ashamed of what you gave up?"

"You know better than that," he snaps.

In return, she harrumphs.

His tone drops to a growl. "Why is modern encryption easier to understand than a woman? If I change to fox form, they'll criticize you for a choice I made."

"I didn't ask you to."

"True. But I couldn't let you suffer with a broken tama nor let you face Inari-sama's ire. You're a damned Guardian, after all. And I'm sure someone ordered you to seek the healing you needed."

Suddenly, a dish clunks on the counter. Aunt Hisako says, "That was not public knowledge. So I'll ask you not to just openly speak of such things. And I'm not your mate. I could have found someone else."

"You wouldn't have let Yoshirou-san help, either. Besides, I won't pursue someone who obviously doesn't want me."

Damn lack of privacy. With a flick of my fingers, a blue glow covers the doorway, blocking out the conversation. "How about we put up soundproof barriers since we're all stuck here?"

Great Uncle Nobu blinks and shakes his head. "We should have done that right away. Kind of hard to think with the stress we've been under."

Su-chan mouths, "Thank you."

The next morning as she lounges on the porch, Aunt Hisako yawns and rests her head on her paws while I chop wood in the damp spring air. Plum trees in the yard give the hint of buds.

I ask, "How are you doing?"

Her shrug is non-committal. "My magic isn't leaking out of me. I am whole, despite the strangeness of someone else's energy inside my ki well. Beyond that? I don't know."

"What's bothering you?"

She looks away. "He's given up on me."

"Hoji? So why's it matter to you now?"

"I... I don't know. It was easier before he sacrificed so much."

She feels indebted. My axe lodges into the log. Lifting it then bringing it down on the stump, wedges the axe head farther down. A few more taps make the first piece a nice size for tonight's firewood. As I repeat the process, my aunt stares into the forest.

"When I watched him so patient and gentle with the kits, I know he needs to help raise them."

Another crack and split. "He'd like that."

"And he's become your friend. Probably talked you into helping him deal with me." Her tone turns thick and sullen, and her bottom lip sticks out.

"Yes, friend. But I also remember what it was like being on the wrong side of you. It sucked. You know I limped for two days after you ran over my foot with that cart."

Her unladylike guffaw makes me grin. She knows I wouldn't bring it up if it wasn't ironic. But she grows serious again. "I saw who you could be when you rescued me."

Crack. One more piece for the evening fire.

"Drop the smirk, Nephew. Yes, he rescued me, too. But this isn't the same."

"If you say so."

Aunt Hisako grumbles at her phone as the two families take turns in the evening bath. "Where is that photo of the twins?"

"Do you want help?" Hoji's deep voice is only loud enough for those of us close by to hear.

"No. But I'll take the help, anyway."

His face softens as she shoves the phone his way. Instead of taking it, he scoots behind her, reaching around and placing the device in her hands.

Su-chan, Jiro and I do our best to concentrate on practicing our electricity-based magic with Yuri and Taka so Hoji and Aunt Hisako can talk.

"Swipe until we can find the photos icon, like this." He demonstrates. "You do it."

So she repeats the action.

"Now tap this one. It's your photos."

"But what if I can't find it again?"

"You're a smart lady. Just because you haven't kept up with technology for several decades doesn't mean you can't learn it now."

Instead of answering, she pshaws him.

"Are you saying you're not up to the task?"

That earns him a glare.

"Alrighty. Try sending me a photo of them both so I can have a copy."

"With this symbol?" She points to the square with the arrow.

"Yep. You're getting it." He guides her through sharing phone to phone. "That wasn't so hard, was it?"

She shrugs and sheepishly says, "I guess not. It just feels so foreign."

"Hisako-san, you'll adjust. You helped several humans learn magic from scratch. You can do this."

Then she gazes at the floor. "You didn't have to help me. Thank you."

"Glad to. I want you to keep the pictures and memories of the twins. And to not be afraid of using technology."

"You're hoping I'll share?"

Nodding, he runs a hand through his hair. "I'll share the pictures and recordings I take, too. More importantly, I think kitsune-kind can secure our place as leaders regarding technology in the spirit realm."

Then he opens up something on his phone. "For too long, yokai relied on only magic. But being able to use and merge the two puts us at an advantage, and others will come to us for that knowledge. That's why I push so hard to get research grants like the one I'm working on at Jidai University."

She says, "Then I will learn anything you can teach me and be grateful. It's a brilliant move to put our dwindling race to the forefront—providing for our safety and security, too. I wouldn't have expected this when I first met you. Just because Yoshirou's death was hard on me, doesn't mean I shouldn't live in the present."

To give them privacy, I tilt my head toward Jiro's room. We get an eye roll from my aunt. But she and Hoji need this time to connect, no matter what they choose.

Aunt Hisako breaks the pause. "Hoji-san. Thank you for the truce. I'd like to be your friend, at least for the sake of the twins."

13

WAR

"Tatsuya," Aunt Hisako grips my elbow as I pass by. "The war council summoned me. Soujou-bou says to be ready."

"War?" I blink and whip around.

She nods and her nine tails hang low, instead of fanning out behind her. "Oni forces have been gathering around Kyuunan. It's divided the oni as a people. That's all I can say. Oh, and I've told my parents and let the kits know that I'll be gone."

"What about the Date clan?"

Then her head droops. "Will you tell them?" My moment's hesitation before I can agree makes her sigh. "I shouldn't avoid him. Hoji-san will want to ensure he has contact with the kits, in case the worst happens. I'll do it now."

She takes a few steps, halts, and raises a privacy shield. "Normally, League business isn't to be shared. But you should know, Mishima is no longer a Guardian. Soujou-sama said the traitor tried to recruit you."

I just stand there, slack mouthed. *They kicked him out? Holy shit.* My instincts were spot on. *How often does a member get ousted?*

She taps my forehead. "Tatsuya…"

So, I shake my head and blink.

"Thought I was going to have to thunk you on the noggin to get you to come back to earth. Anyway, it was a blow to Soujou-sama."

I say, "I bet. So, he trusts his members implicitly?"

"He lends us his power. That's a lot of trust."

"Where's Mishima now?"

"You didn't ask what happened to him. But I'll answer both questions. Soujou-sama stripped Mishima of his seal, then the coward baku fled via a portal before the Tengu King could summon the council. He's banned from stepping foot on Soujou-sama's land and the yokai court will put a price on his head. I do not know what punishment they will enact."

That's why Soujou-sensei was rubbing the spot on his hand.

"You need to watch your back. Soujou-sama and Hayashi-san were impressed with how you handled the situation. But you made Mishima an enemy."

It brings a nod from me. *Wait. Who?* "Hayashi-san is the snow maiden?"

"Yes."

"Could there be anyone working with Mishima? Could someone have controlled him?"

But, she waves a hand as if to dismiss the thought. "Every League member has protections against being puppeteered. So it's unlikely there are multiple traitors."

"You trust Hayashi-san?"

Her lips purse and the privacy shield drops. "Yes. Now, I must be going."

Thundering tromping announces Jiro and the kits as they shove a stack of papers toward Aunt Hisako. "Take these talismans with you!"

Oh, the beaming on their faces as she accepts them, complementing their handwriting and how it will enhance the spell. I've never seen Jiro so proud as the trio scurries away.

Then Great Uncle Nobu insists Aunt Hisako wears armor. "A silver nine-tailed fox will be a target."

"But they'll hear the rattle of those lacquered plates from a mile away. We don't have a lighter, modern version, do we? It's been well over a century since I fought in a war." Despite fussing, she changes into her young human form and stands ready with arms and legs spread.

He responds, "It's not that noisy, especially compared to other styles. Though I'll add a silencing spell. This armor protected me in every war I've fought in, so it will bring you luck. Modern armor doesn't intimidate like the old style does."

Great Uncle Nobu floats the heavy layers of the traditional gear toward her. The shin and thigh guard plates magically tie to her legs and waist. Then the vambraces slip on first the right arm and tie, then the left. She blows a lock of hair out of the way as the chest and back plate slide over one arm, tie themselves up and the shoulder armor attaches to those plates.

Next, a white sash winds several times around her waist and Great Uncle Nobu slips a wakizashi short sword into it as the fearsome faceplate covers his daughter's beautiful visage. He also adds the kabuto helmet and secures the ties as he tenderly meets her gaze.

In under a minute, she's geared up. All the historic videos I'd seen say it takes much longer. So it's not just Soujou-bou who can gear up quickly.

She retrieves her naginata and waves a hand to create a blue glow above her other palm, before tucking the polearm into some ethereal space. The light also disappears.

Whoa. My index finger raises. "Uhm. Aunt, how did you just do that? You did the same thing with your journals back at your house."

Her eyes crinkle and the hint of her mouth through the mask turns up. "It'd be a good thing for you to know. I can spare the time to give you the gist. Practice while I'm gone. Once you get it, share the spell with Su-chan, Hoji-san, and Jiro-kun.

"To create a dimensional pocket, you use the word 'ana', drawing the kanji for it in your mind while imagining a void, like the distance between portals. This creates a hole in space and time. You think of the point where you'll attach it, like your hand or something else. If it doesn't connect to you or a place you know well, anything you put in it will be lost forever."

She repeats the actions for me as Hoji strides in with brows furrowed. Halting in his tracks, his breath catches.

She says warmly, "Thank you again, Hoji. I couldn't do my duty without your sacrifice."

So, Great Uncle Nobu and I step out to give them a moment. They aren't an item but have a unique connection through the kits and the events which brought the two clans together. Then we hear the sizzle of a portal.

Aunt Hisako is about to step through. We wish her luck and pile a few protection spells on her, then wave as she leaves. Hoji's hand drops to his side after the portal closes.

Then the itch between my shoulder blades that says something isn't right urges me to follow my aunt. *But Soujou-bou ordered me to be ready. Not to go yet.*

My feet trace a path around and around the den. I will obey my teacher and trust him to make the right call. *Even if this wait kills me.*

Hoji joins my pacing. *Poor guy has it bad.* Gotta be hard to see the one you care about and gave so much for heading to battle.

Oh yeah. "Hey, Hoji, do you know how to make a dimensional pocket? Aunt Hisako just showed me."

A banshee shriek cuts through the wee hours of the morning, pulling me from Su-chan's arms and the clash of metal and shouting rings through the house.

I scramble for the sword Hiro gave me. *Not mine anymore. Shit.*

But with magic, a sword isn't required. *Remember that.*

Then I glance at my girlfriend. I've seen that look of utter determination on her face before. There's no way she'd stay behind, even if I ask.

She grabs a batch of Chou and potions I don't recognize. At least we had the sense to wear pjs. Our feet slap the stone floor, giving us away to any intruders.

Meanwhile, Aunt Hisako tumbles through a glowing gate and closes a stack of portals behind it, which shuts off the howl of several oni behind her. Everyone in the room rushes to her side as she pushes herself up from the roll.

"Tatsuya! Soujou-bou has need of you. Take Yuki's katana above the stand for this armor. It will serve you well. Father enchanted it years ago to act as a shield, and it automatically renews. Have my mother assist you into armor. You'll need it."

As I help my aunt up, Su-chan asks. "What's happening?"

"Ibaraki knew our plans. Either Mishima tapped the meetings or there's another traitor. We believe the Oni Queen's after a relic we'd hidden in Nono-gawa," Aunt Hisako pants.

What relic?

Hoji, in human form, tucks his katana into his belt despite my having taught him the dimensional pocket trick. Old habits must die hard.

But she holds up a hand. "Hoji-san, Soujou-bou does not want us kitsune there. We have a separate task."

Continuing his preparations, he purses his lips.

Don't be a little shit, just when I was trusting you. So I step into his path, letting him collide with me. "Hoji-san."

"I heard. I'm not just going to sit on my ass when I can provide protection here. Get going already! Soujou-bou called you!"

With a quick clap on his shoulder, I dash off to the armor room. Su-chan's wearing her special embroidered coat and lugging her bag of potions. She joins me near the armor displays. Then Great Aunt Asako and Grandma Miwa whisper words to transfer armor from the stands and adjust them to fit each of us.

"Wait. Soujou-bou didn't ask you to come, Su-chan."

"He can tell me 'No' then. They're attacking my home. I've got a ton of natural magic that we can use and you know darn well we work great as a team."

Grandma Miwa tightens the strap under Su-chan's chin, then puts the grimacing mask over her adorable face, attaching it to the helmet. I've never been afraid of Su-chan, but the determination in her eyes sends a shiver through me.

Downright sexy. Then my stomach tightens. Will my bravado match hers? What if something happens to her?

Suddenly, Great Aunt Asako thunks my helmet with her fist, causing my neck to jar. "Did you hear a word I said, great nephew? Or were you too in awe of your girlfriend?"

My bottom lip sucks in and my head tucks down. "Sorry."

Her chuckle unwinds a bit of the tension inside. "A fierce lady warrior does that to males. As I was saying, since you're not used to wearing armor, it may slow you down. Miwa-san and I will enhance it, so there is only a negligible difference."

My Su-chan's a warrior, for sure.

Next, Aunt Hisako pads in, now out of her armor and in fox form. She nods in approval. "I had hoped you two would have more training before you faced battle together. This fight is dire. So, let me give you a telepathy spell. Hold out your hands." Her nose touches each of our palms, which glow, and a staticky warmth fills us.

I catch Su-chan's eyes lingering on me. Admiration flows in, but her thoughts trickle through, too. 'Mmm. Handsome!'

I test if it's two-way with a voluntary push of a single sentence, instead of a tidal wave of every thought. 'When we return, I'm all yours.'

Her smile confirms it.

"Focus!" My aunt's tail thwacks my leg as she continues, "Beyond allowing you to communicate in private, you'll be able to draw on each other's ki from a distance. It doubles as a warning system for when one of you is in trouble and pinpoints your location. Yuki developed the ability, and we used it often."

Will I live up to his legacy?

Su-chan says aloud, "Baka."

But I didn't intend that to go through the link. It's way too easy to push a thought.

Inspecting our armor, my aunt makes her way around each of us. "The spell combination is difficult. I'll teach you both when there is time." She sighs. "I've had to hold so much back because the council won't give me permission for more than basic training. Right now, my master needs you. Portal to my house—you'll see the dome. Though, you can't portal into the fray because of the barrier."

Nonogawa's a battlefield. It makes my heart sink.

"I know, Nephew. It's hard when it's your home. It took Soujou-sama threatening to throw me through the portal to get me to leave."

Next, Hoji shoves a device at each of us that attaches to our shoulders. "Take these. They're a functional prototype of a ki storage system outside the ki well in each of us. It doesn't rely on dark magic, just electricity. Understand?

"Touch the top if you need ki. I've been developing them via a research grant funded by an anonymous group of yokai calling themselves the LOG. Now that I have a good inkling of who they are and their intentions, I'm willing to let these into the wild to help."

League of Guardians. Could they be more obvious? "You're a genius! Thank you. Show me more of how they work when Su-chan and I return." I grip his shoulder while my aunts and grandmother tuck talismans into various spots in our armor.

When I scribe a sizzling circle in the air, the gate reveals an iridescent dome with lights flashing inside it across the river. Boom! Crack! Boom! The echoes send a shudder through my ki-well. I have to ask. "Can't the residents feel that?"

Aunt Hisako says, "No, the barrier keeps knowledge of the battle minimized for humans."

How is that possible?

Then side by side, Su-chan and I step through. Vials, attached to various points on her armor, clink, and I see a glint of black under one sleeve. Chou's next to her skin. *How does she stand it?*

We jog over the bridge to the dome, getting a few odd looks along the way. One of the townsfolk hollers at us, "You two dressing up for cosplay or something?"

They really can't see or hear the battle raging inside the dome? *Crazy.*

When we reach the barrier, a half-meter sized yokai made of broken dishes blocks our path, pointing a glinting butcher knife as if it was a sword at my chest.

"Only members of the League may join the battle." He taps my armor to emphasize his point. "For your safety."

If I move the knife out of the way, he'll only get more annoying. When I don't answer, his voice drops. "Don't make me repeat myself, boy."

A raggedy, gray-splotched fabric dragon joins him and growls.

If I'd not heard of these tough little household guardians before, I'd laugh. But here they are. Meeting each new-to-me yokai is a rush.

Behind him, bursts of light beyond the shimmering barrier crash like thunder and vibrate through the ground. The shock wave goes through the plates in my armor as earthquake alarms blare from phones in the surrounding homes.

Steeling my nerve, I hold out my palm like I saw Aunt Hisako do those months ago. "Soujou-sensei requested." The burning glow returns from the day my teacher branded me.

"What about her?" The yokai pokes his weapon in Su-chan's direction.

If he touches her... "She's with me."

Then the cloth dragon swirls around Su-chan. Its companion, the pottery spirit, is not quite focused on her, but on something behind us. It nods and steps aside to lift the barrier as if it's the edge of a kid's blanket fort. We duck under. Then my jaw drops.

Overhead, clouds roil and swirl. Raijin, the god of thunder—a red oni with wild, stark-white hair waving in the wind—stands in the sky with a circle of drums, pounding them with a fierceness that makes my knees wobble.

Rumbling crashes in the sky, and lightning rolls in balls over the ground toward a line of advancing enemies, knocking rows of them down at a time. *Glad Raijin's on our side!*

Su-chan and I dash to Soujou-bou's banner. The tengu king issues orders, gesturing toward a mounted brigade, as he strides toward the battle with his katana in hand. He nods in my direction.

The koma inu, from the League's Council, brandishes Honjou Masamune as she marches beside Soujou-bou. But the katana's blade hums, vibrating enough that I hear it meters away. So she slaps it as if to shut it up.

As I pass, my lips purse and the guardian dog barks, "You set it against me, yakuza, by telling it you handed it over only to Soujou-sama!"

"I tried to treat the sword with respect!" I hiss back. *Not like she'll listen. But I had to try!*

Then League ranks part for masked riders who pull their long bows from nowhere and nock arrows. Their plates of iron braided with silk rattle with the horses' trotting.

Soujou-sensei raises his hand. When it falls, a rain of arrows flies into the sky and toward the marching horde. They repeat the volley, picking off the enemy until the oncoming mass is close. In return, a hail of black arrows flies toward our line. Someone shouts, "Ki drainers incoming!"

Instantly, the mounted archer replaces the bows with huge, long- handled nagamachi swords. With a mighty shout that echoes throughout the dome, they spur their horses to race toward Ibaraki's oncoming army. Some of them fall, screaming, hit by the black arrows.

I wince as a ki-bomb explodes, extinguishing the life of a powerful yokai.

Then Hayashi, the yuki onna, calls out, "Umeji-san! Soujou-sama needs you to help maintain our shield wall."

Seeing my confusion, she points out an area to the north. "The tengu reconnaissance reported an enemy battalion heading that way. Go quickly!"

No disdain? Maybe Aunt Hisako's trust in her is right.

War cries draw my attention as a tsunami of red, green, and blue-skinned oni crashes against the shield wall of the League army. The colorful mass raises stories into the air and threatens to spill over onto our forces below as we race to our assignment.

My blood runs cold.

To stop them, a group of tengu priests raise their voices in harmony, creating a powerful cyan shine on our soldiers, which pushes the wave in the other direction. Despite that, the wind covers us in oni stench, causing my stomach to churn.

We skirt behind the lines of yokai, who belong to the League. Their glares bore into me. They think we stole the magic we have. *No time to worry about their judgment, though.*

So Su-chan and I report to a tengu banner bearer. "Soujou-sama sent us."

His eyes narrow, but I show my seal and he points a wing toward a raven bird-man with tall horns on his helmet. "Check in with Captain Higashi."

Higashi shows us how to help maintain the barrier spell, and so we join the armored priests chanting a simple phrase for the deepest use of kotodama I've seen. Then Su-chan's and my voices blend in with tengu priests' in an unearthly, chilling harmony. The magic released from the spoken word glows white like sunshine before joining the blue shield wall.

Out of nowhere, Su-chan swats at something behind her, disrupting the flow of her words, sending the unified sound off and the glow wavers. So, one of the tengu shoves her. She gives a quick bow of apology to step away and swats again.

Through the thought connection, Su-chan shouts, 'Shion, knock it off!'

My head swivels as I shut my mouth to keep from disrupting the flow of the chant. That earns me a shove from another tengu to keep going, but I cast magical sight as Su-chan weaves and dodges to get away from an invisible foe. Drawing my sword, I whisper a shield into place around my Su-chan.

Suddenly, Shion shimmers into sight before me, undulating in serpentine curls. His words puncture the link. 'You would challenge a river god with that pathetic sword? Did the League find you unworthy of wielding Honjou Masamune?'

Don't fall for the bait. 'You won't possess her.' Su-chan wouldn't like my speaking for her, so I add, 'Ask for her help.'

'I will join this fight. I need the body that holds my magic. See any others lying around?'

Su-chan's fists clench. 'I don't want to be a puppet ever again! But you were a Guardian, and I have yet to find a Guardian teacher to become one and join Tatsu in his post. Soujou-bou told me that was a requirement for us humans—find a mentor and fill the post as a pair. Will you train me?'

The blue dragon spirit flies in loose coils around her. 'I will not take another apprentice after the last betrayal.'

Now, Su-chan's teeth grind loud enough to hear. More of the old item yokai—umbrellas, brooms, canes, jackets, and all manner of household things—surround Su-chan, Shion, and me. We're a disruption.

Get this over with.

So, I growl through our connection. 'Help us hold the shield wall or leave! You were a Guardian, for fuck's sake. Live up to that!'

A ripple runs through Shion, and his spines stand on end. The circle of yokai surrounding us closes in.

Stand your ground.

Releasing my sword with one hand, I offer it to the umbrella yokai closest to me. "Join the connection so we don't interrupt the chanting."

Now if I can figure this out. Taking a deep breath, I push the link open as I picture the newcomer joining the conversation. Instead of just her, the little yokai jolts and joins hands with the others surrounding us. A flood of questions rush in, causing Su-chan and I to cover our helmets with our hands.

'Shut up!' I scream in my head.

The item yokai all take a step back and send waves of displeasure through the connection. But they go silent.

Quickly, I take a shaky breath. 'I allowed the one of you into the link, so you'd know we're dealing with Shion-san, a former member of your ranks. Did any of you know him?'

Several of them nod, with eyes going wide. A few whispers of 'Shion-san, is it really you?' make the dragon look around from yokai to yokai.

'It is.' He nods and turns to Su-chan. 'Very well, I will only direct you. Remove the protection on your neck.'

Just then, war cries of a troop of oni echo their thundering against our shield wall. Slowly, she tips her head forward and pulls back the embroidered protective designs under her armor.

'Su-chan! No!' My hand slaps on her nape. 'What if he turned evil after his death, seeking revenge?'

'You do not take the word of a Guardian?' the dragon rasps.

'Let go, Tatsu.' Her eyes meet mine and the resolution there makes me take a step back.

It's her choice, idiot.

Instead of entering the vulnerable spot, Shion places his claws flat onto her skin. Shrinking to the size of a kitten, he settles onto her shoulder. 'Let us do our duty.'

We rejoin after several scathing glances as the warrior priests lean into the shield wall against the battering of the screaming oni. But, when one priest recognizes the dragon spirit, his eyes go wide and he whispers, "Shion…"

I jostle him, since he was the one who shoved me. But we resume our chanting of the incantation.

Movement from a translucent form catches my attention. My words falter. *I know the ghost.*

Kentarou's hands float in front of him and he calls, "Aniki!"

Big brother. He still calls me that, even though I let him down? Next, his ghostly fingers touch the wall, distorting it as he draws his hand away and his own glow grows brighter. He's pulling energy from the spell like Shion did.

My words falter out of tune as a heavy numbness settles inside. *Why did it have to be him?*

But warm fingers press to the unarmored part of my forearm, sending a rush of sunshine heat into me. *Thank you, Su-chan.* With her here, I can face anything.

Swallowing back the bile at my little brother being used as a pawn for Ibaraki, I take a deep breath and steady myself.

In invitation, Kentarou holds out a hand. "You're on the wrong side, Aniki. We've come for what is rightfully the Lady Ibaraki's. Join us!"

Face your ghosts. So I belt the song out louder, pouring ki into it. But I don't have the nerve to block his voice.

When the second group of oni and ghosts crashes into the shield wall, more of my old mob brothers join Kentarou in sucking away the wall's energy. The section they work on fades and flickers. Their puce glow is sickening—tainted magic.

Then words puncture my thoughts. 'Tell them the cost before I go to the top of the shield wall.' That's not Su-chan, but Shion. *Not going without me!*

Removing myself from the chanters, I shout above the din. "Ibaraki is using you! She's taking your ki to power her magic and intends to wipe out an entire race of people for the sins of one."

My girlfriend, with the dragon perched on her shoulder, steps back and crouches. I mimic her movements, retrieve a fistful of banishment talismans from my pocket with one hand, and draw my katana with the other. A spell enhanced leap hurtles us at the apparitions. *Forgive me, little brother.*

Then I whisper a phrase for zeroing in on the target as I fling ofuda papers at the ghosts. The shield wall sputters, but the tengu priests sing louder and push more energy into it.

Kentarou dodges. Slap, slap! Two spirits of my old yakuza clan dissolve into mist and the talismans sizzle into nonexistence. *Rest in peace, brothers.*

In response, the remaining ghosts pull ki so fast they aren't able to absorb it all and the extra turns to a glowing light. Shion's transparent form leaps at one of the dead yakuza, crushing the ghost in his jaws and absorbing the spell energy. My yakuza brother howls a nightmare-fueling shriek as Su-chan releases Chou on another.

That's when a boy peeks out a window from a house below. His parents snatch him back inside and a pottery soldier breaks away from his formation to put a ward on their house. He shouts, "Secured! They won't remember what they saw."

As our shield wall falls and the smaller yokai melt into the rear of the formation, a troop of oni surges toward us. My knees knock, but I get one last glance at Su-chan and brace for the fight.

Then black arrows pelt our lines, and we can do nothing to help those hit. All we can do is back away before the ki-bombs go off. Every explosion makes me jump.

Soujou-sama's booming voice carries over the din, "Envoys, Guardians, Salvage Crew!" His hand falls to signal the charge. "For Nonogawa!"

So Su-chan and I join the war cry echoing through the valley. Leading the elite soldiers, Soujou-bou carves a swath through the horde with his sword.

As Raijin continues pounding the circle of drums above us, lightning arcs down from the sky, rolling into the seething mass ahead. The strikes tear holes in the enemy's front line.

I block the path of a blue oni who broke through the League ranks and he lifts his club. Su-chan flings her razor vine while I chuck a banishment spell at his unprotected chest. With a chilling scream, he crumbles to dust.

Then Soujou-bou stumbles. A throng of oni piles onto him, slashing and stabbing as an archer aims for the mound of yokai.

"No!" I scream.

All around us, the same thing happens to other prominent League members and I attach one more protection ofuda to Su-chan.

Slapping a portal talisman into the air, I rush to my teacher. It doesn't matter how much ki I burn through, flinging away and slicing through one oni after another. When I see his hand emerge from the mound, I use kotodama to dodge the strikes and grab it. I shove ki through the connection, using a tap from the battery from Hoji, and pull my teacher free.

At the same time, a blinding light cracks through another group of oni surrounding the koma inu dog Guardian, sending the attackers scattering in every direction. Raijin's drumbeats send flashes of lightning to target one pile after another.

But freeing the powerful council members only makes them more vulnerable to the ki arrows. A beautiful phoenix goes down. Whether it's from the arrows, I can't tell.

Behind me, I hear a trumpeted bleat and turn to lock gazes with a baku. My insides twist. *Mishima.*

Honjou Masamune lays just ahead; its hum turns to a screech. As I reach down to shove it back toward the koma inu, Mishima's paw snatches it up.

Then a black arrow hits the koma inu, who howls in agony as she tries to rip the thing from her shoulder. Her ki well shrinks before there's an explosion.

"Baka, yakuza!" The traitor baku books it away from the scene. My katana's slash isn't fast enough to reach him, but he stops in his tracks, staring down at the sword.

Why's he standing there? So I cast true seeing as I reach for the katana, and spot a thread reattaching to his neck.

Honjou shrieks into my mind, 'Ibaraki controlled the baku! Made him attack Soujou-bou! Don't let him take me!'

Shit. Where is the bitch? My lungs belt out, "Cut the control thread to Mishima!" as I leap after the baku and he dodges my swings at the puppet string. Then he takes off with Honjou Masamune. My feet bound off the heads of anyone in my way. A shadow covers me and loud rustling swoops in from overhead. Claws scrape at my helmet.

Crack! My protection talisman winks out of existence as I raise my sword once more, only to run smack dab into the enemy's barrier.

Where's Mishima?

Next, a thundering roar comes from the river. Water rushes in like a tsunami around my legs. The blue dragon tosses swaths of the oni aside like toys as it swims toward me. Crashing into the puce glow of the enemy controlled shield, the dragon's teeth rip into the barrier. *Shion!*

So, he and I alternate attacks.

'They're re-enforcing it! See the magic draining from our own shields? Go underneath! I'll open the way. That's what Ibaraki and Mishima did. The baku went toward the park with Honjou Masamune.' Shion's voice pounds its way into my head, shooting through my skull. It's so forceful compared to Su-chan. *How's he a solid form?*

When the serpent bites at it again, a ki signature I know well glows under its scales. "Su-chan?!"

'I'm ok, Tatsu. Do as he says.'

As long as she's alright.

Then the road shakes as if an earthquake went through.

'There's a crack underground. Go!' Shion shouts.

Slapping a portal ofuda onto the street, I whisper 'Hotaru Park'. The gate sputters and glitches but opens, so I dive through to roll out of the fall. Mishima brandishes Honjou Masamune in the air, before rushing me. "It's your fault Soujou-bou kicked me out!"

I've got one shot.

Using time dilation, I leap at the baku with my katana in hand. Honjou wails in agony as light erupts and the sword from Tsuchimikado creates a blue shield. Honjou Masamune plows into it, stopping inches from my face.

At the same time, Sekiguchi, running up, shouts and slashes with his naginata. "You will not pass!"

Where'd he come from?

Behind the shield wall, Shion bellows. "Stand down, Sekiguchi! This isn't the old days! You don't have to defend my river."

Jolting me from the distraction, Honjou Masamune shrieks 'No!' as Mishima forces it to slice through the air. So I dive for Sekiguchi, but my shield can't cover him in time.

The kappa crumples to the ground. Mishima wrenches the sword from his victim, then slaps a talisman into the air as a circle sizzles around it. Wet red drips from the blade.

Sekiguchi's arm and the naginata lay a meter from his body, but the gash in the kappa's side makes me fear the worst. I have to fight down the bile in my throat. My feet pound the grass after the traitor. "Murderer!"

A few of the League are catching up, but there's no time to wait. Mishima's about to step through a portal. My legs burn as I use a spell to increase my speed as more war cries carry up the valley.

That's when I leap with a speed boost, in order to tackle and pin him to the ground, using ki to extinguish his portal. He throws me off like a dishrag into a tree, knocking the wind out of me. Gasping, I slap a healing talisman on my side.

Then the baku flips to a stand before shoving Honjou Masamune under my chin and pinning me against the tree. The katana vibrates violently, thrumming a screaming protest that batters into my head.

"Who has the sword of legend now? As if a yakuza would ever be worthy to wield Honjou Masamune!" Mishima sneers as he uses the tip of the blade to lift my chin, forcing me to meet his eyes.

I growl, "Honjou Masamune doesn't accept you! So who's the unworthy one?" Then a familiar prick sends my hand flying to the back of my neck. With a thought, I sever it.

Ibaraki, the green-skinned oni queen, emerges from the grove to stand beside the baku. Her garish blouse and caked on makeup clashes with her sickly skin tone. But she walks with the same sense of power and entitlement Date Sari did. How much did Ibaraki learn from the kitsune who enslaved her?

"Enough!" Ibaraki shouts. "Umeji-san, join us or die. You took much from me. But Honjou Masamune is vital to my plans. The sword is stubborn, and I need you to wield her.

"The League is hesitant to take you because of your past. You know what it is to be bound to those who don't value you beyond what you can bring them.

"Instead, help shape the future of Japan. We can fix so many injustices together. If you wield it for my purposes, I'll spare the kitsune."

As if she'd do that. She'd written that awful letter threatening to take everything dear from me. *Find out more.* "Why are you punishing an entire race for the sins of one you already killed?"

"They're all tricksters. The witch's father thought he, too, could use my kind. It just shows they're all evil! Didn't realize the whole clan was the same. Did you, Umeji?"

They're not.

She continues, "Your kitsune spirit betrays what you are, Umeji-kun. The Date clan may be your kin, but each of them hides secrets. You'll never be truly one of them. Join me and you can save their miserable hides. I won't offer again."

Hoji and Grandma Miwa aren't like that!

"You don't need him!" Mishima's jaw tightens as he fumes. "My race, we're holy beings! Evil flees from us! I can make Honjou Masamune accept me."

Delusional. At least I knew what I was. "Mishima, you're no more holy than I was at my worst."

To Ibaraki, I spit, "You'll never become Shogun."

The oni queen simply sneers. "I'll relish telling every kitsune before they die you could have saved them."

Bitch.

When the back of my neck prickles again, I use ki to shove the shaking blade aside. Then I snatch the string that tried to connect, winding it around my hand. "I won't be your puppet, Ibaraki. You should have known that from your time as my great grandmother's slave!"

Then, as tension builds in the string, Ibaraki's eyes go wide. I yank her toward me and she spins off-centered, stumbling. A kick to her back slams her face first into the same tree I'd hit just a few moments before.

Coming to her aid, the baku raises Honjou Masamune, which bucks in his grip, and he slices through the thread I hold. Ibaraki groans, standing again.

One last chance, baku. "Mishima-san, hand over the sword. I'll vouch that you were being controlled," I say as I hold out my hand.

Instead, his head jerks back. "You don't know what you're up against."

What'd she promise him? And why the control thread? *Oh. She doesn't trust him.*

Behind me, the tromping of heavy feet pound the ground. *Help?* But the stench says otherwise.

Ibaraki's words snarl. "Unlike you, my magic well isn't stolen. The abilities I have were hard won. And you don't have the League to back you. They're occupied by my forces scattered throughout Japan. You have no idea the power that sword can deal."

Then the oni band encircles us and Mishima advances, unsteadily. His muscles are so taut as he fights for control they might snap with a light tap. His ki well is ridiculously low. He didn't use that much magic already, did he? Click. *He's using it up, fighting the sword.*

So I raise Tsuchimikado's katana, though my arms shake. I don't want to kill again. *But these two'll hunt my family and friends.*

Hiro always said not to let others force you to react. So, I whisper a word to boost my speed and get ahead of their actions.

Honjou Masamune arcs a jerking line through the air toward me. Instantly, a glowing shield materializes as I block. A slash with magic at the baku's wrists makes him tuck his injured arms in and trumpet a grating howl. Honjou Masamune clatters from his grip.

As I reach to snag the sword, a meaty blue hand grabs my wrist and twists. Pain shoots through my shoulder and another oni grabs my other arm. I can't wriggle out of their grasp. *Think your way out of this.*

Ibaraki motions for Mishima and spits in my face. "An inexperienced student shouldn't have challenged the likes of the Oni Queen."

When Mishima's hand opens, it reveals a black spot surrounded by angry red where Soujou-bou's seal had been.

"Umeji-kun's ahead!" Soujou-bou's voice calls from behind me.

Finally!

But Ibaraki scribes a glowing circle in the air. "Leave the human. When we deliver a pile of kitsune heads to his door, Umeji'll change his mind."

"But we don't need the yakuza trash!" Mishima whines.

"You can't control the sword. He can."

Beyond the portal lies a strange city in darkness and a sickly sweet scent wafts through. Before I can escape, something slams into my skull, leaving me to crumple to the ground, clutching my head.

The crackle of a portal closing and my teacher's voice hollering, "Not Umeji-kun, too!" are all I can process as my head throbs so hard I'm immobilized.

Soon, Soujou-bou, leading a contingent, leans over. His voice quavers. "You're alive! We lost many today, and the battle is still raging in Nonogawa. Shimazu, Honjou Masamune's wielder, is among the dead."

I groan. "The koma inu?"

"Yes. She was the only one Honjou Masamune didn't outright refuse, apart from you. Did you retrieve it?"

My head swims as I stand and stare at the ground. "I'm sorry. Mishima and Ibaraki escaped with the sword."

Instead of sharing my master's joy at seeing me among the living, the yuki onna, who had warmed to not quite scornful, is colder than ever. "We saw you reaching for the legendary blade after you had returned it to its rightful place with the League."

My head jerks up. "What? I was gonna shove it back to the koma inu! That's the truth, Sensei! You gotta believe..."

But my teacher's voice cuts me off. "You disobeyed your last order. We have never withdrawn from a battle until this day. And the Salvage Crew has more work than they can handle. The League will enter human records, despite our attempts to remain out of their history."

My failure is theirs.

Then Soujou-bou's voice hardens. "When Honjou Masamune was forged, a prophet foretold the sword would unite all yokai. Not just anyone can carry it. It creates a lifelong bond with its wielder. The treasure here in Nonogawa wasn't what Ibaraki wanted. It was Honjou Masamune. Now she is lost to us."

Wait a minute, Mishima was privy to that, too. "So Ibaraki knew and had a spy in the ranks?" *And worse.* "She organized me handing over the blade, didn't she?"

"Enough!" Soujou-bou growls as his hand slashes through the air. "It is highly unlikely you and Ohno Suzu will become Guardians. To have even a chance, you'd have to undo the damage you've caused. I'm not sure you're up to the task."

A final warning? Shit. "But..."

"No excuses." Soujou-bou's head shakes. "You'd led me to believe the old yakuza stubbornness and pride would not get in your way. But you abandoned your orders to go off on your own, causing us to lose the sword. And I'd hoped Ohno-san could deal with the powerful magic inside her."

Soujou-bou gathers the League and shouts orders for cleanup to begin. Behind his back, Hayashi sneers, "I saw what you were trying to do and swear the Council will never approve the likes of you."

I tried to get Honjou back for the League! Su-chan couldn't stop Shion from possessing her! It wasn't her fault! Unable to bear looking at my teacher's retreating back, I let my fists ball up. My feet glue to the ground and heat fills my cheeks. *I will get that sword back.*

Behind us a terrible howl overpowers even Soujou-bou's loud voice, causing my head to swivel.

Shion thrashes, ripping the roofs off buildings and tossing them aside like toys. "Where is the one who hurt my Sekiguchi!" His wailing agony echoes in the valley around us as every tree spirit repeats the sentiment.

Then my heart sinks as I see Su-chan's spirit inside the dragon pulsate wildly, only to darken.

"Now we have to stop that mess, too," Soujou-bou laments.

"Su-chan!" On instinct, I scribe an arc in the air and scramble through the portal close by her. *Damned dragon!* My feet pound the ground, but dodging the fleeing crowd slows me down. Some of the League members and townsfolk jump through the gate before I let it close.

'He won't let me go! Help me!' Su-chan's plea through our connection stabs my heart.

So, I step into the path of the dragon and sheathe my katana. I don't know what Shion has done with my girlfriend, but I won't risk her. "Shion, let her go!"

In a spell enhanced leap, I latch on to the dragon's head as the beast swooshes past. The warm scales give way like skin. Su-chan's inner glow weakens by the second. *Ki theft? Or something else?*

So I mutter an extreme time dilation spell on the dragon, using the battery to help power it. The flight becomes an agonizing crawl and Su-chan's energy wanes faster and faster. "You're using up her energy! Stop it, Shion!"

Then Soujou-bou and his contingent shout something I can't make out. *Please, don't hurt Su-chan!*

Chou wriggles off one horn toward me as the dragon increases its serpentine wriggling and continues its desperate search. Click. "Chou, have you tried draining her of her ki to get Shion to stop?"

Removing her life's energy might be her only chance. The irony of taking from the woman who's always given of her energy and helped so freely makes my stomach lurch.

'He won't let me go!' Su-chan pleads again as she's subjected to her worst nightmare.

"Forgive me." Pressing Chou to the spot at the back of the dragon's neck, I command, "Drain her ki. All of it."

"I will avenge my lover! You cannot stop me, human!" Shion bucks and weaves, trying to throw me off. To compensate, I whisper a spell to latch myself to the dragon.

Then the blob flinches but complies.

'Su-chan, give me your energy so we can stop Shion.' No response. With shaking hands, I see if she'll let me draw energy and it comes without theft. As the soft sunshine warmth enters my ki well, the pulsing glow inside her fades causing the lump to tighten in my throat. *Kami-sama don't let us kill her. Please.*

The dragon shudders under me, rasping, "Fool! You don't know what you are doing!"

"You're killing Su-chan—your student and my mate! Sacrificing her won't bring Sekiguchi back!"

"His murderer must die!"

But I shout, "Soujou-bou will hunt Mishima and Ibaraki down. I'll help him. We can't allow those two to kill anymore, nor exterminate kitsune-kind."

"Sekiguchi was the only one to understand me! I must-" Finally, the dragon goes limp, crashing to the ground as the light inside extinguishes.

"Su-chan!" My throat constricts so much it's hard to speak. "Shion, let go of her!" I want to pound the dragon spirit's face in for taking her over, but it would hurt my Su-chan. "She trusted you to teach her, not possess her! Let her go!"

Behind me, a weak voice commands, "Stop here."

Carrying Sekiguchi, several small household item yokai halt before the dragon's body, allowing the kappa's blood soaked, webbed hand to rest next to mine on Shion's scaly neck. A warmth I'd never heard from the kappa fills his words. "Shion, I lived without you for a century, hoping all the while to find you again. Leave this destructive path, or you will turn into a monster!"

"You're alive?" Shion squeaks.

"Don't underestimate my will to live for the chance to be with you again. Release the girl. Or have you gone so far down this dark path that you'll take over an innocent and kill her? That is something our relationship can't bear."

"You're alive!" Shion sobs and his body shudders.

Then dragon scales meld into human flesh and the armor she went into battle with, and I scramble to cradle my girlfriend to my chest while pouring ki into her. "Hold on, Su-chan."

"Shion, keep me company while they try to revive the girl. Healing me will be unpleasant," Sekiguchi says as the stretcher bearers continue on to a healing tent.

Next, familiar voices shout in unison, "Suzu!"

Su-chan's dad, Ohno Yasu, drops to his knees beside us, pressing illuminated hands to her temples. Her mom and brothers join him, and we chant together. I can't make out the words well, but I do my best to say the healing spell in what I can only guess to be in the old Ainu language.

In a moment, Su-chan's message pushes through the connection between us. 'Thanks for freeing me. Now I release you.'

My limbs shake and my ribs crush my chest so hard that my heart might not be pumping any more. I shout at her, holding her tight. "Stay with me! Don't you dare give up! You hear me, Su-chan! You're the one who encouraged me to look beyond my past. The one who fought for me to come back from the brink after Hiro died. The one who didn't want anything, but to be with me."

What can I do to stop this? Give back. My limbs turn heavy, and my mind goes fuzzy as I feed her every ounce of ki I have.

"Whatever you're doing, Umeji, keep doing it!" Yasu shouts.

But I'm tapped.

Click. Su-chan's battery from Hoji! Grabbing the device attached to her shoulder, I apply it to the skin between her gauntlet and sleeve. 'I'm here for you, Su-chan!'

Finally, her eyes flutter open and tears flow. The glow returns in her chest, now blue again. She rasps the thought, 'The prophecy came true.'

Thank you, kami-sama. "That wasn't you, and you won't face the town alone," I say and my lips press to her forehead as I sit there rocking her.

Her family keeps chanting and applying potions. Sobs wrack her as she curls up tighter in my arms, while I cling to her and sniffle, too.

Who gives a fuck if the whole town sees? It might help for them to witness people who value her after what just happened.

Ibaraki, Mishima, and Shion have much to answer for. *This is their fault.*

14

Cost

Su-chan's father, Yasu, says, "We need to get her back to the clinic. She's not out of danger yet."

"The closest hospital is in Shimosaki. That might be too far."

But he and his wife wave away my concern. "Suzu-chan never told you?"

"Told me what?"

"Let's just get her there. She's weak. Carry her," Yasu commands and motions for me to follow. Yukiko scurries ahead.

I know better than letting someone speak for Su-chan. If it's not far, she might manage it. "Can you walk?" I ask.

"Carry me, please," Su-chan whispers.

When we reach the Ohno house, I assume we'll get in their van, but a spell-based sign appears on the side of the outbuilding in their yard that says Magical Medical Clinic. If I had a free hand, it'd wipe over my face. *Idiot.*

Su-chan whispers, "When I brought you home to treat you for ki shock, a birthing mom occupied the clinic, so you didn't get to go in. Unless you're a magic user, you won't see the sign."

"There are that many ki users in Nonogawa?"

As Yasu holds the door open for us, he says, "Not just our little town. Yokai and other ki users come from all over the valley, if they can't go to a hospital. Though, we only have one exam area. Two in a pinch if we use the storage above us." He motions to the single bed in the tiny clinic. "Put her there while I fetch potion ingredients."

Tromping up the steep stairs, he leaves Su-chan and me alone for a moment. The scuffling of feet and rustling says Yukiko is in the room above us, too.

"You ok?" I whisper, setting her down and tucking a lock of hair behind her ear and out of her face. "I mean, Shion possessed you, and I suspect he was going to use all the energy you had."

She nods and her lips purse.

Always so brave. "If you want to talk, I'm here."

"I-I can't right now. Maybe later." Her whole body convulses. So I encompass her again.

"Take your time."

"But they said we can't likely be Guar..." Her head butts into my sternum as the seal kicks in.

Yeah, that sucks. Becoming a Guardian was my purpose and the reason I followed my aunt to Kyoto. But I've got to be the calm in the storm for Su-chan, here and now. Breathing deep doesn't ease the tightening in my chest, though. "You're the priority. Always have been."

Soon, Yasu returns with steaming water and sets a bunch of vials on the table before fetching a mortar and pestle. In the meantime, Yukiko holds the door with her foot as she lugs a blanket and a bucket. She says, "I'll prepare the bath."

"Are you gonna use that funky emotion altering potion like when you treated me for magical shock?" My hand goes to the back of my neck as the dread of feeling so helpless floods in.

Yasu shakes his head. He's always short on words. Unless he grills me.

Yukiko is the one to answer. "Not this time. We need to infuse her with ki and stop the energy from being taken from her well for a while. We'll wrap her in a potion-soaked blanket. Though later, a good hot soak will go a long way for you both to heal the mind and body."

"Need help?" I ask.

"Just feed Suzu-chan ki if she gets too low again." Yukiko says as she thumbs through a worn tome entitled Herbalism, Potions, and Magical Healing. "Here's the one we need."

At least there's still some ki in my battery.

Next, Yasu hands me a swimsuit. "Go change."

"Thanks." Good thing I'll have dry clothes to wear, unlike the last time where I had to borrow pajamas. *Talk about awkward.*

When I return, Yasu and Yukiko prepare the potion in a harmony that only comes from decades of working together. *Will Su-chan and I be like that someday?*

A sharp pine scent fills the air as Yasu pours the bright green potion into the bucket. Yukiko soaks the blanket as she requests, "Umeji-kun, would you help Suzu-chan into the tub? This is going to be messy."

Once Su-chan and I get in, they wrap her in the steaming, infused blanket. She rubs her arms as if she's still cold. Though I hiss from the heat as I pull her onto my lap. "Hey, you doing a little better?"

She curls into me but nods ever so slightly.

"We've got you, Daughter," Yukiko says. Then the blanket encompassing Su-chan emanates a blue glow. "The magic is kicking in to seal her well for a few hours."

Draping a dry towel around my shoulders, Yasu asks, "Tatsuya-kun, I wouldn't offer. But considering what you and Suzu-chan have been dealing with, it may be wise for you to know a few of our recipes. Would you like to learn?"

Around other humans, the Ohno clan is so secretive about their healing work. *A serious concession.* "Please." Then I scrunch my eyes shut as the shame fills me again. "Su-chan and I likely just lost our big chance to replace my aunt in her duties."

"What duties?" Yasu asks.

As I'm about to open my mouth to speak about the League, my mouth slams shut. "I'm not allowed to say. Sealed."

He chuckles, "Fair enough." Then his face darkens. "I've never seen Suzu-chan this off."

She won't like us talking about her. *Doesn't her dad know?* "Sorry, Su-chan. Hanging around me means it may continue that way."

"Yeah," her words come out as a bare peep, "But you keep sticking around."

"You can't scare me off. Just don't make me a pet like Chou."

My reward? A giggle.

Then she asks, "Where is Chou-chan?"

So Yasu sets down the rag he was cleaning with and scoops the black blob off the floor as it rolls toward us. He sets the pet on the side of the tub closest to Su-chan.

"Chou-chan, stay out of the tub. I don't know what might happen if you absorb that potion."

Nevertheless, a black tentacle extends from the blob as she reaches toward her owner.

Clearing his throat, Yasu scolds. "Remember what happened when you were curious about the blender?"

Chou shrinks. Instead of staying back though, she launches herself and clamps onto Su-chan's head. Then the blob gives a raspberry in Yasu's direction.

He just raises an eyebrow, shaking his rag at her to reinforce his words. "I can tell you just fed to capacity by your aura. But if you ever want me to feed you again, you'll have to learn some manners."

Ignoring him, the black slime settles on Su-chan's shoulder, avoiding the blanket. There's a light glow where the blob meets my girlfriend's skin.

"Thanks, Chou." Su-chan pats her pet, who leaps back to the safety of the edge of the tub.

What'd Chou do?

Later, when the blanket cools, Su-chan shivers again. Yasu and Yukiko warm up the kotatsu for us and we help Su-chan into dry clothes. She's never been so compliant.

We get her tucked into the warmth and I change before pulling her parents aside, trying to whisper, "This is bad, isn't it?"

Maybe I shouldn't have said anything, because Yukiko's cheerful mask falls as she nods. "Suzu-chan is strong."

"Su-chan's always been the calm in the storm. Seeing her so… I don't even know what it is. But it's freaking me out."

Yasu adds, "She's never shutdown like this. We'll take turns monitoring her."

So I give them a rundown of what happened as I saw it. Everything goes numb as the events replay. *So much blood from Sekiguchi's wounds. Did he make it?*

"From what you said, Suzu-chan's reaction, and the blasted prophecy that's hung over her for years, we may need to bring in extra help. Thank you for telling us."

I failed Sekiguchi. Failed my little brother. Failed Soujou-bou. Failed. *Wait. What'd Yasu just say?*

"You're pale as a ghost. Are you ok, Umeji-kun?" Yukiko asks.

"Uhm," I respond and have to lean on the wall. "Let's check on Su-chan."

Nodding, Yasu guides me. "He's hanging on by sheer will. We'll get him under the kotatsu, too, and poke some food into them both."

They help me crawl in beside Su-chan into the warmth of the heating table. Even though we're propped up against the wall with pillows at our back, her arms wrap around me under the blanket.

Yasu says, "Stay there. I'll fetch help."

Then my eyes scrunch shut as each failure plays over in my head, suffocating me. Interrupting the barrage of memories, Yukiko says, "Put out your hand, Tatsuya-kun. I need to put the mood ring on your finger."

Fight it. "I'll get through this. Put it on Su-chan."

"Are you sure?"

"Yes." Her worst nightmare came true today.

Su-chan doesn't respond. So, I pull her hand out for her mother to slip the ring on it and the color switches to dark gray. *Not good.*

Then her mom asks, "Can you two eat anything? Emotions always go up after a meal."

"Let's try, Su-chan," I suggest as I lift her chin. "Ok?"

She gives only the barest nod.

After Yukiko puts a plate of anpan—red bean paste sweet buns—in front of us, Su-chan stays glued to me. I grab one and put it in her hand. Slowly, she lifts it to her mouth and takes a bite.

Next, I snag a couple for myself. Before I know it, most of the plate is gone. Su-chan is still on her first one. *Better slow down.*

"Suzu-chan, please eat. It will help," her mom pleads.

"Do I need to feed you?" I ask.

But her fist thunks my chest.

"I take that as a 'No'."

Chou rolls out from under the blanket, giving me a start. The blob extends a tentacle like arm and snags a bun. Just as I'm about to say something, Chou shoves it at Su-chan, who takes it in her free hand. Then the ooze repeats the action to shove an anpan at me.

"Let me grab something a little more substantial since you two are handling those." Yukiko rambles as she rummages through a cupboard. "What do we have? The boys have been eating me out of house and home lately. Maybe it's a good thing they're both heading out on their own soon. Oh, they left my protein bars. Those will be just the ticket. You kids need energy right now."

"Can Chou eat these?" I ask as the ooze snags an anpan and drags it under the kotatsu. In return, the blob slaps my leg. *Thief. Those were for us.*

"Chou!" Yukiko scolds.

Then we hear a wet raspberry from under the table. It earns a giggle, through a mouth full of bun, from Su-chan.

So I offer, "Maybe she was just trying to bring a smile?" *Sticking up for that blob. What's the world coming to?*

But Yukiko's eyes roll. In the settling silence, the events from earlier continue to replay and it's hard to breathe.

Soujou-bou rejected you.

Su-chan's suffering.

Everything you worked toward—gone.

Aunt Hisako can't retire now.

All thanks to your failure.

Instead of sinking in the waves of the emotional onslaught, I shove a big bite of protein bar in my mouth and focus on chewing. Su-chan's problems are a bigger issue.

Soon, a sizzle announces a portal opening on the main room's wall while Yasu steps through with a couple of kappa and a Shinto priestess. Su-chan's brothers, along with Matsuo and Mie, pop in via another magical gate. They all bow.

Since I'm stuck, I give a polite nod. Yasu introduces the trio of newcomers. Eikichi and Kai are the kappa brothers, and Mako is the priestess.

Instantly, we're surrounded with more attention than I would ever want. *Put Su-chan's needs first. Because if you don't... Stop this!*

The pair of kappa mutter and wave their glowing hands over my girlfriend and me, while Yukiko zips over with two cups of water at the ready.

Eikichi says, as he accepts the water and pours it into the bowl at the top of his head, "The girl has indeed gone through great trauma to her ki well. So much so that even your powerful potion, Yasu-san, isn't circumventing it. But this young man's link to her should help keep her spirits up until we can get the well to hold ki."

Yasu's eyebrow lifts, but Yukiko is the one to ask. "What link?"

Not now! My head ducks. When her family gives me the stink eye, I dodge. "Long story."

"If it won't hurt her, I will wait." Yasu's arms cross.

Whew. I didn't wanna share that my blunder caused a bond between us that lasts a lifetime. *Or did he mean the mental link?*

Then Ekichi continues, "I am concerned about her magic. The expansion in the young man's well melds well with his own variation. But hers is different."

"Her magic changed a few months ago. She wouldn't talk about it." Yukiko's hands wring, though she accepts the glasses back from the kappa pair.

"Girl, why do you have a dragon's magic?" Eikichi glares, making Su-chan shrink into my side.

Very unlike her. So I jump in to explain what happened with Date Sari and how we got the magic.

While the two kappa discuss the consequences, Yasu asks, "How are you doing Tatsuya-kun?"

The attention makes me squirm. I can't put my hands in my pockets and my father's book isn't close by. "Focusing on Su-chan is helping to fend the worst of this off."

But he tsks. "You need to face that, not push it off. Remember, you can lean on us."

Thank you. "Su-chan's the priority right now."

Next, Mako, the priestess, says as she inspects us, "I came here on the assumption we were dealing with a possession. But this is a very different case. I will do what I can." She chants after she places several items around us.

All of a sudden, Su-chan shudders and shrieks in such a high pitch my ears ring. Her words come in a rush through our mental connection. 'No! Leave me alone! You promised, Shion! Stop it!'

"Suzu-chan!" Yasu shouts. "The ring is black! She's retreating into herself. Everyone, put ki into her and encourage her."

So I pull her tight. Imagining a protective bubble around her, I push the image across the connection. 'I'm here Su-chan. You're safe. We won't let him do that again.'

For the benefit of the others, I say aloud, "She and I have a magical link through a spell. She's reliving the distress."

Kai, the gray-haired kappa, says, "Most like this retreat into themselves and don't return. She may hear you through that connection, though. Keep trying."

Via the link, I plead but keep speaking aloud for the sake of her parents. "Su-chan. Fight this. We need you. I need you."

Then my chest tightens, and a wave washes over me. There's no emotion altering spell to dampen the onslaught this time. *What will Su-chan and her family think of my failure? Or Jiro? Or our friends?*

Su-chan's voice in my head is weak. 'They'll see you're human,' she chides before her presence in my mind fades.

Several more times, the tides of emotion sweep in, pulling sand from under our feet. But we cling to each other. Then, the link goes silent. I scream, "No, no, no! Su-chan! Talk to me! Hang in there!"

Everyone scrunches in around us to lend her energy. They're talking, but I only make out the words 'stopped breathing' and my heart threatens to rip from my chest.

Into our link I bellow, 'Su-chan, don't you dare give up! I'll protect you with my last breath.'

But she chokes out via the connection, 'Take this damned magic out of me!'

"What's happening? Tatsuya, can you tell us?" Yasu desperately asks.

So I push my vocal cords to work even though my throat is tight and raw. "But taking that magic from you will kill you."

Telepathically, she says, 'I don't want to be forced to hurt anyone ever again!'

One of the kappa, in their beak induced accent, says, "She's going dark but there's still a speck of light! Keep pouring ki into them both!"

Next, I pull the battery Hoji gave me from my shoulder and put it against her skin, giving her all the ki and everything I have—save my last spark.

"If we don't stop this, she could turn into a hanya." The priestess' voice waivers, but she resumes her chanting, louder and more fervently.

A hanya? Like a demoness?

That's when something invisible brushes my hand and I cast true sight just in time to see the red string unwind from my pinky finger. My insides crush. There's no future for me without Su-chan. *None.*

Pleading, I croak, "I'll help you learn to never be controlled ever again and look for a way to remove the magic that won't kill you. But I need you to fight this so we can face it. To face the future together."

Yukiko sobs, "Suzu-chan, see how many of us love you! Open your eyes to see us all! Proof you are needed!"

But there's no response and Su-chan's growing cold to the touch, so I force my eyes open and send her what processes in my vision. The room holds our friends and her family. Even Satou and the Nakamura clan are stepping through a portal for her. "See them, Su-chan? All of us care about you. We need you."

Her thoughts turn so soft I can barely sense them. 'They all saw me as the dragon that destroyed our town!'

"That wasn't you, and you won't face the town alone," I shoot back. My lips press to her forehead as I sit there rocking her. 'Right here, right now, they see someone they love. I see the one I want to spend the rest of my life with.'

She mentally volleys in a sob, 'Because you're stuck with me.'

More memories surge in. The sand under my feet threatens to give way. *Kami-sama help her! I'll do anything! Please!*

The cold air from the closing portals only worsens our trembling, and the kotatsu isn't enough warmth to counteract it. Her frigid hands tighten on my shirt sleeves, twisting enough they cut off circulation.

After a moment, a stranger's voice intrudes on my thoughts. 'Look at the girl's ki well. What do you see?'

Two kinds of magic twisting and writhing, like they're at war.

'They are indeed battling. I was the one that allowed the dual nature in you both, so you both carry the burden.'

Inari-sama?

'Tell her.'

It'll be faster through the link. 'Remember when I said my being mated to you for life has a reason? This is it! We have the bond to help you through this. The kami made us both have the two kinds of magic. So neither of us is alone!'

No response.

'I love you!' Granted, I would have waited to tell her such a serious thing, but it was now or never to let her know how much she means to me.

Her eyes fly open and her lip trembles.

Then the stranger's voice fades from my mind. 'Visit the shrine after this.'

Yukiko sobs in relief and Yasu puts an arm around his wife as I tuck Su-chan's head into my shoulder. Via the connection, I say, 'Marry me.'

'But...'

My stomach sinks. She's not saying yes. *Did I ask too much?*

'How can we even think of getting married right now?' she asks telepathically.

'I'll be here for you. No matter what.' Despite the link message I just uttered, my ribs tighten so much they crush my lungs. *Why isn't she saying yes?* Sure, we haven't been dating long. But we live together and we've been through so much already.

Quietly, Su-chan mentally says as she hides her face, 'I don't wanna be alone.'

Only then does the constriction inside loosen. *She needs me, too.* It's not a yes, yet. But it's not a no.

"C-can't breathe," she rasps.

I must have crushed her to me too tightly. "Sorry." So my arms drop, releasing her. How could I be so dumb? But she snatches my hand, dragging it under the kotatsu out of sight and interweaving her fingers in mine. At least it's only people who care for us here. Our interactions have been so public, yet again. But she's not running away. And there's no way I'll leave her side. Ever.

Then Kai runs his free hand over our ki wells. "They're stabilizing rapidly. How is this happening?"

I croak, "A miracle." *And I owe Inari-sama big time.*

Yasu kneels beside us, practically demanding, "Tell us what happened."

But Su-chan just shakes her head. 'I don't think I can talk just yet.'

So I deflect. "We could use something to eat. And I'd like a brush and ink."

Over the next hour, the kappa brothers continue to check our ki levels. Everything seems stable until the priestess says, "There's a kami presence here. Wait... more than one."

Su-chan's head shoots up.

Why can't we catch a break? "What kind of presence? A dragon? He's not welcome here."

My sudden anger makes her head jut back. "But dragons are spirits of protection and good." At my glare, she offers to find out what kind of spirit it is and leaves.

In the interim, Yukiko slides plates of sandwiches in front of us. Su-chan keeps glancing about as she nibbles at one, and I write protection talismans between bites of my own. Su-chan's brother, Ichiro, hangs them around the house as I direct.

After I'm sure Su-chan is stable, I get up to stretch and patrol the dwelling. *That damned dragon will only enter this place over my dead body.*

Soon, the priestess returns. "One of the kami left, but they wouldn't speak to me." Then she bows. "The river kami, Shion, wishes to talk with Suzu-san."

My hand goes automatically to the pocket where Honjou Masamune should be. *Idiot. You have Tsuchimikado's blade now.* Retrieving it from the dimensional storage in my hand brings looks of worry from all around us. "He's the one that did this to Su-chan. I'm not taking any chances. Know I won't unsheathe it unless it's to keep her safe."

Yasu joins me. Glancing at his daughter, he asks, "Are you well enough to go outside?"

After a moment, she answers. "With help, and I'll need the sashiko coat."

My brave girl. "Su-chan, we can banish him so you don't have to see him ever again."

"Don't. I need to face him."

That's when Yukiko scurries in carrying the worse for wear embroidered coat with its talisman patterns to cover the vulnerable spots on Su-chan's body. "I was about to wash it. Good thing I waited."

When we get Su-chan bundled up for the weather, she shoves back her shoulders. "Let's go."

Ken, the younger of Su-chan's two older brothers, holds the door as the crowd steps outside with us. Though I insist on going first. I'm the only one with a weapon. Our breaths form mist tendrils, and the air carries the heavy scent of cedar and the high humidity of approaching rain.

Writhing in impossible knots, Shion floats alongside Sekiguchi as a radish yokai steers the kappa's wheelchair. *The priestess could've said the kappa was with the damn dragon. Good to see him alive.* So I give a quick bow.

But Sekiguchi holds up his hand to halt the attendant. "This is his business."

Shion warily slithers through the air toward us.

'Ready?' I ask.

Su-chan nods. 'Together. As you said.'

"Ohno Suzu-san." Shion's voice resonates around us and the forested hills of the valley ring with her name.

But Su-chan stiffens as Yasu joins our line and anger burns its way through our mental connection.

Her teeth grind so hard I can hear it. Venom bubbles up inside. If I banish him, he could never hurt Su-chan again. Automatically, my hand snags one of the ofuda in my jacket.

'Wait!' Su-chan shouts into my mind, so I release it.

Yasu's gaze goes from the dragon to his daughter to me.

I nod. Yep, that's whose ki capacity she has. "Only she's capable of carrying that much magic."

Su-chan says with an edge I never want to be on the receiving end of, "What do you want?" as my free hand goes to the hilt of my katana.

The dragon's spines bristle, but he turns his head away and lowers. "Your anger is to be expected." Upon touchdown, his forelegs bend as if under the weight of a two ton truck. "Sekiguchi convinced me this was necessary."

So he takes a deep breath. "Never have I, a river god, had to apologize. But it was..." His head touches the ground. "...too tempting to exact revenge through the power that used to be mine once it was in my grasp again. You weren't the one to take my power, yet you allowed me access to it instead of keeping it for yourself. I was wrong to abuse such trust."

My hand slips from the hilt of my blade as I try to pick my jaw up off the ground. Dumbly, Yasu blinks.

Mist rises from the ground around him as the prone dragon awaits my girl-friend's answer. *Second miracle today.* Quickly, I glance at Su-chan, half expecting a holy glow to surround her and Buddha or Inari to have a hand on her shoulder.

"I have your word you won't possess me again?" Su-chan asks as tears form rivulets down her face.

Her simple question makes Shion's head hang. "I swear it. There is no way to be the god I once was."

Suddenly, my brave Su-chan barrels forward, putting a hand on the drag-on's shoulder—only to have it fall through the apparition. "I know why you did. Love is powerful. It drives us to do things that can be amazing or terrible. Instead of dwelling on the past, what if we look for a way to return your magic?"

His eyes pop open. "But that would kill you. You'd end up like me, or worse."

"This magic doesn't belong with me."

"Su-chan!" I blurt in unison with Yasu's shouted, "Daughter!"

What is she thinking?

Her arms cross and her voice turns flat as she glares back at us. "Magically powerful humans have much more of a chance of turning into vengeful yokai than others. It happened in my family. Didn't it, Father?"

Yasu huffs.

Ask another time.

"Ever since Nakamura-san mentioned how the extra power might put me at risk, I researched. Normally, it would kill the one whose magic is being removed. But I found an option."

Shion's head whips to be nose to nose with her.

Though she doesn't back up. "It's dangerous. But Honjou Masamune is the sharpest blade in existence. There's a legend that mentions it being able to cut only what is necessary."

Grabbing her elbow, I tug her around to face me. I can't stop the sharpness in my voice. "Su-chan! What are you thinking? Even if we can get the sword back, I'm not gonna cut you with it!"

Her fists clench and she pulls from my grip. "In the legends, it discerned a leaf from a fish and only cut the leaf despite both being in its way. Therefore, it can cut away magic from my ki well, if I offer it outside of myself. It's Shion's and my best chance!"

"But…" I sputter.

As her eyes narrow, coldness fills me.

"Daughter, that energy attached to your soul. You could lose all of your magic," Yasu adds.

Even so, Su-chan insists, "I think Inari Okami did it somehow with Hoji-san's magic for Nakamura-san."

"It's your body. But…" How do I phrase this right? "…all of us here want to be sure you're not making this choice out of a reaction to what happened today. Because it scares the shit outta me. You said we face this together. Did you mean it?"

When her head lowers, she whispers, "I did."

Then Sekiguchi motions for the radish spirit to push him forward. "Umeji-san is right. Just knowing there's a possibility we can look into and that Su-chan will consider it is enough for today."

"That you have taken the time to research such a sacrifice. I-I don't know what to say." Shion blinks back tears. Turning to Sekiguchi he asks, "Has anyone ever chosen to give up part of their ki well?"

Holding up my hand, I share, "As Su-chan said, Hoji-san likely did. I didn't get to verify. But his sacrifice healed my aunt."

"We can research this together and talk to Nakamura-san and Hoji-san. Our student should rest now, Shion."

Behind us, a throat clears. Everyone's head turns to the elder of the kappa brothers. "We can access the kappa historic text network. My brother and I will help Sekiguchi-san with research. Shion-san, can you access the archives of the League of Guardians?"

The dragon's head dips as he asks, "So the archives are a known entity now?"

"You just confirmed it." Kai winks.

But Shion growls and rushes into his space. "You won't be able to take advantage of my vulnerability again, kappa."

Kai's head bobs, spilling the water in his well. "I shan't try."

When Su-chan shivers, I put an arm around her and give a gentle push to emphasize my words. "Let's get you inside and get some water for Kai."

"I'll have your mother put the kettle on." Yasu opens the door for us.

Before we leave, Sekiguchi calls out, "Do you have any idea where the sword is?"

Breathe. "Only that Mishima and Ibaraki took it. Now we have another reason to find it." Though I don't wanna use Honjou Masamune to cut magic from anyone, let alone Su-chan.

But I won't be able to deter her from pursuing this. My stomach twists, making me queasy again. *I can't lose her too. I just can't.*

Inside, Yukiko must have used a spell to hurry the water for tea, because in no time we're all sipping cups at the table. Su-chan won't look at me and excuses herself to lie down in her room. Dark circles ring her eyes, and she's still pale. She waves me off when I get up.

Why won't she lean on me? My hands tug at my hair as I try to ward off the oncoming headache.

So Yasu whispers, "Tuck her in. Then I'd like to chat." When I raise an eyebrow, he shoos me off. "Go on. Women like support. She didn't want to bother you."

Upstairs, she crawls into her old bed like she belongs there instead of in our futon back at the den. Pulling the blanket over her shoulders, I kneel to kiss the top of her head and smooth the hair from her face. "I'll be back to check on you soon."

As I close the door, my heart shrinks. The last time I tucked her in here was to drop her off after our going away party at the store. How long ago was that? Less than a few months. *Feels like longer.* Yet the time's gone by so fast and so much has changed.

Though, are we ready for marriage? *I sure as hell am. What if Su-chan's not?*

This is getting me nowhere. And there are bigger issues to face—her dad and getting Honjou Masamune back. Speaking of, I should contact Satou and visit the shrine. When I pull my phone out of my coat pocket, my business card case drops. It pops open, spilling its contents on the floor. *Just peachy.*

Those cards represent someone's face. Scooping them up carefully, I get them off the floor as fast as I can. One seems to be stubborn—like it won't let me pick it up. That is, until I see what it says. The sight stops me in my tracks. It's the card from Hiro's message.

Then my head hangs. I lost what he entrusted to my care. Sure, my master commanded me to surrender it, but I had a chance to save it and blundered.

So I shove the card back in the case. A static spark stings my fingers. *What the...?* Winter is almost over and the air doesn't feel dry. When it happens again, I take a hard look at the card.

Hiro, you trying to tell me something? The flame on it appears for a split second before vanishing. *Ok then.*

I shouldn't keep Yasu waiting. Research it after speaking with him and calling Satou.

Sliding into a spot at the heated table, I steel myself. Yasu is unreadable, but he begins. "I've been wanting to ask you. What are your plans after your training?"

Running a hand through my hair, I say, "That's an interesting one. Everything blew up in my face since the battle. I don't know what's next."

He leans in. "Yukiko and I need someone to take over the clinic. I know you're not trained in this. But you seem to be a quick learner. I think Yukiko mentioned both our sons are leaving Nonogawa. We thought Ken would stay and take it over. That's why Suzu-chan was looking at other options and studied massage."

If he knew all my past and failures, he wouldn't want me to help with the family business.

"There isn't a hurry. I just wanted you and Suzu-chan to think about it. You're both very close, aren't you?"

So I simply nod, not wanting to share why I'm bonded to his daughter. Sure, it's helpful for Su-chan right now. But would he see it that way? Or would he think I purposefully attached myself to her? "I'll talk with Su-chan about it. I'd follow her anywhere, and she knows the most about the practice."

His small smile lets some of the tension drain from my shoulders. Then he says, "With Nakamura-san still in Kyoto, know that you can talk with us about anything. Magic users watch out for each other."

He said that before. *If I can't trust him, who can I trust?* So I ask, "Yasu-san, is there a way we can protect Su-chan from being controlled again without having to remove part of the magic inside her? The idea of removing magic is..." I shudder. "And I don't want anyone else using her like that ever again."

"When the barrier fell, and we saw Nonogawa was under siege, my gut said that Su-chan was dealing with the prophecy that's hung over her head for a decade. So we portaled to the dragon."

That's how he and Yukiko got to us on time. "Did you know Shion was a protector of this town?" The stupid seal didn't kick in. Is it just the words Guardian and League? Limitations like that are something I can work with.

"How do you know this?"

I lean in, mirroring him. "Believe me, you won't get much information. And there's a spell on me to keep me from talking about it. Dang annoying. But I can tell you that Date Sari killed him. She took his magic. She was always after ways to make up for her own lack of power, instead of learning to grow stronger on her own."

"Do you think that's part of why Suzu-chan wants the magic removed?" Yasu asks.

"Maybe? Also, Date controlled her in two of our battles. As much as I try, I can't watch her every second. It's best for her to have her own defenses."

"True. So do you think the sword, Honjou Masamune, could help her? I don't want to consider it. But I also know, when she has her mind set on something, she won't let it go."

"Dunno. Did you know that was the sword I carried?"

He just whistles.

"Pretty crappy of fate that I would be the one to end up with that katana, then have the bad luck to have to surrender it and lose it." If I could kick my own ass for it, I would. "It's a sword, though, not a delicate medical instrument. And how the hell would that work? It sounds dangerous."

"We could try it out on something else. I don't want to have the first attempt done on my daughter." He's calm on the outside, but his knuckles crack as he crumples a protein bar wrapper.

"Yeah. I'll volunteer if we can't find anything else."

"No. We'll find something. Su-chan has described how you two can see the magic bound to ki users' souls. We'll need that ability."

"Want to see? It's pretty cool," I say. *Anything to distract us from the freaky topic.*

But he puts up a hand. "Another time. Now, you need to retrieve that sword."

"For many reasons." *Breathe.* "I have two clues. Ibaraki and the traitor, Mishima, have it. But where to find them? I saw a dark city beyond Mishima's portal. No idea what or where it is. The other clue is a card with a seal that appears when I touch it, but no contact info."

"May I see?" Yasu asks.

So I pull out my business card box and slide the strange paper toward him. As before, the logo appears and disappears when I let go of it. Yasu holds it up to the light, turning it over a few times.

He says, "No trace to the naked eye. What if…" then whispers a word of koto-dama that I don't recognize and squints at it. Shaking his head and trying another, he flicks the paper. His face brightens. "There! Can you see it?"

"Ah, no. I didn't recognize the word you used either."

"Oh, sorry. It's an archaic word. Much of our language has traces of Chinese imported with the writing system. If we can find the words older than that, sometimes they have more power. Though your mileage may vary."

"Really? Teach me, please!"

When I can say it right, I hold up the card and push ki into the paper just like I would another spell and the card sizzles with the brightest sparks I've ever seen. Even more spectacular than portal magic. The writing is in a faint glowing script that wriggles as if trying to escape scrutiny.

Yasu, who I didn't see get up, returns with a pen and paper so I can scribble the contact info down. He corrects a few of my chicken scratched kanji attempts because I don't know the symbols. Then the writing fades just as we get the last character down. I try to see if there was more, like an email, but the card won't allow further scrying.

"In Kyoto. That's convenient if you're heading back at some point."

Tucking the paper in my pocket, I bow. "Thank you so much! I couldn't have figured it out on my own."

"As the saying goes, Magic users…" He grins.

"…watch out for each other." The infectious expression spreads to my face as I finish the saying he uses so often.

Then my stomach sinks again. I'm gonna have to tell the mysterious contact I lost the damned sword. *Triple Fuck.*

Yasu pats my shoulder as he gets up. "Yukiko was hollering. I'll be back."

"And I need to make a few calls. Thank you, again."

Filling in Satou leaves him swearing, too. He's at the site where Shion made Su-chan tear apart riverbank buildings. His boss wants to haul her in for questioning. "Tell me you're far from here and getting her help, so this won't happen again."

"We're as far as we can be right now." Which is too close for comfort. But I don't dare say that, even to Satou. "And the dragon gave his word to never do it again. I won't tell you where we're going after this. But I'll check in as I can. Oh—and Aunt Hisako's been healed, thanks to Hoji. Wait a minute…"

"For what? Chief Arai is on hold for this call."

"Uh. Not what I meant. I think I figured something out to help Su-chan. I won't keep you."

"What did this Hoji pay to help our aunt?"

"He won't say, sir. I suspect it had to be a lot in terms of ki power."

"She let him?" he ask as he chuckles. We both know Aunt Hisako's stubbornness.

"It didn't go smoothly. But it was his sister that hurt Aunt Hisako. So he claimed family honor and all of that jazz."

Then Satou's voice cracks. "He's from the Date clan?!"

"Yes, sir. Though, now he's someone I like and maybe even trust. He's teaching us all a new magic."

"Not what his witch sister used?"

"No. It's based on electricity. Not harnessing oni to electronic devices."

"And you're gonna hunt down Honjou Masamune, right?"

The question makes my hands clench. "Yes, sir. I have a lead. Su-chan's dad helped me extract the address from the strange card Hiro left for me."

"There was an address on that thing? The forensics group had a fit about the magical seal on it. How'd you do it?"

I shrug, though he can't see it. I'm about to open my mouth to say and Yasu enters the room, shaking his head.

Now I'm in a bind. So I cover the mic on the phone. "It's PSIA Paranormal Division Business. He wants to know how we got the address."

Yasu's eyes bulge, but he waves the ok.

"It's old Japanese, sir. I can't show you over the phone."

Satou grumbles. I'd bet he's wiping his hand over his face. "Hiro should have recruited you those years ago because you find the things we need. You haven't crossed paths with a luck kami, like Ebisu, have you?"

For privacy, I step out of earshot again. "Not that I know, sir. Instead, I was wondering if I was cursed. Especially since I now owe a kami big time for bringing back Su-chan. I hope they won't demand more than I can pay."

"That'll be interesting." Satou's sarcasm drips through my phone. "By the way, Hiro lost that sword, too. He didn't want to lose it a second time, so he handed it to you."

"I've let him down."

"Baka! I told you so you know you aren't the first."

Sucking in a breath, I mutter, "Gotcha."

"So what are you gonna do now? It better be something useful."

"Hunt down the only lead I have. Any news on Ibaraki or a rogue baku?"

Satou hisses through his teeth and says, "I thought baku were always good."

"Nope. Mishima's a self-important twit."

"His name should help us keep an eye out for him. I'll contact you if I find anything."

Next, I check on Su-chan, who's fast asleep, and let the Ohno clan know I'll be heading to the shrine to give my thanks for Su-chan's recovery. Ken volunteers to drive. I'd rather walk. But I shouldn't leave Su-chan for very long or keep a kami waiting.

"Do you want me to come up there with you? It's such a creepy old shrine." Ken asks as I get out of the Toyota 2000GT that he rebuilt on his own.

Must be nice to have those skills and the cash for the hobby. I shrug. "The shrine is one of my favorites. I don't know how long this will take or even if anyone will be there to listen."

"Suzu-chan would shoot me if I didn't go with you." He closes the door with the same delicacy that he'd hold a baby. So, I follow suit.

Bowing, we head up the stairs I haven't trodden in weeks. It seems more like home than Kyoto. The wind blows gently on my face and the familiar scents of cedar and pine hit me.

Out of habit, I flip down any bibs in the fox statue's faces. *Shouldn't this shrine have a water stand for purification?* Ken's right. It's an odd place. But I wouldn't have it any other way.

We toss coins into the coffer, bow twice, clap and pray. 'I'm here, as you said. Thank you for helping bring Su-chan back.'

After I bow once more, the wind picks up, whipping my hair into my face and swirling the leaves that didn't fall off the trees last autumn.

Spring is peeking through the last hints of winter. So much has happened since I first stepped foot in Nonogawa and the air movement wasn't just a random gust; it increases.

Then Ken says, "You got someone's attention."

I turn around as the back of my neck prickles. "Yeah, but I don't see…" Abruptly, the blast stops, and a white fox steps from behind a tree.

On instinct, I fall to my knees, drop my gaze, and bow. What else can I do?

"Is that…" Ken's words trail off and he bobs deeply.

"Umeji-san, I apologize for the disturbance. Inari-sama said speed was priority over discovery today."

Damn. Not the voice I know. Too delicate. But I shouldn't have expected Yoshirou.

"Inari-sama appreciates your promptness and that you acknowledge the favor you owe, since you said you'd do anything."

At least it was Inari who answered my plea to help Su-chan. *Whew.*

Ken gapes. He can hear the messenger?

Then I gulp at the implication. Inari-sama is a good-hearted deity, but I was foolish to use those exact words. *What's done is done. Live up to your word.*

"You didn't specify it was one request to be fulfilled for such a difficult inter-vention."

Shit. My hand wipes over my face. No matter. Su-chan's life is worth anything I could pay.

"First, find Honjou Masamune. Recover her at all costs."

Everyone wants me to do this, even though I wish it didn't mean I have to figure out how to remove part of the magic inside Su-chan.

"Second, you doubt you have it in you to become a Guardian. Inari-sama is not pleased."

But Soujou-bou said he doubted me and Hayashi said no. *What am I missing here?*

"The kami do not give their support to just everyone, only the most humble and dedicated. Has that spirit left you?"

My breath hitches. Words escape me.

"Have you not seen how fractured the League is right now?"

There was disrespect to Soujou-bou and a betrayal. What else? Was there bickering over the loss of Honjou Masamune? And they can't agree on new blood. *Oh…*

"So you see how important it is for someone to be there who understands unity, yet is new. Yes?"

"I think so. They need more members to protect Japan, because of the sharp decline in yokai numbers."

"Correct. And Soujou-bou needs a dedicated supporter." The messenger kicks at the dirt with a paw. "After centuries of veneration, some of the kami don't understand that anymore. If they see it, they'll recognize it again."

"It's part of unity, isn't it?" No small task, bringing together beings much more powerful than myself.

She nods.

"And Inari chose one of the lowest to show that," I whisper.

Then she smiles. "Inari-sama enjoys a bit of irony here and there. Third-"

I'm so cursed. But I press my forehead to the ground one more time.

"Inari-sama will continue to call on you."

Yep, cursed. "I am at his disposal."

"As you are so fond of saying, everything is a test. But Inari-sama has plans for you. That is all."

Is that good? Because the proverbial piano is always hanging over head threatening to drop.

Finally, the messenger acknowledges my companion. "Inari-sama sends greetings to your clan, Ohno Ken-san. Good day."

After the fox fades from sight, Ken grabs my arm. "Did you really promise anything to help my sister?"

Knock it off! I yank my arm from his grasp. "Yeah. What of it?"

"Nothing. I was just surprised. That's all."

I sure as hell don't know Ken enough to share more. "Mind if I stay to tend the shrine? It needs some TLC. Whoever's watching the place isn't attentive." Dirt covers the floor and windows. Leaves lay scattered inside. Worse, the wind knocked the offerings over.

"You're not freaked out that a messenger fox visited." His hands go to his hips as he puts two and two together. "So this isn't your first time speaking with one?"

My head shakes as I pull out the cleaning supplies from the little closet in the back. "This one is a different messenger. The last one, he was cool, though I admire this one's spunk."

"Are you and Suzu-chan in danger, too?" He asks as he grabs the broom to help, but gets in my way.

How do I say this? "Me? Yes. Su-chan? Maybe. Though not in the same way. She's less of a target."

Scowling, he sweeps for a bit before stopping mid stroke. "I don't want her to go back with you."

Dusting off the offering containers and shelves, I say, "Understood." *Not his choice, though. Nor mine.*

"She's crazy about you. But she's never been in so much danger. I don't want her hurt like this again."

Duh. "You want me to leave her?" My voice turns razor sharp. Why is he butting into business that isn't his instead of supporting Su-chan's choices? If she heard about this, she'd be upset.

Then his hands fly up. "I didn't say that."

It's what you meant.

"Listen, Umeji, I just want her to be safe."

"What about happy? She hates people deciding for her."

That shuts him up.

"Hey, I'll walk back. You have other things to do." The sooner I get back to Su-chan the better, but I could use the space too.

"What about checking on my sister?"

"Then I'll run." *You don't want me around. Why should I catch a ride with you?*

"Don't be an idiot. You were just through some rough stuff, too. Your ki levels aren't restored yet. Besides, you'll see her faster if you ride with me. It's what? An hour's walk from here? I'm not a complete jerk, you know."

And you don't wanna look bad in front of your family.

This attitude won't help. So, I take a deep breath to clear my head. If I want to marry Su-chan, I have to figure out how to maintain the peace with Ken. He's only trying to look after his little sister. "Ok."

When we return, Su-chan is still asleep. I drag myself onto the bed next to her, but my brain won't slow down and I look up the address from that strange card on my phone. It brings up 'Kawahara Vegetables'. That can't be right. So I try again, ensuring I typed it correctly. No dice. *Why can't things be easy for once?*

An urge to slap my phone on Su-chan's bed stand almost overtakes me, but that would wake her up. Instead, I set it down and slip under the covers. Her warmth thaws me after the cold at the shrine. Just nuzzling into her neck is enough to loosen the tightness inside.

Then Su-chan stirs, turning over. "I thought you'd gone somewhere."

"I'm back. Was worried about you." To show it, I kiss her cheek and interlace my fingers with hers.

"Glad you're here," she whispers.

Maybe some things are simple. Simple is good.

A knock at the door and Ichiro's voice greets us. "You two gonna get up? It's almost noon. Lunch is ready."

Su-chan is the one to answer in sleepy slurred words as she yawns. "Huh? Did we sleep that long?"

"Good thing all we heard was snoring in there."

"Shut up, Ichiro!"

Then I whisper as footsteps retreat, "That's what I wanted to say, but I would have used more swear words."

It earns me a giggle before she asks, "So you're not upset about this fiasco?"

"Nope." To prove my point, I nibble on her neck. "Now that Ichiro's gone…"

She shoves me away, but there's a smile. My sunny Su-chan is back. *Maybe things'll be ok after all?*

During lunch, everyone asks how we're feeling. But all the looks direct toward Su-chan. It's so sweet how they're doting on her.

"Are you two returning to Kyoto when you're better?" Yasu asks.

"What do you think? Will you be ready to head back?" I ask. Even though I have things I have to accomplish, would it be best for her to have her family around?

"Yes. As soon as I have the strength. Your family needs to know what happened, especially your aunt."

Aunt Hisako's gonna be ticked.

Su-chan's ki well recovers faster than expected. So despite my growing dread, we head out the next morning for the den.

15

BLADE'S SACRED FLAME

IN THE QUAINT BACK room of the Kawahara Vegetable shop in Kyoto, I run my hand over my mouth. On the way in, I'd passed basket after basket of bamboo shoots, fern sprouts, and a ton of other leafy vegetables I didn't know the name of—some of them spicy, some grassy and earthy scented.

Why'd this person agree to meet me? Sure I mentioned Hiro. But what could these mysterious guys have to do with my aniki, my mob big brother and mentor? Was he a contact from his undercover work with the PSIA?

To stop the swirling of my thoughts, I sip on the fragrant, golden, hot tea a clerk left for me while the owner, an old gentleman, waited on a customer. Clinking the teacup harder than I expected on the table causes a faint blue flash on the door.

Magic? Prickles form on the back of my neck, so I whisper a word of kotodama to cast true seeing. My breath catches. Blue waves undulate over golden walled paintings.

Near the ceiling, the vents that allow air to circulate through the house hint at lavish rooms beyond the walls. But the humble windows of what must be an illusion say otherwise.

How's that possible? The ki expenditure to keep the spell running has to be crazy hard to maintain.

Before I can wrap my head around my surroundings, the door opens and the bent-over elderly man bobs a quick bow. "Sorry to keep you waiting." Wisps of hair in a comb-over don't cover his balding head.

I get up and return his greeting. "No problem, Yamazaki-san. The tea was delicious."

But his keen eyes narrow before his hand waves and my view of the palatial surroundings ceases. A chill runs down my spine and I swallow. *Did I do something wrong?*

"Umeji-kun. That's what you said your name was, yes?" At my nod, he sits with a dignity that looks beyond his station as a shop owner. Pouring a refill in the little teacup with its charming koi fish motif, he continues. "Otsuka Hiro-kun was adamant that we have confirmation before passing on the rest of his possessions to you. That is why you are here, correct?"

My gaze flicks to him, over the cup raised halfway to my lips. Satou, my parole officer and Hiro's partner, should have been the one here for that. "Actually, no. Didn't his possessions go to his family? He has a cousin."

Out of nowhere, Yamazaki slides a fist sized, intricately inlaid wooden box in front of me. Light and dark woods interlace in impossible rippling patterns over the surface, as if the container is a 3D illusion. "He wanted you to have this."

Picking it up reveals a plastic-like clunk from the inside. There's no obvious way to open it, but it's damned familiar as I flip it end over end in my hands. "A puzzle box."

The old man smiles.

"Should I open it here? Because I assume if it was just any puzzle box, you could have mailed it. You're giving it to me in person for a reason."

Then his eyes crinkle. "Yes."

As I push on the box's edges, hoping to reveal a moving part, my brow creases. It's harder to move than I expected.

"You've done these before?" Yamazaki asks.

"Yeah. Hiro-san made me do them often. There was one just like this I had to memorize by heart. He never said why, but this has to be it."

My fingers strain as I push to slide a section that was in the same spot on Hiro's old version. The moving parts are stiff compared to the one I practiced on years ago in a sequence I had to complete in less than two minutes.

Hiro always had reasons for things that seemed dumb. Eventually, I'd learn they had some significance.

Fifteen steps later, I slide the last section open to reveal a hanko—a formal signature stamp. *Is it made from bone?* When I tip it up to see the carving, there's that symbol from the business card Satou had given me upon Hiro's death—a sword and flame in a circle.

I'm about to run my finger over the stamp because it looks brand new, but the old guy snatches it from me fast as lightning. I flinch.

"Young man, if you don't know better, you aren't ready. Otsuka-kun should have told you what that seal represents."

It takes effort to swallow down the bile at the memory of how my aniki's life ended and I bow my apology. "He died before he could. I just got the business card and a note from him promising answers about the katana that turned out to be legendry and has incredible powers." Pulling the note and card from my shirt pocket, I flatten it out on the table.

Next, Yamazaki waves the seal over the card and, like it had when I first saw it, the embossed seal shimmers into view before fading again. "If Otsuka-kun didn't induct you yet, why did he give you access to his seal?"

"Good question. Maybe because he didn't want Honjou Masamune to fall into the wrong hands? But that's the problem. The L-" My mouth snaps shut of its own accord, and I growl. *Damn it!* Aunt Hisako still won't release me from the stupid spell seal, so I can't talk about the League. How the heck am I going to explain this?

"I wondered why it wasn't with you." The walls shimmer before the room darkens and Yamazaki's eyes glow a fiery red. "You will tell me what happened if you wish to leave this room."

I swallow. Another powerful magic user saying I can't leave if they don't like my answer. *What's with these guys?*

"T-there was a spell put on me, so I can't say a certain organization's name. But I was training to join them. They made me surrender the sword, saying only their elite can carry legendary blades. During the battle for Nonogawa, we lost it to Mishima, the traitor baku, and Ibaraki Douji. It wasn't in my possession, but I chased after them, anyway."

My gaze drops and my voice goes quiet. "In the end, they defeated me and portaled away, taking Honjou Masamune."

With pursed lips, Yamazaki nods. "So one of the greatest swords of all time is in the hands of the Oni Queen?"

Constantly have to relive my failures.

The room lightens and returns to its vegetable shop back room illusion. *Who is this guy?*

"Did it connect with you? Could you hear it speak?"

My head shoots up. "It called to me to not let them take it."

"Then you have a way to track her."

What's he talking about?

"If I reveal that secret, you must become one sworn to protect our order. Not a member, yet. And this obligation will not prevent you from becoming one of the League."

He knows about them? At my wide-eyed expression, he waves off my concern. "They are not half as secretive in the yokai community as they think they are. My order could teach them a thing or two. Since Otsuka-kun gave you access to his seal, I will share this.

"That container wasn't just an ordinary puzzle box. It had a lock spell on it and was changed before his death to allow you access. There was a great deal of planning done on your behalf. So I will take that as his recommendation. Normally, the new member would be with their sponsor at this meeting."

Instantly, my throat tightens at the mention that Hiro should have been here. He was there for most everything else in my life. Rasping, I say, "May I learn about this organization first?"

He shakes his head. "I can only tell you we are in charge of the most important weapon artifacts in Japan. That is all."

What's with all these secretive groups? And why me? Only one way to find out. "Are you sure you want someone who was yakuza to keep secrets for you?"

He shrugs as if it's a non issue. "You won't be the first."

Hiro, though he was undercover.

"But you would be the first potential Guardian."

"They don't want me." Pain stabs my chest at having to admit the failure, yet again.

Inari-sama said to not give up. *Idiot.*

"Their loss." My answer earns yet another shrug from Yamazaki. "Good luck. So you will take the vow, even without your mentor present?"

"If Hiro-san wanted me here, he had a reason."

"Very well." He picks up the seal, directing, "Hold out your right hand, palm up." When I do, he hisses. "Soujou-bou already sealed you, yet you're not a Guardian?"

"The seal is there because he disag-" My words cut off again and I stifle a string of swearing.

Suddenly, Yamazaki laughs. "There is disagreement in the League, I take it." He holds up his hand. "Don't verify. You'll only get cut off again. I'll have to put this one a little higher up. For a yakuza, you have several people who believe in you. That's impressive."

Former yakuza. I did. Soujou-bou is upset with me now.

Nevertheless, I present my palm.

He flicks his fingers, causing fire to appear and sticks the hanko stamp in the flame and a dish of salt. "Will you vow to keep our organization secret, with the only exception being that you are ready to bring us a new member?"

"Yes."

He presses the heated stamp into my skin, causing me to flinch as it sizzles. Though there's no scent of burned flesh. When I look down, I don't see the mark. But he passes the stamp over it. "It's sealed to your soul."

I freeze. *What the...?*

Waving it off, he says, "Soujou-bou does the same thing. He just doesn't explain." Without giving me time to process that tidbit, he barrels on. "You are a secret keeper of the Blade's Sacred Flame. Not a full member, mind you. Though you now help protect the most sacred forged works in Japan. Hiro-kun gave you Honjou Masamune to keep it out of Ibaraki's hands, yes?"

"Date Sari's. She was the threat at the time and managed to puppeteer Hiro-san with the help of Ibaraki." Click. These legendary weapons have something special that sets them apart and they're in that group that Ibaraki needs to become Shogun. "So, the items are sacred because our country's blade smithing uses kotodama?"

He grins. "Correct. The smith imbues the soul of the sword at its time of creation. Most will connect on a spiritual level with their wielders, but only if they deem the wielder worthy. This is why I asked if it spoke to you."

My "Wow," sounds lame. But nothing else would be appropriate in front of an elder.

"That connection should only happen with one of our members. If we find a legendary weapon wielder that is not in our circle, we do our best to induct them. But I've gotten ahead of myself."

Then he clears his throat. "Know that we must retrieve Honjou Masamune. You, in particular, because she created a bond. Also, you will never know all of our members. But we have ways of getting in touch with each other if the need arises. You and Otsuka-kun are some of the rare humans."

So, Yamazaki's yokai.

"I see that expression. You deduced correctly. And you'll know if a League member is one of ours if their weapon speaks to them. Do you have questions?"

"Will I be called upon for tasks?"

"Possibly. There are a few things you need to know. Any guesses?"

"You said I have to retrieve Honjou Masamune." *Did I miss something?* As I ponder, my hands stuff into my pockets and play with the book from my father.

"Yes. Since Honjou Masamune saw fit to claim you as her bearer, she will be in distress that you are not the one wielding her. It will take a toll on her soul and her power. If you do not recover her in time, she may lose the ability for her soul to leave the physical shell of her original forging."

That's how she was 'summoned' as a katana when I unsheathed her from the dagger length scabbard.

"The physical blade is likely locked away in some hidden underground collection in Tokyo. That is the best we could surmise before she was lost to us. Otsuka-kun was on the trail but had to hide the summoning hilt when he investigated the kitsune witch."

All the new information swirls in my head, threatening me with overwhelm. Scrunching my eyes shut, I let the facts settle themselves in a logical-ish order. But there are sizable gaps. "So, let me see if I understand. One, the original blade forged to make Honjou Masamune exists, but we don't know where. And two, what I thought was the sword is a summoning device? So it's like a ghost blade?" Soujou-bou had hinted at it, but now it makes sense.

He nods. "She is the spirit of ultimate sharpness. Forged for the great contest between Masamune and Muramasa."

"But the two swordsmiths were born centuries apart, weren't they?" That'd require time travel! My brows dig so deep that they press into my nose.

The reference makes his eyes sparkle. "So you know the stories?"

"I read every myth and folktale I could as a kid. Still enjoy them. My favorites were of the kitsune, but I also enjoyed the tales of the swordsmiths. Especially the ones about Muramasa and Masamune."

Deftly, he pulls a ragged hand-bound book off the shelf. "Then you should enjoy this."

The worn blue cover is in a calligraphy script I have difficulty reading and the title label threatens to fall off the book. The yellow, dog-eared pages give off a musty scent and a quick push of silent kotodama allows me to read the title: 'Smithing Lessons from the Great Master'. *Woah!*

"A duplicate of Muramasa's diary." Then he lifts his teacup as if in salute. "And you are a magic user that hides his ability, for I did not sense this when you first entered my home. But I've seen your magic twice now. Tell me, why do you hide? And how did a yakuza become a magic user? Most teachers refuse criminals, even former ones, as students."

Bang, my insides turn to ice. *Idiot.* You've become so reliant on using magic. It gave you away. Someday that'll get you or those you care about killed. Now, he's expecting an answer. "Well, I rescued a magic user. But I hide because Ibaraki and her minions are hunting for me and-" Ibaraki's overpowered too many already. I don't dare speak about my kitsune kin.

His hand waves off further explanation. "I understand. Just bring back the book when you finish. It's my personal copy."

So I hug the journal to my chest, like I did when Dad gave me the book I carry everywhere. "Thank you so much, Yamazaki-san!" *Talk about a treasure! Dad would have been so jealous.*

"Back to Honjou Masamune. She is a symbol of our nation's strength, only second in importance to the Three Sacred Treasures of the Imperial Regalia—the sword, Kusanagi no Tsurugi; the mirror, Yata no Kagami; and the jewel, Yasakani no Magatama. Do you understand?"

"I think so." I fucked up by handing it over. No one's gonna let me live this down.

"Even though we rarely involve ourselves in human matters, I will assist you in finding Honjou Masamune." Then he scowls. "Don't you give me that expression, Umeji-kun. The sword was in your care before the League lost it. Even though you surrendered it, it still had a connection to you, not to its previous wielder. So you will have the best chance of finding it, and this is where I can assist. I'll teach you on the way."

He gets up to gather his jacket and hat. Heading to the door and putting on his shoes, he says, "Let's go."

"Where are we going?" I ask and rise from the table to follow as my voice raises an octave.

"Tokyo, that's where the body of the sword is. There's no time to waste, young man."

"But-" I swallow. "I need to let my family know where I'm going." They'll be worried if I don't return soon.

"A yakuza caring about that kind of thing?"

Former yakuza. "I've left the criminal life behind, and I wouldn't have come alone for more than information."

"That paranoid?"

"Ibaraki has killed several I knew, including family."

"Yokai, you mean."

What the...? My body stiffens, and I stop in my tracks.

"I'm far older than any of your kitsune clan. Don't forget that."

He's definitely a yokai—ancient and powerful, since he can see right through me.

Then something niggles at the back of my mind, like I should know who or what he is. The name doesn't ring a bell, so his name has to be cover. "Yes, Yamazaki-san. I still need to include my clan in my plans. I have my reasons."

"And to let the League know your actions, no doubt." He harrumphs and puts his hat back on the rack.

"Not them, per se, but they will find out if I leave."

"I expect you and whoever you seem determined to gather here at sunset. Remember Honjou Masamune's strength wanes."

"Thank you, Yamazaki-san." I bow before exiting his shop into the alley and creating a portal to the den. The sun sets at about 6 PM, so I have less than five hours.

16

CONSEQUENCES

WHEN I RETURN TO the edge of Nakamura lands, Su-chan's scream echoes all the way down the hill.

So I scramble back to the den, where she herds the kits outside. "Hurry! We need to get you two to safety!"

Aunt Hisako scampers over, scooping up the little ones to offer a word of comfort.

"But Hoji-san's hurt!" Taka protests.

"We wanna help!" Yuri howls as she clings to Aunt Hisako.

"Not yet. Stay here," my aunt says as I follow her inside.

What the hell happened?

Hoji lies sprawled on the floor as a sizzling ring of black expands around him. Hissing, my aunt screeches to a halt.

"Shit." The word blurts from my mouth. "He's stealing ki."

"This is dire." Aunt Hisako says as she moves closer to examine.

"We just have to stop him, right?" *That's the way it was with me.*

"Not so simple. He's passed out. His body is doing this automatically. That means he was taking ki for quite a while. But why?"

Don't wanna say. Aunt Hisako doesn't need the guilt.

Then Great Uncle Nobu barges in, bellowing. "Not much time to help Hoji. Hisako, think of the kits you carry! Out! And Tatsuya, if your girlfriend could be pregnant, she can't be in here either."

"Got it. What can we do?" I ask.

"We have to contain his ki drain and hope he'll survive until he wakes."

Hang in there, Hoji!

180

"Lend me ki, so I can cast the series of spells. It's demanding." Great Uncle Nobu wades closer as if fording a stream.

When I put my hands on my great uncle's shoulder, I join him and shove against the hazy resistance flowing on the floor, charring it. Forming a box shape around Hoji, Great Uncle Nobu mutters spells one after another. Usually, spells are a single word. This new style is so different. *Ask later.*

But the blackness keeps creeping outward, singeing the floor and my shoes. The drain pries ki from us in a swirling eddy toward Hoji. Footsteps behind us announce help. Then a pair of hands grasps my shoulders.

Great Aunt Asako says, "Keep going, Nobu! Who knows how long Hoji-kun has!"

"Ta-kun?" Su-chan calls as she enters.

"Stay outside, Su-chan! Please! We've got this!" Her glare burns through the shirt on my back, but I focus on giving what ki I can.

"I can help!" she insists. The floor creaks.

Then my voice turns harsh. "Su-chan, I mean it! What if you're pregnant?"

"I'm not!" After a pause, she adds. "At least, I don't think so."

It's possible, though.

Her retreat earns a glance from everyone, but they return to the spell.

"What can I do from here?" Su-chan asks.

Softening my words, I add, "Please, watch over the children. Make sure they don't come in—no matter what happens."

Aunt Hisako moves away from the growing circle, since she's with child. "I'll call Hoji's mother and my sisters. We'll need all the help we can get. I think I know where they went shopping."

"I've got a portal ofuda and a shikigami we can use as a messenger, so you can stay if you want to help," Su-chan says as she dashes to follow my aunt.

Shikigami? Date Sari was amazing at puppet magic. So, Su-chan got that part of Sari's spirit, too. *How did I not know?*

After a few moments, Great Uncle Nobu places two more sides to the box and sweat runs down his forehead as he pants. "This should cut the flow of ki to him. A few more panels to go."

I'm almost tapped, but I give my uncle what I have left.

"Tatsuya, go now before you pass out or you'll become a victim. Reassure the twins. They're probably terrified."

"Will do." Stumbling out the door, I find the kits escaped Su-chan, who's hollering after them. They've been little terrors since they learned to take human form.

Snagging Yuri's hand and Taka's shirt, I drag them to the cherry tree at the edge of the property. "You two need to stay far away from this."

"But Hoji-san!" the kids protest in unison.

"We're doing what we can." Then I collapse at the base of the tree and Su-chan kneels to give me a sunshine warm burst of ki. I explain, "It's very dangerous right now. If you get in the way, it could cost Hoji's life or your own."

Instantly, the kits howl. Maybe I shouldn't have said it so plainly. But it was the truth.

Next, the three Nakamura sisters pop through a portal right outside the door. Aunt Hisako approaches us, while her sisters rush to the den.

She nuzzles the twins. "It'll be alright. When we stop the ki drain, we can save him."

"What's happening, Hisako-san?" Yuri asks as she sniffles.

"Hoji took ki."

It makes the kits gasp.

Aunt Hisako commands, "Stay. I've got to help him."

Just then, another shriek emanates from the house. Su-chan herds the kits down the hill again while I book it after Aunt Hisako, despite the weariness in my legs. Grandma Miwa sobs next to the limp kitsune form of her son as my uncle whispers, "No wonder he wouldn't be in fox form. He's down to one tail!"

Once a kitsune's tail is removed, they can never get it back. They'll lose their ability to be a high-level magic user.

Before this, he'd had three. Now, he'll be less likely to find a mate or to serve as a messenger. *Why'd Inari require so much?*

Turning to Aunt Hisako, Grandma Miwa shouts, "He sacrificed for you! Help him!"

When my aunt tries to enter the room, I block her way. "You're pregnant. There's no way you're going in there."

But her eyes flash. "I've taken steps to protect the kits in my womb. Step aside, Tatsuya. Now."

I've been on the other side of that determination. Don't want to repeat it. So I let her pass.

Tying her kimono sleeves back, she says. "Hoji sacrificed for me out of more than just the Date family honor. I owe him."

Then Grandma Miwa wails, "I can't lose the last of my children!"

Didn't she hear what my aunt said?

"Tatsuya, get Miwa-san out of here. She can help when she's not hysterical." Next, Aunt Hisako puts her hands on her father's shoulders.

Her whispered words sound like a far-off, otherworldly chant and a wave of phosphorescent ki flows like a trail of mist into the room. There's also a response echo as the blue tendril snakes its way through the air and into her.

What the...?

At that moment, Great Uncle Nobu crashes to his knees.

"Father, I'll finish the spell. Go." Aunt Hisako releases her grip, weaving the words with him and picking up the spell where he left off.

"You knew this magic?" he asks, crawling to his feet.

"I connected to your mind. So I know it now." Her voice still carries the mountain echoes.

"But there's a price for what you're doing, Hisako."

"Less than what Hoji paid for me. Let me complete this, or all of us die."

The hazy, charring darkness continues its ominous, rippling expansion past the door. *How far has it reached?*

Helping Grandma Miwa and Great Uncle Nobu out of the dead zone and into the yard reveals the wave of energy coming from the forest—the kodama grove of echoing tree spirits.

Finally, Aunt Hisako shouts, "It's done." The spread halts as the ground smolders in front of the door and the smoke makes our eyes water.

Are we gonna be able to get rid of that stench?

Then my aunt drops to the floor on her hands and knees, out of breath. "Now, to help him survive the shock. Tatsuya, tell Miwa-san to run a steaming bath. Have Su-chan prepare for treating magical shock."

No need to say it. Grandma Miwa was behind me and scrambles toward the tub.

"But I'm out of a few key ingredients. I was going to get more today," Su-chan whispers.

So Grandma Miwa commands, "Get a kappa. They'll have them."

"Sekiguchi is wounded. I don't know where he and Shion are. Other options?" I ask. Su-chan's been hard on my stash of portal ofuda and there's been no time to replenish them.

With brows furrowed, Great Uncle Nobu adds, "He's the only kappa nearby. Does anyone know of another?"

"Tatsu, please fetch my father. Do you have enough energy?" Su-chan asks.

Great Uncle Nobu shoots me a look. Countering, Aunt Hisako says, "Ohno Yasu is an excellent healer and his clinic helps yokai of all species."

But Nonogawa's a long way. My legs are wobbling already. "I'll do my best."

"Baka!" Su-chan chides and slaps my arm to flood me with sunshine warmth. "Go! The clock is ticking for Hoji!"

Yasu and I return a few moments later. Inside the bath area, everyone crowds around. Aunt Hisako is already in the tub, dressed only in her underwear, holding the unconscious Hoji. The air is so hot and steamy it's hard to breathe as the ki stream still flows in. Though now, it connects to Hoji. *How much will the kodama give for one kitsune life?*

While Hoji lays in Aunt Hisako's arms, she strokes the tips of his ears and ponders aloud. "How could I have let things come to this? He sacrificed for me. Another time that it took extreme measures to see the value of someone."

Kinda intimate, isn't it?

Since I'm standing around, Yasu puts me to work chopping herbs.

Then Hoji stirs. "Because our people have always been hunted. Trust doesn't come easily."

Great Uncle Nobu adds, "And there were all the spoiled brats who wanted to marry my beautiful daughter so she could serve them. Not treasure her in return."

But Hoji's not been that way.

Aunt Hisako turns toward the door. "The trees are saying they can't give much more ki, or they'll be defenseless."

At that, the blue wave fades and an echo reverberates around us. "Remember your promise."

My aunt's voice has the same strange vibration as she replies, "Thank you, kodama-san. Tell the forest I will keep that promise and will never forget what you all did for my people today."

Hoji groans. When his head raises, it only makes it a few centimeters before crashing back down.

To make room to work, Yasu shoos everyone else out except Su-chan and me. "He's out of immediate danger, but Suzu and I need room to finish our work."

Next, Yasu asks, "Hoji-san, how do you feel?"

"Terrible." His voice cracks.

Aunt Hisako strokes his ears again, and his spine stiffens. So she whispers, "Relax, then we can deal with the repercussions of your taking ki."

Instead, he growls. "What do you want from me? I'm just a ki-thief to you all now."

"Hush and listen."

"Like I have a choice." Settling, he lays his head on her shoulder and she leans back.

"With your sacrifice, you showed you weren't the spoiled brat you first appeared to be, and your unselfishness brought your character into focus."

But he turns his head away, giving a short rumble to get to the point.

"So I assume you've been coping with having less magic through drawing ki here and there," Aunt Hisako asks.

His muscles tense again, and he struggles to get up.

"I'm trying to understand. Not judge. You didn't take it from living beings. So how?"

He sighs. "The electricity I deal with every day."

Makes sense. He teaches how to use it, after all.

"Now, are you done interrogating me?"

So, Aunt Hisako strokes his fur again. "We need to understand what we'll be up against."

Meanwhile, Su-chan measures ingredients into a mortar as Yasu observes the interchange. His tone is neutral to avoid agitation. "You're addicted to drawing ki to cope with the loss of power. When you passed out, your body did what it was used to—it took ki."

Nodding, Aunt Hisako says, "You're going to need someone to help you through to the other side of this."

Hoji only whines. "It's gonna be rough, isn't it?"

"I'm here. We'll get through it together, if you let me help."

"So you can hold that I stole ki over my head for the rest of my life? No, thank you."

Stop being a putz, Hoji. She's not like that.

185

After a moment, she blows out a breath and says. "I took ki, too. Over a hundred years ago."

Yasu pauses, but goes back to grinding another set of herbs.

"You're just saying that, so I'll agree," Hoji counters.

Unruffled by the argument, Yasu sends me to fetch more wood for the fire.

When I return, it's Yasu, not Hoji, who asks, "Tatsuya-kun, can you tell us if your aunt took ki? We have a dispute."

I set the firewood down in a neat stack by the tub so it's easy to feed into the heating stove. And I reason Aunt Hisako needs to win this argument for the sake of her people.

Still, getting involved in an argument makes my insides tighten. "I found out after I had taken ki too, not understanding what was happening. I just needed to stop Date Sari the first time we fought her. She accused my aunt of taking ki and other awful things."

Then I can't meet Hoji's eyes. He keeps having to learn the shit his sister did. *Don't go into details.* "After I recovered, Aunt Hisako read me her diary entries. She'd given in and performed the forbidden magic to save her son after Sari struck him with lightning. His spirit hadn't left his body yet. So there was a small chance that it would work."

Hoji hisses through his teeth. "My sister tried to ruin everything in your lives over the death of her beloved Ii-san, didn't she?"

"But she didn't succeed. My family flourished despite her attempts to wipe us out," Aunt Hisako counters.

"No wonder you thought ill of me. I remind you of her."

"Not anymore. Now, I want to at least help you through this. And we can see where we want to go from there. It's time I took a husband from my species."

As in be his wife? My jaw drops. That's a hell of a hint, Aunt.

Wait. There's something she hasn't explained. So I clear my throat. "Aunt, what did you do to finish the spell box around Hoji-san? It sounds like you made a sacrifice, too."

"I did. Though we can discuss that later," she says and waves it off.

But Hoji shakes his head. "No. I need the facts."

"We'll speak when you are out of danger."

"You will tell me now, or you will get the hell out of my sight." A low growl emanates from his throat as he wriggles out of her grip.

Instead, my aunt laughs heartily, making the fur on Hoji's head fluff. "Samurai spirit to the core."

I have to stifle a chuckle at the glare he gives combined with the only dry hair, being on his head, puffing up to make him look more like a mushroom than a grumpy fox.

When Aunt Hisako can quell her reaction, she says, "I made a deal with the forest here in Kyoto. I'd hoped to finish training Tatsuya in Nonogawa, but my promise will keep me here for decades."

"Explain." Hoji punctuates the word.

She's still expecting me to be a Guardian, too. *How is that gonna work?* "Aunt, Soujou-bou and Hayashi-san said-"

"Pshaw. We just have to convince the stubborn old birdbrains to change their minds."

I gape. *She called the Council that?*

Unfazed, she continues, "In the meantime, Tatsuya, I'll ask my predecessor to assist when you return to Nonogawa. But I should be able to train you to take over the Guardianship from here, thanks to portal spells."

"What did you sacrifice?" Hoji growls.

"I was getting there! I promised to help re-establish the sentient forests for the kodama. There are so few of them left, like our own kind. It was a reasonable request on their part."

"So you're not going back to Nonogawa?" Suddenly, pain creeps up the back of my neck. Aunt Hisako was the reason people accepted me there. *How the hell am I gonna make that work now?*

"No, Tatsuya. I've maintained an old-woman disguise for over half a century for the sake of my family. It's time to retire it. You and Kazuo will take care of things in my absence."

Damn.

Next, the sun peeking through the window so low in the sky reminds me. "Since the situation is under control, I need to book it to my meeting at sunset with a lead on Honjou Masamune. Do you all have support ready in case there's an attack?"

Aunt Hisako nods as Su-chan and Yasu clean up.

17

THE HUNT BEGINS

Tugging my girlfriend into the hallway, I share, "Su-chan, I'd like you to come."

Her expression turns dark. "We need to recover that sword. I'm glad you're not thinking about going alone."

"We? The one who bears the blame for losing Honjou Masamune is me. I'm just not sure what to make of this contact."

"I couldn't help you when you needed it and the reason the L-" Her mouth clamps shut. "Gah! The reason Soujou-bou couldn't get to you sooner. Besides, you insisted we face things together."

Turning into a destructive dragon is going to haunt her for a long time, but she's right. So, I squeeze her hand. "Together."

When we've gathered a stack of talismans, Great Uncle Nobu accompanies Sekiguchi to the main room. The kappa shows up walking on his own and sporting a gun-metal gray prosthesis to replace his lost arm.

"I will accompany you, if only because I feel I need to be there, too." The section above Sekiguchi's beak wrinkles in a scowl. "This premonition won't leave me alone."

Wow, that was a fast recovery for such a serious wound! "Are you sure you're healed enough to go?"

"I am, thanks to a certain group's funding. So, I will join you at the appropriate time."

"And you know where we're going?"

Sekiguchi nods. "I'm familiar with the area. A powerful presence lingers there."

Just then, Jiro peeks in. "Woah! Sekiguchi-san, your new arm is so cool!"

"I'm still getting used to how it changes my magic. But I'm grateful to the medical research lab at Kyoto Jidai Arcane University for letting me be a test subject for this prototype." The kappa holds out his hand, flexing it for all of us to see.

That's the school Hoji teaches for.

"It works just like your other arm?" Su-chan asks.

"Mostly. The inscriptions on the titanium replace the nerves to provide the sense of touch. Though the joints will need special care, since I'm an aquatic yokai."

I lean in for a better view. The metal fingers have open articulations to allow for the hand's movement. "How does it change your magic?"

So he whispers a word of kotodama and runes flash over the entire surface. "The metal. It gives a different feel to the ki flow. They had to meld the connections to my remaining nerves." Grimacing, he confesses, "It was... unpleasant. Though they did an excellent job. I shouldn't have to deal with ghost pain."

Jiro asks, "Ghost pain?"

Jumping in, Su-chan clarifies, "When someone loses a body part, their nerve endings transmit pain signals as if the body part is there."

"Regarding changes to my magic, Shion didn't recognize my ki signature. We'll see if there's a metallic tint to my spells now and if they're as powerful. Since I'm only the second with this technology, they can't be sure of the effects." Sekiguchi makes a fist and releases a few times as he says, "Robotics and magic. It still amazes me, and I've seen a lot in my centuries."

Click. The battle at Nonogawa. "Was Ibaraki Douji the first to have the prototype?"

As if it's natural, Sekiguchi's metal hand goes to his chin. "They didn't say. But it's a logical conclusion since she had a similar prosthesis. But it's time you two are off."

Then Jiro asks, "Where are you guys going? Can I help?"

"We're tracing a lead on Honjou Masamune. Yamazaki-san wanted me to go with him."

Great Uncle Nobu says, "Let the boy tag along. He needs a few adventures to test his abilities. And his magic style will be handy."

Is Jiro gonna be safe? I don't have a good feeling about this, but I don't dare contradict an elder. And I can't say no to the boy's big brown eyes as he pleads. Three of us should be able to watch over him. "Will you stay out of trouble?"

He nods as he bounces on his toes before running off to verify with his mom. Reluctantly, she agrees.

While I wait for Jiro to grab his jacket, I fill Satou in, too. He's relieved that Aunt Hisako isn't coming with us, but he's concerned that she and Hoji were decoys in the battle over Nonogawa.

In a few moments, Su-chan, Jiro and I portal to behind Yamazaki's house, just as the sun melts into the horizon. We're late. Taking a deep breath, I steel myself. It's best to be early and be the one waiting for the other party, especially when dealing with someone much older and more powerful than us.

Dread fills my voice. "Let's book it to the front. I don't want to keep this guy waiting any longer."

But Su-chan grimaces. "You say that like he might smite you. So what is Yamazaki-san?"

"No clue. He only said he was older than the kitsune I know, and his magic is off the scales. He could snap his fingers and we'd be dead."

As we take our first jogging steps, the back door opens. "It took you long enough. Young people these days can't abide the common courtesies."

We all bow in unison, and I speak for the group, "Sorry, Yamazaki-san. There was an emergency at home."

Then his eyes soften and he holds open the door. "Come in and tell me what happened."

He ushers us to a simple guest room with cushions on the tatami mats and an exquisite sumi ink painting in the alcove. My old yakuza boss used space like this to show off his wealth, so I know quality when I see it. But Yamazaki's a vegetable shop owner. *Or is he?* There was that hint of palatial rooms being hidden by a wall of costly magic.

Movement in the painting catches my attention, and a bird swoops through it. So I rub my eyes, but the bird is gone. *Not a simple shop owner at all.*

When we sit, wards flash around his door. He says, "No prying eyes or ears will get in here. I assume the emergency was with the kitsune, yes?"

We all nod, and I share what happened with Hoji, but leave his name out.

"So your family will have their hands full. Tell me you didn't leave them unguarded."

"My aunt and her parents are capable and have connections ready to help."

"Good. Now, I will show you how to track our quarry. Come with me." When the crew steps forward, he says, "Just Umeji-san. And you..." Yamazaki points to Jiro, "Young man, the wards here are not for you to copy."

Jiro startles, jumping several inches off the ground before bowing. "Sorry, sir. I was just trying to understand them and make sure our magically enhanced devices wouldn't interfere."

Don't talk to an elder as if they could be wrong! I glare, shaking my head at Jiro.

"I-I didn't mean... I-I just..." Jiro bows instead of sticking his foot farther in his mouth. "Sorry, sir!"

But Yamazaki's eyes narrow and he holds out his hand. "Let me see, boy."

When Jiro offers the phone with shaking hands, the old man runs a palm over it. The yellow EMF field shows up and his head tilts.

"Interesting. It's about time you whippersnappers figured out how to manipulate electricity. I've read about the theory from a fellow named Date. If you'd like, I could introduce you to him. 'Denki', electricity's kanji, was aptly chosen after all, with 'ki' in its name."

Then with a wiggle of his fingers, Yamazaki causes a blue glow to mesh with the yellow around the phone. The spell turns a green so alive it puts the old, sickly 70s avocado color that Date Sari's corrupted magic gave off to shame.

"Date Hoji-san is my teacher, sir."

And I add, putting a hand on the boy's shoulder, "Jiro is a prodigy in this new style of magic."

"Indeed?" Yamazaki grins. "Well then. Examine what I have done and duplicate it for any of the other enhanced devices your group has."

Jiro lights up so much his face rivals the glow of all the magic in the room. "Y-yes, sir!"

Curiously, Su-chan peeks over his shoulder as the boy dives in to dissect the new spell.

Then Yamazaki waves for me to follow him upstairs when Jiro says, "I didn't know merging the two magic styles was possible! Hoji-sensei has always had me be so careful to separate them. He's gonna freak when he sees this! Now, is this a layer or a function..."

As Yamazaki holds the door open for me, his eyes twinkle. "That should keep him busy. Youngsters like him always enjoy a challenge. I assume he is on this quest because of his talent."

"And his teachers couldn't join us. Sir, you just changed a new technology in the blink of an eye. How?" I ask.

"I keep up with research, especially when it could relate to magic. His teacher, Date, is the one who stole ki, yes?"

So, I give the minutest of nods. "Both Jiro and Hoji have been through a lot."

"I suspect that is the way of things. Our kind finds change difficult, Ume-ji-kun. Yokai, who haven't had to change for millennia, will have to adapt or become obsolete. All we've done is hide in plain sight for centuries." Then Yamazaki's lips purse. "I'm afraid those left behind will be the victims of a new power vacuum."

"You adapted. My family is, too. The PSIA is doing its best to do so. What if many more are, too?"

"But you didn't mention the League of Guardians."

I gulp. Saying something won't work, but not speaking will reveal just as much.

Then he closes the door and points to a cushion for me before flipping a light switch. Instead of bulbs turning on, the room lights up with glowing lines of circuit-like kanji.

I can only gawk at the spiraled filigree in the ceiling.

But he laughs, waving off my reaction. "I had Date Hoji-san install that. You can bet your bottom yen I studied it until I understood it." Clearing his throat, he says, "You are the first connection to the Guardians to consider what I have to say about modernizing. Likely the youngest. How old are you, Umeji-kun?"

"Twenty-four, sir. But I'm not sure they'll let me j-" Join anymore. *Fuck this seal on me.*

He nods before snapping his fingers to make the water simmer in the unplugged electric kettle and meticulously pours the brew into the cooling bowl.

"I am impatient for tea, but it's not quite the same unless you steep it right. But we can speed up the heating of the water without affecting the taste. So while we wait, let me show you how to communicate with Honjou Masamune. She is likely panicking that you haven't reached out to her yet."

And she's depending on me. Everyone is. "Let's do this."

"When you first received the sword, and she materialized when wielded, she would have offered the bond. Though you didn't know to look for it. At some point afterward, you accepted her of your own volition. It would have been subtle. That Hiro trusted you and Honjou Masamune chose you, speaks well. The bond is a connection at the soul level. Unique to the pair and it was through that telepathic connection that she reached out to you."

"Like the communication link between Su-chan and I at the last battle?" I ask.

"Similar. Are you capable of sensing links between beings?"

"Like puppeteering strings..." I flinch when his stare bores into me. "Date Sari did that to several people I know. Or maybe like the red string of fate for lovers?"

He nods. "The second, despite having the word 'fate' in it, is also voluntary, but at the deepest level. The connection to Honjou Masamune for you is like that. Since you did not know of the nature of the link, she could not establish communication until she was so desperate she pushed a substantial amount of her energy through for words to form."

"Do I have to be in the same situation to return the communication?"

"No. Especially since you initiated a telepathy spell."

"Uhm, sir. My aunt set that communication link up for Su-chan and I."

He pauses. "Well, we all start somewhere. It's easiest with an existing link, like physical contact or an emotional connection. Since you don't know me, I'm going to put my hand on your shoulder while I pour the tea. Try as hard as you can to send me a message. If I receive it, I'll send a thought back."

As I take a deep breath, my mind of course chooses that moment to go blank, but I concentrate hard on Yamazaki's hand on my shoulder. *What the fuck do I say?*

He jerks. 'Anything you want. And you don't have to shout... or swear. Though, I am surprised you got it first try.'

So, I shrink in on myself. *Sorry!*

Then his voice enters my mind again. 'You've done everything with brute force so far, haven't you? We need to work on your subtlety. Not only will you avoid startling those you communicate with, but you'll save ki for all your magic—extending your reserve even farther.'

I blink. 'That's possible? How?'

'I'm getting there, young man. Patience.'

At the censure, my face scrunches like when mom scolded me for stealing from the cookie jar at home, but it softens when he slides a cup of green tea in front of me. Then a plate joins it with an intricate purple wisteria treat sitting alongside the most adorable little dinosaur one. The traditional seasonal wagashi sweet combined with such a whimsical offering makes me grin. *Disarmed by cuteness.*

'I'm glad you like them. Now, try breathing and letting go of the thought as you send it.'

I do so, imagining letting a feather drop. 'Like this?'

'Much better. Enjoy your tea.' Then he lets go of my shoulder.

How are Su-chan and Jiro doing downstairs?

'They are fine. Young Jiro-kun is showing the lady how the spell is done and adding it to her phone.'

That makes me jolt. 'We're still connected?'

'Yes. Now, close the connection, so your thoughts can stay private.'

Though there's a hesitancy from him. He's expecting a slam, isn't he?

I don't know how to do this, but I imagine the connection as a portal. Instead of letting it slam shut, I have it fade out of sight.

With a delicate slurp, he finishes his tea. "Now that you won't scare Honjou Masamune and reveal you're communicating with her, I'm going to have you find that specific thread. Then we'll head out."

"You're coming with us?"

"Do you not want me to?"

Instantly, my hands cross in front of me. "That's not what I meant!"

"Otsuka-san was right about you. Good at the core, just got mixed up in the wrong crowd. Anyway, my connections in Tokyo may prove useful. Let's find that thread between you and Honjou Masamune."

So using a word of kotodama again, I cast true sight and look for a type of thread I'd not seen before. But the number of lines that appear is mind-boggling. *I'm connected to that many others?*

"What do you see?"

"A huge web of strings I can't separate."

He laughs. "Which one vibrates when you say the sword's name?"

Can it be that simple? "Honjou Masamune."

Pling! A faint thread thrums away. So, I reach out in order to keep track of it.

Pling! This time, the vibration returns. She knows! *Sweet!* "Should I say something?"

"Not right now. The sun has set. We're about to miss our ride."

Quickly, I dismiss the spell and follow him back downstairs. That's when there's a knock at the door. Yamazaki opens it and sweeps his hand in a grand gesture. "I assume the disguised kappa is joining us, too."

The stringy hair, metallic hand peeking out from the suit sleeve, and his widening golden eyes give him away before Sekiguchi gives the deepest bow I've ever seen. "I am your humble servant, master. It would be an honor."

"Is everyone ready for a ride in style?" Yamazaki asks as he dons his hat and grabs his cane and pipe. "It's been a while since anyone rode with me in the procession."

Jiro's eyes light up. "You mean a limo, sir?"

But Yamazaki shakes his head and winks. "You'll see."

As we step out the door, eight bulky human-ish servants with elongated necks bow deep and long before they lift the poles on a gold trimmed covered box. Yamazaki snaps his fingers, and the box expands to be large enough for our entire group.

Su-chan places a palm over her heart, uttering, "A palanquin!"

Out of nowhere, more yokai gather behind the box and bow, much like my clan had to bow to our leader in the yakuza. Yamazaki returns the greeting with a perfunctory dip as if it's his due.

When he steps into the box, his body shifts to be much shorter, and his head elongates to be large and bulbous. While his form looks stumpy, he has the bearing of one who's led others for a long time.

The king of the yokai. "We're in the presence of the most powerful..." So I drop to a reverent bow.

Yamazaki says, "Get in. We're holding up the procession."

When we do, the palanquin bearers ask, "Nurarihyon-sama, where is the Night Parade headed?"

"Tokyo, on the double," the yokai king, that used to be disguised as Yamazaki, declares.

"N-night p-parade?" Jiro asks.

"What do you have to fear, my young yokai friend?"

"I-I guess I am a yokai, aren't I? Thank you, sir, for showing me how to mix the magic types."

"And for the ride!" The rest of us chime in unison.

Nurarihyon chuckles. "There will be rumors of you being spirited away."

As soon as we hit the cushions, the palanquin lifts from the ground, jostling us all.

Unruffled, like such a parade is normal, the king of the yokai says, "Hang on to the hand loops if you must. This ride may be bumpy since it is not my usual route. And you will continue to refer to me as Yamazaki-san. I will not be revealing my nature on this trip unless it is necessary."

So I slip my hand around Su-chan's on the strap.

I've been privileged to be among so many yokai straight out of legend. Dad would be amazed!

"Yes, Yamazaki-san," we echo as fast, heavy foot falls slap the street. Sitting in silence, we hear the steps fade, but the ride turns bumpier, and the palanquin pitches backward.

"Look out the windows if you like." Yamazaki motions as if offering a tempting treat.

Sekiguchi is the first to dare lifting the black curtain. We all crane to see. Mist fills the streets below as we rise into the sky and the houses fall away. Jiro can't resist and whips the curtain up to get a better view to gawk at the retreating scenery behind us. The jostling speeds up and soon we're above the clouds. Then a glow encompasses the procession and everything fades.

Spirited away, for sure!

"It's not as fast as a direct portal, but I have standards and expectations to maintain," Yamazaki remarks. "And you'll be safer entering Tokyo with this procession. Though the small group of you can sneak into places if need be."

18

KABUKICHOU

WHEN THE WORLD MATERIALIZES around us again, we're descending over Tokyo Bay toward the heart of my hometown. My stomach tightens and my hands go clammy. It's hard to breathe, but we're too high to exit the palanquin.

"Tatsu, are you ok?" Su-chan asks.

"Didn't think I'd return." I refuse to gaze out the window, unlike the others. Closing the curtain doesn't stop the memories—the deaths, abandonment, horrible things I've done, and all I saw. So much I should forget, but can't.

"Are you sure you'll be alright, Umeji-san?" Sekiguchi echoes my girlfriend.

I should be able to fight off the sharp tightening in my chest by the time we get out. Remember, we're doing this to save kitsune-kind and retrieve the sword. *I won't get sucked in again.* So I give a curt "Yes."

"Then connect with Honjou Masamune," Yamazaki says.

As I suck in a calming breath and re-establish the spell to perceive the silver threads that connect me to others, I whisper the sword's name to receive that distinctive thrum.

Out of curiosity I do the same for Su-chan—the lone red thread, so easy to distinguish.

She jumps as the thrum hits her. "What was that?"

"A test using the thread between us. I know what to expect now. Sorry." I duck my head as she glares.

Is there a way other than names to tell the strings apart? *Such a confusing web.* A guy could go crazy considering every thread and the connections we have to each other. Though it creates the case for kindness.

Shaking my head, I select the thread to Honjou Masamune and, feather soft, push a message through. 'We're in Tokyo looking for you.'

The return? A sigh of relief.

'Any hints you can give?' I ask.

No answer, but there's a distinct dimming in the line. "Something's wrong. The connection thread is harder to see."

So Yamazaki sweeps his hand in front of me and speaks the name of the sword. After brushing his fingers over the line, his hand freezes and retreats. "The connection shouldn't fade like that."

I ask why, but he has no answers.

When the thudding footsteps and jostling stop, a servant opens the palanquin doors. We hop out into cool, but stale air.

Posters depicting cute girls in school uniforms surround us on the basement hall walls. A sign says 'pat' and 1800 yen.

Aww, shit. This is not where I want Su-chan and Jiro to be. Of course, the yokai king would pick a place like this. He's known for visiting brothels; this is just a few steps away.

Worse, I don't know which yakuza clan controls this area. Who knows what happened in the power vacuum when my clan was wiped out? If anyone recognizes me, things could get ugly.

Then Yamazaki holds up a hand. "We will be visible in five seconds. Act as if you've been there all the while. There's no time to waste." He looks at his watch. "It's about 11 PM, so most places are still open." All the yokai in the procession disperse through walls, or disguise themselves to blend in.

"What did the sword tell you?" Sekiguchi asks.

"She's relieved we're on our way." My brow crinkles at the fading thread. Click. "What if I put energy into the fading connection?"

"Ooh! That might help," Su-chan says.

Yamazaki says, "Not too much. If it energizes her, the enemy may notice. It could give away our advantage."

"Gotcha." So I add just enough ki to make the line brighten.

"Sekiguchi-san and I are going to check with a few contacts," Yamazaki says and asks for my cell phone number before heading into the establishment.

Grabbing Su-chan's hand and tapping Jiro's head to get his attention off the wall of cute masseuses, I snap, "Let's go," and lead them to street level.

Su-chan's head swivels from side to side, trying to take in all the lights, people, and sounds of the night-time streets. She whispers, "This is amazing! But why doesn't everyone go home at night?"

"It's a lot to take in, especially after living in a quiet little town." Every nerve buzzes with the immense amount of input. Back in my old groove, I scan our surroundings for anomalies and guide Su-chan and Jiro around the insistent host and hostess club touts.

While we wait to cross the street, Su-chan's wide-eyed gawking at everything and clinging to my arm as I lead our group makes me walk a little taller, despite my unease.

"The big city is 24/7. Normally Tokyo is safe, but this is one of the more notorious places at night. And close to my old stomping grounds." *Too bad we don't have time to play tourist.* Su-chan would love the shopping and Jiro would be ga-ga over Akihabara. "Someday, we should come back to see the fun side of the Tokyo area."

Then a thrum hitting my ki well startles me back to our purpose. After a few tries, I single out the thread. That way I can watch it and just maybe it'll help us track the sword. The vibration came from my right, so I look down the major street.

"You used to live here?" Jiro asks.

"Yeah." Though, my response comes out so flat it dampens the excitement on his face.

A few moments later, the boy's stomach growls. "Can we eat soon?"

Idiot. He's not used to being on the job and we didn't get dinner.

"Let me see... There's a back-alley sukiyaki place that should be open. Best in Japan." My lips purse as I place my bearings, and a little lightness enters my steps. *Sugita's sukiyaki. One of the best things about this district.* "Can you see the famous Kabukichou gate?"

Quickly, I give another thrum of the connection thread and the vibration leads deeper into the district. *Please, don't let me meet up with old connections.*

"Cool!" Jiro exclaims as he whips out his phone for a picture.

But I squeeze his shoulder after the photo. "I was serious. We need to keep our guard up here. Can't be lookin' like tourists. You too, Su-chan."

"I haven't seen you this edgy since we discovered your tattoos," she mutters.

As Su-chan lets go of my hand to guide Jiro, whose eyes continue to be drawn to the nightlife and neon signs, a high-pitched squeal pierces the night. "Tatsuya!"

Instantly, my hands fly up to ward off the woman, who looks like she came out of a hostess club job, barreling right for me.

Chisa. Oh fuck, not now! My heart stops as my brain flashes images of what we shared, all of it brazen. But her farewell, 'This life isn't for me. Goodbye, Tatsuya,' doesn't crush me this time.

"I can't believe I found you!" Slender arms wrap around my chest as I try to back away, and she collides with me, attaching like Velcro. Her lavender perfume is so strong my nose wrinkles.

Shouldn't have returned. "Iwate Chisa." My tone lacks any warmth as I spit the name and peel her hands off me.

Why is she here? She'd left, saying she was going back to her parents somewhere up in the Tohoku region. God, the heartbreak and alcohol I went through. But now? I wouldn't ask for her back if my life depended on it. Su-chan values me for who I am, instead of a meal ticket.

"I've been looking all over for you! Where have you been? The old clan house turned into a bar that shows off the bullet holes from the last gunfight. What the hell happened?" Her words tumble out all at once, just like old times.

But my throat clears. "Let go, Iwate-san."

"What's with the formality? You know me better than that."

Su-chan's mouth falls open before she squeaks, "Tatsu, who's this?"

Then Chisa swings around to re-attach possessively to my bicep, but I extricate myself before putting an arm around Su-chan. "Enough, Iwate-san. Su-chan's my girl."

Chisa's head draws back and her lip quavers. "But you said, if I ever came back, you'd still-"

"I'm sorry." *Liar.* My bow is so stiff my back cracks.

She just sneers, "The word of a yakuza is worth nothing! I thought you were more than that." Then her gaze lights on Jiro. "Who's the kid? Yours?"

Meanwhile, Jiro's head swivels between Chisa and me.

"You got engaged, Iwate-san. I moved on. End of discussion. The kid's a friend of the family." *She doesn't need to know more.*

"But Shigure wasn't you."

Su-chan goes rigid in my embrace and whispers, "Jiro-kun, let's give them space to talk."

"Can we go to the combini?" Jiro points to the Seven Eleven store across the street.

"Stay. I have nothing to say to Iwate-san." The words are so frigid they could turn the bay into an ice skating rink.

"The boss was right. You never valued me. Men never do," Chisa spits.

Pain stabs my head over the brewing argument. But a familiar green glow catches my attention. "You're wearing one of those damned rings! Where'd you get it? Are you working for Ibaraki Douji?" Stomping into her space, I force her to back up several paces.

Then her look turns steely as she plants herself in place. "Now you're interested? I never pegged you as one out for the power Ibaraki-sama offers. Even Hiro wouldn't view me that way. Guess I'll see what he's up to and where the Hiragi clan moved."

"The jealousy trick won't work, Iwate," I say while conjuring a sound privacy spell to protect our group from those who would gobble up juicy rumors for the information market. My hand whips up to squeeze Chisa's arm as I growl, "Hiro's dead. The Hiragi Clan is gone, and I'm not yakuza anymore." Tightening my grip, I get in her face. "Now, where'd you get such a dangerous object?"

She flinches before her old, masked smile returns. "You always were a terrible liar."

Can't let her get the upper hand. She was so good at wrapping people around her finger. Passers-by are already carving a wide swath to avoid us on the tight streets. We're drawing too much attention, even if they can't hear us. *End this.*

"The one behind those rings destroyed the Hiragi clan and will do the same to you. People who wear those rings turn into oni!"

Su-chan joins me. "There's no coming back from that. You don't have to go down the same road, Iwate-san."

You've got a heart of gold.

To my ex, I say, "Chisa, you deserve better than turning into an oni!"

"That oni bit... not true-"

Su-chan interrupts, "I've seen it happen."

"Don't let Ibaraki control you. You're too strong a person for that. So take the ring off." While I don't want her back in my life, I can't let Ibaraki use her, either.

Instead, her palms ball up and a sickly green fire appears. "She gave me power. The power finally to control my destiny!"

Su-chan and I both raise shields. Trying again, I say, "If she taught you magic, great. But what she didn't likely tell you is that she takes the drain for the ki use. She becomes more powerful and makes you dependent on her."

That's when someone yells "Yakuza causing trouble!" and everyone around us scatters.

"Not yakuza!" I shout as I shake my head. *They can't hear you through the privacy spell.* "And not a fight." *I hope.*

"Pesky yokai popping up all the time now," a passer-by mutters, skittering away.

A ton of yokai here?

Next, Su-chan's calm observation brings me back. "Tatsu, Iwate-san has no glow inside her. Everything she has is from that ring.".

Didn't see it. Is being around Chisa scrambling my brain? "Iwate-san, your power comes at a price. Please, just take the ring off. For your safety."

"Not true! She gave me power!" Chisa protests.

"In trade for your life!"

Her shoulders sag and her lip trembles as Chisa points at Su-chan. "Why does she get to call you Tatsu?"

Where's she get off being so rude? "Your safety is the important thing."

"But you wouldn't let me call you that. She's not even as pretty as me."

"Prettier." *End this.* So I step out of the shield raised against her magic and motion for Su-chan and Jiro to stay behind it. Though, Su-chan's eyes meet mine and her worry hits me hard.

"Chisa. Take off the ring. Please."

Defiantly, my ex's hands raise, and that sickly green color intensifies. Before I can react, something springs in front of me. Time slows. Su-chan's arms spread canted as if she's about to do a cartwheel. On instinct, I create a new shield in front of both of us and my arms slide around to catch her before she topples and the blast hits.

Pulling Su-chan to me, I glare at Chisa. "Su-chan, please put up an illusion, otherwise the cops'll be breathing down our necks."

When the glow settles into place, Su-chan steps out of my arms and preps a flickering blue fireball. She says, "Iwate-san, why'd you attack us? Ibaraki's ring will kill you!"

That's new. When did Su-chan learn the fireball trick?

Jiro adds, "Those rings control people, Iwate-san. Believe me, you don't want to be controlled. It happened to me and it was awful!"

"Y-you..." She points at me. "...only ever saw my face and body."

She's desperate. I shoot back, "Don't give me that look. You were more than that and you know it. You left." Then my hands spread. "Ibaraki Douji killed many people I cared about. Do I need to refer you to the police and PSIA?"

"You're serious?"

Bingo. "No bluff. My great grandmother, Date Sari, enslaved Ibaraki Douji—but Ibaraki gained a huge amount of power from it. To make that bargain, Date did something so despicable and dark I won't tell you what it was."

"Sure, she took the power drain and was enslaved, as you said. But she didn't do anything to deserve it!" Chisa shouts.

"All lies." Her lack of answer has me forging ahead. "It was so she could steal the power of a dragon, a river god. Sari and Ibaraki Douji murdered that dragon."

Chisa only shakes her head.

Come on! You, of all people in my past, should believe me.

"Hiro's dead because of Date Sari and Ibaraki. He couldn't take his ring off in time and his last order to me was-" My words gum up and I choke out, "Was to kill him so he didn't turn. Even if you won't tell us where you got it, just take off the damned ring."

It makes Chisa blanch.

"Beyond that, those two killed members of my family and enslaved the spirits of my old clan. Did Ibaraki leave those inconvenient tidbits out? You're playing with a fire that will consume you."

"But it can't be," Chisa whispers.

"It's true. Date Sari's brother and I found her notes. I'll spare you the grizzly details, but the investigation team confirmed it was dragon blood on the pages. And I was the one who had to fight Ken's and the clan's ghosts because of Ibaraki!" I shout, unable to stop my fists from balling up so tight that the knuckles crack.

The blood drains from Chisa's face and I glance around for a trash can. There isn't one thanks to the government eliminating them after the sarin gas bombings years ago.

Finally, Chisa works the ring off her finger. A black band mars her delicate knuckles where the ring was. "What should I do with it?"

"I dunno." Throw it away? Turn it over to my teacher?

As if on cue, Jiro's stomach growls again. "Uhm. Can we talk over some food? I'm starving! Umeji-san promised us the best sukiyaki in Tokyo."

So I glance at Su-chan. Her lip sucks in, then she nods. Not what I'd planned, and I don't trust my ex farther than I can throw her. But I say, "Chisa, come with us. My treat."

Chisa shoves the band at me and looks away. "I work for your enemy! How can you invite me like it's no big deal? Just take the stupid ring!"

Will that thing mess with our plans to find Honjou Masamune? But what happens to Chisa?

Then Su-chan drops her hologram spell and takes the ring, relieving me of the decision. "You look like you could use a good meal."

Click. Chisa's cheeks are hollow and her arms bone-thin. *That's my Su-chan. Always doing the right thing. What happened while I was gone?* We shouldn't let my ex walk away hungry, especially when she has a connection with Ibaraki and maybe the katana.

"Come on. You know old Sugita-san would never poison food."

Giving in, she sighs. "How will he handle seeing you again?"

"We're about to find out."

19

B**ETTER** **T****HAN THE** **O****LD** **D****AYS**

WE ARRIVE AT THE tight, dark alley that houses my favorite place to eat in all of Tokyo. Just the sight of the aging white brick building with its wooden facade and a short, tile-roofed overhang causes a lump in my throat. *God, I missed the sukiyaki here.* Paper lanterns give off a warm radiance that accent the shop's name and the lucky cat statue waves in the window, beckoning us inside. But it's the aroma of the broth and meat wafting from the door that takes me back years.

The karaoke bar next door also gives me a sharp pang. Hiro, Kentarou, and I used to sing and drink away our troubles there. Today, the two businesses don't look like they've changed one bit. But me? The only things I have from my yakuza days are my tattoos, scars, and memories.

So I drink in the enticing aroma. Four years ago, this shop was on my protection payments beat. *He'll probably kick me out.*

Here goes nothing. I take a deep breath, pass through the shoulder-high noren curtain, and open the door. The little pub-like bar still has the same aging light fixtures over the half dozen dark wood tables.

"Irasshaimase!" the owner hollers a welcome, bobs and scurries over with a smile on his face until his eyes light on me. Stopping in his tracks, he shouts, "You!?" His finger raises, and he points to the door, commanding, "Out! I don't serve your kind anymore! There are laws to protect us now, you know!"

Not to be dissuaded, I bend in a long, low, respectful bow. "Sugita-san, I'm truly sorry for the trouble I caused you in the past." He harrumphs. But I want to at least do a little something to make up for what I did. "I left my old life behind. I'm here as a paying customer to show my small-town friends what the world's best sukiyaki is like."

205

"The only way I'll serve you and your rabble friends is if you pay double." Then tilting his head at Chisa, he says, "She stiffed me last month."

"More than fair, considering the trouble I caused. I'll pay before the food is served."

Chisa gapes. But I just shrug. It's important that Sugita knows I'm genuine. In the end, he gives a curt nod.

The guy's not a pushover anymore. "Thank you."

He waves us over to a table and Su-chan has Jiro scoot to the wall, so she's between him and Chisa. The boy can't keep his eyes off my ex. *Su-chan, I owe you big time.*

Thankfully, Sugita's servings are generous. Jiro's growing like a weed, so he'll eat a lot. Sugita hands me my change and tilts his head. "You've changed, Umeji-san."

My ear to ear grin makes him smile too. "I get to be the person I was before the yakuza. It feels good. You've changed, too."

"Damned right. You fresh out of the slammer?" he asks.

"For good."

"The girl's been looking for you. Maybe she can stop haunting my shop."

That's when a vibration from the thread to Honjou Masamune makes a circle around Chisa. *How's she connected?* Is the sword trying to tell us something?

Then my expression morphs to a polite neutral. "I wasn't expecting to run into her again."

He disappears into the kitchen.

Scooting in, across from Jiro, gives me the view of both the front door and the kitchen entrance.

Returning, Sugita brings out a flat round pan filled with the salty-sweet soy sauce and rice wine simmering broth before flipping on the heating element in the middle of the table.

Then plates of thinly sliced Kobe beef and bite sized vegetables—tiny enoki mushrooms, star-cut carrots, tofu squares, Napa cabbage, green onions, and clear mung bean noodles are placed with care. Lastly, he sets bowls with fresh raw eggs, plates, and chopsticks in front of each of us.

The sight makes my mouth water, and my stomach growls its agreement. "Damn, I missed your sukiyaki, Sugita-san."

"Please, enjoy your meal." The restaurant owner bows and leaves us to eat.

In unison, we press our hands together and say, "Itadakimasu," in gratitude for the meal. Then I gesture for the group to start.

"What a treat!" Su-chan glows at the sight of the expensive meats. When I drop a slice of beef into the broth, she asks, "You don't cook the meat first?"

"It's a Kanto region thing." Chisa brightens at a safe topic. "My mom, from Tokyo, and dad, from Osaka, made sukiyaki differently, and I learned both ways. This simmering sauce will also be stronger for that reason, but I find each delicious."

Everyone puts a few pieces in to cook, and we crack the eggs into bowls while we wait.

"So where are you living now, Umeji?" Chisa asks.

Dropping the 'san' suffix? We're not close like that anymore. "A little town in Okayama prefecture." *No details.* Don't want her showing up in Nonogawa.

To Su-chan, she queries, "Has our big city boy adapted to small town life?"

Chisa's less modest outfit and her control of the conversation verify my suspicion she's working as a hostess. With her chopsticks, she snaps up a piece of beef that I'd put in.

So, I give her a raised eyebrow. She returns that same adorable grin and meek duck of her head that used to melt me. Instead, I glare and shake my head. *Knock it off.*

Whether Su-chan is oblivious or choosing not to react to Chisa's flirting, I can't tell. But she takes the question about my fitting in at face value instead of the potential jab it could have been. "He stuck out at first because he tried so hard to keep his head down. Now he's himself around everyone. Though I noticed his Tokyo accent returned as soon as we arrived." She grins and gives me a shove.

Avoiding everyone's gaze over the attention, I snag a slice of beef so at least I get one bite. Everyone's scarfing up the tender tidbits. The meat melts in my mouth and I sigh, contented.

Next, Chisa says, "Adaptable as always. So what brought you three to Tokyo? I'd have thought sightseeing, with the young mister... Forgive me. I didn't catch your name."

Liar. But kudos for including him.

Before my young friend can give his full name, I answer, "He's Jiro, one reason I've kept on the straight and narrow."

The boy looks down to hide his beaming face. "Umeji-san helped me deal with the bullies at school."

Sounds like I made threats. My palm wipes over my face.

At Chisa's raised eyebrow, he waves his hands desperately, "N-not like that! I asked what could be done, and he connected me with Matsuo-sensei, who teaches Aikido."

Then I introduce her to Su-chan, too—as with Jiro, only by personal name. *The less Chisa knows, the better.* "Now that you've met everyone, I have to ask. Are you safe?" Her searching for me is so damned suspicious. *Why would she leave the guy she was engaged to?* Something big had to bring her back.

In her next vie for attention, Chisa sports a pouting lip. "So direct." At my eye roll, she continues, "I'm not in trouble, if that's what you're asking."

"Just tell me, already. Why were you looking for me?" In emphasis, my hand slaps the table.

But her gaze falls to her plate, and she gobbles down another bite, as if she might not get more. "It was my job to keep an eye out for you."

"And report when I arrived," I growl. *Why?* "What kind of trouble are you in?"

Quickly, she waves her hands. "No, no! It's just that where I work won't let me go. The place gets rough, but they pay well. One of Ibaraki-sama's reps recruited me, then I pledged to work in Sumichou. Though, it wasn't what I expected. At all."

Working for Ibaraki would suck and Chisa's playing up the pity. "Where's this Sumichou? Do you need out?"

She laughs. "Sweet as always, but you can't help me. Sumichou is an access limited district below Kabukichou. It's been around for a long time and isn't listed with the government. A yakuza wash up who's got a bit of magic behind him is no match for the group that runs the area. Not even with your new friends."

That damned attitude. It's why we always used to fight.

Focus! Sumichou must be the underground area I saw when Ibaraki and Mishima escaped through the portal.

Then Chisa continues, "Your expression says you weren't here to rescue a damsel in distress, anyway." She scarfs down a few more bites before getting up. "Thanks for the meal."

Good riddance.

About 5 minutes after she leaves, my brain is still churning as I down the last enoki mushroom. Why'd the sword's thread wrap around her? *Don't let her be our lead.*

"Isn't that Chisa's phone?" Jiro asks.

The pastel-pink, rhinestone covered cell sits on the table. *Is she listening in? Are our phones being blocked or monitored?*

So, I whisper a word of kotodama to check for hazards. Then I snatch Jiro's hand in midair as he grabs for it.

"What's wrong?" he asks as I release his wrist.

"Leaving items at a scene is a trap tactic. Give me a minute."

Though, Su-chan beats me to wrapping the phone in a luminescent blue shield and picking it up. "There."

That works too. "Now, Jiro, what can you detect?"

His spell reveals a tracking app.

Su-chan's eyes narrow. "So she was looking for you and she's being monitored. Not an accident."

"Hoji-sensei told me about businesses tracking employees on their phones. The workers say they're sick. But with the app, the company can catch them if they do something else," Jiro adds.

"You're learning about that stuff already?" *Way smarter than I was at his age.*

"Hoji-sensei says it's spying and if I ever did something like that, he'd throttle me."

My ex is smart. Though, now that I'm not wrapped around her finger, I can see through her manipulation. "Assuming Chisa was a plant, she'd expect to be bait."

Then Su-chan clears her throat. "She certainly vied for your attention."

Flashes of what Chisa and I shared return, causing me to look away. "Sorry she made you uncomfortable," I say, patting Su-chan's hand. *Time to change the subject!* "Jiro, as our resident tech mage, can you track the tracking app?"

"You won't turn me in?" He grins like a Cheshire cat now that I've given him a puzzle to solve.

I'm about to answer when Su-chan grimaces. "Tatsu, don't encourage him to do anything illegal!" Turning to the boy, she says, "I think it's time to take you home."

With how he's sulking, he might portal right back.

"It's tracking an illegal tracker. Look, I know I'm just a kid. But I'm having to deal with a lot of adult problems, and you need my help. Neither of you have my tech magic skills.

"Umeji-san, you and Hoji-sensei said I was a prodigy. I won't let it go to my head. But it makes me the best to track Chisa-san after we give her phone back."

My gut tightens. Not listening to that instinct cost me three years ago. Is it because we've got Jiro involved, or is it having to deal with Chisa again? Great Uncle Nobu said the boy should accompany us. *Is he right? Then verify what's got your gander up.* "We haven't tried asking around yet."

"I'm gonna disable the tracker for now." Jiro says as he waves a hand over the phone, and swipes through floating golden menus faster than I can read them. The screen flashes and he closes the menus. "There."

Wizard. That's why Great Uncle Nobu wanted us to bring him. *So it's Chisa setting me off.*

Just as Sugita asks if we need anything else, the phone chimes and the screen changes to a bright pink. A clock ticks down for two minutes, showing a precision down to the millisecond in a chilling black typeface with a little icon of a circle and a curved line sticking out of it.

"Bomb!" My hand snatches the phone and I shove past the owner. "Sorry!" I holler as I burst through the door, "Get Jiro home!"

But Jiro screams, "Umeji-san!"

Behind me, footsteps pound the pavement and Su-chan shouts my name. *Why couldn't they have listened?*

On the way here, we passed by walled off construction that looked abandoned. Pushing for every ounce of speed, I can't quite dodge a pair of weaving dark suited salary men exiting a bar. One of them falls, only to yell at me. I'll apologize when I get back. *If I survive.*

Only a minute and fifteen seconds left. How far was that construction?

Idiot. Portal! Skidding to a stop, I lean over to catch my breath.

Su-chan and Jiro halt beside me, panting hard. As I scribe an arc, I suck in air, too. Then I hear, "What's that guy doing? A thief, by the way he was running."

Watchers be damned. I'm saving their asses. My arm raises to chuck the device through the hole into Tokyo Bay, waiting on the other side.

Suddenly, a high pitched, all too cutesy voice says, "Please, remember to move away from any bystanders for the scan." *What. The. Hell?*

Jiro screeches. "It's not a bomb! Come on, let me help!"

So, I hand over the phone. Though I won't close the portal, just in case. Jiro's already working before I can pop up an illusion to cover us.

"Mortal presences detected. Scan cannot proceed."

I shout, "Stop that thing!" as Jiro waves his hand over the phone, revealing a purple button that reads 'Cancel'. The countdown says thirty seconds as the phone's high-pitched female voice turns stern. "Please, move out of sight or Akumakai will revoke your access."

His finger hovers over the digital button and I command, "Do it!"

When he presses the screen, the freaky countdown stops. My heart beats again, and I close the portal to the bay.

After a moment, Su-chan asks, "Access to what?"

"Sumichou? Let's apologize to Sugita-san and the guy in the alley I bowled over, then figure that out." People are staring, so it's time to leave. I rub my hands over my face a few times as I try to piece the new information together with what I can remember. "The Akumakai—my clan tried to work out a deal with them."

"Who would name their clan something that screams 'Evil Corp'? How dumb!" Su-chan bites her lip, but she can't hold back a laugh.

"I'm with you on that. But no matter how much the name sounds like it's from a b-rated anime, they're the real deal." As we hoof it back, we wrack our brains for what to do next.

Chisa's waiting in front of the shop. "I never took you for a phone thief."

So I hold up the device and, pointing inside, say, "I have questions. Let me talk to Sugita-san for two seconds. Then I'll be right back with your phone."

The restaurant owner hustles over. "Everything ok? That lady was ready to spit nails at you. I tried to tell her what we saw."

Bobbing an apology, I explain. "Yeah, it's some kind of freaky access code. Sorry for our rudeness!"

He waves it off. "You thought of the safety of me and my shop. Now, give that woman her phone so she can stop driving customers away."

Outside, Chisa's arms cross, and she taps her foot. The street light overhead emphasizes her glower. Years ago, despite my being a tough yakuza, her disapproval would have had me backtracking. She snaps, "My phone. Now, Tatsuya."

As she holds out her hand, I demand, "Chisa, what the fuck are you doing with the Akumakai?" and slap the device into her hand.

She stomps off. When I grab her arm, she growls, "Not your business."

"You were hunting for me. And now you tell me it's not my business? The Akumakai isn't a game. They're dangerous in the extreme. Every yakuza clan wanted to ally with them. So what's your involvement?"

She wriggles out of my grip. "Baka! A girl's got to make a living. And I just missed the opportunity to get to my shift. You've put me in a bind."

"You really don't want to be working for them. What were you thinking?"

But she glances at the screen. "If I don't get there soon, my boss will kill me. Not exaggerating. As it is, I'll pay for my transgression. I have to get to the next gate opening. Now." Poking at her phone, her hand shakes so hard I can't read the text. "Too far to make it. Shit. Shit. Shit!"

She's not faking the panic. Or she's a better liar now. *Do I let her take the hit for this?* Balling up my fists doesn't ease the dread winding up my insides. "We'll get you where you need to be."

So she shoves the map on the screen in my face, too close to focus. With sarcasm dripping in her words, she demands. "Then get me behind the Post Office at the north end of the district before the timer's up."

I take a step back and snag the phone to verify. All the way across Kabukichou. Too long to walk. "Gotcha. Let's step out of sight."

Her eyes narrow, but she does as I ask. *Jeez.* Not like I'm gonna try anything, just make a portal.

Then Su-chan pokes me as she whispers, "Magic users watch out for each other."

Code for don't go alone. *Idiot.* Despite your gut telling you something was up, you were rushing in to save your ex. *All on your own.* Su-chan's smart enough to see Chisa could be a viper ready to strike. "Together."

"Jiro and I will put up cover," Su-chan offers.

Scribing an arc into the air, there's resistance. *Odd.* Instead of fighting the magic, I try for the alley next to the Post Office. This time, the portal activates.

Chisa's face lights up. "Thank you, Tatsuya! You saved me!" Before I can stop her, she kisses my cheek and rushes through. I freeze.

On the other side, she says, "Close that..." waving at the portal, "that whatever it is, or my access point won't open."

"When do you get off your shift? We need to talk."

Then her voice turns cutesy. "Still can't get enough of me? Tomorrow 6 AM. They keep our shifts short, so we stay fresh for the customers."

But I scowl, wiping off my face where her lips had been. "Not what I meant. Meet us at Doutor Coffee in the morning."

"You buying?"

"Sure." Finally, I close the portal as the timer on her app announces a new two-minute countdown.

My easy-going facade falls and my head drops. I don't want her back in my life at all. And Su-chan is glaring. But how the hell can I let Chisa walk into the hands of the Akumakai?

The rumors I heard of them when I was in the Hiragi Clan made even our dirty business look like child's play. Taking a few deep breaths allows me to meet Su-chan's gaze.

"Tatsu?" Su-chan's knitted brows say I'm in trouble.

So I bow a few extra beats to show my regret for not intercepting the kiss quick enough. "Sorry, I didn't expect that. I'll make it clear to her when we meet in the morning."

"She's the one you missed when she left?" Su-chan asks.

Rubbing the back of my head, I nod.

"You still think I'm prettier?"

"Much more." *And you treat me like an equal, not a cash cow.*

When Su-chan interlaces her fingers in mine, my insides unwind a little.

How are we gonna deal with Ibaraki and the Akumakai knowing we're here?

Then my phone chirps, causing our little group to jump. A text message from Yamazaki says he and Sekiguchi have news and gives an address to a snack bar I know well.

20

Dangerous Leads

We order a round of sake, though I buy a strawberry Ramune soda for Jiro. Yamazaki leads with a toast. "Kanpai!"

Being able to join in, Jiro grins ear to ear as he clinks his bottle against our cups. The kid's always so happy around me and my friend Matsuo. *More at home around adults than his peers, isn't he?*

Then Sekiguchi says, "I'm very pleased to see Kabukichou cleaning up and ridding itself of crime lords."

I nod. "Me, too, as ironic as it is."

Su-chan pokes me as if to emphasize my point.

"About our news." The kappa leans in. "We discovered rumors of an antique weapons collection specializing in the old masters of Japan in an underground district called Sumichou. Though I'm afraid we don't know how to get there. It requires specialized clearance."

My crew beams, but I just wish it didn't have to do with Chisa.

Sekiguchi continues, "There are also whispers of a resistance movement."

While Su-chan pours more sake, I double check the threads to Honjou Masamune and my ex. Chisa's looks more faint than the sword's. I add, "We might have a connection. But the line to her is dim." *Is she ok?*

So we share our adventure with meeting Chisa and the timer.

Yamazaki puts a hand to his chin as he swirls his drink. "Access out of the area may also be limited. Thus, portals are not a likely option for escape. Also, assume that the enemy knows you are coming."

Sekiguchi adds, "We have the boy, too. Such a brilliant young mage will be a prime target. If he joins us, we must protect him."

Gah. The thought of Jiro being snagged by those who would warp him for his talent makes my gut clench. *Can we avoid bringing him?* "Also, what about your protection, Yamazaki-san?" The Yokai King has an entourage, but I've not seen it since we got here.

"Under normal circumstances, I wouldn't be concerned, but this is Sumichou. I will not be accompanying you for my own reasons. Umeji-kun, did your clan work with the Akumakai?"

"No, sir." *Not that I knew of.* "Though the Hiragi clan was itching for a deal with them."

"So, only I have been there, and it's become even more treacherous." Yamazaki sighs. "We have some time to plan before we meet with Chisa-san. What rumors did you hear when you were in the yakuza? You four need a way in."

That's when Jiro shrinks in on himself as he shoves his phone forward. "I copied the app and snagged Chisa-san's number."

My head swivels. "Jiro!" *Should I be proud or dismayed?*

"Don't tell Hoji-sensei!" he pleads.

Those big brown eyes on his round face melt any resistance. *You're turning me into a push over, kid.* "Che. An ingenious scamp, that's what you are." So I rub the top of his head. "I'd bet Hoji-san would do the same, but we won't tell."

Sekiguchi says, "Transfer it to Umeji-san's phone. This reeks of danger. I'd volunteer, but I don't have one, yet. I'll purchase one tonight."

Mine might as well be the sacrifice. Everyone else's is newer. Reluctantly, I shove my older, inexpensive phone out, even though I haven't had it long. "Transfer it. Then, Jiro, it sounds like we should get you back before we meet Chisa. You and your mom have had enough scares with creeps and bullies."

"About that..." Shaking his head, Yamazaki says, "Putting the only two experts of this magic style in one place while there is danger to the master would be most unwise. Though, I'm not comfortable with Jiro-kun going to Sumichou either."

Tell me about it. "I don't want Jiro-kun near that place."

Kicking the chair leg, the boy sulks.

"You mean well, Umeji-kun," the yokai king says. "But I fear you will need the boy. He's the only one with superior tech magic skills."

Jiro will be in danger, but everyone's telling us to take him into a place that sounds like a hellhole. My fists clench. Though, Yamazaki has a point.

He continues, "My contacts report Sumichou recently started relying on technology."

"Tech magic?" I ask.

"No."

At least we have an advantage.

"You will need both magic and tech to defeat their constant surveillance," Yamazaki points out.

"We need a plan," I say, then eye the sake cup. When I was in the yakuza, I'd drink the issue away and let things fall where they will. But I can't do that. And if I finish it, Su-chan will be obligated to fill it again. I've had several already and need a clear head.

Silence descends. Why isn't anyone sharing ideas? Click. *It's up to me. Argh.*

What-ifs wrestle with each other over and over, and worse, the pressure to come up with a plan makes my head pound.

In the quiet, Yamazaki hails the snack bar owner and pays.

Then Jiro perks up. "So you're not just gonna send me home?"

I shake my head.

So he asks, "While we think, can we walk by the Robot Restaurant?"

Doh. "I think it's closed." *Will it ever open again?*

Yamazaki says, "A little down time may let us see any connections we missed. Let us humor the boy, then rest."

Too bad I can't take them to Tokyo Tower, or the Imperial Palace, or the Ghibli Museum, or a zillion other places that were fun. I'll have to bring them back someday to play tourist. All they get to see today is the questionable side of Tokyo. There really are good things here. And Jiro's request was one of them.

Sekiguchi, true to his word, picks up a simple, pay as you go phone. When we walk past the Robot Restaurant, Jiro plasters his face against the glass to peek in.

"There's a nice shrine a few blocks away. Mind if we pay our respects?" I'd prefer the Inari shrine to the north. But we should save our magic and talismans. So I show Jiro which one on his map app and he dashes ahead to take the lead.

As we weave our way east toward the shrine, Yamazaki shares in a whisper, "You'll need all the help you can get. I wish to share my experience in the underground of Sumichou. I'll do so in the safety of the sacred area."

Ahead of the Yokai King and I, Su-chan, Sekiguchi and Jiro chatter, marveling about the lights and how tall and close the buildings are.

After we leave an offering and pray at the main shrine building with its sweeping-roof and vibrant red and white ornamentation, Jiro and Su-chan meander about the grounds taking pictures. Sekiguchi, Yamazaki, and I all sit on the driest steps out of the way.

Waiting is always the worst. Jitters set in and my hands fidget. Once a plan is in motion, I do better. And Su-chan and Jiro are so innocent. *Don't ruin that.*

"Umeji-san, your face darkened." Sekiguchi puts a hand on my shoulder.

"I'd rather send Su-chan and Jiro to the den instead of dragging them along."

Yamazaki says, "That boy and your lady, they are unique. While I know you don't want to risk either, you'll need both of them to find the sword and get out of Sumichou alive. They don't recognize my authority there, and it will be hard to hide who I am. But you young ones are unknown to the residents."

When the King of the Yokai isn't respected... Daaaaamn.

A light breeze blows through the tree-lined paths and the moist sea air still smells like it might rain again.

"Expect life to be cheap. You'll see trafficking, even children. The hunt for my son was several decades ago, and we barely made it out. The head of the Akumakai knew whose son she had. She slit his throat in front of me out of spite after I was coerced into her deal. The witch worded it in such a way that my end was still binding."

I jerk.

"Did your son survive?" Sekiguchi asks.

Gripping the fabric of his pant legs, Yamazaki nods. After a few moments, he speaks in a husky voice. "He almost didn't. We only escaped because my guards sacrificed themselves to get us out. Afterward, I sent in an army of 1,000 strong to raze the area. She dumped every single one of their heads at my doorstep."

And my friends and I are choosing to go into this godforsaken place? "Ibaraki did that?"

"No." The yokai king shakes his head. "One of her predecessors, a kumiho, named Bak Ae-Ri. Rumor has it she wasn't always ruthless. But something changed her. No one knows what happened. My sources say, the next in line didn't last long before Ibaraki killed him and stuck his head on a pike as a warning to his supporters."

Above us, the clouds grow brighter as they thicken in the night's lights and the temperature drops.

"A small group will have a better chance than the entire contingent," Yamazaki says.

Mishima, I'm gonna throttle you for dragging us into this! "Jiro's so young. If he has to come along, can we disguise him?"

"More than he already is?" Yamazaki raises an eyebrow.

That makes me squirm. *He knows about Jiro's kitsune magic, too.* "Maybe a glamor spell that will draw less attention?"

"I think we can manage something suitable. That reminds me. During our investigation, Sekiguchi and I uncovered an item one of the yokai ladies was given during a shift in Sumichou." He hands over a yellowed business card. "It's a contact from the rebellion. She said not everyone in the district was corrupt."

As I read it, my thumb runs over the worn lettering and wrinkles. Not normal for a business card that's supposed to represent the owner's face. *What did the yokai lady do, stuff it in her bra?* The only text on it is a script that seems to rearrange itself under my gaze.

"To activate the contact, think the name 'Baku', and don't let the card fall into the wrong hands!"

I freeze, fighting down the urge to throw the contact card. The only creature of that species I know is a traitor.

Then Su-chan asks for a group photo. Poor Jiro is yawning and Sekiguchi suggests we find somewhere to rest. So we crash in a reputable hotel for a few hours.

Brrrrringgggggg!

I growl, throwing my arm over my eyes, but my hand hits someone's hair. Too short to be Su-chan's. Then my eyes fly open, and I bolt upright to find I'm next to Jiro.

Sekiguchi's quiet voice urges, "Everyone, please, get up to meet Chisa-san. Yamazaki-san will meet us there and see us off." The kappa, still disguised as a middle-aged salary man with stringy hair, is already dressed.

But the same roiling pit of coldness in my stomach from my yakuza days causes heartburn. *Don't wanna drag my friends in with me.* But Su-chan would just say we do this together. *Sometimes being a man of my word sucks.*

We roust, despite protests and, when we're presentable, we raise our umbrellas and slog through the rain to the Doutor Coffee shop. It sits near the lit-up arch into Kabukichou.

Breakfast perks us up but, when we see a woman collapse outside the window of the shop, Sekiguchi and I rush to help.

We roll her over and my voice comes out in a gasp. "Chisa."

She has no umbrella. Worse, she's soaked, wearing too few clothes for the weather. Her goosebump covered skin has turned from its usual golden glow to ghost white, and the rain trails some rank, oily grime off of her. After a moment, she wheezes and gives a racking cough, spitting up dirty water.

"What did they do to you?" It's all I can do to keep from shaking her senseless. She may be my ex, but I'm not heartless.

"The Cleansssse." Her words slur and her dazed expression turns to a grim smile, "I ssssurvived."

So Sekiguchi kneels as he waves glowing hands over her. "Oh, dear."

"What?" When a healer's worried, it's time to panic.

"I saw this once a few years ago. She doesn't have long. We have to get her help. Warmth first. Carry her inside where we can get her a hot drink." Sekiguchi cradles her shaking form as I open the shop door.

Inside, the barista blanches before barking. "She can't stay here!"

So Yamazaki rises from the table, focusing his gaze on the young man. A wavering glow emanates from his hands tucked behind his back. "We'll get her out of here, but we have to warm her first, as my friend said."

The barista sighs and shoves a plain hot coffee in our direction. "This is all I can do. Don't tell my boss."

No puppeteering? In the legends, the Yokai King gets his way and makes people feel like they were the best for it. *And I got to witness it!*

Yamazaki snatches the coffee after paying, and coaxes Chisa to drink some. "We can get her to my place to recover. It's warded. There won't be a way to track her."

"Th-thank you," she whispers, leaning into Sekiguchi as we exit the store heading for the alley. So I hold up a portal ofuda and Yamazaki nods.

Instead of the old vegetable shop, he chooses a palatial residence and we all gawk. Next, Yamazaki whispers for a servant to start a bath. There, Su-chan and Sekiguchi help Chisa into the warm water.

All I can do is pace. When they emerge, she's wrapped in a thick bathrobe and looking much better.

"What happened, Chisa? You said 'the Cleanse'?" I ask. Something inside prods me to hold her and offer comfort. But I shove the thought away as quickly as it enters my mind. I don't want Chisa back and I won't hurt Su-chan.

She nods as she sips on a warm cup of tea. "In Sumichou, they flush the underground cavern. It's called The Cleanse. They just did one the day before, so I thought I was safe and was going to replace my protection charm from the best of the vendors after my shift. When I heard the alarm sound, I rushed to get something, anything, to help survive the torrent of water. It wasn't the greatest talisman, as you saw."

A million questions try to rush out of my mouth at once, clogging up my voice box as I gape. The stupidest, of course, is the one that escapes, "And you work there?"

"It pays well." When I roll my eyes, she shoots back, "Mr. Yakuza turned hypocrite goody-two-shoes doesn't remember me digging a bullet out of his thigh to avoid the hospital's questions?"

I wince. *That was a shitty day.* "Point taken."

Yamazaki then directs a servant to fetch Chisa breakfast.

"I owe you all," she mumbles between bites.

True. Maybe she'll assist? But how can we keep her from ratting us out? "On that note. We need to get into Sumichou. Will you help us?"

"Tell me you're joking." At the shake of my head, she adds, "You can't take the kid in there. It'll scar him for life!"

"We'll take precautions, but we need to understand how the key works."

For a moment, she fiddles with the sleeve of her robe. "That's why you were so quick to help me."

"Excuse me?" *She ought to know better.* "Forget it. We don't need her."

Then Su-chan urges, "Tatsu, be reasonable."

"But she's a spy!"

"Baka!" Chisa glowers. "This job was my ticket out of the poor district. After that disaster, I don't want to go back. Ever."

So Sekiguchi puts his hands up to show peaceful intentions, and approaches Chisa as he asks, "Is there anything you can tell us?"

"Yeah. The scan is biometrics based. Another person with entry has to recommend you." Chisa hides behind her long hair.

She doesn't want to help. Even after all we did for her.

Heaving in a breath, I try again. "If this is the work it sounds like, they won't let you go and you know it. Don't be an idiot, Chisa. We're your best chance to get out of that job."

"Fine." She slumps before poking her phone a few times and shoving it at me. "I'll give you my recommendation. Just don't get yourselves killed. They've been doing a lot of Cleanses lately, and you won't like what you see."

Next, Sekiguchi kneels before her, and with his hands behind his back, snaps his fingers. A blue glow flashes. "Are there any weapons displays?"

Too direct! I glare at Sekiguchi, but Yamazaki waves me off.

That catches her attention. "Why do you ask?"

She's suspicious. My feet shuffle on the floor as I debate how much to tell her. I don't trust her farther than I can throw her. But Sekiguchi and Yamazaki have a plot. *Trust them, or don't.* "Ibaraki Douji stole something from us. And it's vital we get it back."

"Why would she steal something from you?" The not-so-subtle sneer shows how little she thinks of me now. "Just because you can throw some magic about doesn't mean you'd have anything that she wants."

My eye twitches at the slight and I glance at Yamazaki, who holds up a hand. So, I defer to him.

He says, "Ibaraki took an important sword from a secret organization. The group needs the sword to save an entire race. Please, help us."

Her lips purse, and just when I think she's about to ask what's in it for her, she sighs. "You saved me, so here's what I know, for what it's worth. I work in the bar across from the palace and I saw them bring in a box under heavy guard. Though, I don't think it was your sword because the box was too small. It could have held a dagger, at most."

Jackpot. "Have you heard any rumors about where they might store such a weapon?"

"Nope. I try to keep my head down, though, last week, there was a public execution for someone they thought was working against the leadership."

I grimace and avoid looking at Jiro. *He's so young.*

"That's all I know. Are you done interrogating me yet?"

"Can you give us directions?" Sekiguchi asks.

"Hold out your phone." When I do so, she continues, "Transferring the recommendation and app to your phone only. Open it."

A list comes up in that creepy font. She taps on the one that says gate four. "This is the one I use. Once you're inside, pull up a map for directions. Where might you want to go?"

At my lack of answer, she puts a finger to her lips in thought. "Tatsuya, you never were the hostess bar type. Across the street is a pet shop with the most insane creatures you've ever seen. Since you seem to still be mister-got-bucks, I'll let you know they're the rumor hub and deal in the information trade. It'll be costly."

At last, Yamazaki says, "Chisa-san, you may rest here while the others are away. My servants will attend to your needs. Speaking of... Haru, please fetch the lady another tea." He pats Chisa's hand and steps away. "Then we can discuss finding you respectable employment. You've been seen with us, so you can't return to Sumichou."

A gray-haired, tuxedo-clad butler sweeps in with a steaming brew in another exquisite blue and white China teacup. The servant places it on a tray that appears beside her. Then she gives Yamazaki a second look over the rim of her teacup. Is she evaluating his wealth and attention?

Whatever.

Since Ibaraki's expecting us, we need to prep fool-proof disguises. Yamazaki's butler ushers our group to a secluded courtyard where the crystal-clear pond is chock full of colorful koi fish. A stone path leads across the water and a boulder at the edge would be a magnificent spot to sit and feed the carp. While we wait, Jiro skips from one rock to the other side and back.

Sekiguchi is the last to join us. "Don't worry. Chisa-san will remember nothing before her first contact with the Akumakai and Ibaraki. Yamazaki-san felt memories of our group were too much of a liability since they promised her a higher position in the organization.

"By the way, I'm not sure what plans Yamazaki has for her work. He owns several establishments. So I'd wager a position in one of those."

"Thanks. I won't ask how you got that tidbit out of her."

But he shrugs. "All I can say is she wasn't coerced."

Good. Patting my shirt pocket ensures the card that Yamazaki gave me is still there. "Now, let's disguise ourselves and get this over with." Though, my insides twist for the umpteenth time over bringing the boy. "Ready, Jiro?"

"Yeah. Is it gonna hurt or anything?"

"Nah. This is a glamor spell. A good one, mind you." When I whisper a word of kotodama, my young friend's face lengthens, and his round cheeks give way to a chiseled jaw and five o'clock shadow. Childish round eyes narrow to hooded ones. His shoulders widen and he grows a little taller than me. To finish, I give him spiked, bleached hair.

Before speaking, he shuffles. "You didn't make me look like an old man, did you?"

"The girls'll fall over you." So, I slap his back. "Should've made you look older."

But Su-chan looks away as she fans herself. "He's gonna break hearts for sure."

Then I open up the selfie app on my phone and Jiro pats his face. "Whoa! Am I gonna have to shave?"

After Jiro finishes his inspection, Sekiguchi says, "Yamazaki-san gave us magic masking tokens. Jiro-kun, you will appear to have weasel magic." Deftly, he attaches a pin to Jiro's collar.

Jiro's face screws up as he asks, "Why a weasel?"

"They're known for bewitching humans and bringing natural disasters."

"What about you?" I ask Su-chan. "You can't be an innocent sheep among wolves." No badass character type suits her.

"Mad scientist! I know how chemicals affect the human body and can pass as an alchemist." Her cackle makes me take a step back. She continues, "I could make designer drugs or blow up a city block."

What happened to my innocent girlfriend?

Sekiguchi nods. "That would be the darkness that fits you best, and you would need to look like..." He pauses, rummaging in his pockets and hands Su-chan a bracelet. "...a kijo, the ogresses who specialize in potions and hexes. You'll need a glamor, too. It's hard enough to hide the dragon magic inside your ki well."

In an instant, her appearance morphs to a middle age visage with gaunt cheeks. Dark circles form under her eyes. Her fingers turn bony, and her flesh has an unnatural yellow-green cast to it. Next, sharp horns protrude from her skull and the deep coffee brown eyes I love turn to a blood red.

Give me my Su-chan back!

"What should you look like?" Su-chan's sweet voice emanating from the female oni disguise gives me the heebie jeebies.

Then Sekiguchi snaps his fingers. "I know the perfect disguise that will let you lean on your old background."

"I don't like this already," I grumble.

"A kotengu."

"But Soujou-bou's tengu are civilized!"

"I thought you'd know the myths where tengu ruffians rivaled the mafias. Legend says the first yakuza boss was one, and he set the tone for all the clans," Sekiguchi explains.

Look those stories up when there's time. Stalling, I let my hands shove into my pockets. "I don't want to act like that again."

His scowl says I'm being uncooperative.

"Fine. Kotengu it is." *Will Su-chan worry I'll revert to the jerk I used to be?*

So Sekiguchi says, "Allow me to create this disguise. I've met more than a handful of the ruffians. With my spell, you won't have to use magic if you want to fly."

"Thanks."

"Don't thank me, yet. The transformation will be uncomfortable." He places a pendant on the cord holding my half of the tama which gives me fox magic. "Take a deep breath," he says. Then his webbed hand glows as it presses to my shoulder.

Suddenly, pain rips through every part of me, I gasp and he whispers a word to suppress it. "Sorry, Umeji-kun. It will be over soon."

My eyes scrunch closed as my shoulders rip open and I sink to my knees. Talons replace fingernails as I cover my face where the bones creak and crunch, rearranging themselves. A sharp, hooked beak emerges from where my nose and mouth were, and feathers erupt from my skin. When I cry out, it emerges as a high-pitched raptor's call.

"Tatsu!" Su-chan screams, kneeling beside me. "Sekiguchi-sensei, is he really transforming?"

He nods. "Shion sent me word of a vision that the Akumakai would scrutinize Umeji-san the most of our group. His disguise must be impenetrable because Ibaraki knows him and his magic."

Then my ribs stretch and my shoulder and chest muscles bulge, ripping my clothes and destroying my only jacket. As quickly as the pain came, it's over. I'm left crouched on the ground, panting.

A big gray beak hinders my vision as Su-chan runs her hand over my head. The stiff feathers moving send revulsion through my skin. *Not natural at all!* But the rawness settles.

After a moment, Sekiguchi says, "Soon, you'll feel normal."

"Whoa! A falcon!" Jiro looks up at me as his mouth hangs open. "C-can I?" His hand hovers over my cheek. I nod. This time it's not so strange.

Inspecting my transformation, I find black dots speckling the white and blush feathers on my chest. My head twists all the way to my back to see the extra limbs on my shoulders covered in sleek blue-gray plumage.

Words escape me.

Stretching my new wings sends air spinning around us. I can't resist. So I crouch and use a word of kotodama to boost a jump. My wings open and beat hard, and I spring into the air. When I look down, I can distinguish the tiniest details of Su-chan's disguise, even the individual hairs on her head.

What kid didn't dream of flying? In ecstasy, I throw my head back and let out a piercing scream. That brief pause of my wings leaves me plummeting. On instinct, they extend again. Flailing, I land just short of a crash.

Jiro covers his mouth, but he's laughing so hard he doubles over. Su-chan joins him.

So I hiss and cluck at the pair. *Why can't I speak?*

Sekiguchi says, "You'll have to use magic to talk. Your mouth and voice box aren't meant for human language. In addition, you'll want to cast a spell for understanding other languages."

Doing both charms nets me a cracking, squeaky voice, much like the other tengu I'd encountered. "Then, you land better," I say and wave my hand in Jiro's direction, using only a minute amount of ki.

He lifts, but his smug smile and forced eye contact don't break as he lands just as lithely as the frisky little weasel he's pretending to be. To top it off, he sticks out his tongue. The new cockiness fits his disguise.

I deserved that.

"Good. The personality overlay is meshing, too." Sekiguchi chuckles.

"Huh?" *What is he talking about?*

"I added a layer to your disguise to ensure you act like a trickster tengu."

I can't even be myself?

"And now for me. As an annoying dog that trips people, very little attention will come my way. I'll appear to be your pet." Sekiguchi applies a belled collar to his own neck before handing a leash to Su-chan.

Then his form shrinks to something that's a cross between a chubby, short-legged dog and a flat-nosed cat, though the tongue is definitely a dog's. Finally, his whiskers twitch as he grunts in pain through the change.

Odd smacking sounds accompany his voice. "We are ready. Please, practice your roles and how to move in character with your new bodies."

"You had to go through a physical change, too, not just a glamor?"

"Yes. This way, most will ignore me. Though I expect to be kicked. Yamazaki said to get going as soon as we had our disguises."

"Let's do this." I slap a talisman into the air and portal to an alley near the gate Chisa used.

When we open up the app on our phones, the creepy, high-pitched voice echoes on each device, "Welcome to Sumichou. Do you agree that your personal safety is your own responsibility? Click 'yes' to continue."

When we do, the countdown shows less than a minute left and we scoot into position.

"Please, remember to move away from any bystanders for the scan, or the Akumakai will revoke your access. Now turn your device so the camera and flash are available."

Our phones pulse as if trying to blind us. Several quick light bursts have me blinking the spots away from my sensitive eyes.

"Scan accepted. Gate opening in three... two... one..."

21

DESCENT

AN IONIZED SPHERE WITH wavering olive green and black swirls expands to just big enough for us to step through. At first it glitches, blocking the view to the other side as if the portal is unsafe. When the gate clears and snaps into place, Sekiguchi hisses at the sight beyond.

"10 seconds until the portal closes. Enter at your own risk or wait three days. The Akumakai does not tolerate fear, hesitation, or snitches," the app directs.

"Jiro. Su-chan. You sure you want to do this?" I shouldn't have phrased it as an option. When they agree, we walk straight into hell.

In the tight alley, a crowd exchanges money in front of a neon lit tank where wriggling, nightmarish fish devour the unrecognizable bodies that sank to the bottom. *A bet to see how long it'll take? Gross.*

Above, a blue-green haze hangs smothering everything in the cavern. It's especially thick over the nearest shop and the stench of sweat and something sickly sweet assaults our noses.

Yokai of all kinds exit with packets of crystals and clear straws. Some just slouch with glazed eyes across the road. Passersby take no heed to what is below them, even stepping on those in the path. The crunch of breaking bones makes my skin crawl.

"Move it! Get in a shop or get outta the way!" Someone shoves me beak-first into the wall, making my eyes water.

Then the rest of the group scurries over with me to flatten flush against the shop while we get our bearings. A thrum of notice to Honjou Masamune nets no response.

Where are we in Sumichou? The ward's government didn't bother to post signs. Before I can ask, our phones chirp. "Please keep moving in the direction indicated for the best traffic flow." Then the creepy yet cheerful voice changes to an urgent tone. "The next Cleanse is 5 hours from now. Please, make preparations or be swept along and fed to the Shachihoko."

"Shit," I blurt.

"What's a Shachihoko?" Jiro asks.

"Dunno."

Suddenly, Sekiguchi, in his dog form, growls and lunges. The passerby who kicked him yells, "I'll punt that damned thing to the next street over if you don't keep it at bay!"

Su-chan scoops up Sekiguchi and speaks a word of kotodama. Raising her hand holding a powerful charge, she flashes her razor-sharp teeth. "It'll be the last thing you do!"

Cowed, the dog kicker skedaddles out of the way.

Is her attitude an overlay, too? My raised eyebrow has her whispering, "His ki was so low. He didn't stand a chance."

She's right. We can't be meek here. Those months in Nonogawa trying to stay out of trouble made me timid. Fluffing out my wings as if I own the walkway and adding a swagger to my step earns me a friendly nudge from Su-chan.

Meanwhile, Jiro pokes at the Cleanse info page on his phone. It lists stores that offer survival kits and a map of safe buildings. "Shachihoko is an enormous sea monster that eats anything and can swallow immense amounts of water." He gulps as he reads aloud.

So, I squeeze his shoulder. "We'll be out of here before then." But the news transmission method doesn't sit well. "Those in charge here keep us reliant on the information only they can distribute."

Around us, yokai mutter. "Why are they doing so many Cleanses?" But one conversation catches my ear.

"Crystalized ki has been so hard to get. What's available is shit."

"Yeah. Three guys keeled over this morning. Each bought from well-known shops."

Quickly, I look up crystalized ki and nudge Su-chan to show her my phone. "Gut instinct says that's the reason for the next cleanse."

The description reads: 'A white, crystal, metametal powder of super condensed ki energy. A faint blue glow will help you distinguish the best grade from inferior ones. It weighs almost nothing and acts like an aerogel in its ability to float away with a puff of air.'

It causes Su-chan to shudder. "Industrialized ki theft."

Jiro asks, "Stealing ki comes with a nasty price, right?"

"Yeah," I say, grimacing at the memory of after I unwittingly did it. I felt so damned cold, both temperature and emotion-wise. It almost killed me. Shoving it aside, I take a breath and cough from the smoke or whatever it is hanging in the air. "First priority, find filtered masks. Many wear them here. Second, ensure we can deal with the Cleanse just in case."

Sekiguchi adds, "An important aside. Almost every single being here is not what they seem."

Interesting.

After we pick up the clear masks that magically filter the air, we follow the app's directions to the pet shop. "It's taking us through every damned street!"

"Like the Ikea floor plan, directing you through the whole place," Su-chan rasps.

Good girl, covering up your voice.

Then we hit the 'Flowers and Swords' ward. I stumble as I hold up the first page of the specialized guide. In big, flashing letters, it states 'Open Air Brothel! See firsthand, the raved-about service you'll receive!'

I have to clear my throat to speak. "Jiro. Keep moving, no matter what they say. Su-chan, link hands with him."

"Well, this will be quite the education," Sekiguchi mutters.

So Su-chan puts the dog down and wraps his leash several times around her wrist. Her knuckles whiten as she grasps my hand and Jiro's.

I wince. "I know you're into some painful kink, but let's save it for later."

She elbows me and squeezes my hand again as if she's worried about me getting swept off into another's arms. *Not gonna happen.* Jiro's the one I'm worried about.

Then moans and swearing wash over our ears. I saw a lot of insane shit in the yakuza. But all the catcalls urging the participants on have my head shaking and trying to ignore my body's response. Graphic ads flood the app so I can't escape the visuals by staring at my phone and I don't dare glance at young Jiro's expression.

With a chime, the app highlights that we're close to our destination, the exotic pet shop on the edge of the red-light row. I poke at it, hoping for an alternate route. *Just get us outta here.*

Then Su-chan releases my hand, halting in the middle of the road.

"I'll have you all begging for more!" A man with a chiseled face, deep-set eyes, and rippling muscles calls out. The bottom half of him seems to be that of an octopus.

"Gimme a minute," she says, making her way toward him. *What the?* I call after her. *Why would she go to him? Disgusting!*

In front of the male prostitute, Su-chan holds her stomach as if she might be sick. She croaks, "What are the odds of finding you?"

"Every yokai comes through Sumichou, Love." Then a tentacle wraps around her arm. "Come with me. I'll make your dreams come true. You can bring your friends for even more fun!"

Her flat "No," causes his head to jerk back. She spits, "Not. With. You. Tarou."

He rolls back his shoulders before running a hand over her cheek. "Did I do you wrong, Sweetie? I see so many customers, but I'll make you feel as special as you truly are."

Countering, Su-chan's voice pitches low in her undisguised voice. "Mie Tarou, what the hell are you doing here? I had to help your sister get through your funeral."

Mie. *Her best friend's surname.*

Tarou's eyes rival dinner plates. "Suzu-san?" Then his jaw shoves forward. "Let's get off the street." Hollering over his shoulder, he clicks something in the app. "Boss, I'm taking a break. Got an issue to deal with before I can serve clients again."

A husky response hails from a bulky female in the back. "Docking your pay, twice."

"Damn. I could've used another ki boost today," Tarou mutters and his shoulders hunch as he grips Su-chan's upper arm. "You will tell me what shit you got messed up with to bring you here in such a horrible-looking state as soon as we get somewhere private. Do you hear me?"

"You first." Su-chan's teeth grind so loud they might crack.

At the same time, snickers surround us. "Tarou-kun, you in trouble with another girl?"

"This little lady dragged in a blast from the past. One I'm not a part of anymore," he mutters toward the jibe.

"Ooh, the witch is gonna get her little heart broke."

Let go of my girl or you'll get a fist to the face.

But Su-chan scowls. "First time he was dead obviously wasn't enough."

"Tarou, hon, you gonna be ok?" a stunning, androgynous worker asks and holds out a hand.

Instead, he waves off the gesture. "I'm gonna miss that ki hit, that's for sure. But I'll be fine."

Su-chan stomps, impetuously, as Tarou tows her to the end of the street. So I grab his wrist and crush. "Let go of her or you'll have more to worry about than another ki hit."

He flinches and releases Su-chan. As he rubs his arm, he says, "The hostess club at the end of the street has a room they let me book for a break, if it's not in use. We'll try that."

It's across the way from the bar Chisa said she worked at and Tarou shows us a shortcut out of this district.

"Bird-boy, see that?" Su-chan points.

My ex's picture is plastered front and center on the billboard. Her ghostly magic disguise doesn't hide her face or the hints of her perfect body. *Hostess bar, my ass.*

Pausing, Tarou asks, "You need to stop there while oni girl and I have a chat? The one you're staring at has the best act! I could get you tickets for a discount."

"Hell, no." He was just being friendly, so I backtrack. "She and I used to be serious."

"Ouch. I get it," Tarou says.

As if he'd understand.

"She's not working now, anyway. Got caught in the Cleanse earlier today." At Tarou's loud gulp, Sekiguchi adds, "She's recuperating."

Running a hand through his hair, he says in a shaky voice. "Good."

Play your part. "You got stakes in the joint?"

"She's the salvation for that place. I was investing in it. My chance outta here, you know?" Turning to Su-chan, he says, "Missy, should you and I have a private chat?"

But Su-chan says, "Bird-boy, you got one of those muffling ofuda on you?"

So I slap a privacy talisman into her hand and she activates it. She growls, "All of us. After the crap you pulled on your family, I ought to slap you into next Tuesday."

Tarou stiffens. "Heard you loud and clear. As a show of good faith, here's a tip. You and your friends will also want to stop by ten doors down for a survival kit. They stock the best."

"After we stop by the pet shop," I say. Then we can get a scope on the target location. I'm so done with this place, and we've been here less than half an hour.

"But, I'm on the clock," Taro sputters.

"To compensate for your pay loss, I'll give you a ki boost."

His eyes widen. "While you're there, I can get you the kits if you send me with the cash."

Before I can reject the scam, Sekiguchi cuts in. "I'll go along and pay for them so he can't run off."

"Agreed."

Then Jiro strides toward the pet shop, giving off a predator vibe, even stepping on some unfortunate soul on the ground. Though, there's a minute flash as he uses a spell to make it a light step. *His mom should put him in drama club.*

Me? I spend a bit of ki to toss them to the wall. "Damned tired of stepping on the near corpses here."

It's their best chance of survival and for me not to stick out. Others follow suit, adding them in a pathetic pile of nonresponsive bodies. Their ki is low, but they aren't dead. Though, if they don't wake before the Cleanse, it'll be for nothing. *I had to try.*

My heart sinks when we arrive. The shop we'll do reconnaissance from has all kinds of beings that shouldn't be pets—a kodama clinging to a tiny wilted bonsai tree; a red and gold shrimp-like creature with humanoid hands and feet in a cramped aquarium; a pair of furry river boys huddling together and shrinking away from gazes; and a kojin shark child crying and weaving sea silk like his life depends on it. A machine scoops up the pearl tears from the kojin child as fast as they fall.

At the same time, Sekiguchi snarls his head off as someone kicks him again, so Tarou takes his leash from Su-chan. "Meet you at the hostess club two doors down when you're done."

"We won't be long," I say.

Nodding, Tarou urges Sekiguchi toward the shop with the Cleanse survival kits.

Su-chan covers her mouth to suppress a cry of despair at the state of the sapient beings for sale.

So I whisper, "We need to go in."

Her hand tightens on mine, and she shoves her shoulders back, bracing herself. She says, "I dealt with one horror today. I can do it again."

Together, we shove open the door and the bell rings. A ridiculously long-necked shopkeeper zips over faster than humanly possible. "Welcome!" she coos before her face darkens. "I apologize that the selection in my shop is not up to par today. New stock will arrive tomorrow."

Su-chan lifts one of the bonsai's branches as the tiny, translucent tree spirit's leaf ears lay flat and it swipes at her hand. "This one's tree needs more root and better care to thrive."

"These sad remnants are the only ones to survive the last Cleanse. I was putting up the ward when the water arrived. If they don't sell soon, I'll have to sacrifice them as my tribute to Crystal Row." The shopkeeper waves her hand. "Everything is half off today. That kodama will fade in a day or so anyway without the right care."

"How much?" Su-chan asks, unable to keep the emotion out of her voice.

Of course, she'd try to save it. We can't free them all, but maybe we can make a difference for one.

"50,000 yen, firm," the shopkeeper states.

"More than I have right now." Instead, Su-chan touches the tree, giving it a minuscule amount of ki. The kodama brightens with the energy boost and pats Su-chan. "You're welcome, little one. That will get you through for a while."

Then the shopkeeper's long neck cranes around Su-chan. "Why would an oni who hexes others do that for a creature she can't take from the shop? No benefit."

"Yokai populations are decreasing at an alarming rate. I do what I can." Su-chan sputters as she puts her hands on her hips.

You're drawing attention. "Let's go. There's nothing for us here."

But Su-chan shakes her head. "Not yet, Bird-boy."

She knows I'll stand by her, no matter the cost. *What's she getting us into now?*

To the long-necked woman, she flashes a sharp toothed grin. "Wouldn't it be better if yokai as a group were free from having to hide?"

The shopkeeper's words turn hushed, and she runs a hand over her mouth in a zipping motion. "Careful how you speak here. Someone might turn you in, myself included. I'm only warning you because you did me a favor, not that it will do these ki deprived creatures any good."

In my peripheral vision, I catch Jiro holding up a finger to his lips as he sneaks one of his favorite snacks to each of the remaining 'pets'. They stuff it greedily into their maws.

Instantly, the shop owner's long neck cranes over to him. "Stop feeding them junk food unless you're buying them!"

Drawing himself up to full height, Jiro retorts, "I know how they feel." Then he points to the kojin and asks, "How much for that one?"

"You have expensive tastes, young weasel. He's not for sale."

But he moves into her personal space, making her snake-like neck crane back. "Everything in Sumichou is for sale, from what I see. So how much?"

"Are you threatening me? That would be unwise, boy."

He crosses his arms. "Bargaining."

"I'd only part with him for four kilos of the highest grade of crystalized ki. Since that grade's not available, and you don't look like you can afford it, you're out of luck. I get more from him for the information trade than you'd ever be able to pay."

Next, Jiro fiddles with his phone. I put a hand on his shoulder and establish a mental connection. 'Unless you have a plan, this is not the way to go.'

'I do. Need cover.' He turns to check with the kojin, who nods.

'I'm more interested in the info.'

'This will come in handy! I promise!' he says through the link.

'Later. Right now, look up what we need for the Cleanse.'

But Jiro sucks in his lip.

'What are you up to?' I glare.

'Gonna hack the phone restrictions. The kojin gave me an idea.'

Before I can tell him to forget it, a buzz goes off around us and the shopkeeper shoves Jiro. His spell bubble bursts, revealing a thread to the kojin.

She clips it with razor-like nails. "You! Out! No magic connections to the pets!"

So I point to the door, "Weasel, you're more trouble than you're worth!"

"Whatever," Jiro grumbles, but he lifts his hand so only I can see the ki aura radiating from his phone.

When he's slouching against the wall outside, I approach the shopkeeper again. "Miss, I apologize. He's hard to keep under control, but I owe his mom."

Playing along, Su-chan looks around. "Doesn't look like he stole anything this time."

"Call me Megumi. I'd know if he even tried, 'cause my mage does the best wards." She bows in introduction.

My hand runs over my chin as if in thought and I say, "You mentioned information for sale."

"Always. 10K for a 5-minute chat with my kojin and me." Her head stays put while her neck swivels and she gestures toward the shark child.

She's interested. *But damn, her neck is unnerving to watch.*

"And do you guarantee that what we request isn't ratted out?" I ask.

Her toothy grin makes me swallow. "Each day I wait to share it, costs 10k more yen. You know how it is. Gotta make money where I can."

No choice. So I shove my taloned hands into my pockets as if considering her outrageous price.

With merchants on the up and up, I wouldn't try to bargain. But this is the underworld. "We'll re-energize the pets for a significant discount on the info and the kodama."

Su-chan's expression says I'm the best boyfriend in the world.

"25% off the price of the information given. Not the delay price. Still generous!"

"Considering that we charge 5k for a small ki recharge? Ki's expensive, as you well know. Not worth it for us." Crossing my arms, I add, "Throw in two and a half days' delay and you have a deal."

That's still a steal for her, even if my sweet Su-chan would have done it for free. We gotta look comfortable in the underground.

Megumi's lips purse as if she's not sure, but she gazes over her current stock. "Deal."

Reviving the poor creatures trapped in this store takes us a few moments. The shark child is last, and his set jaw says he's not happy about waiting.

He doesn't believe us. I ask, "What's your name?"

"Shiro." His snapped answer screams defiance.

It means 'white'? Must be figurative because his skin is like a starless night sky. "You've had the short end of the stick a few too many times, haven't you, Shiro-kun? So I'll tell you what. I'll give you extra ki in your boost if what you share is useful. Here's a bit to prove it."

Then My hand goes to his shoulder. He flinches, but I let the sunshine warmth of ki flow into him for a second before cutting it off.

"That's not stale energy." He gapes.

With a click, the shopkeeper has a stopwatch going. "As soon as you asked, your time started. A second over 5 minutes costs you another 10K."

Not on her phone? She's skimming under the noses of the leaders. "Notify us at the four minute mark."

Su-chan puts up a block for our conversation with the kojin and I enact a spell of my own, making it look like I'm helping her hold up the shield. Then I mutter a time dilation spell on top of it to skirt the time limit.

The shopkeeper frowns. "You need to include me in that privacy curtain."

But I shrug and open a hole in the shield. "Should've included that in the terms. Your kojin can tell you everything." Then the hole closes. *She'll call time early, now.*

To keep Megumi from reading my lips, I turn my back to her. "Shiro, we'll be asking for a lot here. There's a sword display in the palace. We need the best way to get in and know what security is in place."

The kojin jerks back. "That kind of info could cost my life!"

"What kind of assurance do you need?"

"Full ki charge, proof you won't snitch where you got the info, and I want out from under her thumb. We're burning your five minutes."

Then I motion toward the yokai passing the shop in slow motion. "Don't worry about the time limit. The ki charge should be our assurance since it's fresh. You want to escape?"

He laughs. "I thought you were a couple of total noobs. But you sure fooled Megumi. I want freedom, but she'll never let me go. My information collection makes her too much money. So it's got to be an escape or a deal with her."

"We'll be taking a lot of risk filling your ki well. We often need every ounce of magic we can muster."

"What are you? Some kind of wanna-be heroes?"

But I shrug. "When do you want your ki charge? Can it wait until our way out of Sumichou?"

"No way. Before you leave. Blood pact to seal the deal for my freedom, 'cause I won't just take the word of a kotengu."

Judgment. *Like when I was yakuza.* "Fine." Using a talon, I prick my finger and his.

Next, Su-chan steps forward. "Let me do the charge."

The kojin mutters, "As if a female oni who hands out hexes like they're candy is better."

To make the point, my hand squeezes his shoulder hard enough he winces. "You don't have to like us, but you won't ever talk bad about her. Got that, punk?"

He pales and nods.

"Tell us what we need before I change my mind, because the deal depends on you. You can sit here and rot if you don't cooperate."

"Ok! Ok!"

This better be worth the ki! I whisper kotodama to seal the blood promise and a light flashes from the cuts. A new string forms between us. *Can he see it?*

Without delay, he starts the info dump. "Word on the street says they have high-powered weapons on display under the throne room. The guards said so just outside the shop."

"Tell us something we don't already know. What kind of security do they have? How do we get there?"

"No clue. I'm not in the Underground."

"Underground? Keep talking."

"Che. You really are noobs, just street smart ones."

Then my eyes narrow. "Don't make me repeat myself."

"The rebels. They stop by here sometimes, thinking it's a safe place to pass their messages. I don't tell Megumi about them, because I want 'em to succeed."

"We wanna join."

"How do I know you're not a spy?"

"You won't until we rescue you out of this hellhole."

"Fine. They have a call sign you send in a text."

"To what number?" *Is he terrified, or just playing us to use up time?*

He coughs a few times to cover saying it. "Spell out Kappa Baku Phoenix as one word in hiragana. They're the leaders."

Baku—like on the card I have. "Thank you. Any of the guards' protocols you can help us with?"

"They base everything on the human yakuza. The leadership took over a clan."

That makes me grimace. "Can you tell me more about them and their underlings?"

"If you're not a financial genius like Megumi or the owners of the brothels of the Flowers and Swords district, the best place to be is in the Akumakai. Their ranks include every kind of yokai." He pauses. "I see that look. Here's what you need to know. The clan's id is in their suits, so you just have to get one and access to one of their phones to blend in."

He cuts off as a ripple runs over our protection spell. I glare at Megumi for interfering, but she says, "Finish it later. The guard patrol will be here any second, and you're damned conspicuous."

"Anything else we need to know, kid?"

"The prison and connection to Crystal row are next to the display." He frowns. "And the clan is awful to everyone outside their ranks."

"Understood. You were most helpful." I stand between the window and the kojin so Su-chan can finish recharging his ki.

He perks up before wiping the smile off his face and going back to looking dejected. I can't blame him for the slip. The warm glow of an energy transfusion is a rush.

Then the shop bell dings and Megumi glides back over to me while giving a smile that looks pasted on. She hollers at the newcomers, "Irrashaimase! Welcome! You must be looking for a new pet. I'll be with you in just a moment."

To me she says, "Your purchase will cost you 15K yen. For the kodama, the down payment will be the same."

Liar.

Meanwhile, a giant bear and rat, both kitted out in riot gear, swagger in drunk on the power their position gives. Their hands caress their batons as if hoping to use them soon. Pistols are strapped to their hips and a shield to each of their backs. They've seen action and the sickening sweet smell that permeates the district rolls off them.

I'm not stupid, lady. "You said 10K." She blanches as the guards poke at the little kodama's banzai, laughing as the tree spirit tries to bite their batons.

"10K won't hold your deposit on the kodama," she mutters. "If someone else can pay the full amount, I won't hesitate to sell to them."

And I'll lose the deposit. But Su-chan is already attached to the little tree spirit. I'll try for her sake. "Gotcha. I'm putting a tracker on it, so I'll know if you sell it."

Megumi scowls as I stick an ofuda on the pot. But she brightens as I hand over the last bill of that size in my wallet plus a handsome 'tip' and wink.

In the yakuza, I learned how different the underground economy was. Tips aren't normal, but a little extra always helps smooth this kind of transaction. She rewards me with a softened expression.

We better not have more big expenses. Most working people don't make 15K yen in a day after taxes and I only earned minimum wage working at a grocery store.

"Were those the same wilted-looking ones you had yesterday?" One guard half asks, half states.

Megumi turns on the charm. "It's amazing what a little water, the right fertilizer, and a good plant mage can do. This little one was worth the price."

Quickly, I grab Su-chan's hand, tugging her along. "We'll be back for the little tree spirit. Don't you worry."

Su-chan's lip quivers. It'd melt me, if it wasn't on her wrinkled oni disguise.

"You gonna have the tribute for the boss tonight, Megumi-chan? You only get one free pass and you used yours already."

As soon as we're out of the store, Su-chan heaves in a big breath. "That was hard."

I whisper, "I know. We'll get you the kodama."

"And the others."

She's such a compassionate woman. It's part of what made me fall for her. So I offer a compromise. "We'll help the kojin, at least."

Motioning away from the store, I say, "Come on, Weasel-boy. We got a job to do. Let's see if the others are done."

22

CHAT WITH THE DEAD

THE RECEPTIONIST AT THE hostess bar welcomes us.

"Is Tarou-san here, yet?" I ask.

Swanky club music flows out, the beats gently vibrating in my chest. *Which reminds me, I haven't felt a thrum from Honjou since before we got here.* Worry tightens my insides even further.

"Sorry, sir." The ghost smiles sweetly.

How did she put on all that makeup? Objects go right through apparitions like her.

"Can we book you all a table and hostess while you wait for dear Tarou-kun? Our girls are adept with multiple customers."

On cue, a nature spirit hostess decked out in vivid blue robes that reveal much of her chest waves at Jiro and blows him a kiss. She grins, showing her fangs at his blush. Her golden hair, done up in a mix of deadly spikes and a traditional courtesan's do, contrasts with her earthy brown skin.

Expensive! I shake my head. "Thanks anyway."

But Jiro waves back.

"What about your friend? He seems quite taken with Yasha-chan. She'd take a quick customer before she goes on break."

My young friend silently pleads.

It's what we get for bringing a kid. "Well, Weasel-boy. You got the cash this place requires?"

He flicks through the app on his phone and flashes a coupon with a triumphant chuff. "Five minutes free."

So, I snag the phone and scroll down. "It says with an hour's purchase."

His face falls when the receptionist calls to Yasha, "Break time for you."

She snaps her fingers as if to say too bad and saunters over to run a finger under Jiro's chin. "I like the fuzzy ones, even when they're in disguise. So cute. Book me sometime." Then she bobs a greeting to someone behind us. "Hey, Tarou-kun. You working a side job on your day off?"

A meaty hand slaps my back. "For this crew. They've promised excellent payment."

The clock's ticking! I swipe a quick message on my phone and flash the screen to Tarou. 'The weasel's underage hormones are causing trouble. Book us the room.'

But he looks Jiro up and down. "I see what you mean."

Can he tell from the boy's ki signature?

Then Sekiguchi says, "We couldn't get the kits. Every shop is sold out because of the increasing number of cleanses. Minimize your magic use."

Shit. We spent a lot of energy at the pet shop. Though Su-chan would have done it, anyway.

Tarou helps us book a private chat room with his gold status discount. Unfortunately, I don't have the cash. So Su-chan pulls out her wallet. Slipping my hands into my pockets, I kick at the street. *She shouldn't have to pay for things.*

Next, the receptionist points down the hall. "Third door on the right. No drinks, messy magic spells except to survive the Cleanse, and no sex unless you pay the cleanup fee in advance."

Jiro is still gawking at Yasha, so I seize his arm. "Come on, lover boy."

"Me?" His voice cracks as he protests.

Once his feet are moving, I tap his head. "Yes, you. Time to focus."

When we close the door to the room, Su-chan pokes Tarou's chest. "You will explain being here in Sumichou, right now! Such a deception will shock your family!"

Tarou squirms under her penetrating gaze. "They can't find out. You got that? I was D-E-A-D, dead! Just because I turned into a yokai doesn't mean I should go back!"

To stop the argument, I put up a hand and force my words to be softer than I would with anyone else. "Su-chan, mind if we save this for later? We're on the clock."

She pouts. "I can't keep this from Mie-chan. She deserves to know."

"I agree. After the job." So, I show Jiro how to look for surveillance devices in the dim space. Ylang ylang incense hangs in the air. We check the table, light fixtures, cushy furniture, and pictures.

Tarou assures us the rooms are bug free, but I pop up a privacy spell anyway that excludes him and he rolls his eyes. "What kinda noobs are you, anyway?"

"We want the octo-perv in on this," Su-chan says.

Uncharacteristic saltiness. "I don't trust him. What kind of guy ditches their family?"

She scrunches her eyes shut for a second, as if fighting an internal battle. "Despite being super mad at him. I believe Mie-chan's little brother won't give us away. He knows what I dealt with in Hokkaido and never said a word to anyone about it. He also had a good reason for leaving home."

Su-chan wouldn't say that without reason. So, we bring Tarou into the bubble and fill the others in on the info from Shiro.

He says, "Why do you want in so badly? Look, I wouldn't ask. But I might help, if there's something in it for me."

But I just glare. "My trust is hard earned."

Casually, he leans back. "I've got to know what you're up to and why. I trust my sister's bestie to not be involved in something evil. But you could have her fooled."

It causes Su-chan to tut. "Bird-boy, there, is ex-yakuza and yet he earned your sister's trust. She'd tell you to let that tidbit parse between your two brain cells."

"Him?" He points to me as his brows furrow.

So I let a trace of the feathered disguise on my shoulder fade before pulling back my collar to reveal irezumi tattoos.

That makes him swallow. "What about the others?"

"My healing arts teacher and a genius young mage. We've been through a lot together," Su-chan says.

Then he pokes at the shield around us as if testing it. "That's serious magic. How about I share info you need as a sign of good faith?"

Something niggles at the back of my mind. Mie's brother showing up out of the blue and being so helpful smells suspicious. We don't need misleading intel.

Before he continues, I snap a lie detection spell into place and Tarou winces. "The code the kojin gave you is a honeypot. He meant well, considering everything else he gave you is correct." His eyes narrow. "Stop scowling at me."

In for a penny, in for a pound. I pull out the business card with the wriggling script and place it in front of Tarou. "We want in."

From nowhere, Tarou's hand whips a dagger to my throat. "Password. Now."

Su-chan shrieks, "Tarou!"

Glaring harder, I lock eyes with him and snag his hand out of the air. Then using my bodyweight, I slam his wrist to the table with a crunch.

Tarou yelps and the dagger clatters to the floor as I focus on the name Yamazaki told me. "Baku." The card flashes blue.

Finally, Tarou withdraws, holding his arm to his chest for a moment before there's a flash of light. He still shakes out his hand after the light healing.

So I growl, "In my yakuza days, that would've gotten you killed."

He whispers, and the dagger returns to his hand, where he tucks it into a dimensional pocket. "You pass. Gotta be extra careful."

No apology? "You appear to at least be legit now."

"You got connections, too, to have that card. Lucky you came across me instead of a snitch. I'm part of the Sumichou Underground, that's why I have to be so careful. Not a leader. But like everyone here, I want a better life. There was a message from Baku saying a few of us died just after midnight. Then there was the Cleanse.

"From what I can tell, a good half the population is in the Underground. Maybe more. We don't reveal ourselves unless it's worth the sacrifice. That knowledge could get me and you stuck on the ki extraction machines. Or worse."

Su-chan's been spot on about so much. Sucking in a breath between my teeth, I give in to her belief in her best friend's brother. "We're gonna steal back a sword. One I lost and cost me a position in the L..." I growl as my throat closes. "Damn it! I hate that seal." On instinct, my hand runs through the feathers at the crown of my head. It feels weird when I was expecting hair. *Keep your cool, idiot.*

After a moment, I continue, "For a group I can't name. I wanted in so bad I could taste it, but I have no chance unless I regain that sword."

"It's not just any sword? And the Akumakai has it?"

"Honjou Masamune. I have to retrieve her to stop Ibaraki Douji. The Oni Queen seems to meddle in everything I come across."

Tarou whistles. "Yes. Bringing shame to the Akumakai and relieving them of powerful weapons—that's worth the risk. I can get you uniforms and chips to tune your IDs. Put down your privacy shield so I can text the group board. Su-chan, what's your number?"

I offer mine instead and drop the spell. *Octo-perv doesn't need her contact info.*

Hastily, he pokes at his phone and mine chirps a moment later. He says, "That's the location to pick them up with directions to tune the fake registration to yourselves."

Then Sekiguchi asks, "How accurate are they about the Cleanse's timing?"

"Once a two-minute alarm goes out, it's accurate. You guys will need backup, at the rate you're blowing through ki. They designated some buildings as shelters. Know which one is closest to your location at all times."

"But the app says you just need a shield bubble and a strong tether. If we aren't tapped, we can handle it."

Jiro asks, "How do we get more ki? Mine's not refilling."

But Tarou shakes his head. "Right now? Safe crystalized ki is hard to find. Everything here runs on it. FYI, no one uses their own magic unless they're forced to. You're gaining attention with your use. For the Cleanse, you'll want a doubled force field if you can manage it. It's better to be inside a building. Otherwise, you get buffeted, even in a shield."

"Thanks for the advice." I bob my gratitude.

Next, Su-chan says, "Please, consider contacting your sister. She's had it rough over the years of thinking you were dead."

Tarou squeezes her hand. "I will. If something happens to you, I'll do it to be there for her. I'm not the only one in deep right now, you know. My break is up. Good luck."

23

History of Comments

When heading to the coin lockers, we come across reward posters with photos of our human forms. None of us can tear our gazes from the price the Akumakai put on our heads—100k yen a piece, dead or alive.

Even swear words escape me. *It had to be Chisa.* Despite knowing she was a spy, her betrayal is still a kick in the gut. Behind us, someone chatters, "Think those four are on the hunt for that human lot?"

Bile burns my throat. If Chisa's memory wasn't wiped... *You'd do what?* Revenge is out of the question, no matter how tempting.

Finally, my tongue works again and I mutter, "Let's go, the clock's ticking."

The cleaning crew uniforms are in the specified locker, but we're short one. Did someone else snag it? Nothing fits well, and there's no time to have them altered. The fabric looks clean, but still has the sickly sweet taint of crystalized ki. We'll have to make the best of it.

'Who's going to be the trainee?' I open a link to the group and ask.

Everyone else looks to Jiro.

'What if I'm the one who sticks out instead of the youngest of us?' I suggest.

But Sekiguchi says, 'We need someone with experience to lead. You can't do that as a trainee.'

Next, we change, but there's nowhere in Sumichou to set up our IDs in private. Even the restrooms have cameras.

So, it's back to the hostess bar.

They insist we book a girl, since Tarou isn't with us. When I text him, he recommends Yasha, saying she's the most reliable. It won't take long for her booking to be done, so we wait. The swanky club music pummels our ears.

She perks up when she sees Jiro again and winks. "Couldn't resist, could you?"

Shyly, he looks down, shuffling his feet.

"Oh, the innocent ones are so adorable! Do you know how rare that is in a client?" She takes Jiro's arm and the scent of jasmine wafts over us. "Shall I get us all some drinks?"

We can't take chances, even if Tarou recommended Yasha. Anyone paid to act like they care isn't trustworthy. Besides, Jiro is way too young to be a sugar daddy.

"Yasha-san, a couple of things, since I'm the one handing over the cash. One, nothing more than a little flirting with Jiro, and two, no alcohol for him. Got it?"

Her face goes unreadable, but she nods. "Just how old are you, Jiro-kun?"

Gulping, he gazes at the table. "Almost thirteen."

Under the consent law. No doubt about it.

She whistles. "No wonder you act so shy." To me she asks, "So you're his big brother?"

"Something like that."

"I'll grab drinks, keeping the age in mind. Then we can head to the room to chat."

When she returns with a tray of cocktails and a yuzu sparkling water, she guides us to the same room we were in with Tarou. We make ourselves comfortable in the cushy seats and she hands us each a drink.

Gotta do this, even though Yasha's powerful. The crew is depending on me. "We need your help hacking our IDs. I'll place a seal that stops you from talking about what you see or hear during this session. That should save you from questioning. Are you agreed? Otherwise, we can ensure you don't witness anything."

Yasha's look turns steely. "What kind of seal?"

"Only the kind that makes it so you can't talk. Nothing more."

"Tarou recommended me. There's a reason for that. I'm not a stupid human, if you haven't noticed." Then Yasha snaps her fingers and we're surrounded by a box of darkness.

We hear a breath, and a wheel of fire appears behind Yasha. Her eyes turn hard. Then a sword appears in her hand.

Oh shit. One of the mythical defenders of Buddhism and bodyguards to the gods.

Instantly, her voice drops to low and menacing. "I don't know what you are playing at. But you will tell me what you are up to if you wish to leave this room alive.

The young weasel boy, being the exception. I'll just blank his memory. No one outside this spell will be any wiser."

How can she be here in this evil underworld? As a hostess, who pretends to be interested in others, no less. *Did I just get us all killed?* Being in control went to my head. Gauging her ki shows she's low but still has much more than I do.

Then flames light her face, highlighting her razor-like teeth. I shudder, but I won't kowtow. *Can't look weak.* My old drawl returns as I spread my hands. "Yasha-san, I apologize. It's vital to pull this job off."

"And if I don't agree to the seal?"

"Then we exclude you from the plan."

She asks, "Jiro-kun, do you trust this yakuza? Don't look at me that way. It's written all over his actions and he just spoke like one."

Without hesitation, Jiro answers. "He used to be yakuza. But he saved me several times. First time was by telling me the yakuza weren't a solution. Then he helped me find an aikido teacher. I don't trust many people, but I trust him and my teachers." Jiro holds up his phone. "Both my aikido and magic sensei can each tell you it's the truth."

"You won't be able to call outside of Sumichou." Yasha waves away his suggestion.

But Jiro's face screws up, though he keeps quiet.

"Then let me share," Sekiguchi says.

"A pet? No thanks."

Sekiguchi hops off the chair. To Su-chan, he says as he ditches the leash, "This would be demeaning if you still looked like you owned me." Then he reveals his original form for only a second. His new metal arm glints in the light.

Yasha sucks in a breath and immediately releases the surrounding blackness. "An actual kappa! Here? No wonder you all use disguises."

Then I tilt my head, but she doesn't offer further explanation.

When Sekiguchi and Su-chan testify about me, my head turns away. Hopefully, the feathers of my disguise cover my burning cheeks because I hate being the center of attention. And hearing what they thought of me at first is rough. My fingers tap on the table while the hostess considers.

In the end, Yasha covers her mouth as she says. "Only one of you is a full-blooded yokai. That's never a good thing in this town. Alright, mobster, seal me or kick me outta this, but Jiro-kun stays with me either way."

Former mobster. "We need his ID hacked, too. Not just ours." Prepping the spell Aunt Hisako taught me saps ki.

Yasha asks, "Are you sure you can spare the magic for the spell?"

No. But I shrug. "The head of the Akumakai steals ki without penalty. We suspect Ibaraki Douji is that leader. The one who held her in bondage had a dark spell for taking ki, too." So I apply the seal and a flash of blue signals it's setup and waiting for input. "I need Honjou Masamune back to stop Ibaraki from killing an entire yokai species and taking over Japan. She's more powerful than her previous master, who my girlfriend and I defeated."

Yasha exclaims, "The Honjou Masamune? You think that sword will let a yakuza possess it?"

My hand taps my wrist to signal how short on time we are. "Former yakuza, and she did before."

"She?"

I nod and whisper to finish the seal and what the hostess can't speak about.

Yasha holds out her hand. So, I slap my phone into it. She says, "I'll do the IDs for 10K yen each, which is a steal, considering the risk I'm taking. But you, too, will swear to secrecy. I'll know if you rat me out." Then she flicks her fingers and static runs over us, head to toe.

"I'll pay." Sekiguchi pulls his wallet from a dimensional pocket in his dog paw and hands over the cash. After Yasha fiddles with the settings on my phone, she transfers something.

Leaning in close, Jiro's entranced by her hack. It's the first time since he laid eyes on her that something else was more interesting. "So you changed the ID in the database? How?"

"Smart lad." She shows him the command and gives him the file to follow along on his phone. He'll set up Sekiguchi's ID.

In a flash, Jiro configures the group to look like a cleaning crew. Though the scan doesn't like him, the one of us who has the least natural magic.

He holds his phone up to me and says via the link. 'I wish Hoji-sensei was here. He'd find the problem in the code. This is harder than the last hack I did.'

'How do we get past this? The scanner issue relates to the amount of ki. We can't just transfer it around.' Then my lips purse. 'Or can we?'

So I bring Su-chan and Sekiguchi in on the conversation. 'Can we share ki and take it back?'

Meanwhile, Yasha sips her drink, surveying our silent interchange like a hawk.

Su-chan's face scrunches up. 'Maybe? Like, just not letting it go?'

Unsure, I say, 'Let's try it with Jiro. He can give it back if something goes wrong.'

'How much do you think we need to give him?'

'No idea.' Nevertheless, I gather up half my available ki and pour it into Jiro. A momentary flash from the app allows him to register. When he gives the ki back, there's about ten percent less than I gave him.

'The transfer eats some.'

Sekiguchi says aloud, "I'm worried about you guys running so low."

"You folks spend ki like you're above ground," Yasha adds.

"We're used to our wells replenishing. We'll have to learn to make do," I add.

"Yes!" Suddenly, Jiro lights up and types like mad on his phone. "I've been poking at the app's security and look at this!"

We crane to see, and find a text message from Hoji describing the vulnerabilities in the magic that blocks communication. Jiro croons, "I created a link to the outside!"

"You did what?" I can't keep from blurting.

His fists tighten as he defends his actions. "It might come in handy!"

Via the mental link, I share. 'I just hope they can't trace it to you, Jiro.' Thinking better of my answer, I pat his shoulder. "Brilliant, though. Just keep us in the loop on what you're doing."

The next message from Hoji reads, 'Nobu-sensei thinks you should go for a degree in magic and computer security.'

But Yasha grabs his phone. "How in the seven hells did you get outside access?" To the rest of us, she demands, "Is this Hoji a bad influence?"

I can't disagree with Yasha's concern. Jiro's amazing for a kid, and I don't have a good feeling about his on-the-fly hacking here in Sumichou. Not that we have a better option right now. Besides, Nobu-san said we'd need the boy.

"Hoji's fine. One of the first to combine magic and tech." The rest of my crew nods agreement.

Then Yasha asks, "Will you give me his contact info?"

"We'll ask him after we're done with this job," I offer.

"If you survive."

Next, I revert to the link. 'Their server's security isn't great, is it?'

Jiro opens his mouth, but seems to think better of leaving the conversation in the open. "Sorry, Yasha-san."

She just shrugs. "I get paid by the hour."

So, Jiro says via the link, 'Hoji-sensei says most yokai aren't tech smart. Maybe that's why?' He holds up another message. 'The differences in code sections hint at various levels of programming ability. What can you find in the menus? Anything we can take advantage of?'

The boy's hands glow as he sifts through menus faster than I can navigate a music playlist.

'Save your ki. What if they trace you? It's not just my life that's at stake.' I shake my head. 'Use normal methods to search.'

The light surrounding Jiro's hands fades. But he protests, 'It's safe. Hoji-sensei's watching my phone through a... tether. That's the word, right?'

'Save your magic. While you poke around in the code, I'm gonna hunt for a schematic of the palace.'

Sekiguchi asks, "When's our shift start?"

"Twenty-five minutes."

"Not much time to get this right," Su-chan says as she huddles over her phone. "I'm gonna skim the guard handbook since I just found it."

When I spot a seedy store with the blueprints, I give a fist pump. 'Anyone got cash? I'm out and we need accurate schematics. The guaranteed set is 20K yen. Also, let's leave this link open for the duration of our time in Sumichou. It'll cost less ki than re-creating it each time we need it.'

Sekiguchi hands me the two bills, hardly denting the cash he has. That's 60K he just handed out during this meeting! I bob my thanks.

"Whoa." Jiro gasps. The boy doesn't hide his screen, even though I'd like him to, considering what it shows.

'I found a set of encrypted comments,' he says. 'It took me a bit to get it. There's these alien-looking symbols—like ancient characters. And they're saved in sound files. I'm gonna play them.'

Sekiguchi's thoughts turn concerned over the link. 'Do we have time? What if it's a trap like the honeypot Tarou warned us about, or a virus?'

'In for a penny, in for a pound. We need all the info we can get. Let me be the one to take the risk with the file. If anything goes wrong, you all can scramble,' I say.

Instead of waiting, Jiro's about to tap his cell. 'It'll go to the link.'

'Jiro!' I snap. 'Stop being so impulsive! We work as a team! You got that?'

'Y-yes, Umeji-san.' The boy shrinks and pulls his knees up to his chest.

Yasha's eyebrow raises as she continues watching.

But Su-chan's the one that jumps in. 'Jiro-kun, we just want to decide things together. Tatsu's our lead.'

'It's more than that. I just...' *wouldn't be able to handle it if we lost him.* 'I don't want you to take unnecessary risks. You're part of the team, and we need your talent and your brains.' He's still sulking. So, I blow out a breath. 'Do you know why I got mad?'

Jiro shakes his head.

'A team has each other's backs. But I can't do that for you if I don't know what's coming. And...' Words gum up even in my thoughts, but I force them out. 'Because you're like a little brother to me.'

He lights up and sends the files to my phone. To show I meant what I said, he gets the honor of pressing play.

At first, there's crackling in the audio with a rushing of what must be a tsunami, and screams before a hushed voice begins.

Call me Kappa. I'm taking refuge as I speak and leaving snippet recordings of what happened as time allows. The rushing waters are the only thing loud enough to drown out the microphones on the spy cameras placed everywhere. You, lucky app user, have accessed my record as the head of the rebellion against the current leadership of the Akumakai.

Yasha's phone blips and she gapes. "You've accessed the secret files! But there's no sound. You hooked it to a private link network? Tell me Jiro didn't do that..."

When Jiro looks at me, I nod.

"That's why you dared bring such a young one to Sumichou," Yasha slaps the boy on the back.

"Play the rest," I say, and close my eyes to concentrate.

You may doubt my account since you'll find no one else to speak of the incident. Everyone the Akumakai could prove rebelled was swept away with a series of Cleanses or put on the damned ki extractors. No warning was given before the acidic flood waters swept through our tunnels and caverns. I only hope those I know have enough magic to survive.

You should know of the hell that brought us to the point we'd rebel. Even self-willed Yokai know we need a powerful leader. We'll put up with a ton of shit before we hit the limit.

As soon as the previous Oyabun's head was stuck on a pike at the main entrance, things went downhill for our district. Ishida Chihiro wasn't a terrible leader. So I want to know why he was overthrown.

Within a month, life was unbearable. Whoever the secretive new leader is, their demand for crystalized ki is insatiable. They don't care about the culture here or our lives.

Even the most minor infraction of the ever-increasing laws means being sentenced to operating the extractors. They made me take every atom of ki from people they condemned. The only chance the poor bastards had to survive was if their ki refresh rate was fast enough to keep them from passing on. To what? Who knows! Do the dead in the factories even have a soul remaining after such torture? ##

Then they sealed Sumichou and turned off our ki's natural refresh ability. Something like that requires the darkest magic. To what end? It limits the crystal available.

When I was sentenced to work on the machines, I swore no more. No yokai, even the most depraved among us, should have to drain the life force of another being. Finding two other workers of like mind, Baku and Phoenix, we coded directions for freedom into the very application that runs Sumichou. We managed it in a way that the Akumakai can't eradicate. It's a virus on every phone in Japan, and possibly the entire world. Baku is the genius behind it. He was the one to keep our memories alive, even if we don't survive.

For a month, we did reconnaissance and planned. We took over each factory in Crystal Row, gathering everyone we could. Then we equipped our little army with all the condensed ki they could carry to power their magic plus the weapons of the guards we overpowered. I hated the killing, but to free the yokai here from this hell was going to cost lives. An uncountable number.

We made it to the throne room of the Palace. Even had the damned green witch cornered in an anti-spell cage I could put a sword through. She kept dodging. When I finally landed a blow to her chest, I was content to be ending the destroyer of my home. She howled, not in pain, but a phrase we couldn't make out.

Something ripped my sword from my hand. It did the same for all the weapons and bags of crystal ki my comrades held and stripped every method of defense from us, save our fists. I conjured a sword based on energy, but it fizzled upon touching the witch. It was like she absorbed the ki.

Next, the cage surrounding her evaporated and, one by one, each of the rebels around me fell. What dark magic was she using? When I saw the black circle growing on the ground, I knew. ##

But the mystery of how she didn't pay the price for the ki theft still stymies me. Was an extraction machine placed inside the throne?

I helped Baku and Phoenix create a stack of portals to escape and minimize the possibility of being traced. By then, she'd subdued the other rebels. Those that remained fell to their knees, panting before turning to ash. I scrambled away, but stumbled, and every step burned like I couldn't breathe.

Gradually, the drain lessened, and I ran smack dab into a group of guards. I stole enough energy from one of them to make a portal out. Now, I'm shaking and freezing from the deadly cost. If I can manage it, I'll try to make one last set of recordings. ##

You hold the only records of the rebellion and my identity. They've had hounds on my trail since last night.

The hunters have cornered me and cut off magical access, so I'll perform a complete memory wipe on myself. Otherwise, the green witch will force me to give up my comrades, then she'll extract my ki and toss my body into the next Cleanse to erase any proof I existed. I included the amnesia spell with this feed, should you need it.

<< click to access spell >> ##

Now, I pass the torch to you. Carry on the rebellion. You have all the documents and the proof of what the Akumakai is doing under the oni witch we believe to be taking revenge on her former master. Work with Baku and Phoenix. The Sumichou Underground must survive to free our district, one of the last refuges for yokai in the world.

Take up the name of Kappa and carry the torch. Bring down the green witch. Remind her that her days are numbered, even if she kills m- ##

Loud static causes us all to jump, and a flashing message on my phone says, 'Unrecoverable Error.' Everyone's haunted eyes flick to me.

There was so much packed into those messages. My taloned fingers pull at the feathers on my head to fend off the coming headache.

So the leader of the underground did a mind wipe? *And they're likely dead.* "It's got to be Ibaraki. Everything leads to her. But she's even more powerful than she appeared in the last battle. And she can drain ki to steal the magic ability of everyone around her... Shit. Why didn't she do that in the battle for our home?"

"Y-you were in a battle with Ibaraki Douji?" Yasha stammers. "What the hell are you? Tell me you're not the four on the wanted posters!"

Responding to that last accusation would give too much away. So I barrel into a diverting but truthful answer. "Not good enough for the task my master gave me. She took Honjou from us there."

Yasha huffs, "Che. You're insane. Large groups haven't been able to bring her down. What makes you think you can?"

But my hand sweeps over our little group. "We just need to retrieve the sword. Figuring the rest out isn't our job."

"Count me out. I have a different mission." When I'm about to ask, she cuts me off. "You'll be the perfect distraction for us. That's all you need to know."

She's part of this Underground. They're planning something to go down at the same time. *And we can use that.*

24

Lions' Den

As Yasha returns to the hostess bar, she says, "Let me know weasel boy is ok when you're done with this crazy mission."

Jiro fiddles with his sleeve, blushing. Yasha's protectiveness must have made an impression.

So I agree and ensure we didn't run over our appointment time slot before paying. Then my crew and I review how a cleaning group should act.

'We can report in for our shift online, but we have to check in at the palace afterward. We have five minutes before that,' Su-chan states into our mental link.

'Don't want to look too eager,' I say as we head out.

'They have a reward for starting your shift on time. It's a small amount of that crystalized ki,' Sekiguchi adds.

'Ok. Let's bring some of that crystal back for my aunt and Satou-san to examine. We'll want to get any information on the activities here we can, especially since they found a way around the price for ki theft. This reeks of Date Sari's work.' My brow furrows as I ponder. 'Makes me wonder if she had anything to do with this place.'

It's hard not to hash over scenarios where things could go wrong. By the time we reach the gate, everything about Sumichou gives me the creeps. I'd rather have my old Glock that I carried in the mob than have to rely on such limited magic and a sword I'm not familiar with. Not that I'd take being back in the mob to have the Glock again. My heart sinks. *Shitty setup for a job.*

'You just turned scary,' Su-chan says as she pokes me.

She's right. My lope, my posture, my expression—everything about me says 'back off'. It all returned to how I was in the yakuza and it was way too easy to slip into that mode again. While that's not who I am anymore, I have a part to play.

Ahead, the towering palace is an incongruous mix of modern steel and glass combined with traditional white plaster and tile. Search lights comb the outside. More than once we have to shield our eyes from the blinding glare off the building.

A sizzling moat and two-story wall surround the palace. On each corner, there's a sentry tower. The gate's heavy iron doors are only half open for foot traffic. They're stopping everyone entering, comparing them to the reward poster with my crew's human faces.

At the top of the wall, pikes protrude from gory heads. Yet another reason we shouldn't have brought Jiro along. This place'll scar him for life.

Su-chan grimaces, pointing out, 'Those towers hold strong mages tripped out on that nasty crystal.'

Jiro adds, 'The eye on the tower sends all the information for the app. They try to run every part of life here.' Aloud, he says, "We report at the North Gate. Looks like it's over there." To my consternation, the boy stays buried in his phone. 'Wish we could link with the app. The FAQ says it's possible, but I didn't want to risk it.'

Now I know how Hiro always felt when I'd pick up something before he could. *Old.* "Get your head outta that phone and keep your eyes peeled," I snap, but resist slapping the top of his head like Hiro used to do to me.

Still, Jiro flinches, so I add via our link, 'It's cover, but also common sense here. We need to be gruff.' *Can I balance this role with the old yakuza side?* Shaking my head to clear it doesn't help. *Focus.*

The North Gate is smaller, but no less imposing and just as fortified. A group of guards reporting in steps into some sort of scanner booth. One of the new guards fidgets as if she doesn't want to be there, and the spotlight highlights them as we approach.

Suddenly, a siren blares and the female guard books it out of the booth. From thin air, soldiers tackle and beat her while she tries to scramble away. But it's in vain. As they subdue her, she cries, "The Akumakai's days are numbered!" before she goes limp.

Dead? My eyes close for a moment of respect for the brave rebellion member. 'Can't let that be us,' the thought pierces our group link before I can reel it in.

'Agreed,' Sekiguchi says.

Then Jiro gulps. *It's sinking in just how deep we're in, isn't it?* And we can't back out now.

'Watch what the rest of the guards do.' Keep the crew safe. *That's your biggest job, Umeji.*

A few of the just-scanned guards look back, but their leader says, "She was the noob. Best to watch for those new ones, guards or otherwise."

Putting the negative focus on others. Bastard. Though, his words give me an idea. 'Follow my lead.'

It's hard not to gape at the metal and glass gate contraption with its blinking lights and the spider yokai at the other end of it. Su-chan tenses. 'Creepy bug.'

'You can do this.' I have to resist giving her hand a squeeze or reminding her she looks freaky in her female oni disguise.

The spider's badge reads Tezuka, and he speaks so apathetically his voice comes out like a robot, "More noobs. Enter and hold up the ID on your app. We'll verify your scan matches what's in the database and check for anything suspicious."

Let him think we're one of them. "Too bad you have to deal with riffraff like that among the guards." I point my thumb toward the rebel being hauled off. "Don't they know who has the power in Sumichou? Better to be on the winning side. Am I right?"

So Jiro crosses his arms and nods. "Dumb rebels."

"Need some help roughing that one up?" I ask.

Instantly, Tezuka perks up but shakes his head. "The machines will deal with that one. Too bad it looks like she wiped her memory. Anyway, step in. Prepare yourselves. We test every noob from janitors to soldiers, since we have need of a few particular traits. If you survive this skill test, then we'll see if there are better-paying jobs to fit your talent."

Forcing us to show our hand. Aww, shit.

Glancing at his screen, then at us again, Tezuka asks. "The boss needs a few techies. Any of you got that kind of knowledge?"

Jiro raises his hand and I add, "We're all decent with whatever tech you can throw at us, but this guy, he's a wizard."

So Tezuka nods, giving a grim smirk. "Survive first. Five minutes, starting when you get in the test chamber."

My teeth grind. 'Let's get this over with.'

When we enter, the doors seal behind us. This didn't happen to the other guards! My palms turn clammy and the feathers down my back threaten to stand on end.

Below the windows, panels open. The stench of raw innards fills the chamber and shrill shrieks echo upward.

Jiro flips through his phone fast as lightning. At the same time, Su-chan and I pop shields around our group and, as one, we pull out our weapons.

But when I seal the entry point, the spell dissipates.

Tezuka's now animated voice breaks into the moment. "Tsk-tsk. No avoiding the test."

Sicko.

The incessant cries grow louder, sending shivers down my spine. Half-meter long, quivering slugs with suckers for feet emerge. If one stops, others use their rotating teeth to saw through and devour it. The monsters converge on us.

"What the hell are they?" I holler.

"The Eyeless ones. Leeches that move fast," Jiro announces. "It says they move in groups and can eat through anything short of three-centimeter steel plate."

"I'll contain the damned things." We don't dare use our link. It'd give that advantage away, so I pop up a privacy bubble. "Jiro, you're in charge of watching the other panels. Expect them to open, too."

Next, I surround a group of the creatures with a spell and squeeze the barrier down to a point. In a gory explosion, they burst. "Su-chan, keep the shields up. Sekiguchi, take out anything that gets through. I'll handle the groups. If you find a weakness, call it out," I shout above the racket, wishing I didn't have to use our real names.

Scraping metal confirms my fears. *We're doing too good.*

Jiro shouts, "Panels near the door opening! Tons of them coming!"

"Same things?" I ask as I crush another group and Su-chan adjusts the shield to let weapon jabs through. *That'll drain ki.*

"Yeah."

"Jiro, do you understand how to surround and crush them?" *Man, I wish we had full ki reserves!*

"Uh-huh, but I'm gonna try something..." He looks rather green, though he keeps going.

My stomach roils too from the sickening, slick disaster around us. *Concentrate.* "Quickly!"

Next, Jiro's phone floats in front of him as a glowing keyboard appears. He types like mad and flips through screens. *What's he gonna be capable of when we're outta this?*

He hollers, "This says they have a kill switch. Sending the file. Protect your ears. I just hope it doesn't break our phones, 'cause I gotta make this really loud!"

"How many spells do you want us to maintain?" Su-chan squeaks.

"Just do it!" I shout.

Then our phones chime upon file receipt and we enable the protection spells. The extra magic I have to maintain saps a ton of ki. When we hit the play buttons, our phones sync to emit the sound in unison.

Boom! Whum, whum, whum. Boom! Whum, whum, whum.

The vibrations rip through us, almost knocking me over. Glass shatters. Even with my hearing shielded, my head and ears throb so hard they hurt.

Boom! Whum, whum, whum.

The Eyeless Ones near us splatter. Other slugs scramble away out of the broken windows of the chamber.

Meanwhile, a siren blares and an announcement comes over every phone. "Eyeless Ones containment required." Our audience scatters, screaming. At least the ones that aren't down on the ground with blood running from their ears.

My gut ties itself into knots. "Get this under control before that containment crew arrives!"

Quickly, Su-chan targets the strays as she whips out her potions and shikigami talisman puppets, while I attempt closing the open panels again. This time, they stay sealed. Once Su-chan and I handle the surrounding slugs, we drop our shields and split up to handle the stray Eyeless Ones while Sekiguchi covers our young tech mage.

Jiro messages via the link, 'I'm gonna up the volume to reach the rest of them.'

The thought of having to increase all our personal shields makes me shout. "Don't you dare! This is hard enough to deal with!"

He shrinks. "But..."

"No."

His glumness seeps through the connection.

'Jiro, the shields are draining us. What happens if we're too low on ki to handle the next challenge?'

'Oh. I'll shut it down.'

It takes a few minutes to destroy the rest of the carnivorous slugs. Security cordons off the area around the gate just as we finish, and a voice barks through what sounds like a megaphone on our phones' announcements. "Everyone, stop where you are!"

Complying, I shout to a ghost inside a heavily armored robot, "We dealt with them, sir!"

"A cleaning crew handled this mess?" His eyebrow raises as he continues, "However, releasing the Eyeless Ones on palace property is a serious crime that could cost countless lives unless every single one of the slugs is dealt with."

"Tell that to those testing us with the damned things."

In a flash, the ghost rounds on me, having his metal substitute body tap my sternum hard enough to leave a bruise. "You have a problem with the rules?"

"No, sir." *Just the testing methods used on us.*

So, Jiro asks to approach and shows the ghost how he tracked the Eyeless Ones via temperature readings. "We got every one of them, sir."

"You didn't track their ki signature?"

"That seemed to shift. Heat was more reliable."

Then the ghost nods. "Correct, young weasel." He catches Tezuka's attention and points to Jiro, then himself, before commanding his troops to verify Jiro's readings.

Tezuka's head tilts back, and he lets out a full bellied laugh. "That was the most excitement I've had in months. What are you four doing as cleaning crew?"

Since I'm the team lead, my old habits for a quick answer kick in. "Too new here to find something better. Have any leads for us?"

"Well, you've certainly earned your crystal for the day, but the fix for the scanner will come out of your cash pay. Replacing it will be costly. The good news is you won't have to remain as cleaning crew for long. Pay for other jobs is better with a higher ki allotment, so you can replace the gate sooner."

Cash pay isn't as good as crystalized ki. *They want us hooked.* "The only requirement was to survive. We also contained the mess. That should earn us a break."

Tezuka shakes his head. "Instead, I have some advice. Come here, feathered de-struct-o-matic." He whispers, "First, that weasel of yours—keep him happy. Teams will vie for his favor. Tech competent yokai are scarce and the Containment Unit already says it has dibs. Second, keep an eye out for that human group. I'd suspect you as a group of four, but your ki signatures don't match human ones."

"Noted. I'll keep humoring the weasel." *Thank you, Yamazaki, for the disguises.*

"Transferring your crystalized ki ration ticket to the app now. Collect it at logistics, then report for your shift." He taps on a screen and an image appears on my phone. "Here's a map."

As we pass through the gate, cracks in the palace's window glass stand out as Tezuka orders a new testing booth.

I opt to share a few observations with the group via our private link. 'We aren't the first to break the chamber. Also, Tezuka never broke a sweat, so they see weird shit all the time. And the glass on the palace windows is bulletproof. Can tell by the crack pattern—it's seen action already. Interesting, no?'

Instead of traditional plaster on the walls of the compound, a closer glance says it's cement, which makes the palace a veritable fortress.

While we follow the map to our check in, I have Jiro look up crystalized ki and how to use it. We'll need to know.

Corridors of sleek, modern glass and metal clash with ornate, traditional wood accents. The app seems to route us around an unlabeled central core, which the map I purchased doesn't have.

At logistics, they verify our IDs and swear us in, requiring us to put the palace and Akumakai's needs first, before giving us our allotment of crystalized ki. The glowing powder gives me the creeps. I know what it cost. Energy from the eyedropper-sized squeeze applicator is stale—like smelling moldy bread.

Then the clerk snarls, "Remember to keep the dropper. You buy the next one if you lose it." When we tuck our bags into our uniform pockets, she asks, "You aren't going to use the crystals now? They lose potency fast. Three hours old is as fresh as we peons can get."

Improvise with those yakuza smarts! There was talk about bad batches. My eyebrow raises and I lean in. "How have the others been handling today's allotment?"

She says, "Each batch is different. Depends on the poor sods they sourced it from. I don't ask more than that. You know how it is. The risk of crystal is always worth the reward."

So we step aside for the next group. I open up my bag and squeeze a drop of the super fine crystals into my palm. There's no warmth with this ki. Energy, but it's weak and... lifeless. Like I'd expect liquid mercury to feel.

When no apparent side effects surface, I finish the vial and the crew follows my lead with a test before using theirs. But Su-chan screams when the first drop touches her skin.

"What's wrong?" I ask as our crew crowds around and Su-chan examines her palm.

"Disgusting!" she grumbles and shoves the vial in my direction. "There's no way that stuff is touching me ever again."

Behind us, others snicker, "What a priss! That female oni doesn't know how good she has it, getting a daily ration."

'Quiet! You're drawing attention!' I hiss through our mental link.

'Tatsu…' Her tone carries a warning.

Taking a calming breath, I say, 'Sorry.' Man, it's hard to lead when you're close to your teammates and trying not to revert to your old ways.

But her expression softens. 'Sorry, I was so loud. It's not good ki at all. Totally unnatural. And have you noticed how small everyone's ki pool is here?'

Now that you say so. 'Think that has to do with the dependence on these crystals?'

'Why are they hooked on it? Don't their ki wells refill?' Jiro asks.

'Good question. Su-chan, I know you don't like the stuff. Please, use what you have since our ki is limited here. We don't have to do it again once we get out of this place.'

She grimaces. 'Ok. But only because of the possibility of not accessing more ki. Never again.' After the crystal dose, she's much greener than her female oni disguise and her hand covers her mouth. 'I feel sick.'

'You gonna be ok?' I ask, wishing I could take her hand. But that would draw even more attention.

'Dunno.'

Sekiguchi interrupts. I'd almost forgotten he was there. Since he's so short now, he hides well as a little dog yokai. 'It might be some kind of reaction. Ohno-chan has so much natural magic of her own, plus a dragon's, too. She's never been exposed to polluted environments or corrupted energy. What if I trade ki with her?'

She swallows hard and nods. When the exchange is complete, Sekiguchi runs to the corner to wretch.

'Bad batch?'

'I could feel it,' Su-chan says.

"Hey, clean up after your damned mutt and get it outta the way! Otherwise I'll put it on the machines. We've been short of 'volunteers', if ya know what I mean," a burly boar yokai half snorts, half slurs as he kicks the dog.

So Sekiguchi races over to Su-chan, who scoops him up, and I spend ki to ditch the vomit. I should have saved my magic, but we don't have cleaning supplies on us, and the last thing we need is a fight.

The boar wanders off muttering, "Who's so well off they give crystal to a pet?"

In return, I mumble loud enough for him to hear, "Those who don't want to deal with a bad batch."

Pivoting on his foot, he scowls but his features relax as it dawns on him. "You use the mutt as a tester?"

"Could save our lives. Though, get something extra dumb. This one here is a little too smart and doesn't want to be our guinea pig."

On cue, Sekiguchi growls. Via the link he says, 'We'll have to be careful about others seeing me get anything. Have you noticed there's a general ki drain in this building? It's not big, but that might explain a lot.'

Glancing at my phone, it reads T-1 hour and 7 minutes to the Cleanse and flashes a warning that we need to get our assignment, or our palace access will be revoked.

Jiro flips through our options. 'Should we sign up for the next shift?'

"Slackers!"

Instantly, we all jump, but a meaty hand slaps a head in another group browsing the options. "Your next crystal ration is halved." The blue-skinned oni's voice echoes through the chamber.

This one is more intelligent than the others I've encountered. His yellow eyes light on me.

'Do it. Let's go,' I say as the oni brute heads toward us.

The app points us down a far hallway.

'Don't run,' I direct the group. 'It'll draw more attention.' So I set the pace and we stride purposefully, as if we know what we're doing.

The old rolling swagger returns to my steps, and Jiro adopts one of his own. Sekiguchi, with his tongue lolling, trots along, tugging Su-chan's arm with his leash. Other crews seem to file in, heading the same direction.

We end up in a cramped, dim room where a scowling hag demands the trio in front of us get to work in the cells for those held at Crystal Row. She gives them a swift kick in the backside to speed them on their way. *A babaa yokai. The kind that eats people. Damn.*

"Maga-san, we have new cleaners," a crisply dressed tengu bird man holds up his phone to the hag.

There's something about this one. So, I check the app for the names of the staff leadership team. The tengu's picture says Garu.

Harrumphing, she growls at her tablet and taps, not even glancing at us. "Put them in for the crew we lost in the last Cleanse."

His discerning stare makes my stomach tighten. *Can he see through our disguises?*

But Garu says, "Anyone can fill that slot. What if we let a disappointing group have that duty? We can reward this crew for being on time by letting them clean the antechamber? The assigned ones are late, and the Oyabun is expecting visitors in a few hours. We need a crew in there ASAP." His hands wring as if to stress the need not to disappoint the Akumakai leaders.

The head honcho's having guests. A help or hindrance?

Not missing a beat, the tengu continues, "My oversight should have this crew done with the room in time. They may prove useful as cleaners and more, according to the report from Tezuka-san. Is that acceptable?"

Maga's eyes, caked with tacky makeup, harden. "I hold you responsible for any chaos, Garu."

"As you wish, Maga-san." He bows and motions for us to follow.

The walls of the twisting, four-person wide hallways have fragile paper and lattice shoji doors glowing with the energy to re-enforce them. No ki expense spared. The polished, dark wooden floors squeak under our feet. In the yakuza I wasn't ninja quiet, but I'd been decent at clandestine work. Here, I can't walk light enough to keep the boards from announcing each step.

Above us, the ceiling grows more ornate with colorful motifs on gold tiles. Open slats above the shoji let fresh air flow between rooms. Yet, the air outside the palace is stale like the crystal ki. *Piped in from above ground or filtered?*

When we round a corner, Garu slides back a panel to reveal a breathtaking room with elegantly painted nature scenes on the screens and gold lattice work in the ceiling. How could the inside of this palace be so lovely, when the outside is a horrible clashing mix of modern and traditional?

Sekiguchi intakes a breath before murmuring, "A replica of Nijo?"

The palace that Tokugawa built for himself. So, the Akumakai's been mimicking the old shogunate for a while.

"Correct. Each area is modeled after a famous castle. You visited?" Garu remains stoic, despite a supposed pet talking.

"A few years ago," Sekiguchi says. "Private tour with my owner."

"I've not been fortunate enough to see it. Perhaps some day." The tengu waves his hands, which emit a dull blue glow. Though his ki well is ridiculously low.

How's he managing spells?

"It's safe to talk now. My particular talent allows me to see the magic you four share. Few of us manage that level of trust." When Garu whispers a word of kotodama, 'truth', it reeks of musty ki as it slams into us. "But first, I need a bit of information. You are the crew I was told to expect, yes?"

He's on to us! I step in front of the others, lowering into a fighting stance. He could give us away with the snap of his fingers. My legs twitch. 'Run!'

Though Su-chan coughs, sucking in air like it's hard to breathe, and Sekiguchi growls.

Instead, Garu motions for us to stand down. "Do not be so foolish as to expose your purpose. Many yokai have risked themselves to get you this far."

"We're the crew," I say.

"You do not have long, especially with your lady reacting to the tainted crystalized ki that powers my magic. It happens to those particularly pure, like water spirits." His head tilts and juts in a bird-like manner.

Emulate that to look more like a kotengu.

"Her intolerance raises questions which I will not ask. Earlier, you invoked Baku's name, thus earning my help."

Another cough makes me whip around. Su-chan clutches her throat, and the others crowd around offering help and questions.

Commanding, "Step back!" I pop a filtering bubble around her. *Please, work!*

Then the magic field spits foul ki into my face as I bob and weave, trying to look into her eyes for verification that it helps. When she gives a thumbs up, it allows me to breathe again.

"Let us use your lady's helplessness as a distraction, now that you have a suitable solution." Garu points to the ceiling and tosses her a rag. "She should be the one to dust up there. The polluted ki settles to the ground. Then your spell will be less difficult to maintain."

Gesturing to the rest of us with a sweep of his hand, he adds, "Everyone else will beat the cushions, vacuum the tatami along the grain, and polish the low table until it shines. Supplies, including a ladder, are in the panel behind the alcove.

"I will leave you to your tasks. I knew you right away by the waves of fresh ki my contact said to expect. This is your only chance. My associates will use your task as cover. Be thorough and quick about your work."

I nod. "Where do we clean after this?"

"Monitor the time, as 'guests' will be here in thirty-five minutes. After that, I cannot suppress you being noticed. One of you must keep the app open at all times, since turning it off will raise suspicions." Then his magic retreats. "After this area, ensure the front windows are spotless."

He's a liability. But he's hinting at being part of the resistance and said he was helping us. How many yokai in Sumichou are in the Underground? We couldn't have just been that lucky. So the card from Yamazaki got us in?

The repulsive force fills in around us again as Garu waves his hand. "You will not speak of this meeting."

As the spell slaps into place, I share through our group link, 'That's what the crystalized ki does to magic users.'

Next, we bow and get to work. I grab the vacuum. Su-chan wrestles the ladder in place to dust the ceiling. Jiro chooses the polish and a rag, but we have to show him how to use it. And Sekiguchi says he'll sit watch. I was skeptical at first about the kappa pretending to be an annoying dog yokai, but now I see the wisdom.

After a few moments, Su-chan asks, 'What stops the ki from renewing in the residents? Because they're all so low on magic!'

'Perhaps the stolen ki still has an added effect?' Sekiguchi asks.

Meanwhile, I sweep the vacuum over the tatami. 'Good points. There has to be a block too. I felt more energized until I used that stuff. Is it the same for you all?' The crew confirms my suspicion. 'So we have to try to avoid using that crystal again. Severe disadvantage.'

'And Ibaraki doesn't seem diminished by the stolen ki,' Sekiguchi says.

'On the other hand, residents here seem to stretch energy reserves to the max. That gives them an advantage, too,' Su-chan adds.

Click. I snap my fingers. 'Yamazaki taught me to try to use gentleness as I release my spells into existence. He said it would save ki. It's like the magic wants to happen and we just let it do its thing.'

'Really?' Su-chan asks as she tries a simple healing spell on herself. 'Oooh!'

So I add, 'I'd been trying to force my magic to work the way I want by sheer will. But it can manifest with much less effort. So I think that's part of it.'

'Can we take advantage of that?' Jiro's lips purse as his look turns contemplative.

'I am so glad you didn't go down the yakuza road. You are positively scary as a pre-teen.'

Unabashed, he grins like a maniac. 'I'm gonna work with Hoji-sensei to bring all yokai into the digital age. Teach them how to use it for good. He's already recruiting me for Kyoto Jidai Arcane University.'

'The school Hoji works at?'

'Yeah. They only recruit yokai.'

'Awesome!' He'll have the chance I never did.

The cleanup doesn't take long, leaving about twenty precious minutes left we can use to hunt for Honjou Masamune. *Why can't I reach her?*

Shoving aside the butterflies in my stomach, I share, 'Verify how much ki you have, then let's do this! Sekiguchi-san, will you be able to provide a distraction when we get there?'

'Just say the word.' His doggy-disguise tail stump wags as he continues, 'I picked a yokai that gets underfoot with that possibility in mind.'

'Jiro, pull up a map. Nothing too specific. Let's make a best guess at how to reach the sword display. Shiro said it should be by an entrance to Crystal Row.'

So, we dust as we go, pretending to touch up. Sure, Garu said he'd protect us from being spotted. *But is he reliable?* The Underground has different values.

Jiro's head buries in his phone as he zooms the map out from our location.

'Everyone else, turn off your phones and pull the battery and chip when we hit the next corner. I think it's a blind spot in the cameras.'

'Won't they notice we went off-line?' Sekiguchi asks.

'Either way, we have to move fast. Remember what Hoji taught us about converting electricity? That can be our cover in a pinch. We're all low on ki. Though only admit we can do that if you have to.'

The squeaking floors make my skin crawl. I can't spare the energy to keep our movement silent, so swift will have to do. Then a frame on the wall catches my eye and my neck prickles. "That painting..."

'We were in this section just a moment ago. Weren't we?' Sekiguchi sighs.

So, I ask, 'Could the app or magic be misleading us?'

Quickly, Jiro pokes at his phone again. 'I'm gonna try the gentle push thing,' he says as his hands glow. 'Hard to tell.'

Taking a mental picture, I scan for entrances toward the center of the building. But, something's screwy. 'The palace is messing with my sense of direction.'

'We only have so much time.' Sekiguchi sniffs the air. 'Extra magic and metal this way.'

Then Jiro's voice hikes. 'Your disguise allows you the senses of a dog?'

Sekiguchi huffs as he trots off, stating, 'I'm not human, remember? I always have superior senses.'

To cut off further grumbling, I say, 'Then lead us.'

"What are you doing!?" A sudden, raspy cry makes us skitter to a halt as we hit a crossway in the corridor. The same voice continues, "My family and I need that crystal!"

Sekiguchi nods toward a rat guard pinning a cleaner to a solid section of wall. Another rat frisks the cleaner, snagging their pouch of unused crystal ki.

Su-chan shares with grit, 'I don't like leaving that poor cleaner.'

'Neither do I. But-' I cringe when my foot hits a squeaky board. 'Shit!'

"We've got company," one guard snarls.

The cleaner's single eye widens. He's hoping we'll save him. *But we don't have time!*

'An ushirogami,' Sekiguchi shares, 'The kind that sneaks up behind people to feed on their fear. It must have scared the guards.'

Next, the pitiful yokai's hands tremble as it shields its shaggy-haired head.

"No witnesses, or we take a one-way trip to Crystal Row," the rat guard snaps.

"Shin, this is gonna draw attention. And those cleaners have a lot more ki than we do. Should we call for backup?" the other rat asks.

Their ki is so low, they won't be standing for long.

"Idiot! This can't be helped. They're just cleaners and they're unarmed. If they were worth anything at all, they'd have better jobs. Get them!" the first rat barks.

The second takes his time advancing on us, and his face brightens. "They smell so good! They've been outside!"

True to his role, Sekiguchi growls. 'Keeping others so desperate is a volatile way to keep them controlled.'

'Everything about this place is wrong,' Su-chan says and pulls a few potions from her dimensional pocket as I draw my katana.

'I don't think it used to be.' Sekiguchi flicks his tail to turn invisible as he rushes toward the oncoming guard and Su-chan spends precious ki, erecting a screen to reflect the hall behind us. This one isn't as bright as hers usually are. But it'll cover the fight.

Jiro provides a silencing spell, sucking energy from his phone to power it. Meanwhile, Sekiguchi's paws hitting the wood slab floor give faint hints at where he is. With claws scrabbling, Sekiguchi halts in front of the attacking rat yokai, who lets out an oof and flails as he crashes to the floor.

Good boy! I pounce on the fallen guard, using a nerve pinch to knock him out. Then I snag his phone. Having his tracker should make those watching think the pair is still on patrol, even if it's off the regular track. So, our path'll look legit.

All of a sudden, the eyes of the senior rat widen before instincts kick in. He races down the hall on all fours.

Coward! Never leave your partner!

'Su-chan!' I shout through our link as I book it for the cleaner.

'On it!' she hollers and black blob whizzes past my ear.

The close call makes me whip around to glare. 'Gah!'

'You're a walking door,' she says as she sticks out her tongue.

Thump. The guard crumples to the floor as Chou sucks down ki like she'd not been fed in weeks. Jiro retrieves this guard's phone, too.

Next, Sekiguchi asks, 'What do we do with these poor sods?'

But a prickle on the back of my neck makes me jump and my feathers fluff.

"Sorry to scare you," the ushirogami cleaner bows.

He just fed off my fright. *Jerk.* Though, he looks so low on ki I can't blame him.

The cleaner bows again, deeper this time. "Th-thank you."

"You're welcome. Go clean where you need to now." I make a shooing motion.

"You'll need to hide those bodies."

"Just knocked out. Any idea where we can stash them?"

So he nods and motions for us to follow, then sighs. "I won't snitch on those who just saved me, even though it's obvious you don't belong here in Sumichou. You could have mugged me..." He motions to the guards. "...and them for extra crystal. The cheap phones you took are worth pennies compared to the payment in energy."

'He can't use the phone's electricity.' Smugly, Jiro bobbles his head.

You said you wouldn't let things go to your head. 'We're on the job. That means wariness at all times. You got that?' I say to smother any quick growth of my young charge's ego.

'Yes, Umeji-san.' Jiro deflates a little, but it seems to process between his ears.

After a moment, the cleaner continues, "Your ki is still fresh, yet you stopped to rescue me. So, you need to avoid others tasting that. Come now. There's a storage area outside the weapons display. That's where I came from cleaning."

Excellent!

When we gather the limp guards, the cleaner snags his ration of crystal back and his hand hovers over the guard's pouch.

"Nope." I shake my head. "We need it."

With a shrug, he leads us to a paneled wall with no apparent handle. His floating body raises and his transparent hand presses one of the golden hexagon crests inset high in the light wood border. The panel slides open to reveal a supplies cabinet.

He says, "The rare sentient cypress in these walls cost more than the emperor's travel budget for a decade."

Su-chan pales and her fists clench. "Th-they used a kodama's tree?"

"Yes, Miss. You leak a rare pure magic. I thought you should know."

Suddenly, her aura grows such a vivid red, I grimace. She's never been this mad, even when Shion used her. *Is she gonna burn down the palace?*

Seeing Su-chan's response, the cleaner shrinks back. "I had no part in the kodama tree deaths!"

But Su-chan growls, "I'll find those responsible."

"Later. We have a job to do." I squeeze her hand after helping dump the unconscious guards into the cabinet.

Volunteering, Sekiguchi says, "I'll help you avenge the kodama, when the time is right."

"Can you help us get to the weapons collection?" I ask the ushirogami.

The cleaner takes the lead, mumbling, "I am in your debt."

A quick check confirms the app doesn't show our path on the map.

"I'll open the door. That is all I can do and retain plausible deniability. This act means I'm not beholden to you, and I shouldn't get dragged off to the machines at Crystal row."

"Understood."

We round the corner, and the cleaner uses the app on a cellphone that's as transparent as he is to open a panel in an uninteresting wall and he gestures us forward. With a sweep of his hand, he also indicates the camera above.

Then my phone vibrates. *Access? Sweet.*

"I'm going to raise my fist, so run off now." When I do, his cower isn't fake. So I whisper, "Thank you" through my clenched beak so my words can't be read, but say aloud, "Get lost before we deal with you like the guards back there."

His gaze drops as he mouths, "Good luck." Flailing his arms in mock alarm, he flees the scene.

Beyond the door lies a set of slick, moss-covered stone stairs going down. There's no railing, and each step looks treacherous.

Digital tablets mounted into the wall run advertisements for various unsavory services in Sumichou and their flashing images light the way in a dizzying disco effect. Worst of all, the stench rolling up rivals anything we've dealt with, and painful groans echo from below.

A chill runs down my spine. *Trap? Does it lead to more than one place?* Either way, we have to investigate.

'I don't like this,' Jiro says.

We have to move slowly to avoid slipping. None of us wants to touch the slimy walls.

'Man, I wish we didn't have to breathe this,' Su-chan whines.

At last, we reach the bottom and find two tunnels, one forking to the right and one continuing straight. The side tunnel is where the now-unbearable stench and terrible sounds emanate. Not only are the feathers on the back of my neck bristling, something in my ki well shudders. The sign reads Crystal Row.

Tearing my gaze away, I motion for the crew to move down the less repulsive tunnel.

Soon, we see a door labeled Weapons Manufacturing. I'd give good money to verify that's where the arrow that hit Hoji came from. No time to investigate, though. Other signs read Backup Generator and Maintenance Corridor. Finally, we reach one labeled 'Special Access Only, No Admittance'.

Then a text appears on my phone, 'Guards contained. Keeping you under the radar as promised. Security system up to you.' *From Garu, I presume.*

Between Jiro and me, we put the camera on a loop and bypass the lock.

Next, my crew emerges into a humidity-controlled room where light glitters off every surface. The glass cases hold a myriad of perfectly maintained weapons and a swarm of cries hits us in a wave of magic that floods our minds.

My head swivels as I try to pick out Honjou Masamune and Sekiguchi whistles. He says through the link, 'Too bad we can't liberate them all. Each weapon is important in the historical record.'

Intensifying, the silent screams bring Sekiguchi and Su-chan to their knees.

Sekiguchi bellows, "Stop! We can't!"

Holding her head as she curls up, Su-chan shouts, "We'll do our best to come back and free you all!"

So I raise my hands, letting a glow fill them and trace a shield around us to stop the onslaught of pleas. The silence rings in my ears. Heaving a sigh of relief, I look for the weapon I came for.

There are so many priceless treasures here. The League would salivate. How many of them are part of the Ring of the Rising Sun—the weapons that would allow someone to usurp the Emperor's throne?

Next, I tug on the thread between me and Honjou Masamune. No response still.

The only one not shining in this entire room is the short, blade-less handle I know well lying next to an ancient, jagged edged sword. The deep tears in the metal make me gape. She must have seen some insane fights. Every other weapon I've seen displayed was in pristine condition.

Taking a shaky breath, I approach the case where Honjou Masamune lays. *Why isn't she responding?* I reach out to touch the glass, but my old instinct to check for traps kicks in. A spark still stings my fingers. Casting a spell of true seeing reveals grotesque, glowing purple characters cover the case.

There's also the ghostly silhouette of a miniature old woman sobbing, with her face turned away. Her lower half melds into the handle of my sword. She's in a tattered, long-sleeve, flowered kimono that would have been more appropriate for a woman in her twenties, as if she's past her prime.

"Honjou Masamune?"

Her head whips up, eyes haunted. She mouths my name, but there's no sound.

"We're getting you out of there!"

But her head shakes. Again, her mouth forms a word I can't make out. So, she frantically waves her hands.

"You'll be out soon."

Sobbing comes from all around the room, along with renewed demands to be freed. Sekiguchi shushes the weapon spirits.

A glance at my phone says we better hurry. 'We have 10 minutes of blackout.'

So, we strain to get a better look at the case.

'I think it's an ancient script.' A glow forms as Su-chan runs her hands over the symbols. 'Dragon characters. But an oni wouldn't know that, would they?'

'Shion told you about it?' Sekiguchi asks.

'I think his magic allows me to read it.' At our expectant expressions, she squints at the glowing symbols and her words come slowly, but none of us understand her. 'It's an isolation spell, and an alarm mashed together. And it's fresh. Like earlier today.'

'That's why Honjou Masamune couldn't respond. So how do we break it? And what is the alarm? A sound? Guards appearing?'

'And how did Ibaraki make the spell? Did she con a black dragon into helping her?' Sekiguchi asks.

Most dragons are holy beings, but black ones are another matter. Every legend I've read about them says they're evil.

Su-chan concentrates on the writing again. 'A sound, I think.'

To help, I use my phone to shoot a short video. 'Ibaraki was stuck with Date Sari and dragon magic for a century. What if she learned it?'

'Either way, dragon spells are hard to counter,' Sekiguchi says.

I play the recording back a few times at various speeds as Su-chan watches over my shoulder and announces, 'The magic has a frequency. Can we use that?'

'Maybe.' As I let my thoughts coalesce, I stroke my chin. 'Can we reduce the spell's energy?'

No answers.

'Ok. I'm gonna try absorbing a smidgen of the magic.' When I reach out toward the purple glow, it sends a crackle to snap at my fingers as if to slap my hand.

"That's ki theft!" Su-chan shouts.

So I growl. 'Fine. What about like noise canceling headphones?'

Sekiguchi brightens. 'Generating an opposite wave to cancel it out?'

'Maybe?' I never finished school, so I missed out on much of the science side of things. I picked up some in the yakuza, but it was mostly computer stuff, and it was a spotty education. Evaluating my friends' ki levels leaves a knot in my stomach. We're all so low. 'But we won't be able to keep the counter frequency going without magic, will we?'

Sekiguchi adds, 'Not only that, our link that we've been leaning on may break. To provide the magic out-of-phase effect, the spell needs to be read backward, continually.'

Raising his hand, Jiro asks, 'Can we record it and put it on repeat?'

'Ooh!' Then I ruffle his hair. 'Excellent thinking.' Another peek at my phone. 'Five minutes of blackout left. Remember, we have the ki batteries from Hoji if we're tapped.'

Su-chan's already sidled up to the spell work. Her determined expression, even as the female oni, reminds me of the first time I knew I'd fallen for her. She's a force of nature.

Meanwhile, Jiro has his phone next to her face as her brows furrow and she leans in to read the small script. Taking a deep breath, she begins with a few syllables. It sounds like gibberish, and she stumbles a few times before putting her hands over her eyes. 'Ugh. It's hard enough to read the right way because it was all instinctual. Backwards? I dunno if I can do this.'

'What if we reverse it after you read it aloud?' I offer as I put a hand on her shoulder.

'Yeah! I think I can do that.' Then Jiro pokes a few menus on his recording app.

This time Su-chan manages it. Some of the meaning seeps through my physical contact with her. *Stronger than any metal, impenetrable... shriek of a hawk if attacked...*

When Jiro plays it backward once, the glow flickers and Honjou's attention darts up to us with a glimmer of hope through her tears. The glitch was most intense when he moved the phone close to it.

'Put the spell on repeat. Then, gently, place the phone on the box,' I say, as I get in position and Sekiguchi guards the doors.

The alarm spell flings purple sparks at us, and Jiro jumps back, holding his hand. So I take the phone. An oval that wavers with the repeating jumble of words spreads from his phone as it hovers above the case.

No alarm sounds. No guards rush in.

Without delay, I dip the corner of the phone into the ward's hole and contact the glass. No shocks. No noise but the tap on the case. Honjou's face lights up.

So I retrieve the sword from the Nakamura clan, and whisper the words that will help cut the thick glass. A portal opening would cost too much ki. *Such a pain!*

Trying to balance speed and precision, I carve a hole in the glass. Honjou's spirit covers her head as the disc crashes down. Her frantic cries through our connection scream to hurry.

"On it!" Sticking my hand into the case, I grasp the sword.

Then a rush of relief and wholeness floods through the silver thread between us. I don't have her out of the case yet, though. As I lean to maneuver the sword, her ghostly form points at the roughed-up blade lying beside where she was. *Her body.*

The distraction makes me bump the handle on the edge of the hole. In my haste to avoid dropping her, my side hits the purple spell work with a shock. Worse, my flailing knocks the phone off the case and an alarm blares. "Shit!"

At the same time, Honjou screams, 'The original forging! You must get it!'

Jiro scrambles for his phone and tucks it in his pocket, but I stop him. "Again! We need the blade."

"Hurry up! They're coming!" Sekiguchi calls.

My young friend pales as he places the device on the case.

"Everyone, grab all the weapons you can carry!" Su-chan shouts.

So Jiro snags a dagger with a fox carved into the blade. Su-chan takes the ancient naginata. As Sekiguchi tucks a hatchet into his dimensional pocket, he whispers with awe, "Kintaro's axe, we'll use you well."

Meanwhile, my pulse pounds in my ears and my hands shake so hard it's difficult to hold the phone still. But when the hole opens, my hand thrusts into the glass and grabs the tang.

Whipping the blade from the protected case, I step back and tuck it into my dimensional pocket. *Don't let me run out of magic!* There's no telling what will happen to that storage space if I do.

Cries of the weapons we're leaving behind fill my chest with heaviness. We'll have to come back for them some day.

But the thudding of boots echoes from the entrance opposite the door we came in. And pounding above us means we lost access to the stairs. So, we dash into the creepy tunnels. The only choice is through Crystal Row.

25

CRYSTAL ROW

THE APP'S COUNTDOWN FLASHES the half-hour mark to the Cleanse as if taunting us. 'We gotta get out of Sumichou ASAP,' I say as we book it away from the weapons room.

Jiro pokes at his phone again. 'Closest exit is two minutes away. But it'll shut down to protect the palace.'

Gotta try, even if-

'They'll be waiting for us,' Sekiguchi's voice tints with sourness.

'Yep.'

The hall's wreaking dank air carries the command, "Shut down the machines and take cover."

That's when a weak voice turns to a wail. "What about us?"

"Not our problem."

Like hell it isn't! Bursting into the dim room where half the lights flicker like they're about to go out, I swallow down bile.

Rows of steel half drums with flashing status screens encase yokai of every kind. Only their heads stick out of the drum. Every face contorts in anguish as the stench of filth, sweat, and the sickly sweet of the crystalized ki assaults us like a baseball bat to the head.

An off-kilter hum dims as workers scurry to vacuum the crystals into a storage bin, then shut off the extractors. Still conscious yokai squawk to be freed.

Blood roars in my ears as I tell my crew 'They won't die on our watch.' Suddenly, my feet pound the floor toward the workers.

Catching one by the sleeve, I swing him around and pull back my fist, ready to beat him senseless for what he's done to those in the machines. His hands fly up.

Idiot! You're not yakuza. So I shake my head to clear it and hiss, "Help us free them or I'll stick you in one of those damned machines!"

He just turns a pasty white.

'There's one for each of us.' With his dagger, Jiro pins a worker against the wall.

Another scrambles for the exit, but Su-chan halts her by throwing Chou. Letting out a growl so feral, Su-chan's sharp teeth cause her captive to faint.

Meanwhile, Sekiguchi trips another and tethers the fallen yokai to a machine using his leash.

The worker in my grasp remains rooted to the spot. So, I bark in his face, "Free them. Now!"

They cower, complying. Precious time evaporates as we release each of the thirty or so yokai and destroy the machines. Even if we can only bash the control panels, it will reduce the number of victims.

But my hands shake. There's not enough time to deal with more. *Gotta get out of here.* "Let the victims take enough ki to survive the Cleanse!"

After Su-chan inspects the glowing sand and gives the thumbs up, everyone rushes to scoop up the crystal, absorbing it. Jiro and Sekiguchi hold the workers at bay.

Then I let my crew go before me. Su-chan's wrinkled nose and grimace say it all. While this crystal may be the freshest possible, it's still awful. There's no warmth, no life—just bare, weakened energy.

"What about us? We won't make it to the shelter in time!" one worker shrieks, his plea rushing out almost as one word.

My mouth opens to say 'no'. *But the Akumakai forced them to do this.* So I say, "If there's any left, take some."

The freed yokai huddle together, creating a tethered bubble shield they can each help maintain. I can't blame them for refusing to let their captors in. Instead, the workers mimic the spell.

Next, our phones blare an ear-piercing siren. "Cleanse initiation in T-5 minutes. Sumichou evacuation gates have closed. Prepare your shelter now."

"Can't stay here." I tilt my head toward the door.

Then Jiro thrusts his phone at me with the app's map. "We're penned in." His jaw sets in a grim line.

"Are we able to portal?" I ask.

Before I finish the sentence, Jiro whips out a piece of paper, but I snatch it and slap the talisman into the air. He can't be the one in trouble if this goes south.

The portal opens to outside the hostess bar, and we dive through as a computer's emotionless voice fills the air. "Portal creation inside the Sumichou district is prohibited. Violators will be tracked and collected for sentencing after the Cleanse."

Sealing off shelter, heavy metal doors slide into place on every building.

"Establishments are now locked down," the Sumichou app states in that emotionless AI voice. "Please deploy protection to weather the Cleanse."

So we zip into an alley. I'm panting and wobbling from low ki and the adrenalin withdrawal. To conserve energy, I pull a pack of gum out of my pocket and write a shield spell on a wrapper. Written wards like this use less energy, but the item is destroyed in the process.

"If we split up to use smaller bubbles, it'll conserve ki." Sekiguchi eyes the wall. "Su-chan and I have the most magic remaining."

Che! Trusting Jiro to someone else grates against my gut instinct. But they both insist. It turns out to be Sekiguchi with Jiro and Su-chan with me.

Next, Jiro holds out his hand and I slap a stick of gum into it.

"Cleanse initiating," my phone announces.

Sekiguchi asks, "How long does the Cleanse last?"

"Five to fifteen minutes," the app announces.

So, we ensure each group has a partially charged phone and an almost full ki battery. Jiro and I slap the talismans to the wall for an anchor as shields pop up around us.

No time for gentle ki use here! I pack as much energy as I can into the ofuda. Though the glow is faint, especially for talismans. Holding up the small crystal packet from my pocket, I ask, "Not sure this ward can hold up to the surge. Can I just add this straight to the ward to avoid ki loss?"

Su-chan shakes her head. "It has to go through you."

No time to waste. I smash it into my palm and reinforce the talisman as the civil defense sirens blare.

Then Jiro takes a shuddering breath. "Here we go."

Building-sized metal hatches fall open above us with loud booms. The falling water roars as Sekiguchi shouts, "This'll be a rough ride! Curl up to minimize injury."

My crew uses the moment to pull energy from the batteries Hoji gave us.

'I'm gonna ask Hoji-sensei if he thinks we can hack the trackers.' Jiro says through the link as he types like a madman on the device.

"Go for it!" I shout. He actually listened, warning us what he was up to!

I see his mouth moving, but there's no sound over the rush of the oncoming flood. Thankfully, Hoji's face appears on the screen. If anyone can hack the tracker in the app, it's Hoji and Jiro. Plus, it'll keep the boy's mind off the insanity.

In seconds, water swells in a rush down the street. A tanuki struggles to splash through it and tethers near us, but his shield's glow flickers. The tightness in the yokai's face says he doubts it will hold. Though, we can't reach him.

Jiro shouts, "What's your phone number? I have a friend who can send help."

The tanuki's eyebrows furrow, but he shouts his number. Jiro taps the send button with a flourish. As the swirls fill in, the glow of the tanuki's shield brightens, and he nods his thanks.

Soon, our bubbles shift and rise as they crash into each other, straining the connection to the building. We're jostled off our feet as the rushing water swallows us.

How do Sumichou residents deal with this all the time? Why isn't everything covered in mold?

We spot a group of frog yokai swimming against the current, but they wash away in the rapids. They're the last beings I can make out before the water turns too dirty.

Then flotsam and jetsam batter our bubbles, causing them to squash so much they might pop. Su-chan and I curl into balls as we get tossed around like toys.

Through our link, Sekiguchi asks, 'Can we reduce the shield sizes?'

'Not without sacrificing oxygen,' I respond, pushing each word through as if my brain turned to Jell-O.

He groans over the link. 'We're gonna have concussions.'

Already, my head aches and I'm seeing stars. So I wrap myself around Su-chan to cushion her. Is that Hoji's voice screaming through the onslaught?

Finally, the words register. "Jiro's shield detached. They lost his phone and battery when they sealed the breach. They've expanded the bubble to lodge between the buildings, but it won't last. Sekiguchi's almost tapped trying to maintain it!"

My words come out slurred. "Gotta... help!"

When Su-chan releases me, I'm flung to the wall, smashing one of my wings, as I try to pull a talisman out of my pocket. Pain shoots through my shoulder.

Gasping, I force my arm to raise and slap the paper on the edge of the bubble. The glow of Jiro and Sekiguchi's shield fades. *Hang on!*

At the same time, my phone helpfully informs me again that portals inside Sumichou are illegal. *Shut up already!*

Then Sekiguchi's dog face contorts as he strains his magic to keep the shield from being swept away. Constant jostling hampers Jiro from crawling into my bubble. I reach through, though my fingers brush past his outstretched hand.

But Sekiguchi barks a spell to shove Jiro through the hole, before going limp.

Sekiguchi! As soon as Jiro's in my bubble, I steel my nerves and bail into the portal, almost squashing my kappa friend.

In a flash, I grab the scruff of his neck and toss him through. But my head rings and blackness threatens to close in. *How much longer?*

Ominous scraping and magic sparks say there's no more time.

"Umeji-san!" Jiro screeches.

Out of desperation, I shout words of kotodama to siphon the last of the ki from Hoji's battery in my pocket. "Energy boost!" Using a spell to propel myself, I fly through the hole again.

My head crashes into Sekiguchi, causing a splitting headache and more dizziness. Su-chan closes the portal behind me just as the other bubble tumbles away.

Everything spins. I just want to close my eyes and hold my head. So I pull energy from my phone's battery to ease the vertigo.

The incoming light grows and the bubble flickers. A muffled voice comes from my phone again, but I can't make it out. One more pull from the phone. Static warmth pours into my body from the device. As I force the ki I have into the shield, Hoji's voice shouts through my phone, "You're pulling too much energy! Stop, or we'll lose contact!"

So, I halt the flow. *Too tired.* As if things couldn't get worse, my energy starved body absorbs ki from the weakening bubble and I can't stop it.

Pop! Our foursome splashes into the receding water. I snag Jiro's arm as we're swept off our feet. By sheer luck, I latch onto the alley corner and the torrent appears to be about waist deep.

Next, Su-chan attaches her feet to the ground via spell and her hand clenches mine. Power rushes into me with that wonderful sunshine warmth.

Thanks to her energy, my grip on Jiro's arm tightens and keeps him from getting swept away.

I don't want to, but I cut off the flow. Su-chan would give me everything, and we're all too short on ki. Can't let her endanger herself. Later, we'll fill up from the remaining batteries.

Besides the magic issues, my skin is on fire. It's more like alcohol being poured on a wound than sea water!

Just when I can't hang on anymore, my feet alight on solid ground. I help Jiro get his footing and keep a hold of him, just in case. *Too close!*

"We gotta move, ASAP!" Though, my head still spins.

Jiro's face tightens, and he nods. Su-chan rushes over to help the tanuki stand. She must have revived Sekiguchi, too.

That's when we hear rhythmic thuds. The tanuki hisses, "Containment Unit! Get out of here!" and he zips around the corner.

As one, we scramble. Others race through the wet streets, too. I pull out my phone for directions. Flickering on my screen has me spewing expletives. "They're jamming us!"

Just then, Hoji's voice comes through the speakers again. "On it! Glad I thought to put a protection spell on your phone!"

When the screen clears, a flashing dot highlights the least busy gate, but it's all the way across the district.

"Give us another option!" I shout as we dash in the indicated direction. Other dots appear on the edges of Sumichou and they're much busier.

Jiro asks, "Why is that one less busy?"

"Trap," Sekiguchi states. His tongue lolls and his stubby dog legs have to move twice as fast as mine to keep up. "I don't want to split up, but it may be the best option for at least some of us to get out."

True, but it could leave some stranded with zero chance of survival. "We stick together. Direct routes are a no go. They'll search those."

As if to prove my point, commands echo off the alley walls behind us. "Halt! Tell us if you've seen this group of four yokai!"

We know that voice—the head of the containment unit and none of us have enough ki to change our disguises.

When we pass a residential district with laundry hanging from the railings, a plan forms. *Is the mental link still active?* I give it a quick test. 'Grab clothes to change into.'

No response. *Fuck.*

So I skitter to a halt and grab as many clothes as I can. The others follow my example. Ducking into a stairway, we ditch our outside layers and throw on the new as best we can. Shimmying, I hop on one bird foot as I work a new set of pants over my feathered body. The guys turn away from Su-chan as she changes.

Our legs already burn, and we can only keep going for so long. When my vision spins again, we take a moment to pull half the energy from our remaining two batteries. A quick ki healing halts the vertigo. At least that allows us to think straight enough to attempt making a plan.

26

FLIGHT

A MESSAGE FROM HOJI pops up on my screen saying he neutralized the new phone's tracking. So, I put the device on silent. A fox icon blinks at the top. Clicking on it shows Hoji's own VPN. *I owe you.*

Ahead, the ground rumbles from the footfalls of heavy robots—the Containment team.

After who knows how long of twisting and turning through narrow passages, we reach a main street. My hand raises as I peek around a corner.

Close to the palace again. My gut winds up so tight it's amazing I can breathe. Too damned close to the constant dread from my yakuza days.

Gently, Honjou Masamune, tucked in the cargo pocket of my pants, thrums and shakes me out of my darkness as her gratitude washes through the silver thread between us. Ibaraki would have used my sword to wipe out innocent yokai. Worth the risk. *If the League demands her return... Fuck them!*

"Rumors say a gate in the palace leads to a tiny little town. I think it's your best chance," Hoji says.

"We just came from that building!" Then my hand slaps my forehead. "The town has to be Kyuunan. That's how Ibaraki controls the area, even though her headquarters are here."

"How do you know?" Hoji asks.

"I had to investigate. A covert group controlled the town." Gnawing the inside of my cheek doesn't keep away the creeping dread. "That's why she could attack Nonogawa so easily. If they have more than one gate, the Akumakai can just come and go at Ibaraki's whim."

Suddenly, the phone buzzes, making my heart stop. There's a message from an unknown caller. 'Surveillance is back online. I've done what I can.'

Garu!

"Man, I don't wanna go back to the palace," Jiro whines.

But Hoji turns snippy. "Got a better idea? Containment has every other gate locked down. If they catch you, you're toast."

"Noted," I say to cut off further argument. *No choice.*

On guard, we follow the map through the alleys off Crystal Row.

The feathers on the back of my neck stand on end, despite my best efforts to exude calmness. As if on cue, a mechanized search team tromps by making us scoot into the shadows.

Thanks to Hoji, we have access to city blueprints. They show a storm drain that leads to the dungeon. Still dangerous, but we're in control again.

"Follow me." A glance at my phone says the battery is only at 38%. *Please, last!*

As covertly as possible, we duck into the drains off a branch from our current location. Weaving through the clear paths is slower than I'd like, and I loathe having to wade through the nasty water. Even the feathers of my disguise rub and make me want to scream.

"My skin feels like someone took a vegetable peeler to it," Sekiguchi grumbles.

Ahead of us, a swarm of mechanical spiders appears at the end of the tunnel. We freeze, and I pull a little juice from my phone to hide us.

Jiro's hands glow as he whispers something, making the spiders go silent and skitter away.

'You dealt with them?' From close call after close call, my heart drums double time in my chest.

Jiro nods.

Ask about it later. 'We can't stay here. Too vulnerable.'

My phone says we can go right or left. Right looks easier, so I choose left. We'll have to crawl through a few tight spots, but if there's a trap, it'll be on the easier route.

When we hit the last spot to crawl through, Su-chan's hips, from her short and chubby disguise, get stuck. *How could I be so stupid?*

That's when my phone flashes a message saying they're purging the water right above us. *Dammit!* 'Su-chan, drop your disguise!'

It's still a tight fit. Checking her over, I flash my phone's light on the scrapes. She rubs her sides, giving me a weak, chagrined smile. 'I'm not doing that again. Ever!'

Then we spot a heavenly beam shining down through the tunnel a head of us. *A gate!* As I heave a breath of relief, the sound of rushing water sends chills right back down my spine.

With no time to waste, we run full tilt toward the light. *Please, let us get out of this!*

Reaching the grate, there's no time to verify it's safe. But the damned thing doesn't give way.

We lift Jiro and he says, 'There's a switch.'

It clicks and the bars raise. We shove him through first, then Su-chan. The flood grows to a roar.

Hastily, I hoist Sekiguchi in shaking hands. As he's scrabbling through, Su-chan's shriek is the last I hear before the water sweeps me away.

The app said the Cleanse flushes into the jaws of a giant sea monster. *Don't let me end like this.* Flailing as I tumble, I try to reach for something. Anything.

My lungs burn. There wasn't a chance to suck in a big breath before the torrent swept me away. What I wouldn't give for more air. I didn't even get to say goodbye to Su-chan. That spurs me to keep fighting. My muscles protest, but I force them to work and resist sucking in a breath of water.

Out of nowhere, something clenches my wrist in an iron grip. *A webbed hand.*

'Got you,' Sekiguchi's strained voice via a renewed link is better than a warm spring day. He reels me in so his arm can slip under mine and around my chest. 'Swim with me. I'll lend you oxygen.'

Even though the air he shares is stale and not enough, it's still the sweetest thing ever. We kick. Despite our efforts, the feet of my bird form do me no favors.

He says, 'Drop your disguise.'

So, I slap the pendant to revert to my original human form. This time it isn't so painful. We swim hard to reach the top of the water. Both of us suck in breaths in loud gasps.

A light appears ahead.

'Any magic left?' I ask.

'A little. Can we grab that grate?'

'Gotta try,' I say. 'On the count of three. One... Two... Three!'

In tandem, we shoot up out of the water with our arms raised. Only my fingers grasp a bar. Sekiguchi's swipe past and he flails midair. Straining, I reach for him as his webbed hand snatches my arm. Though my skin is slick and he slides down. *Shit!*

His grip tightens, just like it did when he caught me in the flow. His weight jerks my shoulder so hard it'll be a wonder if I don't come out of this with a bad sprain. Then he goes up hand over hand, squeezing the daylights out of my muscles. I grimace but say nothing as the rough, rusty metal tears into my palms.

Finally, Sekiguchi grasps the grate with his metal hand and pain shoots through my shoulder as I push to lift my free arm. Then he swings his legs near the ceiling. The familiar blue glow of magic glows on his webbed feet. *Did he attach himself to the top?*

That's when my hand cramps. Man, I wish we had more ki right now. This would be so much easier! As it is, I might manage another mid-level spell before passing out.

Sekiguchi's bony webbed fingers reach through the grate, feeling around the edge for the switch, while I strain to pull myself up to do the same. My hand hits something. A rocker switch.

Clink.

Then footfalls thunder above us. *Shit! Shit! Shit!* At least the water below is receding. Before I can figure out how to pull my hand out of the way, the face of the one I love pops into view.

"Ta-kun!" Su-chan's angelic voice rings a welcome reprieve. She and Jiro pry the grate open as she says, "I had to use the red string of fate between us to track you. I hope you don't need much healing, because I'm super low on ki. Jiro had to loan me some."

Sekiguchi points upward. "You will go up first."

But I shake my head.

He frowns. "I insist. Unlike you, I can swim."

Touché.

When we're both hauled up, we're soaked to the bone. The water will leave a trail for pursuers.

"Stop right there!" a deep voice commands.

Can't we catch a break? I'll try to fight, but damn. I'm wiped out and my head is killing me.

"On it!" Su-chan already has potions in hand and the guard goes down with a crash of glass and a freeze potion. She and I rush over to the open doorway in case there are more.

"Paku? What's going on?" a high-pitched voice calls as a boar head pokes around the corner.

Her mouth opens. Before she can even squeal, I put my sword to her throat. But she reaches for her phone. Honjou shudders in my hand as if resisting. *Understood.* The sword doesn't want to kill someone who's not attacking us.

"Not a peep," I growl. "After the hell of today, I'd not think twice about slitting your throat if you give us any trouble." The boar doesn't have to know I won't actually kill her.

Su-chan's brows furrow. She, too, disapproves, but the priority is getting us out. Then the boar yokai nods and drops her phone. It clatters to the ground face up, flashing an alarm.

We're so cursed.

Deftly, Sekiguchi scoops up the phone with his prosthetic hand, and presses cancel.

"We need the uniforms. Off with it." To hurry her up, I let the sword's tip poke the leather of her armor. Her eyes narrow as she complies and mouths a word that looks suspiciously like 'pervert'.

So, I shake my head. "Not my type, sweetheart."

She whispers, "You're the ones everyone is hunting for."

In response, I wink.

"Back for the rest of the legendary weapons?" she hisses.

"More armor, less talk." Sekiguchi flicks the boar's ear and preps to punch.

She flinches.

I'm already stripping down to ditch my wet clothes.

When the pair is relieved of guard uniforms, phones, weapons, and crystalized ki, we toss the female our two biggest disguises. Then the guards are shoved into a cell and enclosed in a silencing spell.

It's the last of my expendable ki and the magic's glow already sputters. *Ki won't last long.* The boar's eyes flick around, and she pounds the spell's walls.

Only after slipping into the warm, dry clothes, do I notice the stench. *Why do pigs smell so bad?*

Then Sekiguchi dons the other set of armor. He plugs his nose, whining, 'Did they ever bathe?'

Scooping up the boar's spear, I grimace as my head pounds when I check my phone. Dead—from the water.

Sekiguchi turns the weapon in his hand as he asks, "Isn't this the type of spear used to hunt wild pigs? Ironic."

It causes the boar guard to bare her teeth.

'Though I'm exposed in my natural kappa form, I can be more helpful now.' Sekiguchi thumbs through the boar's phone to find possible portals. Only one shows up above us, in the central area the app had blocked off.

When he tries to view the area, an error appears on the screen, 'Access denied'. I try the other guard's phone, too. Same message.

'That's where we go. Charge up on the guards' crystal. Save the phone batteries for later. Jiro, can you have Hoji hack this phone, too?' I say as I hold out the bags to divvy up the ki.

But Su-chan clears her throat. 'Let me check that stuff first.' Her nose wrinkles and she scowls. 'Low grade, but it won't hurt us. I just hope we don't have some addiction at the end of this mess.'

'Same,' I say.

Sekiguchi does a double take at the phone. 'The portal is moving. At least, I think it is.'

How? Sure enough. It's not above us anymore. When it appears the next time, the kanji characters are a little different. 'Or only one gate in a set is open at a time?'

'Is there a pattern?' Su-chan asks.

'Your ID is on the guard's phone now,' Jiro says, and his hands open and close like a grabby little kid. 'Ooh! Lemme see!'

When I flash him the screen, he asks, 'Where else have they appeared?'

So, Sekiguchi and I point to different areas on the map.

Pondering for a moment, Jiro asks, 'What order?' When we point to them as we saw them, Jiro grins maniacally. My poor head can't parse whatever my young friend sees.

Humoring us, Jiro traces a path. 'I think it's a star pattern in a circle around the central room, so the next one will be there.'

'Too far,' Su-chan's voice goes gloomy.

'But Jiro's on to something. We go to one that's close in the pattern,' I say with more confidence than I feel.

When the others agree, I ask Sekiguchi, 'Know how to march? We're gonna have to pretend the others are our prisoners.'

He shakes his head. Man, his background is so different from mine. It's not his fault he wasn't force marched at crazy intervals like I was in the slammer.

Also, it doesn't help that I hate the crystalized ki we're using. We burn through it too damned fast. The shaking in my hands and nasty ache in my head make it hard to concentrate. *Breathe.*

'Follow my example, Sekiguchi. Make it look like you'll prod them hard if they don't obey.' To Su-chan and Jiro, I direct, 'Look defeated. Slump your shoulders, shuffle along, don't look up.'

"Chou, split," Su-chan commands her pet.

So the slime emerges from under her tunic and manifests a globby, black hand to shake in a definitive 'no'. Su-chan's pet still gives me the heebie-jeebies, even after all the times it saved my bacon.

"Please, Chou. I'll give you an extra big ki meal when it's safe."

But the cartoonish hand divides, holding up two fingers.

Su-chan sighs before caving. "Fine."

Complying, the ooze splits with a sickening slurp, and my girlfriend hands me a grapefruit sized portion. 'For just in case.'

Not gonna ask 'for what'. I nod and pull my hood down as far as I can to cover my face and use a small glamor to make a beak poke out.

Now, the fastest way to the next portal opening is the circle hallway around the throne room. A pair of guards approaches us with the most pathetic version of a march I've ever seen.

"Where are you going with this sorry lot?" the round guard asks.

'Look upset we got stopped,' I share with Sekiguchi. Rolling my eyes, I puff out my chest. "I wasn't authorized to share that info."

He uses the butt of his spear to poke my shoulder. "I outrank you. Enlighten me."

Giving a huff, I let my arms cross and I lean back with the practiced arrogance of my yakuza days. "If you want to explain to the Oyabun why we're late getting these prisoners with fresh ki to her for special treatment, then by all means, delay us."

"The boss is looking for a group of misfits..." He scowls.

"I'm pretty sure this is the group, though a couple got away." I point down the hall to the door we came from. "Now, if you'll excuse us. We need to get these mangy beasts to her."

But he gets into my face. "How do you know the boss is a 'she'? You don't have the insignia of her guard."

I shrug, trying to hide the shaking in my knees. "And I'm bringing this lot to her. Ibaraki-sama does not put up with disappointment. Get out of our way or come with us. I'll be sure to let her know you made us late."

Trembling, the guard's cohort's squeaks, "Captain, he knows her name! He's got to be telling the truth."

Whether to test my resolve or think it through, I can't tell, but the leader pauses. It takes every ounce of will to breathe normally.

His companion shakes his head muttering "No, no, no. I'm too low on ki for this."

Finally, the captain grumbles at me, "You were going the wrong way."

Whew. I whisper a prayer of thanks for the foresight to have kept the device. I whip out the boar's phone to give the guard captain a peek at the app. Though, my thumb hides the fox icon from Hoji's VPN.

So the pair continues down the hallway. The other guard squints and counts on his fingers. "But there's the right number of them."

"That group isn't even the right species." Then the captain's voice goes quiet. "We'll see if they go the right way this time."

When the guards are about the round the corner, Sekiguchi prods Jiro with his spear. "Get a move on!"

27

***

BATTLE FOR SUMICHOU

Over our group link I share, 'Don't look back. Keep moving.'

The map, with extended access thanks to Hoji, shows the central pillar, a dais, and a set of entrances in a circle. Only one portal is available at a time.

Footfalls behind us say the guard pair followed, so I veer toward the next gate that will open.

'Book it! We're close!' The thudding of our feet on the squeaky wood makes me want to scream. *Damned nightingale floors.*

Then spurts of Ibaraki's grating voice echo down the hall. Another joins in, dripping with snobbery, causing me to skitter to a stop. *Mishima!*

'Chou can be our eyes if we let her into the link,' Su-chan urges. At my hesitation, she pokes me. 'Do it!'

Ugh. Why does it have to be Chou? Nevertheless, I press the ball of slime to the wall, and she seeps around the corner. Opening the link to Chou, we get a hazy black and white view of a guard contingent. Enthroned, Ibaraki sits on an ornate dais surrounded by a circle of gates. There's a mechanized hum in the room, coming from the throne. Behind her, a portal brightens and opens. Mishima stands, poised with a wakizashi short sword, at her side. But instead of his ant-eater-like trunk, a steel replica gleams.

My blood goes cold. 'Mishima did a mechanical upgrade for Ibaraki's ki theft power!'

Worse yet, a guard lifts a limp body by the neck. "Oyabun, this is one of the Underground leaders. Shall we put her on the extractors?"

'Yasha!' My thought leaks through the link and Jiro flashes me a pleading look.

291

"No, we'll keep her here as a shield and show the rebels what happens to traitors." Then Ibaraki's voice raises. "I shouldn't have listened to your plan to let that blasted yakuza and his cronies near Honjou Masamune. Your trap failed!"

"My plan was perfect. It only fails if they escape with the weapons. Umeji has but one way out of Sumichou—through this throne room. I'll find the traitor who helped him, Oyabun." The baku starts for the door, halting in place.

"Mishima, if you don't recover those weapons immediately and lay the thieves' heads at my feet, I'll drain the ki from you and your soldiers myself, and leave your corpses to the Eyeless Ones! I need those weapons to become Shogun and make Japan a force to be reckoned with again!"

Over the link, I share, 'They think they have us trapped.'

Next, Mishima gloats as he lifts Yasha's chin. "After we defeat the rebels, I'll interrogate this one on the extractors. I've been tailing her for weeks. But she made a mistake meeting with the yakuza. So she'll see him and his lackeys fall today."

Suddenly, gears squeal and the hum in the room stops. A guard jogs up and bows. "Ibaraki-sama, someone sabotaged the throne's mechanisms! Let us evacuate you since you haven't fully recovered from your last battle with the League!" He fidgets. "Even as Oni Queen, you can't sustain the ki drain beyond what your mechanical arm can handle!"

"What is the top priority of the Akumakai, Sergeant?" Ibaraki hisses.

"To put the Akumakai above everything else, Oyabun."

"You just spoke of my weakness. Not in the Akumakai's interests." Ibaraki snarls, lifting a finger to point at the guard who spoke up. He rises into the air, kicking and grasping his throat. "They can't steal my chance to be Shogun, nor will anyone control me again!"

When she releases the guard, he's gone still and collapses in an unnatural position.

'We need a distraction. Wish we knew when the Underground was going to act,' I say to my crew.

'I'll claim to be Kappa, one of the Underground leaders,' Sekiguchi suggests as he's about to remove his helmet.

'Not yet! Let's think this through.' His plan sounds more like a death sentence than a ploy.

Boots on wood behind us emphasize the need to ditch our location. Poking at the phone again, I find the next portal and duck into an alcove to avoid the pair of lackeys.

Then I hand off the guard's phone. 'Jiro, take this. It's got a connection to Hoji. You two see if you can find us a possibility.'

'Best hackers in Japan are on the job.' Jiro grins and texts Hoji.

Cocky kid. So, I ruffle his hair. 'How many batteries and phones do we have?'

The tally, two batteries with a quarter capacity and two phones about half charged. Everyone gets one.

As the guards pass, the captain growls, "They came this way. They may not be on our registers, but they had high enough access to the app that they knew where to go."

Just then, Jiro's phone blares an alarm, making him fumble and almost drop it. *Not now!* But the same tone spews from other phones down the hall.

"We just had a Cleanse! Wait! I heard a phone in the high security sector." The senior guard's voice drops to a whisper.

His cohort says, "Not a Cleanse, Captain! Look!"

What is it? Taking a peek at Jiro's phone reveals a scrolling message. 'Incoming announcement...' I flip the switch to silence it, but it was already set. *What the-?*

Suddenly, the well below my ribs pops open and I double over as spots fill my eyes. A tiny speck of ki enters. My energy starved body greedily absorbs it.

'What's happening? Did someone end the ki block?' Su-chan asks with a groan.

But the particle of energy inside revives us.

Above, a gruff voice booms over crackling speakers. "Breech of the control towers! All units, report to the front gate! I repeat. All units to the-" Hissing static replaces the voices.

"What the-? The app is down! Our last command is to head to the war tower. The Oyabun's guards are gonna have to handle that group," the captain blurts.

When their footfalls recede, I risk poking Chou around the corner again.

The static switches to a few microphone clicks, as if someone is testing the sound. "Residents of Sumichou, this is Phoenix. Thanks to Baku, the Sumichou Underground neutralized the app and the ever-seeing eyes that controlled your lives and cut your access to the natural flow of ki. The throne Ibaraki relies on has been destroyed."

'That voice...' Su-chan taps her forehead. 'Where do we know it from?'

"For too long, we've been slaves in our own city, one that was built to be a yokai haven. But the damned Akumakai stole our very life force and hoarded it for their own use. Today, that changes!"

A squad of Ibaraki's oni troops race past our hiding spot. They're heading to the broadcast towers, too. *Fewer guards to deal with.* 'This is our best chance. Let's go!' I order as we bolt out of our alcove.

But the announcement voice niggles at the back of my brain as it continues. *Su-chan was right.* We know it from somewhere.

"Thanks to our new recruits who provided an opportunity, we can strike the Akumakai while they're weak! The weapons needed to take over Japan were raided, and I have Onikiri, the sword that cut off Ibaraki Douji's arm centuries ago. Today, we take back Sumichou and put Ibaraki's head on a pike!"

Now they claim us? We aren't a part of them!

A roar erupts, and it escalates enough to make the floors shake.

The underground are the "visitors" Garu told us about, aren't they? I say, 'The Underground is taking the palace. Charge up on the batteries! Hurry!'

So, we drain the ki storage to minimize the impacts of our concussions before dashing toward the gate. Though Jiro leaves enough energy to run his phone.

Inside me, the sunshine warmth of natural ki burns after so long without it. Crystalized and electric versions just aren't the same.

'Su-chan and I will distract Ibaraki and the guards while Sekiguchi and Jiro rescue Yasha and book it for the open gate,' I say.

Sekiguchi tosses his helmet aside as we charge screaming into the gated chamber room. Heavy metallic thuds announce the Containment Unit's entrance. Then their commander orders, "Hold the line! Ki bombers, fire!"

A chorus of shouts echoes behind us, along with crashing, shots, and screams of pain.

'Incoming!' I shout over the link. 'Keep watch for those ki drain arrows! Try to make them go off course.' I reach into my pocket and Honjou's anger courses through our connection as she jumps into my hand. When I draw the sword from the sheath, frigid air blasts outward, leaving frost all down my arms. *Honjou carries a serious grudge!*

Over the connection with her, I gripe, 'Hey! Don't freeze my hands! I'm gonna need them!'

The icy torrent directs away from my arms, but it's still damned hard to hold the blade. So, I spend ki to protect myself from Honjou's dangerous cold. If we make it out alive, I'll need gloves rated for Antarctica.

After having to use stale ki and being depleted for so long, my magic is so much stronger than before.

Meanwhile, two guards haul Yasha toward the dais. The others converge around Ibaraki. Seven plus the Containment Unit and Ibaraki—whose metallic prosthesis glows, with magic at full capacity.

Then the containment unit fires into the crowd. Though everyone's so low on ki, the bombs shouldn't go off for a while. One whizzes toward Jiro and I cast a spell for wind to whip it up toward the ceiling.

Jiro thrusts his new dagger in the air as he screams a war cry that makes my blood run cold. I've never seen him so determined. At least one good thing will come of dragging him through Sumichou. He and Sekiguchi book it for Yasha.

On the dais, Ibaraki screeches to her troops as she stands to heft the largest double-bladed axe I've ever seen. "Honjou Masamune is mine! Your lives depend on its retrieval!"

Just then, a crowd's roar fills the chamber. The Containment Unit charges the incoming Underground horde. More of the rebels fall to the ki bomb arrows, though one mage manages to turn the arrow back on the archer who shot it. That one explodes.

Pouring on the speed from a ki-boosted spell, I rush straight for Ibaraki. When Mishima steps in my way, he raises his trunk and Honjou jerks in my hand. She shrieks, 'Don't let me go! I'll snuff myself out before belonging to them again!'

To protect her, I cast a spell to glue Honjou Masamune to my hand. My next step falters. Thankfully, Su-chan catches my wrist. Every moment we contact the ground, ki drains out of us faster than it ever did when Date Sari stole ki.

"Hang on to me!" I shout to Su-chan.

Leaping into the air, I create a floating path above Mishima. Our feet alight, and we're running free from the drain as Su-chan sends an arrow flying off toward the dais.

Mishima springs toward us, slashing his sword into the path just behind my feet. Meanwhile, the guards struggle onto our bridge. Su-chan hurls her pet slime. "Chou, snack time!"

The black ooze forms aerodynamic fins as she sails toward Ibaraki.

Another oni slices through Chou, but the slime just reforms and sticks to his sword. Then she crawls down it to reach the exposed flesh, slurping loudly. Screaming, the guard tries to peel the ooze off.

As three more soldiers try to climb up on our path, I slash, severing limbs. Su-chan tosses a potion that has them clawing their faces and crashing down to the floor with a crunch.

The remaining three all charge, raising shields, not weak ones like other magic I've seen here in Sumichou. The Akumakai got the best of the crystal, for sure.

Suddenly, I jerk when massive amounts of ki rip from my body. Whirling, I see the Oni Queen's demonic grin as she reels in energy like a rope from both Su-chan and I. It absorbs into her metal hand as fast as she can draw it.

At the same time, Mishima pulls his wakizashi from the magic path, sputtering, "You ruined everything! I could have overthrown the League from inside. So now, you die!"

That's when Su-chan bounds from the path. I swipe Honjou through the energy-draining ropes, and I can breathe again. If Su-chan and I can't stop Ibaraki and Mishima, we're dead.

In the periphery, I see Jiro swipe at the only standing guard, and Sekiguchi struggling as he lifts Yasha.

I shout, "Chou, to the green oni!" *Please, listen to me for once.* Switching to the link, I offer, 'If you manage this, I'll give you half my ki since you seem to like it so much.' Though, I shudder at the thought.

The slime flings herself toward Ibaraki faster than she's ever moved before.

Then shouting from the battle with the Underground crescendos. Ibaraki raises her hand again, and the dagger rips from Jiro's grasp to land at her feet. Sekiguchi's spear and Su-chan's potions do, too. At least the floating hamster-ball-like shield around my friends seems to protect them from the energy sapping effects.

Next, Mishima focuses his ki drain on me. When Honjou jerks in my hand again, the glue spell that connects her to me causes my shoulder to pull from its socket. Grunting with the effort, I raise a shield.

"Shion-sensei, I summon you!" Scales cover Su-chan's face and wind whips in swirls as her body elongates, writhing in serpentine knots. The voice that emanates from her mouth is too deep and inhuman, echoing in the room. "Ibaraki!"

Shion allows that?

The Oni Queen's hand whips sideways, causing Chou to fly away, but the ooze bounces right back.

Meanwhile, sinewy legs and sharp claws form to cushion Su-chan's drop like the shocks on a mining truck.

I say to her, 'Mishima first, then Ibaraki!'

No reply. *Please, be in control, Su-chan.*

Raising my sword, I create a glowing platform to leap from. It dissipates after my foot breaks contact. But as I sail through the air, I slam into a barrier a few feet from Mishima. Shaking my head to clear it, I get a glance at the rest of the battle.

The Containment Unit has their hands full with the Underground army. The rebels copy our methods to deal with the energy drain. To counter, the Containment Unit commander shouts, "Release the Eyeless Ones!"

Aww, shit!

While Sekiguchi lifts Yasha into a floating bubble, Jiro has a glowing interface floating in front of him, and his fingers fly across the keyboard. "Protect your ears!" Jiro shouts through the loudspeakers.

Our crew complies as Jiro gives the count down. "Three. Two. One."

Boom, boom, whum! The repeated vibrations rock the walls, even the floor. The Eyeless Ones shriek and I have to dodge a group of them fleeing before they pop, spattering gore.

'Good job, Jiro! Anything you can do about the Containment Unit?'

'Hoji-sensei and I are on it!' he says, with sass. 'And we have Yasha safe and sound.'

So I direct the rest of my crew. 'Sekiguchi, keep everyone away from Jiro! Su-chan and Chou, with me! We need to take out Ibaraki's mechanical arm and Mishima's trunk! They're the keys!'

Sekiguchi pulls the axe from his dimensional pocket as he nods. Popping up another shield, Su-chan and I charge as I belt a war cry. "Ibaraki, today you pay!"

Su-chan, now in full, flying-dragon form, heaves in a breath, smoke pours from her nostrils. Her eyes glow red as if they're a signal. Then she spews fire, boxing in Ibaraki's guards who maneuvered to protect their leader. To counter, a member of the Containment Unit peels away from the fray to focus on my girlfriend.

I'm about to help her. But Su-chan whips her tail, sending the mech suit tumbling. And Mishima bounds toward me, using the energy stair trick. *Copycat!*

"Free Sumichou!" the familiar voice rings over the din. A glance back shows Garu, the tengu who covered for us, leading the crowd.

The distraction costs me as Mishima's ki drain snakes its way around my shield. Honjou yanks toward the baku again and pain shoots through my shoulder as Mishima charges.

That's when the seal on my palm burns. Soujou-bou said it would grant me his power. *Will it work in Sumichou?* Desperately, I whisper his name.

Where my hand connects with Honjou Masamune blazes a brilliant white and travels all the way down my arm, warming the injury and popping my shoulder into place. I wince, but the pain disappears as the glow spreads.

Soujou-bou's voice fills my thoughts like a recording. 'Use my protection wisely as it pulls power from me to heal you and, for a few moments, creates an impenetrable shield that allows only your linked weapon through.'

Hell yeah!

Mishima crashes into the new shield as his wakizashi bounces off. Instinctively, I swing at the opening and Honjou Masamune slices through his sword arm. Another quick slice detaches his trunk. Blood spurts as the baku crumples to the ground, shrieking a spell to cauterize the wounds.

A word of kotodama snaps a cage around him and blocks ki from filling his well.

Then Phoenix's wide eyes light on me. His hand falls as he directs the swell of yokai and screams, "Charge!"

At the same time, Su-chan's dagger-like fangs expose as she opens her jaws wide and lunges. A black blob bounces forward, too.

Ibaraki, taking in all the opponents, raises her mechanical hand to sweep over the crowd.

Won't be a better chance. Instead of letting the Oni Queen suck the energy from my shield and drain my master, I scribe a portal above her and jump through it. Honjou Masamune turns so cold, my palms might freeze to the hilt. Raising the seething blade in my hands, I spend ki to make this attack true.

When I emerge from the portal, Su-chan's dragon form is bleeding but rising for another bite at the remaining Containment Unit suits. More Sumichou denizens flood in, filling the cavernous throne room fast. Some move injured comrades out of the way and others continue the charge, dodging the ki drain as best they can.

My muscles tighten for the coming blow. "For Sumichou!"

Ibaraki pales as she looks up. Her hand flicks to swish me away. But I veer back toward her, thanks to my spell. Then I yelp as my arm takes the brunt again. Honjou Masamune makes contact so hard, the ring sends vibrations through my whole body. A blast of freezing cold shoots into Ibaraki's shoulder, where it connects to her mechanical arm and frost tendrils spread like lightning.

That's when all hell breaks loose.

Honjou bucks in my hands and turns unresponsive—the cold vanishing from the sword. My arms go numb as the drain travels into me. If I hadn't used a spell to hold on to Honjou, she would be ripped from my grasp.

I crash, foot first, into the oni queen as Honjou digs a trench into the metal of her ki absorbing arm. The oni crumples to the ground and my ankle twists, popping painfully. Honjou's path halts despite my last spell.

As I pour energy into my sword, Honjou revives, sputtering curses at the Oni Queen. So I wrench the weapon out of my foe as she tries to scramble up and swing her axe one handed. I have to tumble out of the way.

Meanwhile, the tide of rebels sweeps to the dais. Ibaraki drains ki and flings them off right and left, but not fast enough to keep from being overrun by those smart enough to stay off the ground.

I rush back in, favoring the likely sprained ankle and shouting, "Out of the way! Gonna detach her arm!"

When the rebels part, I raise Honjou. The white shield sputters out. *Ki, do your magic!* Instead of bending the ki to my will, I release it like a petal falling from a cherry tree. 'True strike and cleave through!'

Energy drains from me again with a spectacular gleam, making my knees wobble.

Ibaraki jerks to the side, but Honjou's freezing blast covers the metal, making it creak and forcing the rebels to leap away.

Contact causes an ear-splitting metallic crackle and my sword cleaves through to the ground. But the continued drain drives me to my knees.

That's when a coin sized amount of ki enters my well, giving me just enough energy to stand. Soujou-bou's voice is quiet. 'That is all I can spare, Umeji-kun. Good luck.'

I don't know if he can hear me, but I give my thanks.

The Oni Queen shrieks, rolling away, but the rebels surge after her as she scrabbles toward the open portal. Before we can stop her, Ibaraki hurls herself through and the portal slams closed.

Can't let her escape! I shout, "Jiro! Hoji! Track her!"

"On it!" Jiro shouts. His fingers tear through commands.

Next, Phoenix growls to a guard, "Take the baku's head off now! We'll post it on a pike outside the castle as a reminder of those who would trample Sumichou!"

My gaze whips to the tengu leader of the Underground as he kicks the now defenseless baku being dragged from the cage.

Granted, Mishima's a traitorous bastard. He's taken lives. But this isn't the right way to deal with him!

As the rebels beat the pulp out of Mishima and his gaze goes unfocused, my stomach turns. Garu's actions are too close to my yakuza days.

Struggling to control my voice, I shout. "He'll stand trial before the League!" Suddenly, my palm sears with pain. *I said that name! Was it Soujou-bou's seal?*

But Garu stomps over into my face. "I know your voice! You're that kotengu! Listen, well! The League won't come. They've abandoned us. As leader of the Underground, I, Phoenix, order you!"

"No!" My voice goes deep and threatening.

Out of nowhere, his hand whips through the air to strike my face, jerking my head back. He screams, "Didn't you hear me? We all know what will happen when he's conscious again. This is our only chance to end the Akumakai tyranny. I command it!"

"I don't take orders from you! My crew and I will retrieve the League!"

"The League isn't welcome here! I told you, they abandoned us. If you won't take his head, I will. He and Ibaraki have killed many of my people!" Phoenix caws.

"And mine. But my decision stands!"

Whispers rise around us and coalesce into one. "Kappa."

Sekiguchi strides in his flopping gate to put a hand on my shoulder. "This young man is correct. Ibaraki needs to be handed over to the L..." His words cut off and he scowls. Glaring, he asks, "How did you say it?"

I hold up my hand to show the seal that's still making my palm an angry red. Sekiguchi rolls his eyes.

"You're not Kappa! She was my friend who died in the Cleanse! And you have a spell enhanced metal arm just like Ibaraki. So you'll do the same things she did to us!" Phoenix sputters.

Undaunted, Sekiguchi continues, "My friends and I read the messages from the first Kappa, your companion. I've learned the Akumakai wiped out my kind here because of that codename, but I'm not afraid. I'm here to help."

Voicing my approval, I add, "Sumichou needs a healer."

"I'm an expert in recovery from ki drain and teach it to anyone who will learn. Hear me now, I, Sekiguchi Yuu, am here to take up the mantle of Kappa!"

"They don't know what you're talking about, and the Underground won't accept someone who hasn't lived here! You don't know what we went through!" Phoenix goes to slap Sekiguchi, but this time, I catch the tengu's arm.

My grip tightens on his wrist. "Then they need to hear it. All of Sumichou should know what happened to the first Kappa."

Jiro says, "On it!" and casts a spell to amplify the audio files.

Gasps come from the crowd as the secret messages play and Phoenix growls, unable to stop the chant of "Kappa! Kappa! Kappa!"

Su-chan's dragon form changed, while I wasn't looking, to the one I know and love best. Her voice rings out, "Sekiguchi is a humble leader. He'd never steal ki from anyone! He even listened when he found out that I carry the magic of his beloved, Shion, the river god and former Guardian of Nonogawa. Others shunned me, saying I stole it. Instead, he helped Shion and I find peace."

Then a rebel holds out the metal arm and trunk. So, I snag them before Garu gets any ideas. "We'll take Mishima to the League."

"No! He remains in Sumichou for judgment."

"Then the League comes here."

Phoenix pokes my chest. "You think you're something special because you work with the League? I saw that white shield you had. You think you're hot stuff. On your own, you're nothing."

Baka! My nails dig into my free palm as I spit my words. "I don't work for the League. But, only they have the authority to deal with Mishima. Killing him will bring their judgment, since it's not in self-defense.

"You're right about one thing, though. On my own, I wouldn't have made it here or been able to help you free Sumichou. But my crew and I gave you what you needed to take back this city. Even an ex-yakuza like me knows better than to keep picking fights after achieving a goal. So why do you have such a stick up your ass when you should make peace?"

But Phoenix's shoulders only shake. "How come you have Soujou-bou's seal if you're not a Guardian?"

"I was true to him."

Suddenly, the tengu kicks the ground. "He chose a criminal over me, and now, the residents prefer an outsider they don't know, ta' boot."

He wanted to be in the League?

Just like Hiro used to when he expected my attention, I flick the side of Phoenix's head. It earns me a spectacular scowl, but I wipe the grin off my face. "Be the leader Sumichou should have had. Sekiguchi will need help from those who know this place and the people. I'll fetch the League." To Sekiguchi and Jiro, I say, "Ensure Mishima doesn't get away, and that Phoenix doesn't change his mind about killing the idiot baku."

Next, Hoji's voice comes through Jiro's phone. "We had a fix on Ibaraki, but she disappeared. Must have pulled her phone's battery and sim card. Sorry, Umeji-kun!"

"Shit. Thanks for trying."

Jiro joins our group with an arm tucked around Yasha for support. "We'll track her down, somehow."

Phoenix says, "Access to and from Sumichou will remain limited for the time being. If you insist on this fool's errand to fetch the League, we'll open the gate to Kyoto for you. You may return via a single portal, assuming you can convince the League to assist."

"Thank you." I heave out a deep breath. *We won!* Nevertheless, my entire body shakes from the adrenaline withdrawal and my ankle throbs. There's no time to collapse, though.

Su-chan's eyebrows raise as I half limp, half stride past her toward the gate. She laughs and holds out the shopping bag she always carries. "Such a far cry from the guy who tried to not make waves. Put those bloody appendages in here or you'll scare off everyone in Kyuunan."

28

§

POST BATTLE

WHEN WE STEP THROUGH the gate, it puts us behind a small temple. A few puffy clouds dot the sky and the fresh breeze revives me after the sickening sweet air of Sumichou. Quickly, I tuck Honjou Masamune into my cargo pocket. Can't just wield swords on the street!

Despite the exhaustion from the craziness we went through, it feels so good to have sunshine on my face. Now that we're outside of Sumichou, the ki floods into my well again.

Though my brain assaults me with a to-do list. Satou needs to know that the worst is over. Also, I need to report in, since he's still my parole officer. A few more months of that to go.

Much has changed since he first picked me up and I was fresh out of jail. It'd be more pleasant to talk to him, even in his grumpiest mood. But I need to report to Soujou-bou first, no matter how much my stomach ties itself in knots.

"Ready to face the League?" I ask.

Su-chan nods, though she fidgets.

My sweet girlfriend is always walking into hell with me.

She says, "When this is all done, I'd like a proper tour of Tokyo. We only saw the dark side, but there are good reasons so many people live there."

"There are." Before the moment passes, I intertwine my fingers with hers.

"Would you take me to the Ghibli Museum? I've always wanted to go." Su-chan asks as she squeezes my hand.

"Deal. Might be fun to show you the Ueno Zoo, Sensouji, and the bay too." I never thought I'd want to return to Tokyo. So many terrible memories—being picked on in school, Dad's death, having to join the yakuza, and what I did as a mobster. But

303

there were good ones, too. Through her eyes, maybe I can see the city in a better light. *Should I try to connect with Mom again?*

No. She shut me out.

"Your mood just darkened." Su-chan cradles my cheeks. "Whatever it is, I'll face it with you."

My forehead rests on hers as I soak up the attention like a sun-parched sponge. "Thank you."

"I'm starving. Can we pick up something to eat from the combini across the street?"

At that, my stomach growls. I could eat an entire horse and food should help the post-craziness blues. "I'll stay. If anyone gets a gander at what's in this bag, we'll be dealing with the police," I say. On second thought, I stuff the bag in my dimensional pocket. Can't afford any trouble.

Staring at the seal on my palm, I debate on where we should open the portal to report to the League. It would be so much easier to just walk into Soujou-bou's estate. But he banned portals on his territory, unless we use one of those special talismans.

Will the Council even believe us? Maybe Garu was right that this is a fool's errand. The last time I saw them, the Council rejected both of us.

But Inari-sama wanted me to keep striving to be a Guardian. *Is it really possible to do that now?* At least we retrieved Honjou Masamune.

In the past, only Soujou-bou and my aunt stood up for me. As proof, Soujou-bou put this seal on my hand. Even after losing Honjou Masamune, he lent me his power. So he and Aunt Hisako alone are the ones in the League I trust. For them and for Sumichou, I'll try.

Su-chan returns and hands me a wet wipe. *Gah!* My hands are nasty-dirty with stuff I don't even want to think about. *And how bad to we smell?* Dutifully, I wipe off the Sumichou grime.

Also, my ankle throbs, but I refuse to ask Su-chan to heal it. She's so low on ki right now. So, I mask my limp. *Can't look weak in front of the Council!*

Then we dig into the sandwiches.

Sumichou and getting the League to sentence Mishima is more important than the portal ban. They also need to know Ibaraki got away. So, I'll deal with the consequences of disobedience, because I'm too damned tired to hike up Mt. Kurama.

Holding my supper in one hand, I scribe an arc allowing Su-chan and I to step into the council chamber.

Every head in the room swivels in our direction. Their glares carry heavy disapproval. Was I too arrogant in my exhaustion? *This is an emergency!* If they'd bothered making me a Guardian, I'd have one of those cool red ofuda.

Soujou-bou snaps the portal closed behind us with a swish of his fan and his eyes narrow. "You two dared portal here, despite knowing I forbid it?"

We bow in deep respect. I say, "Sorry, Soujou-sensei. It's an emergency. We just came from Sumichou. Now, the town is free." So I pull the mechanical arm and trunk out of my dimensional pocket, and set them at his feet with the same care I would an antique.

Then I barrel into the explanation. "Ibaraki and Mishima can't make people slaves by draining their ki using these spell enhanced devices again. The Sumichou Underground was going to execute Mishima. They wouldn't let me bring the baku to you, but I insisted the League try him."

Hearing that, the entire council leans in.

"They don't believe you'll come. Sekiguchi and Jiro won't be able to keep Mishima alive for long. And Ibaraki escaped. If I thought there was time, I wouldn't have dared portal here. Therefore, I accept whatever punishment you deem necessary. Su-chan didn't know. Please spare her, Sir."

His eyes widen despite snickers of disbelief from the others. He says, "Sumichou, you say?"

"Yes, sir."

"But how did you get in undetected? They captured every Guardian we sent in—"

His voice cuts off and Hayashi, the yuki onna, finishes the sentence. "Or they turned on us."

I plead, "They need the leadership of the League now that the Akumakai has fallen. Phoenix and Sekiguchi will require help to bring peace."

But my teacher growls the name. "Phoenix? You mean Garu? That worthless tengu survived? So he betrayed us, after all."

Wouldn't wanna be in Garu's shoes. "Sir, Garu and Baku lead the Underground rebellion and can't revitalize the area alone. Sekiguchi will remain to guide rebuilding, but even he won't be enough."

Slowly, Soujou-bou's lips purse. "Tell us what happened."

So I give the speediest version I can and Su-chan adds details I glossed over. We emphasize how important Hoji and Jiro's hacking skills were and that the Underground used our recovery of Honjou Masamune as a distraction.

Raijin asks, holding out his hand in expectation, "So you came to report and return Honjou Masamune to us?"

Then the sword in my grasp shudders and my gut clenches. Yet another way they'll see me as arrogant. But I won't make the same mistake twice. With a steady voice, I respond, "My apologies, Council. Honjou Masamune remains with me. And the other weapons we recovered stay with my crew, unless they wish to relinquish them."

"Those weapons belong to the League! Do you not remember what I swore to you?" The yuki onna's voice echoes off the walls.

That you'd never let me into the League. In defiance, my grip tightens on the scabbard. "Honjou Masamune chose me and you weren't the ones to recover them." My jaw shoves forward. To cover my shaking, I shove another bite of sandwich into my mouth.

Soujou-bou looks from me to Raijin, to Hayashi, and back, then laughs long and hard. Confused, I can't stop my face from screwing up, but I don't dare question my teacher's authority more.

Out of nowhere, he slaps my back, causing me to stumble and wince. "I knew he had it in him." To the Council heads, Soujou-bou says, "You lost the bet," and points his feather fan to the alcove.

The yuki onna's eyes roll, but she snaps, and a pile of sake kegs appear in the indicated spot. "I still won't approve his appointment."

"Hayashi-san, don't forget we outvoted you." Soujou-bou snaps his fingers as he prods, "And the rest of you," Without grumbling, they pay up. I spin around to see an altar appear and a host of offerings settle on it.

To his servant, Kairi, he directs, "Fetch Guardian Nakamura."

"What's going on?" As I try to put two and two together, my head spins.

Su-chan whispers, "Is she to witness our punishment for portaling?"

Even if it's the case, I came here for a purpose. Wobbling, I kneel with my head to the ground in supplication. "Sir, Sumichou needs the League. Please, don't make them wait."

"You two don't want to be the Guardians that represent us?" Soujou-bou asks. *Did I hear that right?* Suddenly, the room is too warm.

Do I? Will Su-chan want to, still?

Wait a fucking moment. The Council should apologize for how they treated us.

Like they would.

When I spot Aunt Hisako padding through a portal, her face is tight as she leans in for my answer. She's the Guardian I trust the most. The one who started my journey. She knew I could do this. So did Inari-sama.

My arms protest, but I force myself to sit up. "No more mind games?"

"Once a part of us, always a part of us, even after you turn the mantle over," Raijin says.

Shit. My teeth grind. He didn't answer my question. *They won't change, will they? Forget it.*

But Inari wanted you here.

Soujou-bou's hand rests on my shoulder. "No more mind games." He turns my exhausted frame to face him. "We tested you more harshly than any other guardian in history. Let me tell you why."

My nod is almost imperceptible as I prep to parse any hidden meanings for the catch. *Don't dash my hopes again, Sensei.*

"With three betrayals in the last century, I had to be sure of your loyalty. I thought you disobeyed me in the Battle for Nonogawa. Though, Shion told us what happened. Now I understand why you went after the sword."

So, I'm forgiven. The tension inside unwinds a smidgen.

"Beyond your past, Umeji-kun, we had concern that you and Su-chan are from a new generation. It's been over two centuries since we had new blood, let alone anyone who bothered to keep up with technology. Our magic always got us through. The League..."

Swallowing, he continues, "...we've fallen behind the times. We need to modernize so we can face new threats. The two of you can help us adapt and protect Japan. So, join us."

They won't apologize. But to hear an explanation is a huge concession. They're trying to change from expecting my generation to obey and put up with whatever we're given from our elders.

Will my generation be tenacious enough to ensure we're heard? Su-chan and I can be the start.

To be the ones that see this day. Holy shit!

The irony that the League needs me, a former yakuza, makes me laugh before I can squelch it. "I'm dreaming, right?"

Su-chan covers her mouth, but she nods. She's having a hard time believing it, too.

Recovering, I add, "We accept."

Soujou-bou's grin tries to expand past his face. "Hold out your hand."

At my compliance, he waves his fan over the seal on my palm. I flinch at the burn but watch enraptured as it morphs to look just like Aunt Hisako's and the spot under my ribs where my well resides aches as it expands.

My aunt's eyes gleam with pride as she pads up beside me.

Then Soujou-bou says, "Ohno Suzu-san, you need my seal, too."

I don't want to miss her moment. While shoving my hand into my pocket, I freeze. Pictures won't be welcomed in this secretive group. *At least not yet.*

"Congratulations, both of you. We'll have the official ceremony soon, and you'll receive your first month's pay then. Oh, and Umeji, I saw you reaching for your phone. Thank you for waiting. You'll have an opportunity for a picture after you get your uniforms."

Awesome!

Aunt Hisako nuzzles us. "I'm so proud of you both! Three Guardians in our family!"

Family? Not so fast, Aunt! Su-chan hasn't said she'd marry me. *Yet.*

"Nakamura-san, you have one last duty to perform." Soujou-bou gives her a warm smile. In acknowledgement, she bows and portals back to the den. To Kairi, he says, "Prepare for the ceremony."

The Council straps on the weapons at their sides as Raijin says, "Show us how to enter Sumichou."

They're looking to me? And I have to ask for something awkward in order to keep a promise. "Soujou-sama?"

"Yes." He stops mid-way through putting his swords into his obi.

Gotta do this. "M-may I have my pay now?"

Immediately, his expression darkens. "Why?"

Does he think I have loads of debt? "I gave my word to free two yokai, sir. It will be expensive."

"You would use your wages to free another?"

"Yes, sir. I can get by until I've paid that off. I don't need much to live on."

Su-chan adds, "I'll help, Soujou-sama. Tatsu and I promised the kojin and little kodama."

Silently, the council's glances bounce between Su-chan and me.

Letting out a guffaw, he produces a scroll. "You never asked if there is compensation for job-related expenses. Show this to whomever you need to pay. Let us go. We don't want to keep Sumichou waiting."

"Come on, Guardian." Su-chan nudges me and emphasizes her last word.

Guardian. At that title, a glow fills my chest and the radiance in her eyes and smile captivates me. I'd follow her anywhere. Even back to Sumichou.

Checking my well, it refreshes at a rate that's almost as fast as when Su-chan gives me ki. The sunshine heat spills in, not just with energy, but with a confidence I've never known before.

Happily, Honjou Masamune hums in my hands, no longer frigid but warm. It adds to the headiness of what will be my first actions for the League.

Breathe. Don't let it go to your head. Then my hand scribes an arc in the air, as if I could do it since the day I was born, right into the cavernous gate room of Sumichou.

Whispers behind me ask, "But how? The Akumakai gated it with a dark magic..."

"Not anymore." Then I wink at Phoenix's squawk of surprise.

Soujou-bou, King of the Tengu, strides through just short of crashing into the trembling Phoenix. He spits, "Garu."

The tengu swallows so hard everyone can hear it. "S-s-soujou-sama, my king." He pitches himself to the floor with his forehead touching the ground. "I'm s-so sorry!"

For what? Is Soujou-bou gonna kill Garu?

"The newest Guardians report you lead the uprising here," the voice of the king thunders.

Responding, the leader of the Underground shakes violently and his voice quavers, "I-I w-wasn't alone, Sire."

"You weren't?"

Phoenix's head remains on the floor. "There were three of us that wanted to change ourselves and the city. Soon, word spread, and we just needed a catalyst. It came when Umeji-san and his crew provided the distraction we needed."

"So, you learned to cooperate and compromise?"

"I'm-" His voice cuts out, but he takes a breath, "I'm learning, Sire."

"Are you capable of working with the League until we establish peace?"

Nodding, he sits up. "Yes, Soujou-sama. If I may be so bold, then what?"

"What do you mean?"

"Not to be disrespectful, but the League rushes in, takes over, and then vanishes while those left behind struggle to find a balance in the void."

Instead of being angry, Soujou-bou puts a hand on his shoulder. "We are learning, too. Umeji-kun and Ohno-chan will stay for a time, but the League won't abandon Sumichou." Motioning to Sekiguchi, he says, "And you will stay?"

The kappa bows. "Yes, Soujou-sama. I need a purpose again, now that my student has a proper teacher, and the spirit of my beloved has hope and peace instead of revenge." Then Sekiguchi's gaze lingers on Su-chan.

She shuffles. "I will keep my promise to Shion about his magic. So, you won't return to Kyoto?"

"Alas, no. Visit when you have the time. I can share recipes and tricks you may need in the field."

Clearing my throat, I say, "We have another promise to keep. May we be excused to fulfill it, Soujou-sama?"

He waves his fan as if to shoo us off. "The word of a Guardian must be kept."

When we teleport into the pet shop, Megumi gapes. "H-how may I help you?"

But Su-chan whispers, "She doesn't recognize us."

Oh yeah. "We were disguised as the tengu and lady oni. I'd left a retaining fee on the kodama and we want the kojin, too."

Suddenly, Megumi's eyes light up and her head weaves toward us on her long neck.

With a wicked grin, I add, "I'm here on business for the League of Guardians."

All eyes in the shop dart to Su-chan and me before the howling for freedom begins. The little kodama makes child-like grabby hands toward Su-chan.

In an instant, Megumi's posture shifts and her arms cross. "You're going to demand them from me, aren't you?"

"No." It's only wise to make good use of the boss's funds. "But since we did Sumichou a huge favor by helping to take down the Akumakai and freeing everyone, I think a discount would be in order."

"So it's true..." Words fall from Megumi's lips and she wilts, having to lean on a counter. "Letting the kodama go at a discount is the least I can do. But I can't part with the kojin."

Next, the shark yokai holds up a finger. "Let me be your assistant manager. You won't have the Akumakai breathing down your neck for protection payments anymore. So you can pay me a salary, and you'll have to call me by my name."

Megumi heaves a sigh. "I could use the help. You'll still do the weaving?"

"If you won't chain me here. After watching you for years, I learned the business. So I'll work on weaving things as I can. But we'll also train the other yokai here to be useful. Then we can hire them out instead of selling them."

Then Megumi puts a finger to her lips. "Interesting."

Before they get too deep in negotiations, I unroll the scroll. Megumi's head jerks back about a meter on her long neck. "From Soujou-bou himself?"

When I peek at the text, it lists the very numbers I'd had in my head with the discount. *Slick! I'll have to ask about that.*

"But how did he know what we'd agree to?"

"I discussed my plans with him." *Close enough to the truth.*

With a grin, Su-chan scrambles over to the bonsai kodama, who's jumping for joy. "Oh, little one, you'll have so many friends!"

Chou slips out of Su-chan's bag and bounds up to the kodama, greeting it exuberantly with pats and wild hand gestures.

On the way to our lodgings, I snag several of the wanted posters. I figure Jiro is going to want to hang one in his room as badly as I do.

That night at our temporary apartment in Sumichou, a package arrives wrapped in a crepe cloth and bearing Soujou-bou's mon crest, the fan. When I open the note, it's blurry, as if dodging my attempt to read it. Blue light flashes where my fingertips make contact. Then the symbols coalesce into words and Soujou-bou's voice fills the room.

'New Guardians, the League has a long and proud tradition. Now that you are joining our ranks, I charge you with the maintenance of our reputation—in your words and deeds, in your manner of dress, and how you protect your assigned location.

'I sent these uniforms to be worn at official gatherings and when you must reveal yourself to the public.

'Wear them to report outside the Council chamber for your first formal assignment in two hours.'

Su-chan unwraps the package. Inside is a pair of indigo dyed kimono with the Guardian lion mon on the front and rear of each shoulder and the middle of the back.

There are also midnight blue hakama trousers and haori jackets, a red obi sash and cords, a white under layer, split toe socks and sandals, and an ancient style black starched hat. Under the clothes, there's one of those beautiful ofuda with red symbols that allows us to portal to Soujou-bou's estate.

Wanting to present ourselves properly, I text Aunt Hisako to ask for help with the traditional uniforms. But Grandma Miwa shows up at our door and tuts at my clumsy attempts. "Hisako-chan should have taught you better than this!"

"Sorry Grandma. She tried. Though, today my hands won't cooperate. They're shaking too bad."

It takes more than an hour to preen us to her standards. "To see one of my kin and his love in Guardian garb..." As she shakes her head, her eyes go misty. "Now, off with you. You'll be late."

Instantly, my stomach fills with butterflies. Su-chan squeezes my hand before I slap the paper into the air.

When we step through onto Soujou-bou's estate grounds lit by torches, about fifty yokai in two lines of Guardians, Envoys, and Salvage Crew members greet us. Hayashi is not among them. Though, Aunt Hisako, in human form, is there, and her eyes sparkle. I also spot Shion, the tengu captain, the dish warrior and the little rag dragon from the battle at Nonogawa. We bow with reverence and the group returns the greeting in unison.

Next, Soujou-bou sits on a cushion at the far end, with the Council behind him. He waves his feather fan, commanding, "Approach and kneel to receive your assignment's crest."

My aunt pins my medallion, embossed with a rice stalk ready for harvest—the symbol of Nonogawa, to my uniform. Shion does the same for Su-chan. I feel a meter taller when my aunt gives mine an approving pat and says, "Umeji Tatsuya-kun and Ohno Suzu-chan, I turn over the duties of protecting Nonogawa to you."

Then a weight settles on my shoulders. *Will I live up to her example?* But glancing at Su-chan reminds me. *We do this together.*

"Nakamura-san, thank you for your decades of service." Soujou-bou gives a long deep bow. "I release you from your obligations, save guiding these two new Guardians." And a wave of clapping comes from the entire contingent.

"Umeji-kun and Su-chan, you already have my seal. Though there is one last thing." The edges of Soujou-bou's eyes crinkle. "I had promised you a picture. Nakamura-san and Shion-san, if you would stay with this pair for a moment, I will have Kairi-kun do the honors."

On the Tengu King's top secret estate? What if something in the background gives the location away?

Aunt Hisako's eyes bulge. The same thoughts were racing through her head, weren't they?

Chuckling, Soujou-bou says, "Even I can adapt. Nakamura-san's fiancé offered ideas that will keep our secrecy. I'll share more in the next meeting."

With that cue, a group of servant tengu shuffle over carrying a folding panel to serve as our backdrop. Kairi bows and herds us to the center before snapping a picture on a phone and showing Soujou-bou how to send it to ours. Council members hover in amazement to watch the transfer happen.

My eyes remain glued to the photo. *We're really Guardians!*

Then, Soujou-bou claps his hands and shouts, "Now! Let us feast!"

Cheers erupt, filling the courtyard with an inhuman roar. Each member slaps us on the back and files into the feast hall. Su-chan and I are last through the buffet of tables piled with meat buns, grilled fish, rice balls, seasonal veggies, desserts and huge casks of sake. There's more than enough for everyone and the party lasts through the night.

Mishima's trial is swift. Su-chan, Jiro and I attend, and Phoenix brings witnesses from Sumichou. In the end, the Council banishes Mishima from the mortal realm, stripping him of magic. Representatives of the baku species send word stating they won't welcome Mishima in their lands.

Not missing a beat, Hoji recruits Jiro into a pilot program at Kyoto Jidai Arcane University for exceptional middle and high school students. Jiro's hacking skills and experiences in Sumichou make him quite popular. Instead of reveling in it, he befriends the kid everyone picks on. Hoji says the pair will leave the rest of the group in the dust in their studies and opportunities.

Rebuilding Sumichou will take years. Beyond restoring and purifying the town, there's rebuilding the hearts and minds of the downtrodden residents. So many are broken in spirit and their ki wells have shrunk to almost nothing. They need to see progress.

Every morning Su-chan leads a ki capacity recovery class while I help with the demolition and cleanup of Crystal Row and the palace.

Sumichou never will be the most reputable. It's off the map for a reason, a place for yokai to be free. The new leaders don't trust the League and vice versa, but hope buds.

Then there's what to do with Shachihoko, the sea monster that devoured the Cleanse floods. The beast depended on the town for its food source. He isn't healthy from all the awful things he fed on, and the thought of how many residents he ate makes me shudder. But Sekiguchi points out Shachihoko, too, was a slave.

The kappa is the only one who wants to contact the massive sea creature. Grudgingly, I accompany him. It takes time to convince the beast he needs to go back to the depths of the ocean. There he can recover and be the terror of the sea again.

Su-chan offers to help Tarou disguise himself and visit his family. He says he'll only go after Sumichou is restored. At least he's considering it.

Yasha says she'll accompany Tarou when he visits. Poor Jiro had no idea the two were close, let alone dating. In the end, Yasha snags a position on the Sumichou district council and quits her hostess job. She wants to ensure there's at least one woman in the leadership.

Back in Nonogawa, Satou gets clearance to visit Sumichou. His report for the PSIA Paranormal Division clears up a host of disappearances.

Besides helping with Sumichou, Su-chan and I portal daily to Soujou-bou's estate for training with him and Shion. Learning is intense and we have little down time. We're both exhausted.

After about a month of the heavy demands, Sekiguchi stops by our lodging one evening to pull Su-chan aside. I can't hear what he says, but her hands fly to her mouth and she pales.

"Is everything alright?" I ask.

She nods. Her mouth opens, but no words come out. A tear trickles down her cheek.

Joining her, I wipe it away. "Take your time."

She tries again, though the words still escape her.

Did Shion try to control her again?

"Shall I tell him?" Sekiguchi asks.

"Uhm-hmm."

Shit. It's gonna be bad.

Without hesitation, Sekiguchi says, "She's expecting. Congratulations! I suspected it right after we helped free Sumichou, but was curious if she'd see the light of the baby's spirit. Alas, Shion insisted I share before she's farther along."

I blink. The world stops. My kappa friend's mouth moves, but there's no sound.

Pregnant? Inside Su-chan's belly, the faintest light pulses.

A baby.

Holy shit!

Nothing's gonna be the same again.

Su-chan flashes me a timid smile, but I can't hear what she says either.

We're gonna be parents.

Will she have to step down from being a Guardian? How did Aunt Hisako handle it?

Wait. Sekiguchi hinted she was pregnant while we were sneaking into this godforsaken place.

Is the baby ok?

Is Su-chan?

"Ta-kun?" Su-chan's voice strains as she tugs my sleeve.

Laughing, Sekiguchi pats my shoulder. "Once he snaps out of it, he'll do fine. I'll give you two love birds some privacy." Then he shuts the door behind him.

Man up.

But she hesitated when I first asked.

Time resumes. Wrapping her in an embrace, I whisper in her ear. My voice breaks on the last couple of words. "You said if we were together everything was gonna be ok. So, marry me. It'll be a new adventure together."

Her fists clench my shirt as her tears soak the fabric. "Together."

Before I became a Guardian, I thought it would make me someone. But that's not how life works. It's how I live every day, through the calm and through the storms.

I owe so much to those who stood by my side and believed in me when the rest of the world refused. Thanks to them, I have a path that I can be proud of, and I won't walk it alone.

29

CAST OF CHARACTERS

I PUT THE MAJOR character, Umeji, at the top of the list. Everyone else that recurs in the story is in English alphabetical order.

Remember that Japanese names have the family name before the personal name. For example, in the name Umeji Tatsuya, Umeji is his family name and Tatsuya is his personal name.

* Indicates the person is a mythological figure
** Indicates possible deviation from well-known myths and folklore

You can find portraits and more details at https://www.worldanvil.com/w/liminal-chronicles under the Meet the Characters sections.

For notes on name suffixes and other name information, see the Cultural Notes section at the beginning of the book.

CHARACTERS
Umeji Tatsuya
(AKA Tatsu, Nephew, Ta-kun)
Former yakuza (mobster) who wants to become the Guardian of Nonogawa.

Arai Ryouta

(AKA Chief Arai)

A ghost and Chief of the PSIA Paranormal Division.

Baku

The tech mastermind of the Sumichou Underground.

Chou

A semi-sapient slime and Ohno Suzu's pet.

Date Hoji

The impetuous little brother to Date Sari. He's a male kitsune (fox spirit).

Date Miwa

(AKA Great Grandmother Miwa, Grandma Miwa)

Recently widowed mother of Hoji and Sari and a kitsune (fox spirit).

Date Sari

A kitsune (fox spirit) who trapped Ibaraki and used her as a ki battery. Nakamura Hisako's mortal enemy.

Garu

Tengu (bird man) who works at the Palace in Sumichou.

Hayashi Ume

A yuki onna (snow maiden) and member of the council for the League of Guardians.

Honjou Masamune

Sword created by the famous smith, Masamune.

Ibaraki Douji*

(AKA Ibaraki, Oni Queen)

Leader of the oni horde.

** The legends are not really clear on if Ibaraki is male or female. Most stories say Ibarkai is male. I chose female to fit this story.

** In the legends, Watanabe no Tsuna severed Ibaraki's arm. Later, Ibaraki stole back the appendage. I add to the myths in this book: a secret medical facility, that only services yokai, attached a prototype metal arm that connects to her nerves with magic. It acts just like a normal arm with some bonuses.

Inari Okami*

(AKA Inari, Inari-sama)

Shinto kami, who is best known as the god of rice cultivation and foxes. High-ranking white foxes are his messengers.

Iwate Chisa

Umeji's ex-girlfriend.

Kairi

Soujou-bou's head servant. He's a tengu (bird man).

Kappa

One of the leaders of the Sumichou Underground.

Kentarou

Umeji's little brother in the yakuza (the mob).

Megumi

Pet shop owner in Sumichou.

Mishima

A self-important baku (a tapir-based chimera) and newest member of the League of Guardians.

Nakamura Asako
(AKA Mother, Great Aunt Asako)
A seven tailed white kitsune (fox spirit). She is Nakamura Hisako's mother.

Nakamura Hisako
(AKA Aunt Hisako, Daughter)
Umeji Tatsuya's aunt and mentor in magic, who is also the Guardian for Nono-gawa. Hisako is a kitsune (fox spirit).

Nakamura Nobu
(AKA Father, Great Uncle Nobu)
A nine tailed white kitsune (fox spirit) and father to Nakamura Hisako.

Nakamura Tsubame
Younger sister to Nakamura Hisako.

Ohno Ichirou
One of Ohno Suzu's older brothers.

Ohno Ken
One of Ohno Suzu's older brothers.

Ohno Suzu
(AKA Su-chan, Ohno-chan, Suzu, Suzu-chan)
Umeji's sweet, headstrong girlfriend.

Ohno Yasu
(AKA Dad)
Ohno Suzu's father.

Ohno Yukiko
(AKA Mom)
Mother of Ohno Suzu.

Otsuka Hiro

(AKA Big Brother, Aniki)

Umeji's big brother in the yakuza (the mob). He was an undercover agent for the PSIA.

Phoenix

One of the leaders of the Sumichou Underground.

Raijin

God of thunder and member of the council for the League of Guardians.

Rin

Ohno Suzu's pet, a semi-sapient Razor Vine.

Satou Kazuo

(AKA Boss, Kazuo, Nephew)

Volunteer Parole Officer for Umeji Tatsuya, nephew to Nakamura Hisako, and PSIA agent in the Paranormal division.

Sekiguchi

A kappa (turtle-like spirit) and talented healer in Kyoto.

Shachihoko

A giant sea monster.

Shion

River god and dragon spirit.

Shirou

Kojin (shark spirit) at Megumi's pet shop.

Soujou-bou*

(AKA Sensei, Soujou-sama)

King of the Tengu (the wild bird men) and Head of the League of Guardians.

** Note: His name is often written without a dash before the 'bou' suffix. I added the dash to show it was a name suffix, like '-san'.

Sugita

Restaurant owner in Kabukichou.

Suzuki Chiyo

Mother to Jiro.

Suzuki Jiro

(AKA Soujirou)

Middle school student who has a shard of Nakamura Hisako's magic.

Note: In Rise he was called Soujirou. I have him use his nickname 'Jiro' to avoid having a name to similar Soujoubou's.

Takahashi

Police officer that works with Satou and Arai.

Tarou

Male prostitute in Sumichou.

Tsuchimikado Yukitada

(AKA Yuki)

Nakamura Hisako's first husband. A samurai and magic user from the 1800s.

Watabe Taka and Yuri

Kitsune (fox spirit) twins. Taka is the boy. Yuri is the girl.

Yamazaki

Important yokai (spirit) whose cover is acting as a vegetable shop owner in Kyoto.

Yasha

Nature spirit and popular hostess.

Yoshirou

A white, nine-tailed fox and Inari's messenger to the Nakamura clan.

30

DICTIONARY AND PRONUNCIATION GUIDE

A STORY SET IN Japan has to have the vocabulary to make it feel like the real deal. I've tried to provide context with the words in the story. But if you need it, here is a list of words you'll come across.

A quick note on spelling: I have tried my best to represent Japanese pronunciation with Roman letters. Numerous ways exist to attempt this. One choice I had to make was how to represent the 'long vowel' sounds, which are held for a beat longer when spoken. I chose what seemed to me to be the simplest option available—a doubled vowel in a word, such as 'torii'. Please note, in the case of the long o, it often appears in hiragana (an alphabet of the symbols for the sounds) as 'ou'. Exceptions such as the location name 'Oosaka' exist. Westerners tend to shorten the sound to Osaka, but it's not correct.

There are also a few that I didn't keep the long vowel for, because they are pretty well entrenched in English with the shorter vowel - such as 'bento', 'dojo', 'tanto', and 'shoji'.

Please remember, these are quick definitions. Each word or phrase can have many more layers than this surface glance. Feel free to explore more than I can offer in a simplified dictionary.

anime
Japanese-style animation.

anpan

Red bean paste sweet buns.

baka

Idiot, dummy.

baku

A mythical tapir-like chimera that eats bad dreams.

-chan

An endearing and cute name suffix often used for children, young women, or by a significant other.

daikon

A large white radish.

donburi

A rice bowl with fish, meat, or vegetables.

futon

A mattress put on the floor for sleeping. Not the American-ized college furniture that folds up into a couch.

geisha

An entertainer trained to dance, sing, converse, serve tea, etc. Dresses in beautiful traditional clothes, and does hair and makeup with traditional style.

genkan

The entryway of a Japanese house.

gyuudon

Beef, onion, and rice bowl.

hakama

Pleated skirt like pants that are worn over the bottom half of a man's kimono.

hiragana

One of the two sound-based syllabaries in Japanese. The first one taught in school.

hoshi no tama

A ball that legend says holds a kitsune's magic and/or soul.

hostess

A woman at a club who gets paid to be attentive to a male client.

Itadakimasu

An expression of thanks for the meal one is about to eat.

kami

A god or powerful spirit.

kanji

The most complex of the Japanese characters systems in writing. Chinese was the language of scholarship in ancient Japan. So, many of the kanji symbols were imported from China in the 6th century.

kanpai

A word said when toasting, like Cheers!

katana

The larger of the two swords samurai carried.

ki

The energy or life force that flows through all things.

kiai

A quick shout made when making an attack in martial arts.

kimono

A long robe with loose sleeves, kept closed with a sash. Formal wear in Japan.

kitsune

A fox. Many myths tell of them being magical tricksters and shape-shifters.

kodama

A tree spirit. The word also means echo.

koma inu

A mythical lion dog guardian.

kotatsu

A low table with a heater under it, covered by a heavy blanket and a tabletop.

kotodama

The belief that words and names have magic or mystical and divine powers. The power can be accessed by speaking or writing them.

kumiho

Korean word for a 9-tailed fox that hunts human males to feast on their liver or heart.

-kun

A friendly name suffix for boys and young men.

miso

A thick fermented soybean paste. Often used as part of a soup base, but can be used in many dishes. Has a distinctive umami taste.

naginata

A pole weapon with a blade on the end. Women were often taught to use this effectively against a samurai with a sword. The long reach of the pole keeps the wielder out of the way of the sword.

Noh

A style of traditional play that uses masks, dance, and song.

noren

The split curtain outside a store. Put out when the shop is open.

ofuda

Paper talisman. For this story, it's the paper a spell is written on.

oni

A large red, blue or green skinned ogre-like creature that has protruding tusks. May also be translated as ogre, troll, or demon (though in English this carries a connotation I didn't feel appropriate).

otedama

A children's juggling game that uses small bean bags.

Ramune

A popular soft drink that comes in many flavors. The bottle has a glass marble as a seal.

sake

A rice-based alcoholic drink and the national beverage of Japan. Can refer to alcohol in general.

-sama

A respectful title suffix put after the name of a person. A higher rank than 'san'. Also, very polite speech from store employees to call their customers. "Okyaku-sama" might be translated "honored customer".

-san

Respectful title put after the name of a person. Can be translated as Mr. _, Mrs. _, or Miss _.

sashiko

A running stitch embroidery usually done in white thread on indigo dyed cloth.

-sensei

Teacher, doctor, or other profession, such as a lawyer—that is an authority figure. Also, a name suffix that denotes the person's position as a teacher, etc.

shikigami

A summoned servant spirit. For this story, they occupy a paper puppet.

shinkansen

Bullet train.

shogun

A military commander that led or later, ruled, feudal era Japan from the late 1100s to 1868.

shoji

A wooden lattice door, covered in rice paper.

tanuki

A raccoon-dog. In mythology, they can transform into human and other shapes. They're often rivals with kitsune.

tatami

A reed mat used as a traditional floor covering. Their length is twice as long as the width. The size varies a little by region. But a room can be described as an X tatami room - where X is the number of tatami that fit in it. Tatami are hard to clean. New tatami have a gentle pine-like scent.

tengu

Mythological bird man. There are two main types. The greater tengu may look like a person with a large nose and wings. The lesser tengu look more like a bird with more crow or bird of prey characteristics.

tokonoma

Alcove to display items like a picture or vase of arranged flowers.

torii

A traditional gate at the entrance of a Shinto shrine, marking the entrance to a sacred space. They're often red.

udon

Thick wheat flour noodles. Or a soup with this type of noodle.

wakizashi

Shorter of the two main swords a samurai wore.

yakuza

The Japanese mob, a mobster.

yokai

A supernatural being.

yuki onna

A mythical snow maiden that drains humans of their life energy.

31

If You Enjoyed This Book

Thank you so much for reading Guardian: Liminal Chronicles Book 2. I'd be thrilled if you left a review on your favorite book shops and review sites. I read every review and love to hear from you all.

Umeji's adventure will continue in Legend: The Liminal Chronicles. Coming in 2025.

32

ABOUT THE AUTHOR

AMY IS AN URBAN fantasy author who writes Japanese myth-based stories to reconnect with the country and culture that captured her heart on both of her trips to Japan. She lives in South Dakota with her supportive husband, two wonderful kids, and three wily and crazy ferrets.

You can read more about her, find the occasional ferret picture, and sign up to receive a free story at amywintersvoss.com.

www.ingramcontent.com/pod-product-compliance
Lightning Source LLC
Chambersburg PA
CBHW071407200726
48294CB00002B/313